SELF-PORTRAIT WITH NOTHING

SELF-PORTRAIT WITH NOTHING

AIMEE POKWATKA

TOR
DOT
COM

A TOM DOHERTY
ASSOCIATES BOOK
NEW YORK

This is a work of fiction. All of the characters, organizations, and events portrayed in this novel are either products of the author's imagination or are used fictitiously.

SELF-PORTRAIT WITH NOTHING

A Tordotcom Book
Published by Tom Doherty Associates
120 Broadway
New York, NY 10271

www.tor.com

Tor® is a registered trademark of Macmillan Publishing Group, LLC.

Library of Congress Cataloging-in-Publication Data

Names: Pokwatka, Aimee, author.
Title: Self-portrait with nothing / Aimee Pokwatka.
Description: First edition. |
New York : Tordotcom/Tom Doherty Associates, 2022.
Identifiers: LCCN 2022010473 (print) | LCCN 2022010474 (ebook) |
ISBN 9781250820846 (hardcover) | ISBN 9781250820853 (ebook)
Subjects: LCGFT: Science fiction. | Novels.
Classification: LCC PS3616.O5566 S45 2022 (print) |
LCC PS3616.O5566 (ebook) | DDC 813'.6—dc23/eng/20220311
LC record available at https://lccn.loc.gov/2022010473
LC ebook record available at https://lccn.loc.gov/2022010474

Our books may be purchased in bulk for promotional, educational, or business use. Please contact your local bookseller or the Macmillan Corporate and Premium Sales Department at 1-800-221-7945, extension 5442, or by email at MacmillanSpecialMarkets@macmillan.com.

First Edition: 2022

Printed in the United States of America

0 9 8 7 6 5 4 3 2 1

for Jason

All sketches wish to be real.

—Tomas Tranströmer,
"The Blue House"

ONE

1

AT THE TIME of her disappearance at age fifty-four, Ula Frost was already a mystery. There were no records of her selling a painting in almost seven years, and she had never given an interview, attended a public showing of her work, or indicated to either the press or any of her clients where she lived. Social media sightings were rare and scattered across four continents. If she owned property, she did not own it under her name. The disappearance was reported to the police by her assistant, Gordon Priddy, who'd only ever communicated with Frost via mail and, once a week, a brief phone call. The mail was directed by Gordon to an address in London, which, upon investigation, turned out to be the terraced home of a man who'd died several years earlier and whose residence had been left unoccupied by his feuding children. The calls were placed through an internet phone service, and when the police attempted to trace their origins, they discovered the source had been obfuscated through IP redirection. Gordon, a middle-aged bachelor who'd found the job in the classified section of the local paper, told authorities that Ula had never missed a call in the twenty-two years he'd been working for her. But now he hadn't heard from her in three weeks.

Gordon answered the police's questions with a distracted but intense concern, though the shallowness of his information quickly frustrated the detective assigned to the case, a man named Jamie Marchand who'd spent two decades with the NYPD before moving to this sleepy Connecticut town—Frost's hometown—where Gordon lived and filed his report. Marchand had been ready for a quieter, easier life, only to find himself responding to opioid overdoses, incidents of domestic violence, and not-infrequent hate crimes directed at the few people in town who looked like him. Occasionally, there was a call about a stray chicken someone found, and once, a llama. This spring, there'd been an uptick in calls about bear sightings, the bear lumbering through affluent residents' backyards, unhurried in its exploration, sniffing the expertly landscaped hydrangeas, pausing to investigate a child's play set, to take a turn on the swings.

Marchand had initially been energized by the possibility of doing some actual detective work for a change but found himself stymied at every turn in his investigation. There were few records of Frost's existence in any of their databases. She'd never been arrested or married. Her sister and presumed sole surviving relative, Tilda Hogan, still lived in their childhood home, but every time Marchand called or stopped by the house, no one answered, except for three greyhounds who would gather at the window and look out at him with unnerving stillness. Gordon sat in Marchand's office for hours, but his response to question after question was *I don't know.* What Gordon did know, or was willing to reveal, was that Frost was extremely selective in accepting new commissions and had not done so for a long time. When Marchand asked Gordon why he thought that was, Gordon shrugged.

"There could be any number of reasons," Gordon told him.

Gordon had gone to art school with his own ambitions but soon realized he had neither the vision nor the tolerance for criticism necessary to carve out a career for himself, and thus devoted himself to delivering to the world the work of other artists, which, in the case of Ula Frost's work, he considered to be a sacred calling. His primary job was maintaining the small collection of the local historical society, which contained a few odd pieces by minor artists who'd passed through town at one time or another, as well as several early pieces by Frost. The historical society was housed in a former general store on Main Street that was built in 1778 and was the closest the town came to having a tourist attraction. Ula Frost, it turned out, had something of a cult following.

Marchand had heard her name, of course, and the stories about her work, but he found the reverence with which some people spoke of her silly and off-putting, and thus had never ventured to the historical society himself. Those who believed the stories believed with fervor. He kept watch for the out-of-state license plates when he drove through town, and locals knew to be careful on Main Street, where Frost tourists paid little attention to road signs and occasionally wandered into traffic. There was no common denominator among the believers in terms of age or class or race, but they all had a distracted quality about them, their faces glazed with daydreams. Frost's work had that effect on people, rendering them oblivious to the real world around them, immersing them instead in worlds that existed, as far as Marchand was concerned, only in their imaginations.

Ula Frost had a cult following for a reason: her portraits—at least those painted in the last twenty-two years—were said to unlock alternate versions of their subjects from parallel universes, bringing them, somehow, into this world, the one that Marchand inhabited. Marchand wondered fleetingly about what alternate versions of himself might exist. A version of himself who'd never watched his own mother die, a version who never got shot while buying a Dr Pepper and a banana at a bodega that was being held up. A version of himself who'd studied harder, gotten better grades or advantages from life, and turned out to be someone completely different. Marchand had always liked building things as a kid. Maybe in a parallel universe there was an architect version of him, who lived in a house he'd designed himself, an A-frame, with those spindly white chairs he saw in magazines and fluffy white rugs. He could imagine that version of himself walking across those rugs, barefoot, holding a mug of hot chocolate, digging in his toes. It felt good, he thought. That rug felt good under his old feet.

The evidence surrounding the claims about Ula Frost's work was ample, though easy enough to explain away. There were photographs of several clients, whose birth records indicated that theirs had been a single birth, with what appeared to be their own twins. Marchand wasn't any good with computers, but he knew what Photoshop could do. The accounts of those who'd managed to purchase a Frost portrait, or rather those who were willing to talk about the experience, were more compelling, though not particularly heartening. The first client to go on record had spoken of it only once. He was a painter himself, an abstractionist named Victor Morgan, who claimed he'd met Frost at an exhibit for an obscure surrealist when they were in their early twenties, only to reconnect years later in a fishing town in France. The fishing town was known for an unusual number of drownings, a fact that had drawn them there, independently, at the same time. In his sole interview, with the fine arts magazine *Ekphrasis*, Morgan refused to answer questions about his relationship with Frost, or whether Frost had anticipated the outcome of the painting when she'd begun painting it. He wanted only for the public to know there was nothing in his life he would ever regret more. French authorities found a photo of the two together after Morgan's death, both of them standing stone-faced in front of some unidentifiable ruin. Morgan's body was discovered a few months after his interview, decomposing in his flat, the portrait slashed to shreds beside him.

Marchand made a few phone calls and learned there were pills involved, and there was no indication of any contact between Frost and Morgan after the portrait was completed. Marchand asked if the investigator on the case at the time had attempted to locate the alleged alternate version of Morgan after Morgan's death. The woman on the other end of the line, who sounded very much like she was smirking, would only say that the case had been closed. The damaged portrait had eventually been released to a team of art historians whose extensive analysis of the work revealed nothing remarkable about the materials or technique. Marchand found a photo of the portrait online and spent too long looking at the gashes running through the canvas, as if the destruction itself were transmitting something of importance. There was an image now stuck in his head—irrational, nagging at him—an image of himself in a pressed suit, wearing the pair of wing tip shoes he admired in the window of a store he walked past every morning knowing full well he'd never be able to afford them.

Many of the other stories, which were widely and sensationally published, played out the same way—in terms of the clients' regret, though never again, as far as Marchand could tell, in terms of the personal connection to Ula Frost. According to Gordon, after Victor Morgan's death, Frost only entertained applications for commissions through the mail. Early on, it was rumored that she distrusted people who typed their letters, and Gordon confirmed that much of the mail he forwarded to the London address arrived in fine, handcrafted envelopes. Sometimes they were scented, sometimes they had wax seals. Sometimes the paper was homemade, imprecisely folded, with dried flowers or leaves or—once—a lock of hair embedded in the pulp. Gordon had been instructed never to open the envelopes he forwarded, and though a number had been seized by the post office under suspicion of containing hazardous or illegal materials, he did not disobey Frost's orders. The letters came from all over the world, and Ula Frost had received thousands of them a year, for years on end.

Gordon's role in the operation seemed to Marchand to be deliberately limited, as if the support he provided was secondary to his function as a touchstone who was able to verify Frost's continued existence. He forwarded the letters, attended to administrative tasks, and, crucially, once a week, he spoke with Ula Frost on the phone. In the years when his work also included screening potential clients, Frost had rarely responded to Gordon's reports with more than a *hmm.* It had been seven years since Frost had assigned this kind of task, though, and as a result, most of their calls since had been brief.

Marchand asked Gordon if he'd ever requested a portrait of himself.

"I wrote a letter once," Gordon said. "I didn't tell her I was sending it. I just stuck it in with the others."

"And what did she say?" Marchand asked. Marchand was chewing on licorice strings, and one fell out the side of his mouth like a tusk. Licorice strings were his thing.

"She never said anything about it," Gordon answered. "I don't know if she even read it or realized it was me."

"You didn't ask her?" Marchand said.

"No, of course not," Gordon told him. "I would've been mortified."

DESPITE THE ANGUISH on Gordon's part, which Marchand felt confident was genuine, he declined to provide Marchand with any of the records he'd kept on Frost's behalf, claiming that would be a violation of her trust. And because there was no evidence that a crime had actually been committed, nor was there even a clear indication of where Frost had been living prior to her disappearance, Marchand could file a missing person report and enter Frost into the Interpol database, but he could not compel Gordon to provide access to any documentation. Gordon returned home to his antique colonial and waited what he thought was a safe interval of time before slipping out to the studio he kept in the back.

The building at the rear of his property had been added in the early 1900s as a workshop, and though Gordon's research failed to uncover what kind of work the original owner had done in it, the studio still smelled faintly like a lit match. Gordon had transformed the space into a kind of tribute to Ula Frost and filled it with prints of her lesser-known work, often acquired through sketchy art dealers on the internet. Sometimes he painted there himself, though he would never presume to compare his impressionistic experiments to anything approaching Frost's brilliance. Her style was difficult to describe—she lacked the pained surrealism of Frida Kahlo, though critics often noted that, like Kahlo, Frost seemed to give physical space to suffering in her work. Her paintings were by no means as overtly feminine as Georgia O'Keeffe's, though they had a way of making the viewer feel like a voyeur. Gordon had been known to involuntarily blush in the presence of Frost's work, even pieces he'd seen many times. She had a fondness for texture, the paint improbably thick on the canvas, and there was a sensation upon looking at them that the paintings reflected and absorbed more than light.

When Gordon had visitors, he kept them clear of his studio.

Gordon had a secret.

Gordon couldn't quite say how it had happened, but one afternoon twelve years prior, he'd stolen a Frost original from the historical society. It was an early painting, juvenilia, donated to the historical society by the local high school, which Frost had attended for three years before dropping out, after they found it swathed in cobwebs in the corner of a humid storage room during a renovation. She'd left it there, along with the contents of her locker—a hairbrush and a pair of sneakers, a backpack of neglected textbooks—most of which had been trashed or repurposed after she and her parents had failed to claim them. The painting was a simple landscape depicting a vernal pond by the field near the edge of town. Gordon had recognized the spot immediately—he'd taken a woman there once on a date, lugging a picnic basket full of charcuterie and cheeses, a loaf of crusty bread, and a chilled bottle of rosé. They'd walked to the center of the field and, as if by magic, fireflies blinked into being around them. Gordon had shaken out the blanket he'd brought, but the woman had touched his arm and pointed to the piles of goose droppings that dotted the field and said, "Maybe we have different ideas about romance."

It was always like that with Gordon. Sometimes he imagined a version of his life where these things didn't constantly happen to him, where this woman, the registrar at a museum of the history of whaling in New England, had instead grabbed him by the face and kissed him, and they'd slow-danced to imaginary music with the fireflies all around them, and then she'd grabbed him by the face and kissed him again, more tenderly this time, and they'd fallen to the ground, unsullied by goose shit, forgetting about the blanket, laughing. Somewhere, Gordon thought, that version of him existed.

The painting he'd stolen depicted that exact spot, except there was a sycamore tree in the center of the field, which, according to numerous artistic renderings in the historical society's collection, had never existed. Like this world, but subtly different. Gordon had loaded it into his trunk with the intention of taking it to a conservator but had brought it home to his studio instead, and when someone at the historical society had asked, he'd told her the conservator had found it was damaged beyond repair, crumbling, really.

"What a shame," the woman had said, returning her attention to the brochure she was designing.

"Yes," Gordon had replied. "A shame."

Gordon hadn't told Marchand about the painting, of course. There were other things he hadn't told him either. Like how in the months leading up to her disappearance, Ula had become uncharacteristically chatty. Well, not chatty—she never asked Gordon about himself—but sometimes she'd call and say, "Still alive," then pause and talk for a while. Once she went on for a full ten minutes about a recent scandal involving a performance artist and the technology company who'd used the artist's work in a commercial which they'd subsequently pulled after outcry from far-right media outlets. He was surprised by the lightness of her voice and by her awareness of both the existence of the scandal and the political landscape in general, as if she inhabited a world apart from the one he did. In the background, he could hear church bells ringing, but he'd been too stunned by Ula's sudden monologue to count the hour. Another time, she'd spoken at length about a pair of children she'd watched playing in a fountain. Gordon tried to picture it, but there weren't many fountains in Connecticut. He'd never traveled much. The children had been surprised by the water, delighted every time it changed direction, even though its choreography followed a predictable pattern. Ula couldn't make sense of their enchantment. Sometimes she asked about her sister and then changed the subject immediately.

The last time Gordon had spoken with her, she was back to her usual terse self.

"Still alive," she'd said. "For now."

It was the *for now* that stuck with Gordon. He wondered if she'd painted some kind of exquisite vision of her own death, which was a heartbreaking possibility to consider, but Gordon couldn't help himself. He looked at the painting on the wall, that one tree haunting everything. No, Ula was still alive. He could feel it.

He busied himself hiding the rest of his records, just in case Marchand came looking. He told himself it was because he was still entrusted with the duty of protecting Ula's privacy, but if he was being honest, he would have admitted this protectiveness was more of himself, of this one undeniable part of his life that made him special. He hid the client list. He hid the logs of return addresses, and the other log—the list of letter writers who couldn't take no for an answer, who when their correspondence went unanswered had shown up at the local post office, camping outside the PO box where Gordon received Ula's mail. A few months ago, there was an older man, in his sixties, with round tortoiseshell glasses and a lanky mop of hair. For a moment, Gordon wondered if he was meeting an older version of himself, come from the future to warn him of some yet unknown catastrophe. But no, the man was there to plead with him, to pull at Gordon's cardigan and weep, oblivious to the scene he was creating. He'd followed Gordon home and waited, parked across the street in his BMW, for three days before giving up.

He wasn't the only one. It happened two or three times a year for all the years that Gordon had worked for Ula.

Gordon finished hiding his files and proceeded to tidy up the studio. But a ledger he remembered putting in the top drawer was missing, and the checkbook for the account into which Ula deposited money was on the wrong side of the desk. Or maybe he simply wasn't remembering correctly. It happened more often these days—checks disappeared, documents were not where he remembered putting them. He was getting older. There was a painting on an easel he'd started but hadn't finished, of a man who looked like him, except he only had half a face. Gordon couldn't see the rest clearly yet, but he wanted desperately for the man to look somehow different, to look happier, or richer, or less alone. He wanted him to be the kind of man who was into horses, who had a stable and a mare whose coat was a warm chestnut color, whom he brushed methodically every evening, listening to some old jazz record, savoring a nice port, while she swished her shiny tail. He wanted the man to be the kind of person who was cool enough to stay put when he heard, as he did now, the arrival of an unfamiliar vehicle in his driveway. Someone who received so many visitors he was weary of them. But Gordon did not receive many visitors. He was not weary of company. And he'd been harboring the secret hope that she'd come for so long. So instead of being cool and staying put, Gordon straightened himself, trying to tamp down the thrill of anticipation, lingering on the possibilities inherent in an unexpected visitor at the door. This Gordon couldn't be cool about it. But somewhere, he thought, in some other place, that man existed.

2

PEPPER RAFFERTY SAT in her lab—its walls lined floor to ceiling with cardboard boxes containing the skeletal remains of a population who'd died thousands of years earlier—and tried to concentrate. The bones presently in front of her weren't archaic, and she'd arranged them on the table as the police had found them—the femurs crossed, the skull fragments scattered like a constellation. Pepper had heard the news about Ula Frost's disappearance on the radio on her way to campus and was having a hard time staying focused. The pelvis was obviously female, which she'd already noted. The partial fusion of the medial clavicular epiphyses and the open sutures in the recovered skull fragments suggested the victim was between eighteen and twenty-five. Someone had loved the owner of these bones. Someone missed her. Someone, somewhere needed Pepper to not screw this up.

There weren't enough facial bones present to reconstruct a reliable image, but after her next class, she'd have her grad students work on gluing the fragments together and running the image through the reconstruction program anyway. It would be a lesson. A lesson on managing expectations.

This body had been buried shallowly near the pond at the edge of town, early in the unusually hot fall, Pepper suspected, as it would take a combination of temperature and soil acidity to produce the accelerated rate of soft tissue decomposition she now observed. Pepper wasn't supposed to know about anything else the police had found, but Jamie Marchand liked her and told her anyway over a cup of hot chocolate in the faculty lounge. The department only stocked the powdered kind, but Pepper kept a bag of Hershey's Kisses on a high shelf in the lounge's kitchen, which she added to their mugs. Jamie had a sweet tooth.

The body, he'd told her, had been found after a recent three-day storm by an elderly woman who'd been instructed to walk more after a hip replacement. She'd seen the fabric first, shreds of pink sweatshirt, before spotting a rib jutting from the ground. Upon excavation, the police had also found a single earring, silver and spider-shaped. The clothing matched that of a girl who'd gone missing at the beginning of the fall semester, a math major who'd disappeared while walking her calculus professor's dog. The dog had turned up in the owner's own yard a week later, missing its tail. Pepper hadn't known the girl, but she'd attended the candlelight vigil. Jamie told Pepper the boyfriend had been suspected at the time because he'd acted strangely when questioned, compulsively repeating a story about how sometimes she got lost when she took walks, how she had a bad sense of direction. There were gnaw marks on the femurs and one humerus. An animal, likely a rodent, had gotten to the body. The fracture pattern of the skull looked suspicious, but it was impossible to tell the difference between perimortem and postmortem trauma with the remains in this condition.

Pepper went through the bones again systematically, rereading her notes. She worried, more than usual, that she was missing something. Somewhere, in an alternate universe, Ula Frost was not missing, and Pepper was able to keep her attention here, where it belonged.

She was sealing everything back into the police-issue bags when the grad students started streaming in. Pepper had never aspired to be a professor—she'd learned at an early age to avoid drawing attention to herself and had initially planned to pursue museum work—but this part of academic life arrived as an unexpected pleasure. She liked it when her students got excited about the same morbid things she got excited about, like the effects of lawn mowers on skeletal remains or the discovery of a female body in the tomb of a Mayan prince.

Pepper had three master's students this year, who were helping her catalog a collection of archaic-period skeletal remains that had been excavated from a farm in Kentucky. The population showed signs of treponemal disease—non-venereal syphilis—a fact she shared selectively with new acquaintances, deploying it as a kind of personality test. The collection was due to be repatriated in less than a month, and she was running out of time to wrap up her research, though late at night, Pepper worried less about her research and more about the void that would be left once this constant in her life was tucked back into the ground. She'd been sitting with these burials nearly every day for five years. And soon they'd be gone, and she still hadn't secured funding for her research proposal for the fall. When she started consulting for the police, she considered it might be time for a shift in her career, but testifying in court was a necessary part of the process, and she always felt so wrong, taking an oath and sitting in front of a jury, calling herself an expert. Her husband, Ike, assured her the imposter syndrome would pass, but it hadn't, and maybe it never would.

Somewhere, in a parallel universe, there was a version of Pepper with perfect posture and tailored suits, who answered the attorneys' questions with confidence and poise. But not in this one.

Today, Jeremiah was the first to arrive, but Naomi and Janet weren't far behind. Jeremiah came in red-eyed most days and listened to jam bands while he worked, but he had exceptionally good vision and often noticed patches of pitting that Pepper wouldn't have seen without a magnifying glass. Naomi had started in cultural anthropology, working with local farms, but she had too many allergies and couldn't handle the fieldwork required for her ethnographic thesis. Once, when they were working late and Pepper ordered pizzas to her office, she returned to the lab to find Naomi talking to the burial on the table, gently explaining which bone she was handling and why.

Janet, who today had a red bandanna tied through her Afro, arrived last and settled in without greetings. Janet was Pepper's favorite because she didn't like to talk about herself, and she seemed most content when she could lock herself into the storage closet they'd commandeered for their X-ray machine. Pepper understood that instinct to avoid being seen. Janet never checked her phone while she was in the lab or discussed her weekend plans, but she hummed while she worked and left every burial she cataloged wrapped more carefully than when she'd found it.

The routine was well established by this point. Naomi launched into a diatribe about her boyfriend, and Jeremiah put in his earbuds. Janet rearranged the tables so she'd have more space. Pepper had an hour until her undergrad class started, and she had identification stations to prepare. She liked to stick random bones into boxes and make her students reach in and examine them blindly, using only their hands. Could they tell her which bone it was, the sex, the age, the condition? Pepper liked it when kids who were sure they were stumped figured it out.

She was sorting through a box of model vertebrae when she heard the knock. The door swung open to reveal a youngish man, midtwenties, wearing a button-down and purple Chucks and hipster glasses. He was holding a notepad and had a leather bag slung over his shoulder.

"Hi," he said. "Are you Dr. Rafferty?"

He seemed to know that she was, like he recognized her from somewhere. A Ph.D. student, she guessed, from another department.

"Yes," she said. She planted her body in the doorway, reluctant to disturb the lab's peace.

"My name is Scott Morrow. I'm with *Ekphrasis.* Do you have some time to talk?"

Pepper's vision blurred, and for a moment, she could see two Scotts standing in the hall. She could feel her students behind her. The music from Jeremiah's headphones got slightly louder as he slid one bud out of his ear.

"I have a class in a few minutes," she said. "And we're working. I'm working. This isn't a good time."

"Oh," Scott said. "Can we arrange a time for later? After class? I'm working on a piece about Ula Frost, and I have a few questions I'd like to ask you."

The first time Pepper testified in court, she'd gotten so nervous upon entering the courthouse she'd rushed straight to the bathroom and vomited. When she was finished, the woman from the next stall—who, when it came time for Pepper to testify, she discovered was the judge—took a paper towel and wet it with cool water and placed it on the back of her neck, then left without saying a word.

That's how Pepper felt now. Like she needed a cool paper towel for the back of her neck.

"I'm pretty busy," Pepper told him. He was wearing cuff links with comic book explosions on them—one said *POW* and the other said *BLAM*. "I have to head home right after class today. My husband." She stopped. She couldn't even think of a proper excuse.

"That's okay," Scott said. "I'm planning to be in town for a few days. I can totally work around your schedule."

"Hey, what are you writing about Ula Frost?" Jeremiah said. "Is this about her going missing?" He was standing beside Pepper now, having abandoned the remains of a male skeleton on which Pepper now noticed pronounced periostitic lesions on the proximal aspects of the tibias. She could smell the amber scent of his cologne, which wasn't quite masking the scent of pot. "I'm basically obsessed with her. I actually considered switching to physics as an undergrad because I wanted to study how her paintings might work."

"Yeah, I'm writing about her disappearance. It's a profile, really. There's a lot people don't know about her. I'm trying to piece together her personal history."

Pepper stood unmoving in the doorway, locking Scott with her best *shut the fuck up* stare.

"Why do you want to talk to Dr. Rafferty?" Jeremiah asked. Because of course he did. Of course that was the next question he'd ask.

"I wrote something about her," Pepper said, before Scott could answer. "Ages ago, when I was working on my master's. I did a paper on her work as it's been interpreted by other cultures."

"Oh, that's so cool," Naomi piped in. She leaned hard from

her chair to get a better look at Scott. "Like, do some cultures think there's a religious connection? I want to read that paper!"

"I'll bring you a copy," Pepper lied. "But yes, global responses to her work vary dramatically depending on a culture's relationship with science and systems of belief. We can discuss it later."

"I have a Frost print in my bedroom," Janet said casually, as if it wasn't the most personal detail she'd ever shared. "That painting of the woman standing in front of a lake, and her reflection has a big scar across her neck but the woman doesn't?"

"You should teach a class about her!" Naomi said.

Scott was still standing in the hall, trying to peer around Pepper's body.

"Sorry," she said. "I've got evidence in here from a case in progress."

"Are we supposed to have some kind of clearance to be in here?" Jeremiah said. "Whoa. My mom is going to like that."

"You have all the clearance you need," Pepper told him. "But you don't have much time to finish with this burial before my undergrads come in, so look alive, okay?"

Jeremiah shrugged and returned to the table. Pepper stepped into the hall and closed the door behind her.

Scott stood there in his stupid purple shoes and smiled. Pepper had never slapped a man, but her hand was hot and itchy at her side. Around the corner, she heard two colleagues talking about a hidden tomb in Egypt that had been discovered using thermal imaging. She kept her voice low.

"Listen, I don't know how you found me, but I have no intention of talking to you about anything," she said. Scott tried to interject, but Pepper didn't let him. "I'm not going to answer any questions. I'm not going to talk to you. I'm going back to my lab, where I'm going to promptly forget about your existence. Don't contact me again."

She turned and slipped back into the lab, closing the door harder than necessary. Everyone looked up, but just for a moment. Pepper returned to the bagged remains and stared not at the bones but at the words printed on the plastic: *Chain of*

Custody. In a parallel universe, there was a version of Pepper who was still working, uninterrupted by a knock at the door. Pepper was a scientist—she didn't really believe in such a romanticized interpretation of parallel universes, but that didn't stop her from thinking about them. In a parallel universe, there was a version of her who'd just stepped out for coffee, or who'd taken a job at a different school, or who'd woken this morning with a fever and called in sick. There was a version of Pepper who'd changed her name and moved to Mexico, where she had a reckless tan and worked at a museum of indigenous art. There was a version of her who managed to stay hidden, who kept the lab door locked and didn't post office hours. In a parallel universe, there was a version of her that was just bone fragments in a bag, or some other receptacle, and all these alternatives she found more appealing than the one currently pressing in around her.

3

IN THE PARKING lot of Rafferty Family Veterinary Hospital, Pepper found a teenage girl with a long ponytail and gold sneakers trying to coax a Great Dane who was almost as tall as she was toward the door. The dog had clearly made up its mind and was passively resisting its owner, rooted in place, turning its head from the girl's treat-filled palm. A man in a Jeep with a cat carrier in the front passenger seat was trying to reverse from his parking spot, but the dog was unmoved by his honking.

"Please, Sarah," the girl whispered. She bit her lip, visibly willing herself not to cry.

"What are you in for?" Pepper asked. She was talking to the dog more than the girl.

"Just blood work," the girl said. "So she can get her arthritis pills refilled."

Pepper cupped the dog's chin and pressed her forehead against the top of her head. She felt the dog press back, the thick bone of her skull, the shining bristles of her coat. "Come on, Sarah," she said. "It won't be too bad. We have peanut butter."

Sarah's big tongue flopped out of her mouth, and she trotted alongside Pepper to the clinic's door, pulling the girl, who stuffed her treats back in her pocket, behind her. Pepper had a sudden, visceral memory of reaching into her own pockets at that age, finding the spongy remnants of a biscuit, that chemical meat smell.

"Thanks," the girl said as Pepper held the door.

Inside, Pepper found Judy, who'd had the same helmet of gray hair Pepper's entire life, on the phone at the reception desk. She waved at Pepper and continued her conversation.

"Now when you say *diarrhea*, do you mean watery, or is it more like pudding?"

She pulled a file from the shelves behind her and clicked her mouse, bringing the ancient printer to life. In the waiting room, a man in a reflective utility company vest scolded his Jack Russell, who struggled against its harness, laser-focused on a towel-wrapped guinea pig chutting in the lap of a boy, maybe eight. Pepper relocated the boy and his mother, who barely looked up from her phone, to an open exam room and continued past the desk, past a girl from the kennel mopping a puddle of urine in the hall, back to the clinic's treatment room, where she found one of her moms scrubbing an abscess on an anesthetized cat and the other kneeling in front of a gray-muzzled black Lab named Albert, a syringe poised in front of his neck.

Lydia, the mom with the cat, pierced the abscess with a scalpel blade and squeezed pus into a wad of gauze. Annie, the mom with the dog, inserted the needle into his neck.

"She didn't answer, but she has an appointment next week," Annie was saying.

Albert caught sight of Pepper and thumped his tail, his body otherwise still. The technician who was restraining him whispered that he was a good boy.

Pepper set her bag on a shelf under the wildly blinking phone. "Who'll be in next week?"

"Tilda Hogan," Lydia said. "Did you hear about Ula Frost? You know they're sisters?"

"Of course," Pepper said. She put on a pair of gloves. "I want to squeeze."

"You always want to do the fun part," Lydia said.

She ceded her spot at the table to Pepper, who'd spent so much time at the clinic as a kid they'd marked her growth by the size of the latex gloves she wore, often while she pretend-operated on her stuffed gorilla while one of her moms performed a real surgery.

Finished with Albert, Annie kissed Pepper on the cheek. She smelled like popcorn. "You should've been here earlier," she said. "We had an amputation."

She returned to Albert's chart as Lydia filled a bowl with

betadine to clean the abscess. Pepper pressed her fingers around the wound, searching for hidden pockets of infection.

"Hey, remember that time you guys adopted me?" she asked.

Lydia brought the bowl to the table. She was wearing the Red Sox jersey Pepper had given her for Christmas under her white coat. "That sounds vaguely familiar," she said. "Do you remember that, Annie?"

Annie didn't look up from her chart. "Mmm," she said. "I remember something at one point with a baby, but you know how my memory is."

"Move your fingers," Lydia said, and began flushing the wound. "What's up, Pepper?"

Pepper gathered the used gauze, now yellowish and threaded with blood. "You didn't ever find out anything more about who left me, did you?"

Annie put down her pen. Lydia scrubbed the wound a little more vigorously than necessary.

"Do you think we have some kind of secret knowledge about your biological parents we're not sharing with you?" Lydia said.

"No," Pepper said. "I didn't mean it like that."

When Pepper was a sophomore in high school, a group of guys had stuffed her in her locker and written *FAG* on the outside. She remembered how the locker smelled like pencils and the cupcake Annie had snuck into her lunch that day. She remembered how quiet she had been. She hadn't even made noise when she heard the teachers gather, the bolt cutters snapping through the padlock on the door. That night, her moms had served her ice cream for dinner.

"That doesn't even make sense," Lydia had said. "On several levels."

The next time someone tried to harass her, Pepper took hold of the boy's arm and bit him as hard as she could, like a dog. The boy's parents had been outraged, but the principal had only given Pepper detention. That night, her moms served ice cream with hot fudge and extra cherries.

"Did something happen?" Annie asked.

Pepper took off her gloves and washed her hands. On the dry-erase board where they logged the day's controlled drugs, some-one had written *3 cc Euthasol* next to a name Pepper recognized. Lydia had a set of scratch marks running all the way up her left forearm. Annie's purple eyeliner had worn into the creases under her eyes.

"I was just thinking about it," Pepper said.

"It's normal to wonder about your birth parents," Annie said. "But you know we don't have any secrets."

Pepper believed her. They still had the dog bed they'd found her on, on their front porch one summer night. Just a tiny, screaming newborn, wrapped in a blanket and left on a dog bed on the porch. Underneath her squirming body, there was a Polish coin with a hole drilled through it, which on Pepper's thirteenth birthday they gave to her on a chain. Pepper had never worn it. And for years, she'd known more about her biological mother than her moms did.

A tech came into the treatment room holding a printout. "The results from the liver panel." She gave them to Annie, who sighed. Lydia unmasked the cat, who was now beginning to wake and claw at the air in confusion.

"I should go," Pepper said.

"Come over tonight," Annie said. "We have ice cream."

"Ike is expecting me," Pepper said. "Thursday is documen-tary night. Maybe tomorrow."

WHEN PEPPER WAS a kid, one of her moms' clients brought them the nest of a baya weaver from India—a bulb-shaped nest that had hung like a pendulum from a palm frond, out of the reach of predators. This is how she imagined her family, the nest around them intricately woven from eucalyptus and sugarcane, stubbornness and humor and gratitude and guilt—a compli-cated shelter built to withstand a monsoon. So she never told her moms what she'd learned when she learned it. She was fifteen, half-asleep under her sunflower-print blanket, when she heard a noise in the street. Her moms were both asleep, and Pepper crept in the dark to the window, where she saw someone opening their mailbox. Someone she recognized. Tilda Hogan, a client who had three rescued greyhounds, one of whom had thyroid problems and who, when he boarded at the clinic, would only take his pills with cream cheese, and only from Pepper. Pepper could see the dogs in the station wagon's back seat, all three of them sticking their heads out the window facing the house. Tilda was slow and careful with the mailbox. Maybe she was bringing a payment for an overdue bill, Pepper thought. Her moms were like that, always working out payment plans with people who couldn't otherwise afford treatment.

But the next morning when Pepper came downstairs, she found her moms whisper-arguing at the table, and they both shut right up when Pepper walked into the room.

"What's happening?" she said. "Are you talking about me?"

Her moms didn't answer, instead pressed their hands together as if to make a pact, something they did absentmindedly when they were stressed, as they'd been doing since the night they first met in vet school, keeping watch over a horse with strangles.

Finally, Lydia said, "Take a seat."

"Did someone die?" Pepper said. They'd named her after one of their dogs, a miniature schnauzer who'd died just before they found her. They hadn't allowed themselves to hope, then, when they'd given her the name, that they'd be able to keep her. But social services had received an anonymous letter, which bore a small, inky handprint that matched Pepper's, indicating that Annie Rafferty was preferred as the adoptive mother. Pepper looked at her moms and felt like someone had died. She felt like someone had died and they were afraid to tell her.

Annie opened an envelope and slid its contents across the table. Lydia scooped up the orange tabby that was weaving between their legs. Pepper had grown up in the midst of an ever-changing menagerie, which at one point included a goat named Frito Pie who'd eaten the side mirror off Lydia's truck.

"This was in the mailbox this morning," Annie said.

It was a cashier's check for $100,000, with a Post-it stuck on top that read *for Pepper*. Pepper looked at it but didn't touch it. Frito Pie had been a fainting goat, who didn't really faint but who froze when panicked.

"Is this a joke?" she asked.

"We don't think so," Annie said.

"We're going to have to take it to the bank and see if it's legit," Lydia said.

"What's it for?" Pepper said. She was thinking about Tilda and the dogs, thinking she should tell them, and then she saw the picture of her swaddled infant self on the dog bed on the living room wall.

"We don't know," Lydia said. "If I had to guess, though, I'd guess maybe one of your biological parents is involved."

The kitchen around Pepper blurred.

"Are you okay?" Annie said.

"Can I have some juice?" she asked. She didn't even like juice. She'd been drinking coffee like her moms since she was nine, but now she wanted juice. Lydia got her a glass of tomato, which was the only juice in the house.

"Are you okay?" Annie repeated.

"Yeah," Pepper said. "Why wouldn't I be?"

THERE WAS A car in the driveway when Pepper got home. It was a long, black Cadillac, recently waxed—the kind of car Pepper imagined a funeral home director would drive. She saw Ike's tall frame move past the window and another figure follow. The car had local plates. Pepper sat in her car and fiddled with the climate control. She was always too hot or too cold. They weren't expecting company. Her phone showed five missed texts from Ike, but she didn't read them. She had papers to grade. Her car was an eleven-year-old Honda with a scraped bumper, and sitting in it next to the Cadillac, she had to suppress an urge to flee, to get on the highway and keep driving. But she was overdue to have a belt replaced. She wouldn't get far, even if she tried.

Ike held the front door open and gave her a look she couldn't read. He was still wearing the sweater vest he'd put on that morning. He'd wanted to drive in together, but Pepper hadn't been sure if she'd need to stay late to work on her case. Or rather, she'd known she wouldn't, but she'd wanted an excuse to drive in alone. Ike was always talking in the car about whatever he was reading, lately a history of American battleships during World War II, and did Pepper know Iowa-class battleships could fire shells that weighed over a ton—as heavy as her car!—as far as twenty-four miles? Pepper had not known, but now that information was lodged forever in her brain. Pepper preferred to listen to music while she drove, so she could practice her lectures in her head and, sometimes, sing.

Ike took Pepper's bag and tucked her hair behind her ear to kiss it. Ike's maternal grandfather was Argentinian and his paternal grandmother Lebanese, and he had a look he liked to call "ethnically ambiguous" that made Pepper worry when he had to fly. She caught people watching him sometimes, trying to figure out what he was. The owner of the Cadillac introduced himself as Bill Williams.

"I'm an attorney," he said, though he looked like a funeral director. He stole a glance at Ike. "Can we sit?"

Pepper felt like someone had died. It was a feeling she got a lot, really, a feeling that the universe she inhabited was so tenuous one wrong move would send everything into disarray. A sense of a shadow lurking behind her, like in a horror movie, patiently waiting for the exact right moment to knock her on her ass. When she was a kid, her moms had worried sometimes— always out of earshot, but Pepper wasn't stupid—that something would happen and they'd lose her. The feeling was hard to shake.

They sat in the living room, across from a shelf of replica pottery that depicted ancient Greek figures contorted in a variety of sexual positions. Ike was a history professor who specialized in the history of sexuality. Bill didn't seem to notice.

"You're making me nervous," Pepper said. "What kind of attorney are you?"

"I mostly do employment work," Bill said. "Except for one client."

Ike had disappeared into the kitchen and now returned with a glass of water, which he didn't give to Pepper but held for her, as if he expected her hands might not be steady. She felt his knee against her own. He smelled like the library, which normally both calmed and aroused her.

"Okay, well, what the hell is going on?" she said.

"I was under the impression you . . . ," Bill said. "Forgive me. I realize this must come as a shock." He was wearing a black turtleneck under a black blazer, and he enunciated his words like someone who'd practiced enunciation. Pepper imagined that he played saxophone in a jazz quartet on the weekends. Or maybe not this version of him. Maybe a version of him in a different world.

He took a sheaf of papers from a briefcase. "You may have seen in the news that the painter Ula Frost has gone missing. Are you familiar with her work?"

"Of course," Pepper said, attempting nonchalance. She could feel Ike's eyes on her like a form of heat.

"Good," Bill said. "I'm here because you are the primary beneficiary named in Ula Frost's will."

Ike put a hand on Pepper's knee and squeezed. She took the water, sipped it, and handed it back without making eye contact.

"What does that mean?" she asked.

"It means, in the case of her death, after the probate process, you'll acquire her assets. We don't have to go over all of this now, but you can imagine her assets are substantial. And in addition to financial assets and real estate, there are a significant number of paintings that, if you agree to Ms. Frost's conditions, would also transfer to your ownership."

Ike's hand was still on her knee, his index finger stroking as if to soothe her. She couldn't look at him.

"Conditions," Pepper said. She wanted to pick up the papers, but her limbs were stiff, like a fainting goat's. "You said *in the case of her death*. But she's only missing?"

"Yes," Bill said.

"So why are you here?" she asked.

"This is the beginning of a process," Bill said. She could tell he'd rehearsed this, the way she rehearsed her lectures in the car. "Ms. Frost has given me clear instructions, as her financial conservator, on how to proceed in a number of scenarios, and this is one of them. Official reports have been filed, of course. In Connecticut, once a person has been declared missing, they can be declared dead in absentia after seven years, or sooner if evidence suggests they're dead."

"So if she doesn't show up in the next seven years, she'll be declared dead and I'll have to sign some papers?"

"Pepper," Ike said.

Pepper stared at her knee, Ike's tense finger. She could feel the moment about to split itself, a charge in the air, but thought maybe she could hold it off for a few minutes by playing dumb.

"It may be possible to obtain a death certificate before that based on circumstantial evidence," Bill said, "like when someone isn't found after a plane crash. We don't know enough right now to say if there's evidence to point in that direction. But it's a little more complicated than that."

Pepper closed her eyes and saw a plane falling out of the sky, and another universe, in which the same plane kept flying. A moment of worlds splitting apart, when one version of a person disappeared while another continued on. She could hear Bill still talking, something about real estate and deeds, but the words weren't sticking.

"Pepper," Ike said again. When she looked at him, she had a flash of double vision and could see two of him, but she blinked and there was only one again. Her eyes were watering. "Don't you want to know why you're the beneficiary?"

"No," she said, and felt the tug as it all began to separate. Going forward, there would always be a universe in which she told him the truth now and a parallel one in which she didn't, and everything continued as it had, just like there were all those other universes that split off when she'd had the opportunity to tell him and did instead of didn't. There were a lot of them, so many versions of Pepper and Ike out there.

"No," she said again. "I know why. Ula Frost is my biological mother."

The room was uncomfortably silent. Bill stared ahead of him and cocked his head, finally noticing the pottery on the shelf. "I'm sorry," he said. "I thought you must've known. And then your husband said you didn't. I just need you to sign a few things, and I'll get out of your hair."

ONCE BILL WAS gone, Ike went to the bedroom and shut the door. After Pepper's revelation, he'd taken his hand off her knee, and she'd signed the paperwork without reading it. While Bill had gathered his things, Ike stood like an old man.

"I read something today about Mary, Queen of Scots," he said. "After she was beheaded, her lips kept moving for fifteen minutes."

Bill had left a folder on the coffee table. "We can talk more after you've had a chance to read this."

"Fifteen minutes," Ike repeated.

Pepper got a beer and sat at the kitchen table. There were plenty of times she could've told him. And there were no good reasons why she didn't. She didn't tell him because she'd never met Ula Frost and never would meet her and it didn't matter. She didn't tell him, because she needed one tiny piece of this universe she could control. She didn't tell him, because she knew he'd do what he always did—gently press her in the direction of understanding something too big for her to fully grasp, like the number of galaxies in the universe. She didn't tell him, because a woman the world revered hadn't wanted her, and she always carried that, a gem of certainty that if she let Ike really, truly know her, he wouldn't want her either. She thought about the Polish coin, tucked in the back of her jewelry box. She was good at tucking things away. She already had two moms. She was all set, mother-wise.

The evening was dissolving into night, and Pepper felt herself growing darker with the world around her, the only light in the kitchen seeping from a lamp left on in the living room. She drank the beer fast and went for another. That's when Ike came out of the bedroom, and she realized he'd probably been waiting for her to join him.

Ike got himself a beer and sat at the table. A few years ago, they'd run out of space for more bookshelves, so they'd taken the doors off some kitchen cabinets and stuffed them full of nonfiction. They didn't need many dishes. They'd agreed years ago that they didn't want kids, though sometimes as Pepper watched the university's day care taking the toddlers on a parade through campus, a line of wagons filled with girls wearing pom-pom hats and freckled boys blowing kisses, she wondered. Somewhere there was a universe in which she wouldn't be a terrible mother.

"How long have you known?" Ike said.

Pepper tapped her wedding ring against her beer bottle, which made a dull sound. "I got suspicious when I was fifteen." She told him the story about Tilda Hogan and the check. "But I wasn't sure until I was in grad school. The Hogans came to the clinic a lot. There was always something little with one of their dogs. A limp or a cough. One time, Tilda saw a snake in the yard and brought them all in to make sure none of them had bite marks. She'd chopped the hell out of the snake with a shovel and had it in a baggie in case we needed to identify it."

"Did you?" Ike asked.

"It was just a baby," Pepper said. "It wasn't old enough to have clear identifying marks." She tapped her ring again. "Even venomous snakes are capable of biting without injecting venom. Only half of their bites are envenomated. They learn to save it."

Ike closed his eyes. Once, at a history department party, an older woman who specialized in early-modern economics and sometimes sent Ike home with handmade beaded earrings for Pepper touched her arm and asked if she knew how lucky she was, which took Pepper completely by surprise. Ike was always talking at her about random trivia, especially when she'd just woken up or gotten home and wasn't ready for it. And he sneezed louder than any person she'd ever known. It wasn't that Pepper didn't love him, she just couldn't stop herself from imagining universes in which her life wasn't locked in with his. She was different in those universes. Lit up.

"Do you want dinner?" she asked.

He shook his head.

She continued. "When I'd come home from school and visit the clinic, Tilda would always be there. Annie made a joke about it one time, that Tilda was better at keeping track of my schedule than she was. Tilda was one of her favorites. She'd been one of their first clients, which meant a lot then." She drank. The beer tasted like metal. "Then Tilda started saying things."

"What kind of things?" Ike asked. He was looking at Pepper as if she were a document he was trying to interpret. She fixed her eyes on the table. It was the first piece of furniture they'd bought together, right after they got engaged, made from reclaimed wood from a one-room schoolhouse in Michigan, where Ike grew up. He'd been giddy about it—they both had—and Pepper had scratched the surface with her bag almost immediately. Ike had countered her self-loathing by taking a needle from the sewing kit and etching a little heart into the corner. "Now," he'd said. "It's not damaged. It's just worn in."

"Tilda would tell me a story," Pepper said. "About going to the doctor, and mention there was a history of heart disease in the family. Or about how her mother's father died from colon cancer."

"She was giving you your medical history," Ike said.

Pepper nodded. "But I wasn't sure if she knew that I suspected or what. And then one day, she was asking me about school, and I told her I worked in the genetics lab. And she said, 'Oh, do you do those tests to see if people are related, like on the talk shows?' And I explained that wasn't what I did but some people in our lab worked on kinship analysis. When the appointment was over, she took out her gum—it was grape—and she stuck it on the exam table right in front of me."

"Subtle," Ike said. "And you tested it?"

"I tested it," Pepper said. She'd swabbed her mouth in a bathroom stall that day, and while she was in there, her supervisor had come in and started talking to her, having recognized her shoes. And she'd stayed in there, claiming an upset stomach, sick with shame, until after her supervisor was gone. Even then, it seemed impossible to talk about.

"So your moms know too?" Ike asked. He'd finished his beer, and she could hear his stomach from across the table. His body was so loud; she'd never understood it.

"Why don't you let me make you something," she said. "Grilled cheese? I think we have some potatoes and smoked salmon."

Ike's jaw shifted. "You didn't tell them either."

Pepper could only shake her head. Her face was hot, and the universe was buckling around her. Maybe in another universe, this same conversation was happening, but Ike wasn't looking at her like this.

"There's no excuse," she said. "I have no excuse for myself."

"Sure you do," Ike said. "You didn't want to hurt them. You didn't want them to worry she might take their place in your life. You didn't want to deal with the fact that you knew about your birth mother's identity, so you just pretended it didn't exist."

"Wow," Pepper said. "Maybe you should've skipped history and gone into psychology instead."

Ike stood and went to the refrigerator. He opened the door, stood in the chilled light, and slammed it shut.

"Is there anything else you want to tell me? Any other secrets you've been keeping the entire time I've known you for some reason that probably doesn't even make sense to you? Now's the time! May as well do this all at once."

"Thank you," Pepper said. "I know you're working so hard to create a space where I might feel comfortable doing that, but now you know everything."

But even that wasn't true. Pepper stood in Ike's way, and she wanted him to push her, but instead he put a gentle hand on her arm as he navigated around her and returned to the bedroom. Pepper sat at the table and tried hard to picture a universe where she'd behaved less stupidly, but all she could see was a million versions of herself, miserable and deserving to be miserable, at this table with a heart on it. The best she could do was imagine a table that had never been scratched in the first place, or one that was inscribed with something different—their initials, skull and crossbones, a knot.

The bedroom was dark, but she could see him, lying on his side, on top of the covers, curled away from the door. She sat at the edge of the bed.

"Now that I think about it, you should probably know some guy came to see me today. This guy from an art magazine who's writing about Ula. He must've figured it out."

Ike sat up and wrapped one hand around her wrist. "Pepper, I met her."

Again the universe split in two, which looked in Pepper's mind like a cell dividing. But Pepper could see that one of the cells was mutated.

"What do you mean, you met her?"

"She came to see me," Ike said. "Just before we got married. I didn't know who she was at the time. I'd never seen a picture of her."

Pepper was grateful for the room's darkness. "What did she want?" She tried to pull her hand away, but Ike held tight.

"Nothing," he said. "Or . . . I don't know. She asked a lot of questions. About me, not about you. She wasn't very pleasant about it."

"That doesn't make sense," Pepper said. This time when she pulled her hand away, Ike let go.

"She was just a strange woman who showed up in my office," he said. "I didn't put it together until the lawyer came and I looked her up on my phone. I guess she must've been making sure I wasn't after you because of her."

A car drove down the street, and its headlights penetrated the window and moved across Pepper's body, the room both dark and light at the same time. It didn't make sense. Ike had met her. Ike had met her and Pepper had not.

"You look just like her," he said, as if he were giving her something.

"Okay," she said. "Do you want a grilled cheese?"

"Okay," he said, and lay back down in the dark.

PEPPER WANTED TO sleep on the couch, but after dinner, Ike took her hand and led her back to the bedroom where they lay awake next to each other, not touching, for a long time. Pepper imagined Ike was doing what he did when he couldn't sleep, which was mentally recite Abraham Lincoln's speeches. He'd told her once that when Lincoln was shot, some witnesses heard Booth say, "I have done it," while others insisted he'd said nothing at all. It was something Ike obsessed about—how two different accounts of the same event could exist and historians would never know which one was true.

When Pepper couldn't sleep—at least since she was fifteen—she imagined the alternate universes that might be out there if alternate universes really existed. A universe where antibiotics had already stopped working. A universe where cancer had a cure. A universe where that man had never become president and started that war, and all the people who'd died and the cities that'd been destroyed still lived and stood perfectly intact. A universe where she hadn't met Ike in the hotel lobby of a conference about the evolution of human sexuality. A universe where they'd met but hadn't skipped out on the conference in favor of drinking hurricanes at the hotel bar and ended up in Ike's room shortly thereafter. A universe where they'd broken up that time she told him she couldn't see herself married instead of staying together. A universe where the pregnancy scare had been an actual pregnancy, and now they had a couple of kids, and two dogs and a cat, who was the boss of them all, and it was chaos and she mostly loved it. A universe where a terrorist attack had or hadn't been successful, a universe where a virus had or hadn't mutated and spread. A universe where there wasn't a mass shooting every single day, or a universe where there were even more. A universe where children didn't drink poisoned water, where hundreds of millions of people didn't go to bed hungry, where the earth's temperature wasn't steadily rising, where solvable problems had been solved. A universe where Annie had found the lump in her breast a few months later. A universe where Pepper had told Ike sooner and they'd avoided this mess. A universe where she didn't always keep secrets, where saying things out loud wasn't impossibly difficult for her, where she said things out loud whenever she felt like it and was a totally different person. A universe where she wasn't so terrified she'd inherited an instinct to abandon people that she tried to make them abandon her first. A universe where her infant body had been found by a fox, who'd dragged her by the nape of her neck into the woods. A universe where someone else had adopted her. A universe where she'd never been left alone on a dog bed in the night, where Ula Frost had kept her and was the only mother she'd ever known, and she lived a life with a different shape, where maybe she could sleep.

4

PEPPER HADN'T PLANNED to call Scott, but the next morning, she found herself staring at her phone rather than gathering her bag for work. Scott had sent her an email that she'd deleted immediately but kept rereading from her trash folder. It was a Friday morning. Usually, Pepper had office hours on Friday mornings, and no one ever showed up, which made it her favorite part of the week. She told herself to get up and go, but she didn't. Her hand sweat on the phone. Her legs didn't lift her from her chair. Her fingers came dangerously close to Scott's number on the screen.

Pepper didn't want to give Ula Frost more space in her brain than she already had. She also didn't want to keep thinking about how Scott had found her. She didn't want to worry about the professional implications if Scott wrote about her and everyone in the academic community knew she was Ula Frost's daughter. But more than that, she didn't want to keep wondering what else Scott might know about Ula. Why she'd left Pepper the way she had. What her life had been like all these years. How much of what Pepper disliked about herself had come from Ula, and how much was her own.

But she did. She did want to know. Her body wouldn't let her keep denying it. Coffee, she told herself. She made the call. A single cup of coffee couldn't hurt.

When they got to the coffee place, Pepper expected Scott to park, but he pulled into the drive-thru instead.

"I thought we were going to talk," she said.

"We are," he said. The morning was muggy, and the windshield was plagued with a creeping fog that Scott couldn't tame with the defroster. "I have questions. But we have an appointment first."

Scott ordered his latte with soy milk and a caramel drizzle. Pepper pried the lid from her coffee and poured four packets of sugar inside, spilling granules onto the car's leather seats.

She snapped the lid back onto her cup. She'd woken that morning in an empty bed, Ike already out for a run. Usually, he took his phone so Pepper could track his progress and reassure herself that he was safe, but today, he'd left everything but his keys.

"So how did you find out?" Pepper said. She didn't want to keep worrying about it, but she was anyway.

"I read your paper," Scott said.

Pepper turned her head toward the window. "My paper."

In grad school, after Pepper had run Tilda's DNA and confirmed they were related, she'd spent one feverish semester in the stacks of the library, reading everything she could find about Ula Frost. The art books were on the twelfth floor—an eerie labyrinth that smelled like sweat and glue—and Pepper had sat cross-legged on a couch near the elevator, a tower of books beside her. Even people who thought the stories about Ula's work were pernicious nonsense couldn't seem to stop themselves from writing about her. There were theories about how the paintings might actually work, and theories about how Ula might be duping people into believing they work. Interviews with former clients, some of whose claims had been debunked. Interviews with other artists, and their interpretations of both the art and the hype around it. Detailed analyses of Ula's entire known body of work. Discussions of possible influences—cultural, scientific, and philosophical. Ula's career as a case study on the spread of urban legends. A thesis situating Ula's popularity in the history of urban legends. Psychological texts exploring the desire for alternate universes to exist. A collection of fictional letters between Ula and her subjects' alternate selves. But almost nothing about the artist herself. Pepper had written the paper for one of her seminars because she couldn't focus on anything else.

"It was a good paper," Scott said. "I looked you up to see if you'd written more about her."

"I haven't," Pepper said.

"I know," Scott said. "But your picture is on the department website."

Pepper considered throwing herself out of the car. Scott wasn't driving that fast. She'd never broken a bone before. She wasn't sure who'd sign her cast, but she'd always kind of wanted one.

"So what about my picture?" she said.

Scott looked at her for too long, which made her worry he was going to crash. You could only look at people for that long when you were driving in a movie. "You know what she looks like."

"I know what she looks like," Pepper said. Ula had a habit of suing anyone who published a photo of her, but there were photos out there. Sometimes she popped up in odd places—a restaurant in Morocco, a ballet in Cuba, Disneyland. One time, she'd trashed a hotel room in Vegas and someone had recognized her running through the lobby, security close behind. There were enough people who recognized her. And it was clear in the way Scott looked at Pepper, while driving like someone who'd never seen a body pulled from a car accident, that he recognized her in Pepper, too.

"I can't blame you for not wanting people to know," Scott said. "There are some real nutcases among her followers."

Pepper had been so distracted by everything with Ike that she'd nearly forgotten about Ula's disappearance, and the possibility that this woman she'd never met might be gone.

"Do you think one of her followers might have done something to her?" she asked.

Scott's phone buzzed in his pocket, but he didn't answer it. "I don't know. She's so secretive it's hard to imagine anyone could find her if she didn't want to be found. Like I said, I have a lot of questions."

He turned onto Main Street, where the dogwoods were just starting to bloom. The street was lined with antique houses, all tastefully painted, picturesquely New England. A few years ago, a group of Buddhist monks had filed plans to build a temple on the other side of town, but the town council voted them down. It wouldn't fit with the town's aesthetic, had been the reason. Now Scott turned again, onto the road that led to the high school.

"Where are we going?" she said.

"According to her birth certificate, Ula Frost is fifty-four years old. And you're thirty-six," Scott said.

"How do you know that?" Pepper said.

"Your marriage license," he said. "So that means Ula was eighteen when you were born. And according to the yearbooks I found in the library, she was at the high school for at least part of her junior year, and then I'm guessing she dropped out. So it seems pretty likely that getting pregnant had something to do with that."

There was a man wearing neon orange-and-yellow leggings running on the shoulder of the road. Pepper wondered where Ike was. Sometimes he went to the path by the old railroad tracks with all the signs warning about coyotes. If you saw a coyote, the most important thing was not to turn your back to it.

Now the high school loomed before them, through the persistent ghost of fog on the windshield's glass, the same long, beige brick expanse it had always been. The flag was at half-mast for some reason.

"Probably no one is still at the high school from when she was there," Pepper said, though she knew it wasn't true. Two of her former classmates were current teachers. She knew exactly who was still there and who wasn't.

Scott sipped his latte. "A few people are still there."

"What about coffee?" Pepper said.

"You have coffee," Scott said. "And we have an appointment."

The school day had already started, and the parking lot was full of cars too expensive for students to afford, the bumpers plastered with stickers for bands. The security guard at the booth by the entrance barely looked up when Scott gave his name.

"I don't know why you brought me here," Pepper told him.

IN THE MAIN office, the secretary had them sign their names and gave them badges for their shirts. Pepper hadn't been to the high school once in the years since she'd graduated— half her life ago—but it still felt wrong to be treated like a visitor. The building smelled the same, like floor cleaner and pizza, even though lunch wouldn't be served for hours. She remembered the chocolate chip cookies from the cafeteria, underdone and mixed with too much salt, with an unexpected pang of affection.

The principal, a woman named Dr. Bergman, came from her office to greet them. She was short and wide with the hair of an eighties pop star and wore a blazer with velvet lapels. In the hall, Pepper saw a girl rush to her locker, where she stared at the mirror inside while pressing a tissue to her chin. She'd picked at something till it bled. The girl held pressure on the tissue for a minute before dabbing the spot carefully with powder. The whole time, she kept checking up and down the hallway, making sure no one could see her. When she turned to go back to class, she saw Pepper watching and fled before Pepper could react.

The principal was looking at Pepper expectantly, but she hadn't been listening.

"Was it ninety-eight when you graduated?" Scott asked.

Pepper hated him so much already. "Something like that," she said.

"Feeling nostalgic?" Dr. Bergman asked.

Pepper could see her old locker from the office, three down from the fire extinguisher. They'd moved her there to deter attacks. She smiled and nodded.

"It must look very different to you," Dr. Bergman said. "We've completed quite a list of renovations in the past few years, thanks to contributions from generous alumni." Pepper

and Scott followed her down the hall, where Pepper didn't notice anything she'd qualify as improvement. Maybe the carpet
was new. It still looked like it would give you a nasty rug burn if
someone tripped you and you fell on it.

"We get a couple of inquiries like this every year," Dr. Bergman continued. "Ula Frost is our best-known alumna, though
our graduates have been successful in many fields. We just
had a visit from an alumna who has a highly respected physical therapy practice." She stopped in front of the art room and
knocked before opening the door. Across the hall, Pepper could
hear a teacher lecturing on the Civil War. He was talking about
how the North and South named the same battles after different things—the North bodies of water and the South nearby
towns—so every battle had two names.

In the art room, Mr. Ashcroft reclined at his desk, oblivious
to their arrival. Dr. Bergman stepped in front of him and waved
her hand, and he looked up from his newspaper.

"Gene!" Dr. Bergman shouted. "This is the man from the art
magazine who wanted to speak with you. About Ula Frost."

Mr. Ashcroft gave Scott a once-over and made an evalua-
tive face. Then he looked at Pepper. Bob Dylan was playing
on the ancient CD player next to his desk. That's what Pepper remembered about high school art class—memorizing
the lyrics to Dylan songs. Ashcroft had given suggestions, not
assignments. Sometimes, when Pepper and her friends had
been bored, they'd taken paper and paint from the closet and
screwed around for a while. Pepper had once gotten ambitious
and attempted an imitation of a Rothko painting she'd seen on
a recent museum trip with her moms. Ashcroft had toured the
room at the end of class.

"I expected better from you," he'd said.

Now he examined her face in a way that made her uneasy.
"You know, you look exactly like her."

Pepper eyed Scott. She wasn't sure what he'd told Dr. Bergman about why she was accompanying him. "Oh no," she said.
"I'm just here to . . . I'm here in a professional capacity."

"Right," Scott said. "Dr. Rafferty is advising me on cultural interpretations of Ula Frost's work."

Dr. Bergman smiled blankly. "That's nice," she said. "I'll leave you to chat. I'll be in my office if you need anything."

She left the door open behind her. Pepper could hear a French class singing "Les Champs-Élysées," competing with Dylan, who was singing about a tightrope walker.

"Well, I don't know what you want me to tell you," Ashcroft said. "She never listened to anything I said."

Scott laughed in the way men laugh when they're trying to get something. "Do you mind?" he asked, and pulled a chair to Ashcroft's desk. Pepper half expected him to straddle it, but he sat like a normal person.

"Can you tell me what she was like?" Scott asked. "As a student."

Ashcroft leaned back, put his feet on the desk, and crossed his arms. He was wearing a purple jacket with a paisley-print shirt, and snakeskin shoes almost worn through at the soles. Pepper wondered if he even knew what Ula was like as a student or if he made up a different version of her for every journalist who came asking.

"I'm sorry," Scott said, much louder. "Can you tell me what Ms. Frost was like as a student?"

"I can hear, son," Ashcroft said. "I'm not deaf." He skipped a few tracks on the CD until he arrived at a song Pepper recognized. A fragment rose to her mind's surface, a fortune-teller warning about a lightning strike. "I remember her. Ula Frost was a brat. That's what she was like."

"What do you mean she was a brat?" Scott asked.

"Girls that age, they're mostly brats," Ashcroft said. "But she was beyond that. She came in at the end of the day sometimes and took paint from the closet home with her."

"And you didn't stop her," Pepper said.

"I'm not trying to stop a kid from painting," Ashcroft said. "But she never asked. Never said a kind word to a classmate. She was a talent, even then. Everyone knew it. Sometimes those other kids would ask her to look at something they were working on, and she'd ignore them. Couldn't be bothered by anyone else. Her parents came to see me a few times, with catalogs from art schools, trying to figure out what to do with her. Her mother didn't have any illusions. But that kid had no respect for her. I wasn't sad to see her go. No one was, even if we all knew she'd go on to be a big shot."

"So you knew she was leaving?" Scott said.

"It's not that big a school, son," Ashcroft said. He closed his eyes for a moment, caught by something in the music. Pepper wondered how many times he'd listened to these songs. "When something like that happens, everyone knows."

Scott's phone was buzzing again, and he put a hand in his pocket and silenced it. "You mean about her being pregnant."

Ashcroft gave Pepper an unambiguous can-you-believe-this-asshole look, which unknotted something inside her. The French class was still singing—two lovers, a long night. On one of the room's walls there were prints by Mondrian, Hopper, and Ernst; on another an oversize poster with a lot of distressed people on a raft. Pepper didn't know the artist, but she liked the dark clouds hanging over the wretchedness. Another wall was covered with student work—a few paintings of girls with multicolored hair draped across their faces, a portrait of a man in a suit with the head of a fish, another painting of what looked like a huge owl eye. A sloppy pointillist butterfly. There was a series of three black-and-white skulls with typewritten text going through them. Pepper recognized a few lines from *Hamlet*.

"You're from some magazine?" Ashcroft said.

"*Ekphrasis,*" Scott said. "I can show you my credentials if you'd like, sir."

Ashcroft coughed. Pepper stopped in front of a portrait of a boy with a gaping hole in his head.

"I don't want your fucking credentials. Give us the room, son."

Scott fidgeted with his cuff links, then offered Pepper his chair, which she didn't take. She wasn't the one who cared about Ula Frost. She already knew more than she wanted. This is what she told herself. Scott pulled something from his bag and passed it to Pepper before leaving and closing the door. A yearbook.

"I remember you," Ashcroft said. The yearbook had once been a shiny silver, but the foil was mostly worn to gray. "I remember thinking you looked just like her. And your age was about right."

"I don't know anything about that," Pepper said. "I mean, I put it together, but I've never met her."

Ashcroft nodded. "She was young," he said. "And she would've been a shit mother. It's a wonder her parents didn't raise you, but I'm sure they had their reasons." He held out his hands, and it took Pepper longer than it should have to realize he was reaching for the yearbook. He flipped through the pages in a way that made Pepper think he was trying to look absentminded to hide his purpose. Now that he bent and flexed his fingers, she could see he had arthritis in his hands. Pepper's own hands retracted into fists. "You were always a quiet one. Just trying to avoid being noticed." He stopped on a page in the yearbook and squinted. "So are you going to ask me?"

There was a new song playing, a song with a lot of harmonica, and Pepper knew all the lyrics even though she hadn't heard them in such a long time. She'd have to read up on the neurology of memory. She didn't understand where those words had been since the last time she'd thought of them.

"I know I should," she said. The song went on and on, the harmonica fast as an emergency. She was hoping maybe now he'd refuse, sensing her hesitance. She wanted to know, but she didn't. She couldn't see the universes around her clearly, the ones about to split off from this moment. A few kids ran down the hall, shouting nonsense. "Do you know who my father is?"

Ashcroft pressed the yearbook flat against his desk and pointed to a picture. Pepper felt the room around her waver. She sat. Three boys, in track uniforms, their arms around each other.

They looked out of breath, flushed from exertion, like they'd only stopped running to pose for this photo and seconds later were back on the track.

"The one in the middle," he said. "The tall one."

Pepper rotated the book and touched the boy's name with her finger. Michael Orlando. He was tall and skinny, and he had thick, wavy hair, like hers. He looked like a boy from a movie about summer camp, the kid who befriends the outcast who's being bullied. He just looked like a normal kid. The word *kid* was stuck in her head. He and Ula were both kids then.

"Do you know where he is now?" she asked. She could think of a few people in town with the same last name, but no Michaels.

"He died," Ashcroft said. "That summer. He was on a motorcycle without a helmet, like an idiot." He looked at the dates imprinted on the yearbook's spine. "If you find the one for the next year, there's some kind of tribute to him. He had a brother, a few years older. Can't quite remember the name."

"Oh," Pepper said.

She ran her hand over the yearbook, trying to process but not actually processing. She hadn't wanted to know. In another universe, she didn't and never would. She could have gone on not knowing. This didn't change anything.

Ashcroft put one hand on hers, which startled her. "You seem like you turned out pretty good," he said.

"Yeah," Pepper said. She thought, *I got lucky,* but couldn't say it out loud. She made it to the door and remembered herself, turned back, and said thank you. Scott was waiting in the hall, texting as fast as she'd ever seen anyone text, and she walked past him toward the exit, giving the office a weak wave on her way out. Scott was behind her, and he stopped her by grabbing the crook of her arm.

"What did he tell you?" he said.

The flag was still at half-mast. Pepper didn't know why it surprised her, why she thought it might be any different now. Inside she could hear the bell ring, the end of one period, the beginning of another.

IKE SHOULD'VE BEEN back from his run, but he didn't respond when Pepper texted him. She didn't call, because she knew she couldn't handle the sound of his voice. She just wanted to feel less alone.

i know you're still mad

She texted like an old woman.

but i really need you

She hated being so cryptic, but she didn't want to slow-text the whole story in front of Scott, who was still rapid-firing off his own missives next to her in the parking lot. He'd turned the air conditioner up high to cool the car down, which muted the sound of their fingers. It wasn't hot outside, but inside the car, light became heat and was trapped. Something folksy was playing on the radio. If Pepper had been alone, she would've chosen a song with screaming.

Scott put down his phone and pulled a backpack from the back seat, from which he drew more yearbooks.

"I don't know which years to check," he said. He flipped through a few, scanning the *O*s in each grade. He handed one to Pepper, in which she found a freshman version of Michael Orlando. He looked like he could've been eight to her. She could never tell how old kids were. He was wearing a T-shirt with cartoon characters on it. He had freckles on his cheeks, and she touched her own, instinctively. Her face was the same shape as his, an overlong, horselike oval.

"The local paper has their archive online," she said. She knew this because sometimes, after she worked on a case for Jamie Marchand, she'd look up whoever's bones she'd examined.

When the bones were a woman's, there was almost always a record in the police blotter, a history of assault. Every time a man hit a woman, the worlds fanned out like a deck of cards, shuffled versions of the same woman, versions who escaped and slept in different bedrooms, painted different colors, or with floral wallpaper, safe. Sometimes at night, lying in bed next to Ike, who breathed so loudly, Pepper imagined other versions of herself, sleeping next to other men, who loved her more or less than Ike did.

"Okay, this is something," Scott said, looking up from his phone. "No obituary, but there's someone named Phillip Orlando. Have you heard of him?"

"Dr. Orlando?" Pepper said. "Yeah, he's my dentist."

She kept looking at her phone, but wherever Ike was, he wasn't responding. She thought about texting *SOS SOS SOS* but stopped herself.

"He seems about the right age," Scott said. His phone buzzed again, and he grimaced.

"What the hell is going on with you?" she asked.

"Nothing," Scott said. He texted something back. "Just my girlfriend."

"Do you need to call her?" Pepper said. There were some kids out front of the school now, with a shovel and a tray of impatiens. They seemed to be arguing over where to plant them. "I can get out."

"It's fine," Scott said. "Her dad is sick, and she's just venting about her family. It'll be fine."

"You're in trouble," Pepper said.

Scott sighed. "She knows I can't be there. It's complicated. It's fine." His phone buzzed again.

"Seems pretty fine," Pepper said. She lit on a selfish hope that Scott's own disaster might be enough to distract him from hers. "What does she do?"

"She's an artist," Scott said. "She makes these kinetic sculptures—they're powered by the wind. Huge, hypnotic things. She's amazing."

"So why aren't you there? This can't be more important," Pepper said.

Scott looked at her with disbelief. "Are you kidding?" he said. "It's *Ula Frost*. Ula Frost is missing."

"Who cares?" Pepper said. She ground her teeth to keep from crying. She wouldn't let herself cry in a car that cost more than her undergraduate education.

Scott put the car in reverse. Pepper had never had a cavity. At the end of her last appointment, Dr. Orlando had ordered her to go buy herself a doughnut. They were on Pepper's street before she realized Scott was driving her home. Ike's car wasn't in the driveway.

"I'm going to have to make some calls," Scott said. "If I can verify that Phillip Orlando is Michael's brother, I'll set up a time to go see him. Do you want to come?"

The summer before, she and Ike had pulled out the boxwoods in front of the house after carpenter ants had gotten into the wood siding behind them. It had been a million degrees out and there were ants everywhere and Pepper hated yard work, but by the end of it, they were both sweaty and dirt-streaked and making out like teenagers in the front yard. Sometimes she'd think about little moments like that and realize they were pretty happy, most of the time. She just never realized it while it was happening. The rhododendrons they'd planted as replacements for the boxwoods had buds on them.

"Do you ever treat your girlfriend like shit?" she asked. She didn't know why she said it that way. "Like, I'm sure you love her, but do you ever feel like you've been so ugly to her, even though she's the person you love?" *Or is it just me,* Pepper thought.

Scott gathered the yearbooks and handed them to Pepper. "I'll call you when I figure out what's going on with the dentist."

"Okay," Pepper said, and got out of the car. There was a twinge in one of her molars, which she knew was psychosomatic.

She waited until Scott had driven away to go inside, leaving the yearbooks in a neat stack on the porch.

SOS SOS SOS

        i'm in a faculty meeting

sorry

        SOS SOS SOS

haaa

        you okay?

i have a dad

        hold on

THEY WENT TO see Phillip Orlando that evening. It was strange seeing him in his own home, away from the sterile trays and vinyl chairs of his office. He was skinny and had the hunch of someone who bent over for a living, and he wore chinos and a sweater that was too big for him. His house was warm and smelled like garlic bread. Pepper had always liked him because his teeth were crooked and a human shade of yellow, so she didn't have to worry he was judging her too much.

His wife, Dot, came from the kitchen and hugged both Pepper and Scott hello. She had the demeanor of a kindergarten teacher, full of energy but firm. Pepper declined her offer of a drink, but Dot brought her coffee anyway. It was in a mug with different species of fish on it.

"It's been a long time since someone asked about Michael," she said. "It's always nice to hear his name."

Scott sat in the living room's sole mauve upholstered chair, so Pepper was forced to sit on the couch next to Phillip. She stayed close to the arm. Ike had offered to go with her, but she'd told him she needed to do it alone, afraid of having him there to witness her fumbling or to press her forward if she lost her nerve. When Scott called, Phillip had only vaguely remembered Ula Frost. It was obvious to Scott he didn't know there'd been a baby, and Scott didn't tell him on the phone. It was a lot to drop on your dentist. They'd have to ease into it.

"I got a box down from the attic," Phillip said.

He began arranging its contents on the coffee table, and an

ache took hold of Pepper's body. She sipped her coffee even though she knew she wouldn't sleep now, focusing on the mug's rainbow trout, its speckled belly, iridescent pink.

"Most of this is from when we were kids." There was a stuffed monkey and a discolored recorder and a notebook that was water damaged. Pepper almost touched the recorder but didn't. She thought about Michael's saliva, dried inside. Sitting next to Phillip, she noticed his ears were squared off, like hers.

"He was always one part quiet and one part wild," Phillip said. "Even as a kid. He went missing one day—I wasn't quite in high school, so he would've been maybe eight then. Our parents looked everywhere. Not in the house, not in the basement, not in the backyard. They ended up calling the police and they came and took the report, and once they'd left, we heard giggling and there he was, up on the roof. He'd been lying up there under a blanket the whole time. Thought he was being funny."

Scott flipped through the notebook without looking at Pepper. He'd been guarded in the car when Pepper had tried to make small talk about his family. She didn't like that he knew so much about her while she knew so little about him.

"I wish there were more to show you," Phillip continued. "I was at college when he died, and our mother stuffed most everything into trash bags. Not to throw away, but she needed it out of sight, I suppose. And they sat in the basement for a long time. I didn't find them until after she died and we were clearing out the house, but most of it was so mildewed we had to toss it." He swallowed. "I was glad she wasn't there for it."

From the bottom of the box, he pulled a jean jacket and a binder. "This," he said. "I remember seeing some drawings in here. He never drew. They must've been from his friend Ula."

Pepper took the binder and opened it. There was trigonometry homework in the front, and a report on the Cuban missile crisis. His handwriting was hard to read, the letters shrunken and close together, compressed.

"He was a good student," Phillip said. "He got in trouble a lot, skipping school and that kind of thing, but he was smart.

Liked math. Liked to go sit by the creek and fish. I wasn't around much those years before he died. I wish I'd known him better."

Pepper flipped through the homework and found a note in someone else's handwriting. *That bitch with the penny loafers likes you.* Was it Ula's writing? Pepper had attended a session on handwriting analysis at a forensics conference once, but all she could remember was that serial killers tended to have extreme height differentials in their lettering. There was a photocopied diagram of a frog's internal organs, and notes from history class, the pencil faded. Something about Napoléon. Then Pepper got to the back of the binder, where she found a folder pocket with three heavy sheets of paper. On one, there was a sketch of Michael's face. His eyes were half-closed, and his hair was swept back as if by a gust of wind. On the second was a tree, the bark intricately detailed, a length of frayed rope hanging from the uppermost branch. The third page was crossed with crease marks and looked blank at first, but when Pepper flipped it over, she found a row of geometric shapes and dots.

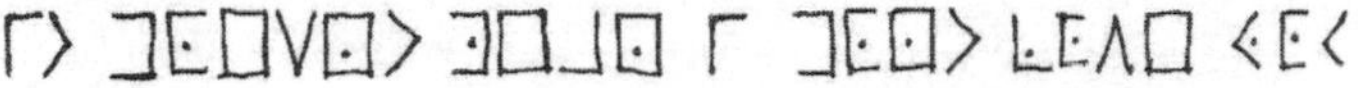

Scott took the page from her hand. "What in the world is this?"

He passed it to Phillip, who shook his head. "No idea."

"It's pigpen," Pepper said. She felt the room's attention tilt toward her. "It's a code. They used it during the Civil War. Union soldiers in Confederate prisons."

The study of the history of sexuality relied on primary sources, which meant Ike spent a lot of time reading collections of diaries and letters. Years ago, he'd found a diary written entirely in pigpen, and Pepper had helped him decode it, the two of them sitting up late, heads literally together as they squinted at the same copy of the cipher. She took a picture with her phone and texted it to Ike. The diary they'd read together had been mostly comprised of entries about the weather, except for one in which the prisoner had fantasized in explicit and heartbreaking detail about his wife. Ike later learned the soldier never made it home.

"Do you remember Ula?" Scott asked.

"Not really," Phillip said. "My parents didn't like her. I remember they said she was disrespectful. I didn't get the impression it was very serious. I asked him about his girlfriend once, and he just shrugged. The time I met her, she wasn't friendly at all. She was sitting on the steps, waiting for Mikey. She barely said a word to me."

"Did your parents have any contact with her after Michael died?" Scott said. "Or do you remember seeing her parents around?"

Phillip thought about it for a minute. "No, not that I can remember. I don't think she was even at the funeral."

it doesn't mean i don't love you

Scott was still puzzling over the code. Phillip set the sketch of Michael's face on his lap. Pepper wanted to leave. She didn't want anyone to say another word. There was no reason to make this more painful than it already was. In some universe it was inevitable, but it didn't have to be this one.

> the pigpen
> that's what it says
> it doesn't mean i don't love you

But Phillip was rubbing his thumb over the stuffed monkey's hand. He had so little of his brother—a stuffed monkey, a drawing, a recorder. And Pepper had chosen to come here. And she knew: this was the universe where it was inevitable.

"Did you ever hear a rumor that Ula Frost was pregnant?" she asked. "Around that time?"

Phillip sank back into the couch. "No," he said quietly. He took the monkey's hands and pressed them together. "Was she?"

Scott kept his eyes on the shapes and dots, the sureness gone out of him. The mantel was crowded with photographs of Phillip's kids and grandkids, all of them smiling, showing off their teeth.

"We think so," Pepper said. "I have reason to believe that Ula Frost is my biological mother."

Phillip turned fully in her direction and touched her face, which he'd done before, many times, in the course of an exam. His eyes filled as yet another universe came into being. Pepper imagined the version of herself in that universe, the one who wasn't doing this, which calmed her. Somewhere she wasn't doing this at all. And then Phillip put his arms around her so tightly, as if he were reaching through this universe to another one, different from the one Pepper was imagining, where his brother was still alive.

"Don't let me forget," he said. He was practically kissing her ear. "I have floss for you. And a new toothbrush to take home."

5

WHEN PEPPER ARRIVED at the local post office on Saturday morning, she steeled herself by imagining a universe in which mail simply did not exist. The problem with the local post office was that there were only two clerks—a woman named Dee, who distributed her resentment with an admirable equanimity, and a man in his sixties named Wally. Wally was a mouth breather who told everyone he was a poet and who, without deviation, examined each customer's outgoing mail and struck up an overly loud conversation about it. He'd worked there forever. When Pepper was applying to grad school, he'd made sure everyone in line behind her knew his opinions of the schools to which she was applying. When she was submitting a paper to a journal, he subjected her to an onslaught of questions about her hypothesis, the methods of statistical analysis, the peer review process. Pepper answered as minimally as possible. She valued her privacy. But clearly, Wally thought they had a rapport. He was fond of quoting the poetry of Robert Frost. He always told Pepper she looked like she needed to spend more time outdoors.

Scott had already been there the day before, and though Wally had been cagey about Ula Frost's post office box, he'd encouraged Scott to make himself at home in the lobby in case someone showed up to check it. When Pepper arrived to meet him, Wally winked at her from behind the counter.

"This is exciting," he said. "I feel like I'm part of a sting."

Pepper settled next to Scott on one of the stools at the counter by the window. The post office boxes were in an adjacent, glass-walled room. Scott handed her a postcard-size form for sending registered mail.

"Look like you're doing something," he told her.

"Do you do this a lot?" Pepper asked.

Scott wrote a name on the registered mail slip: *Jasper Johns.* "The art world is full of intrigue," he said. She eyed him until he cracked a smile. "I just started with this magazine. I did investigative reporting for a newspaper before."

Pepper knew. Ike had looked Scott up and discovered he was the middle son of a media magnate who owned both the newspaper and the magazine. Her antipathy was softened by Scott's failure to disclose this information.

"Why'd you switch jobs?" she asked. Then: "Oh, the girlfriend."

"Among other reasons," Scott said. He smoothed his shirt, which was already wrinkle-free. "Ula Frost's work isn't something people take lightly."

Pepper could feel Scott watching her as she wrote on her postcard: *Meave Leakey.* The post office was sun-streaked and warm, like a greenhouse. Her phone buzzed. That morning when Pepper had tried to kiss Ike goodbye, he'd turned his head so all she could kiss was his cheek.

> just got a weird phone call
> was it about car warranties
> because sometimes i answer those calls
> and start talking about diseases
> so they might be concerned about me
> it was not about car warranties
> though now i am also concerned about you

Pepper swiveled her stool so Scott couldn't see her screen. She and Ike had barely spoken since the visit from the lawyer. They didn't fight often, but fighting she could handle. It was silence on Ike's part that worried her. His parents had worked long hours, his mother as a nurse and his father as a contractor, and when they got home, they'd been too tired to fight. They'd let everything build up quietly, until they'd agreed finally, without fanfare, to a divorce. Ike had never approached their own fights with that kind of apathy before. The worst fight they'd ever had, which started over a dirty kitchen but wasn't about a dirty kitchen at all, ended with Ike sitting at Pepper's side of the bed for hours while she lay silent and wretched, wishing he'd give up but also wishing he wouldn't, until he put one hand in her hair and broke her.

> the call was about a loan
>
> for what
>
> i just paid the mortgage
>
> no a different loan
>
> taken out against your property in london?
>
> oh right my property in london
>
> that's where i stash my numerous
>
> british lovers

She could feel Scott trying to see what she was typing and re-angled her body.

> we enjoy postcoital scones
>
> with clotted cream
>
> pepper
>
> i'm looking now
>
> i think this is a legit company

At the counter, Wally was helping a brusque man in a suit who did not care to discuss why he was sending a package to a hospital in Arizona.

> they said they received notification
>
> that the title is being transferred
>
> to your name
>
> as a gift
>
> by ula frost
>
> what
>
> but there's a lien against the property

how could ula frost give me property
if she's missing
can someone just put property in your
name
> starting to feel like we should've read all that
> paperwork
> the lawyer left

Pepper flipped her postcard over and began drawing a wobbly spiral on the back. She decided not to panic over this. This was the kind of thing you panicked over only to find, after worrying a hole through your stomach, it was all a mistake. You didn't just acquire property in London without knowing about it. It seemed like the kind of thing that required money, paperwork, effort.

"How long do you think this is going to take?" she asked Scott. Saturday afternoons, she and Ike took a long walk together. It wasn't something she usually looked forward to, but it was the beginning of the season where the field with the yellow flowers was full of white moths. "There's probably not much chance anyone is going to show up, right?"

"I have reason to believe the box gets checked on Saturdays," Scott said.

The line at the counter had moved, and Wally was now grilling a frazzled mother about a breast pump she was returning. She had a baby strapped to her chest, and the baby was screaming. Pepper had signed papers for the lawyer without reading them. "It just didn't work," the mother said.

Pepper's spiral had nearly reached the edge of the paper when Scott touched her arm. There was a middle-aged guy with floppy hair and round glasses standing in front of box 701—Ula's box. He scanned the room before taking a silver key from around his neck and opening it. At his register, Wally rubbed his hands together and wagged his eyebrows dramatically.

When Scott entered the room, the man with glasses startled

and turned, pressing his back against the box behind him as if to hide it.

"Excuse me," Scott said.

"Yes?" the man said. Seeing Pepper, he stood straighter and adjusted his cardigan, which was misbuttoned.

Scott introduced himself. "I'm working on a piece about Ula Frost. This is her post office box, correct?"

The man with the glasses looked past him as if he were considering making a run for it. "Yes," he said. "But I don't talk to journalists."

"You must know about her disappearance, though," Scott said.

The man with the glasses glared. "Of course I do," he said. "I'm the one who reported it. And she's going to be furious, I'm sure, that those indiscreet police let it slip to the media. Furious," he repeated. "Now it's a whole thing, and she'll hate that."

"So you're in contact with Ula Frost?" Scott said.

The man sighed, though Pepper detected a hint of thrill under the façade of frustration. "I'm Gordon Priddy," he said. "Ula's assistant." He seemed like he was going to say more but instead gave Pepper a long look. "Who are you? Another reporter?"

Scott cocked his head at Pepper.

Again she was struck by a sense of her presence here, the unfolding of this universe, as inevitable. "I'm Pepper Rafferty," she said. "I'm Ula Frost's daughter."

Gordon was silent as he considered this. He turned to the open box, pulled out a handful of letters. There was a pale blue envelope, speckled like an eggshell, and a thick manila one that had been bent to fit in the box. An envelope made from a red doily, a magenta one embossed with gold-foil shells, an envelope made from turquoise fabric and wound over and over with twine. Gordon locked the box and returned the key to his neck before turning back to them.

"Ula Frost doesn't have a daughter," he said.

"Guess you don't know your boss as well as you thought," Scott said. "I wonder what else she's been keeping from you."

Gordon stuffed the letters into his bag, blinking. "You don't know what you're talking about. I know plenty. I handle many things for Ula. She trusts me."

"Did you share all this privileged information with the police?" Scott asked. "Sounds like it might be helpful to their investigation."

"There's nothing to investigate," Gordon said.

"What makes you say that?" Scott asked. "Have you heard from her since she disappeared?"

"No," Gordon said. "That's not what I meant."

"Then what did you mean?" Scott said.

Pepper took a step back. As an undergrad, she'd assisted with a research project on chimpanzee play behavior and sat for hours each day at the zoo, watching the juvenile males try on alpha status, puffing their chests and beating on them. They'd take turns climbing atop the alpha, who'd wrestle them briefly before pinning them with what Pepper had unscientifically considered bemusement.

"I meant there's nothing to investigate because no one knows where Ula was before she disappeared," Gordon said.

"You don't know where she lives?" Scott said. "But you're her assistant. What about where she stores her work?"

"She's a very private woman. If she wanted someone to know where she was, they would," he said. He looked at Pepper in a way that felt hostile. "Do you know?"

Sometimes when stuck in an uncomfortable situation, Pepper slipped back into observation mode. Gordon touched his bag, protective of its contents. Ula Frost had given her a property in London. There were calluses on the pads of the thumb and middle finger of Gordon's left hand, which he rubbed together now in a silent snapping motion. A nervous habit.

"You must be worried about her," Pepper said, initiating a change in strategy. "This is so hard."

Scott put a hand on Gordon's shoulder, mimicking intimacy, following Pepper's lead. "I'm sorry," he said. "I shouldn't have raised my voice. Surely, between the three of us, we can find something that will point us in her direction. Can you help us?"

Gordon's fingers stopped moving. The chimpanzees were bonding now. Pepper imagined Scott reaching out and grooming Gordon's hair, checking his scalp for insects. But then Gordon's eyes landed on the window and hardened. Pepper looked out, following his gaze, but the parking lot was empty except for their cars.

"No," Gordon said. "I'm not going to be a part of this. This isn't what she would want."

Scott tried to stop him, but Gordon was quick, and his fingers, Pepper noticed, started up again as he rushed through the door.

SCOTT WAS ALREADY on his phone, so Pepper texted Ike that she'd be home in time for their walk. It was colder outside than it looked. Pepper was easily fooled by the presence of sunlight.

> so i read all the paperwork
> full of surprises!
> and i confirmed with the lawyer
> we will indeed be responsible
> for an obscene loan
> ula took against the property in london
> the deed for which
> you already signed

Pepper tried to get Scott's attention so she could leave, but he waved a hand dismissively. Ike was supposed to be on sabbatical the next academic year, studying a collection of diaries from the Oregon Trail that had just arrived from Wyoming, which meant he'd receive only part of his salary. They'd planned for this, but not for an obscene bill on top of it. It was bad enough that their furnace was old, their roof was old, the refrigerator had been making noises. Pepper was always waiting for disaster to strike.

HOWEVER
i have just found religion and i am praying
the lawyer has instructions
to repay the loan
starting to warm to this woman
on one condition
jk let's go back to denying her existence
altogether

pepper
the whole inheritance is conditional
you only get it if you sign an agreement
saying you won't sell any of the paintings

what paintings

the ones you're going to inherit

oh that's all

that's all
you sign the agreement now
the lawyer pays off the loan

Pepper watched her screen—Ike typed something else, stopped, started again.

which she clearly didn't need

Scott got off the phone and took out his keys. Pepper didn't care why Ula had taken out the loan. All Pepper had to do was sign another piece of paper and this particular crisis would be averted. How many paintings could there be? Their garage was a mess, but they could make room. Or loan them to a museum. She read the placards at museums; it was a thing people who owned paintings did. All kinds of deranged people loved Ula's work. The museums would be thrilled. Pepper didn't care about the paintings. She cared about Ike being able to take his sabbatical.

"I found the address," Scott said.

"What address?" Pepper said. She thought about London, but her mind couldn't form an image of this property that Ula, for whatever reason, wanted her to have.

"That guy is hiding something," Scott said.

Pepper considered telling Scott about London but didn't. "So?"

"I don't give up that easily," he said.

SCOTT HAD A plan that seemed ill conceived to Pepper, but he needed her help, and if he found something, she wanted to see it. She texted Ike that she was going to miss their walk after all, and Ike didn't respond. There was still something she hadn't told him yet. Sometimes Pepper felt this impulse rise in her, the impulse to push Ike hard enough that he wouldn't pull her back. She wasn't great at resisting it. The not-telling was a way of pushing. The telling would also be pushing, because it came with the admission of not-telling for so long. There were only so many times you could push someone before they moved fully out of your way.

Scott parked around the corner from Gordon's house, and Pepper walked alone, past the yards of the neighborhood. In another universe, she and Ike were walking together. In another universe, he was out walking with someone else, and he was happier for it. The yellow flowers and white moths radiated quiet light whether Pepper witnessed them or not. The snow had come early that winter, falling over leaves that hadn't yet been raked, and now spring had revealed the grass as dead and clumped with decay. A few people on Gordon's street were out, trying to mitigate the damage. There was an elderly couple hunched over the small flower bed surrounding their mailbox, planting lilies. They glared at Pepper as she stepped carefully around them, united by their certainty that she didn't belong there.

The walk leading to Gordon's door was uneven brick, treacherous enough that Pepper nearly twisted an ankle. There was a wreath of yellow leaves hanging from the door. There was no knocker, no bell. She wasn't convinced Gordon would even be home. He answered the door with a look of disappointment.

"Were you expecting someone else?" Pepper said.

Gordon held the door halfway closed. Pepper thought she saw a cat slinking in the dark foyer behind him.

"I was expecting to be left alone," he said. "If she wanted me to talk to you, she would've told me."

Pepper looked at her feet, the mat she was standing on. It was brand-new, tastefully coordinated with the house's gray paint.

"There's something I need to know," she said. Standing on this doormat, she wasn't sure why she'd agreed to this plan. She had questions but had devoted so much of her adult life to avoiding their answers.

Gordon looked past her, bitter at her existence, which was something Pepper could understand. "She's your mother," he said. "What could I tell you that you don't already know?"

Pepper thought she heard something from behind the house. Her voice felt stuck in her throat and came out sounding shrunken. "You could tell me what she's like," she said.

Gordon studied her a moment, processing the question. Pepper felt like a kid who knew nothing about sex, watching a sex scene. Like she didn't even know how much she didn't know.

"I talked to her every week," Gordon said. "For twenty-two years. The first fifteen, she was busy. She was decisive. She had me send her the local paper every week. She had lists for me. There was something wired about the way she spoke. I imagine she drank a lot of coffee." A car drove down the street, and Gordon stepped out from the doorway to watch it. "Seven years ago, that's when she stopped taking commissions. She was different after that. She'd call sometimes, out of the blue, and ask me questions about records she'd never given me access to. She'd order me to send her something and the next week, she'd have forgotten about it. Sometimes she sounded normal. Sometimes she was angry." There was a sadness in his voice, like he could feel it too, the way this action was splitting him off, and now there was a universe in which he'd never betrayed Ula's trust and this one, the one where he had. It was an impossible thing, living under the weight of your other selves. "I'm not sure I could say what she's like."

"Do you think something happened?" Pepper asked. "There must've been some reason why she stopped taking commissions. What happened seven years ago?"

"All she told me was that she was focusing her energy elsewhere," Gordon said.

Pepper thought about it. Seven years ago. Seven years ago, she got married. There was a noise from behind the house, and this time, Gordon heard it too. He stepped off the porch. Pepper had to stop him.

"There's something else," she said, too loudly. She didn't know what the something else was. Gordon stopped, though, and waited.

"When was the last time . . ." There was something else. "The last time she was here?"

Gordon listened for more noises, but the street was quiet except for the sound of a neighbor dragging a bag of mulch. "In town?"

"Yes," Pepper said. "That you know of."

Gordon looked at Pepper like she was the one hiding something, which she was.

"I have no idea," Gordon said, though they both knew that he was hiding something too. "She's never been to see me, as long as I've been working for her."

"That's not my question," Pepper said.

"If she didn't come to see me, how would I know she was here?" Gordon said.

"Have you seen her?" Pepper asked. A door slammed somewhere down the street, which made them both flinch. "Would she know you if she saw you? Have you ever sent her a picture? Or FaceTimed?"

Gordon shook his head, increasingly suspicious. "No, no." He moved again toward the back of the house.

"Let me give you something," Pepper said, reaching into her

purse. She didn't have anything to give him. In her purse, there were balled-up receipts, faded shopping lists, a tube of lip balm that had come uncapped. She pulled out a small notepad and a pen and wrote her phone number and email address. "In case you need to get in touch."

Pepper wrote as slowly as possible, focusing on the ghostlike impression her pen was making on the pages beneath. She tore the page from the notepad unevenly.

"Her handwriting," Gordon said. He tucked the page in his cardigan's pocket. "Her handwriting is unexpectedly messy, a mix of cursive and print." He was heading around the house, and there was nothing Pepper could do now but follow him. "Like yours."

Behind the house, there was a small outbuilding with black-out curtains covering the windows. Gordon unlocked the door and checked inside. Unsatisfied, he strode across the yard and peered over the fence at the rear of the property.

"Were you expecting someone?" Pepper said. She hoped Scott had gotten what he needed.

Gordon gazed out at the street again. "She's going to be furious with me," he said. "Just furious."

6

THE HUMANITIES BUILDING was usually empty on Sunday mornings, but today Pepper heard voices somewhere in the sociology department. She unlocked her lab before following the noise around the corner, where she found the door to Dr. Levin's office open. Pepper didn't know Dr. Levin well, but they'd each attended talks given by the other, Pepper standing to ask a question about Dr. Levin's work studying Deadheads on the road when the audience fell silent during the Q and A.

Dr. Levin's office emitted a red glow and was obscured by a curtain of beads hanging in the doorway. Pepper slapped her sneakers against the floor as she approached, making herself known.

Reaching a hand through the beads, she knocked twice on the door.

"Hmm?" said the voice inside.

As she crossed the threshold, the beads dragged across Pepper's body like a chill. "It's just me," she said. "I'm working down the hall. Didn't want to scare you."

Dr. Levin smiled and closed her eyes and nodded. On her desk was a delicate glass teapot with a golden flower blooming inside. The red light, Pepper now saw, came from a lava lamp. She was listening to NPR, something about fraternities.

"Carry on," Dr. Levin said.

Pepper settled into the lab, relieved to focus on anything unrelated to Ula Frost. She'd successfully diverted Ula's assistant long enough for Scott to find what he needed—not records but a painting by Ula, which, upon investigation, Scott realized was unaccounted for in Ula's catalog, and which gave Scott the leverage he needed to get Gordon to provide him with records. Pepper was ambivalent about her role in the operation, but at least if Ula never turned up, Pepper wouldn't have to worry that her reluctance to get involved had been a contributing factor. Scott had left unceremoniously after getting what he needed, returning to New York to research the client list. And tomorrow, Pepper would meet with the lawyer, sign the agreement, free them from the cursed lien. The only alternative was to hire an attorney of their own to fight the transfer of ownership, but based on the free consultation Ike arranged through the college's legal services, a court battle would cost far more than they could afford. If Pepper signed the agreement, they could sell the London property, fix the roof, replace the fridge, buy a newer used car. They could hire a fancy lawyer to safeguard against Pepper's carelessness in the future. She gave herself permission to forget about the whole mess, for now.

This was spring break week, and Pepper's in-box was dominated by emails from students, late papers, or flimsy excuses for why something hadn't been turned in. There was an email dated two days ago, informing Pepper that she'd not been selected for the research grant she'd applied for, funding to collaborate with an acquaintance at another university on a collection of remains from North Carolina. The last email was from Jamie Marchand, letting Pepper know they'd arrested the boyfriend in the case she'd consulted on. When they searched his apartment, they found what they believed was the murder weapon, a bloodstained rock wrapped in a scarf on a shelf in the back of his closet. It could be months before a trial date was set. But they got him.

Pepper climbed a stepladder and pulled a box from the top of a stack. Cataloging remains steadied her. A six-thousand-year-old skeleton wanted nothing from her that she wasn't prepared to give. The air in the lab was dusty and familiar. Her mind stuck on the image of the rock on the boyfriend's shelf. Like a souvenir. Somewhere there was a universe where that girl was still alive, having broken up with her boyfriend months before. He'd forgotten to text her back and she'd decided he wasn't worth it, or she'd found a number she didn't recognize in his phone. Somewhere there was a universe in which he killed her but never got caught, and lived to a hundred with that rock always on his shelf, the blood on its surface eventually crumbling away. The box Pepper needed was filled with infant and juvenile remains. The bones were comingled— the babies had all been buried together. She set out the bags and her calipers. When she recorded the measurements in her log and checked them against growth charts, she often found they were classified as prenatal. Sometimes there were small rocks mixed in. Whoever had excavated the site hadn't been able to tell the difference between an infant's bones and pebbles.

Pepper was lining up a row of long bones the size of matchsticks when she heard more noise in the hall. She'd left the lights off in the lab, because it was sunny and the buzz from the overhead lights gave her a headache. She listened to the footsteps, their deliberate pace. It sounded like two people who were looking for something. The footsteps stopped a few doors down. It didn't sound like Dr. Levin.

Pepper pocketed her phone. Reception in this building was sketchy at best, which she liked during class but not when she was alone. She'd left the door to the lab cracked open. Sometimes maintenance worked in the building on Sundays, but the maintenance guy was a whistler. The footsteps approached the lab door and stopped.

"Hello?" Pepper said. She was sitting with her back to the door, her body so tense now she couldn't turn around. She was being paranoid, she told herself. A side effect of lingering too long on the dead girl, the rock.

No one answered. She thought she could hear breathing. She put her fingers on the infant bones before her—tiny femurs, tiny ribs. She didn't know why she was so afraid. She heard someone step into the room.

"Greetings," the man said.

Pepper jumped up from her chair and spun around, holding her phone in front of her as if the fact that she had a phone might make this man think twice about whatever he intended to do.

She wondered how many of the murder victims she'd examined in her career had been holding their phones when they died.

"Oh dear," the man said. He took a step back and held up his hands to show they were empty. "I didn't mean to startle you." He was slight with dark eyebrows and Andy Warhol hair. An accent, maybe Scandinavian. He was wearing a shirt with a print too small for Pepper to make out, buttoned all the way up. Behind him, another man stepped into the room—broad with a shiny bald head, horn-rimmed glasses, and an argyle sweater.

"Terribly sorry," the second man said, with a cartoony bow. "What a fright we must've given you. Forgive us, Dr. Rafferty."

Pepper kept hold of her phone. Her name was on the door to her office but not the lab. "Are you looking for someone?"

She stepped forward, trying to press them into the hall, but both men held their ground, just inside the doorway.

"We're looking for you, in fact," said the first man. "My name is Roscoe Larsen. This is my associate Christian Bruno." Neither man initiated a handshake. "We're from the Everett Group. Perhaps you've heard of us?"

"No," Pepper said. She stepped around them and flipped on the lights. She could hear NPR from down the hall, the volume likely too loud for Dr. Levin to hear anything over it. "How did you get into the building?"

The men both offered tight-lipped smiles. Her phone buzzed in her hand.

so here's a story

Ike had already left for the library when Pepper woke that morning. The new diaries he'd acquired from Wyoming were part of a special collection on the westward journey, and he was helping prepare educational materials to accompany them. And avoiding her, probably.

"You shouldn't be in the building," Pepper said. Ike's message made her feel braver, like she was no longer standing there alone.

"It's not open today. If you'd like to make an appointment, my email address is listed on the department website."

i'm reading the new diaries

"We won't take too much of your time," Roscoe said. "We can see that you're busy."

there's one by this woman named kit

Pepper pressed her phone against her thigh. "Yes," she said. She waved a hand at the infant remains on the table as if the dead required a sense of urgency. "I'm in the middle of something."

Again, she tried to herd the men into the hall, but they stayed where they were, impassible, blocking the doorway.

"I'll get right to the point," Roscoe said. Pepper's phone continued to buzz against her leg. "We're here because we understand you are to inherit the work of Ula Frost."

"Where did you hear that?" Pepper said.

Roscoe smiled that tight, unnerving smile again. "Oh, here and there," he said. "It is obvious enough why to anyone standing in front of you." Now that he was so close, Pepper could see that the print on his shirt was tiny knives. "The Everett Group is a society of art collectors," Roscoe continued. "You must have read by now about the furor created by the possibility of Ms. Frost's work becoming available to the public."

"No," Pepper said. "I haven't read anything about it." Her phone quieted, which made her feel vulnerable again. There was nothing in the office she could use as a weapon. She had books and a cabinet full of animal skulls, a coffee mug a month overdue for washing. She didn't even have a stapler. "And any inheritance I receive will likely be years away. I've never met Ula Frost. For all I know, she's just not answering her messages."

Pepper didn't want to take her eyes off these men, but her phone was buzzing again. Across campus, Ike was tapping at his screen, her sole connection to the world beyond this room.

"Sorry," she said. "My husband gets worried when I don't respond."

> so kit joined a wagon train alone in ohio
> very unusual for a woman to go alone
> she's supposed to be going as a school-
> teacher
> all the other women have like ten kids
> she's told them her parents died in a fire
>
> strange men

"Sometimes a man needs a woman's reassurance," Christian said. He hadn't spoken much, but his voice was deep and resonant, like the voice of a giant. He seemed to be getting broader, filling even more of the doorway. "We understand you are not currently in ownership of Ms. Frost's work. But we would like to know that you will be amenable to dealing with us once you are."

> the men have certain ideas about women
> that kit does not subscribe to

Pepper smiled her cheeriest smile. She'd developed this strategy for dealing with men who didn't want to listen through a long process of trial and error during her academic career. The lawyer was already preparing the paperwork, in which Pepper would agree not to sell Ula's paintings in exchange for repayment of the loan against the property, and nothing would stop her from signing it. The property wasn't worthless. The money from selling the property could change her and Ike's lives.

"Who knows!" she said. "Maybe I'll sell everything. Anything's possible!"

"We are not interested in maybe," Roscoe said. He advanced into Pepper's personal space. "It is of the utmost importance that Ula Frost's work remains safe. We'd like your assurances, please. We are prepared to exceed any offer you may receive."

"I don't even know what a fair price would be," Pepper said. It didn't seem wise to tell them about the lawyer and the agreement. She thought she heard something in the hall. Maybe the men would turn to look. "And what makes you so certain she's not going to turn up in a few days?"

> but then i get a little further into the diary
> and kit says something about a secret
> she's keeping a secret from everyone

Pepper felt Christian take a step closer as she read. She faked exasperation at her phone.

> men in lab

"Ula Frost's work has rarely gone to auction before," Roscoe said. "Prices, they are hard to estimate. But I think you would find many collectors willing to pay several million dollars for a prominent piece."

> what men

Pepper's head swam with the research she'd done on Ula's work. She'd been prolific before she started taking commissions for portraits, supposedly painting people out of other universes. But Pepper wouldn't get anything if she didn't sign the agreement not to sell. Why would Ula make that the condition?

> pepper

There was a noise in the hall. A real noise this time. Christian put one hand in his pocket.

"Dr. Rafferty," Dr. Levin said from the hall, her voice high and singsong. The men stepped all the way into the lab, leaving the doorway open as Dr. Levin appeared. She was wearing a long, multicolored kaftan, indigo and fuchsia and teal.

"I thought you should know security is coming." She kept her eyes on Pepper. "I got an email. Something about an issue with one of the doors. I didn't want you to worry when you heard them."

Christian gave Dr. Levin a stunted bow.

"Excuse us, madam," Roscoe said. "We must be going. We've had a fruitful visit. We trust the door will cause you no further problems."

pepper

The men disappeared down the hall. Pepper listened as the door to the stairs around the corner opened and closed.

gone now

Dr. Levin stood with Pepper until the quiet was interrupted by the ding of the elevator, which opened to reveal a young Black man from campus security holding a walkie-talkie.

"Lovely man," Dr. Levin said. "What a blessing to have you. Can I make you a cup of marigold tea? The moon is in the Sign of the Virgin, so the marigold's virtues are fully intact."

The young man seemed confused but followed her anyway, and Dr. Levin didn't look back. Pepper returned the infant remains to their box with shaking hands. She wasn't sure she could muster the nerve to leave the building alone. She sat at the table and waited for it to pass.

what's the secret
>what secret
>are you okay
i'll explain later
what's the secret
>i don't know yet
>i'm not that far in
>it just reminded me of you

Somewhere there was a universe in which Pepper's conversation with those men had gone differently, but she couldn't let herself think about that now.

> you should skip ahead
>> you know i'd never do that
> i'm flummoxed by your patience
> has kit fucked anyone at least
>> no
>> it's all just cholera and buffalo chips
> that's disappointing
>> disappointment all around

Pepper gathered her bag.

>> you leaving soon

She forced her hands to steady long enough to lock the lab's door.

> will you keep texting me

Embarrassed by her own fear, she counted to three and found the momentum to start walking.

>>> on the oregon trail when people got married
>>> sometimes they'd push their wagon way out
>>> in the prairie
>>> for privacy
>>> and all the assholes on the train
>>> would sneak out and start singing to them
>>> at top volume

The stairs were clear, the first-floor hall was clear. Outside the building, a girl in short shorts was fixing a slipped bike chain. Pepper had parked in the faculty lot in the back.

sometimes people just went crazy
from all the walking
one woman came back from doing laundry
and told her husband she'd clubbed their kid
to death
on a rock

There were two cars in the lot, other than Pepper's. She didn't see anyone else around. It was as if those men had disappeared into thin air.

and when he went to check
she set their wagon on fire
the kid was fine tho
you probably know more than i do about
cholera
are you still there

yeah
in the car

7

PEPPER ENTERED THROUGH the clinic's side door, just as Lydia was slipping from an exam room into the hall. This part of the clinic was a narrow strip of hallway, all the exam rooms feeding into the hall on one side. The other side was lined with cabinets full of medications, under which was a long counter, today bearing a box of bagels alongside a fecal sample waiting to be taken to the lab.

Pepper had lost her nerve in the parking lot. She hadn't told her moms anything yet, and Ike was waiting for her to do it. It was bad enough she'd kept it from him. But she'd forgotten about the Monday rush, and now was clearly not a good time for this conversation. When she arrived at the clinic, the lot was full of owners bringing in animals with problems they'd attempted to manage over the weekend and clients picking up boarded pets. She'd wait until another day, when she could talk to them at home and they could have some time to process. She couldn't waltz in and tell them what she knew and expect them to keep seeing patients. It wouldn't be fair.

Lydia closed the exam room door behind her and squeezed Pepper's shoulder. There was a single red claw mark on her neck. "I'm glad you're here," she said. "I have a euthanasia. Can you help me? We're slammed."

Pepper couldn't say no. She followed Lydia back to the treatment room and watched as she began filling a syringe with thick pink liquid from a vial in the controlled drugs cabinet. She wrote on the dry-erase board: *Cordelia Clements, 5 cc.* Pepper went to the kennel to find a blanket. The teenage kennel staff had their arms around each other, their mouths close but not kissing. They pulled apart when they saw Pepper. The girl was petite and had an eyebrow ring. The boy looked too many years older than the girl. Pepper dug through some towels and took the nicest faded comforter in the pile, pink with green banana leaves. She still had a stash of peanut butter cups in the hall, and she pocketed one before joining Lydia in the exam room.

Cordelia was a Dalmatian, and her owners knelt on either side of her, rubbing her ears. They were a younger couple, and the woman held a baby girl who had gray eyes and wild lashes and who grabbed immediately for Pepper's hair. The woman and her husband were both dressed in suits, like they'd come straight from work.

"The medication we use is a form of anesthesia," Lydia told them. The woman nodded and blinked back tears. "It shuts down the central nervous system first, so she won't feel anything, but she may pant or yelp or act disoriented, which is a normal response to anesthesia. It's called the excitement phase. But it's not pain."

The woman handed the baby to her husband, who sat on the room's little bench next to a stack of pamphlets about heartworms. He put the baby on his knee and bounced her, and the baby laughed. Cordelia walked in circles, like she wanted to lie down but couldn't find a way to be comfortable. Pepper spread the blanket on the floor.

"This is more than I usually give," Lydia said, "but since she's on barbiturates for her seizures, there's a chance she has a tolerance."

The woman kissed Cordelia on the head, and then kissed her again and again. "I'm so sorry," the woman told her.

Pepper handed the woman the peanut butter cup from her pocket without speaking. Her job was to hold off the vein and make sure her mom didn't get bitten. She'd done it once, in high school, while they were euthanizing a mastiff with bone cancer named Rudolf. He'd always been so gentle, and she wasn't restraining him properly, and once the meds started working, he'd lurched forward and bit Lydia on the scalp. She'd waited until her lunch break to go have the wound stapled because she had a full morning of appointments, plus two surgeries on the schedule. Pepper had felt sick, but Lydia hadn't made a big deal about it. "Just another scar," she'd said. "At least this one's well hidden."

The woman unwrapped the peanut butter cup, and Cordelia took it in one bite. Pepper put an arm around the dog's torso, pinning it to her body. She could hear the man on the bench crying as the baby babbled. She held off the vein. Her mother inserted the needle, and Pepper let up, opening the pathway as Lydia started the injection. Cordelia slumped in Pepper's arms. Pepper had helped with hundreds of euthanasias but was always unnerved by how quickly life could leave a body. She set Cordelia gently onto the comforter. She was already gone, but her body looked the same. The woman folded over her, weeping. Pepper's mom put a hand on her shoulder. Pepper capped the syringe and stepped into the hall.

In the treatment room, she found Annie on a step stool, perched over a cardboard box with a towel inside. Annie was short and often had to use a step stool to reach high shelves. As a kid, Pepper was always tripping over a stool left wherever Annie had last needed it.

"Give me a hand, will you?"

Pepper looked in the box and found five squirming kittens, so new their eyes were still shut.

"Judy bottle-fed them up front," Annie said. "But they need to poop." In the wild, the kittens' mother would lick their butts to stimulate a bowel movement. Annie took a wad of gauze from the shelf and ran it under warm water before handing it to Pepper. "Their mother got hit by a car. You're their mother now."

Pepper took the gauze and picked up one of the kittens as Annie grabbed a chart and disappeared through the door. The kitten was mewling in the tiniest possible way. Pepper rubbed the gauze over its bottom. She tried to think of something she could tell Ike when she got home, about why she'd chickened out. There was a euthanasia and kittens who needed to poop. It was too much today, and Pepper was a coward. The kitten pooped, and she cleaned it and returned it to its nest and started on the next one with fresh gauze.

Lydia returned to treatment, followed by a tech. "They're going to take a little time. Let me know when they leave. She's a cremation. Can you get a bag ready?"

The tech went to the kennel as Annie came back through the swinging door, unflustered. The kitten was all white with one black spot. Warm water slid down Pepper's hand. She thought about the note in Michael Orlando's folder, the pigpen masking the meaning. Sometimes people kept secrets because they were ashamed to say the thing out loud.

"Do you guys have a minute?"

They both looked at her like she was a hallucination. The dogs in the kennel quieted as if in anticipation of Cordelia's body.

"Sure," Annie said. "What's up?"

Pepper felt dizzy as she walked into the X-ray room off treatment. Someone had left the processor on, and it was buzzing. The kitten in her hand was scrabbling at the air, so she held it close to her chest.

"Something happened," she said. "There's something I have to tell you."

Lydia put down the chart she'd been reading. She looked at Annie. Pepper sat on the X-ray table and felt its cool white surface beneath her.

"Okay," Lydia said. "We're here. We're listening."

The kitten was trying to burrow into Pepper's shirt, and she felt its tiny needle claws against her chest. It was warm and scared, and it was hurting her.

THEY WENT TO Tilda's house that evening. Climbing into her moms' back seat, Pepper felt like a kid who was being chauffeured home from a slumber party after bad behavior. When she'd told them, they'd snapped into action—hugs and plans first, questions later. They didn't need processing time. Pepper was the only member of her family who needed a stupidly long time to process.

Tilda's house was in the woods. She'd asked Pepper to dog-sit once in high school, but Pepper had said no—she'd had other plans—and Tilda hadn't asked again. Now the car climbed the winding driveway, and through the trees, Pepper saw it—a pink Victorian, perched like a cake on the hill. The garden around the house swayed with color, purple alliums and yellow tulips and striped grasses that were waist-high. Tilda came to the porch in her overalls, all three dogs quiet at her side. The yard was scattered with little stone statues—rabbits and angels, a large, open hand. Annie rushed up the steps, and Tilda folded her into her arms. Pepper heard sniffling. Lydia put a hand on Annie's shoulder.

From the yard, Pepper watched the knot of women, all of whom were so much braver than she was. Again, Pepper tamped down the urge to flee. She'd spent so many years fighting it. Maybe she'd staved it off for so long by disallowing herself membership in this family. One of the dogs—Theo, Pepper's favorite—came down the stairs and leaned against her leg.

Tilda kissed Annie's cheek and sent her and Lydia inside. It was just Pepper and Tilda and the dogs then. Tilda was tall with wiry, muscled arms—she'd always looked to Pepper like the exact kind of woman who'd surround herself with greyhounds. Pepper followed Theo up the stairs and knelt to pet him. He rested his chin in her cupped hand.

"I waited a long time for you to say something," Tilda said. "I would've said something myself . . ."

Pepper waited for her to say more, but instead Tilda bent and rubbed Theo's ears. Pepper thought she understood. Even now, with all of them knowing, it still felt impossible.

Theo nudged Pepper upward with his head, so she stood. For one single second, she felt as if she were standing in the right universe, a universe where things were as they're meant to be, even her.

"I'm sorry," she said. "I don't know how to make this right."

Tilda pulled her in, and Pepper let her. "Sweet girl," she said. "I've been waiting such a long time to do this."

TILDA'S HUSBAND, NEIL, had baked cookies, thumbprints filled with apricot jam he'd made the summer before from one of their trees. Pepper had never talked to Neil much—Tilda was the one in charge of the dogs—but every year, he'd brought a bowl of blackberries to the clinic, his hands covered in scratches, because Pepper had once told him they were her favorite. When she joined her moms in the living room, two of the dogs dug themselves under a blanket in the corner and curled up, yin and yang–style. Theo lay at Pepper's feet.

The living room was dim and so full of paintings there was hardly any space on the walls between them. Some were in tarnished metal frames, some in black plastic ones. Some hung off-kilter from nails. There were a lot of still lifes—fruit and flies or flowers and brass knuckles. There was a series that involved dead poultry, painted alongside dishes filled with herbs and bloody knives. There was one where everything looked unripe. Another composed of white objects, including a few bones and teeth. The only color came from what appeared to be a single, glossy, red press-on fingernail.

Pepper thought of the men from her office. If they knew about Pepper, they knew about Tilda. "Does anyone know you have these?"

"We have a security system," Neil said.

"Not by choice," Tilda said. "Those men just showed up and installed it. Ula sent them. The damn squirrels are always setting it off. One of these days, I'm going to rip it out of the wall myself."

"Tilda prefers her gun," Neil added. He offered more cookies, and Annie piled them on her napkin. "It belonged to their father. Don't worry, we have an agreement that she doesn't keep it loaded. But she's not above waving it around."

"So you're in touch with Ula?" Annie said.

Tilda looked at her lap. "Ula is in touch with us," she said. "Sometimes. I wouldn't say we're in touch with her. We wouldn't know how to get in touch with her. It's better for everyone that way."

Pepper took a cookie so she'd have something to do.

"What do you think about the stories?" Annie said. "About the alternate universes? Have you ever seen anything that made you think it was true?"

Pepper knew her moms were like her, too steeped in science to be able to buy the fantasy, but also too full of goddamn longing not to think about it. She bit into the cookie. The apricot jam was sweeter than she'd expected, only a little tart.

"I wouldn't put it past her," Tilda said, as if that answered anything. She turned to Pepper. "You must have so many questions."

Pepper should've had so many questions, but none were forming in her brain, which was stuck on the white painting, the bones. Snake, she thought, vertebrae and ribs, and the teeth were likely canine. Maybe Ula had found them in the yard.

"I have a question," Lydia said, and Pepper was so thankful. Lydia hesitated. When she spoke again, her voice wavered. "Why us?"

Tilda let the room be quiet for a minute. Pepper liked that about her, that she was comfortable with silence. They had the same long fingers, the same hawk nose.

"Ula was a difficult kid," she said. "She was always that way, as long as I can remember. She gave our parents fits." Tilda was a few years older than Ula and had the resigned competence of the responsible older sister. Both their parents had died while Pepper was in college, and Tilda had been the one left to care for them. "She never wore anything our mother bought for her. She started cutting her own hair when she was nine and refused to let anyone else touch it. And it continued as she got older. She wouldn't eat meals at the table, only in her room. She'd lock herself in there for days, missing school, painting. She never showed our parents her work. Never wanted to talk to them about it. She had that boy, Michael, who I don't think she ever called her boyfriend." Her gaze was on Pepper, but she was looking through her. "She talked to me, though. She'd come in my room sometimes at night and sit at the foot of my bed. I wasn't allowed to say anything. If I talked, she'd leave. But she never really wanted to be alone."

Pepper tried to imagine a young Ula, curled at the end of Tilda's bed, but in her mind she could only see herself.

Tilda continued. "She didn't tell me she was pregnant. I just looked at her one day and knew. I tried to talk to her about it. Our parents were Catholic, but there were places we could've gone. But she shook her head. I don't know why she decided to keep it." At the word *it*, Pepper felt herself flicker. There were universes where she didn't exist, which was not the comfort she expected it to be. "I'm sure it had to do with Michael. She never let anyone see her cry, but I could hear her. It was hard. She was always hard. There was a cruelty in her, but not all the way through. And maybe she had seen something. I never understood how her mind worked.

"She stayed home mostly once she was showing. We had to hide it from our parents, which wasn't as hard as it should've been. I was still living at home, trying to save a little money. She stopped going to school, and our parents had given up trying to make her do anything. And then one night, she came into my room and said when the baby was born she was leaving. And I knew it. I'd known it was coming. She'd been in her room for so long, painting the same landscape over and over again, and I could see she needed to leave. You'd just opened up your practice. I'd only met you a few times. But I thought, Ula would be such a terrible mother—what if this baby could have two good ones instead? I asked her, and she agreed. So that was that."

Neil took a handkerchief from his pocket and offered it to Lydia. It was white and thin with a lace border. Lydia held it to her face before offering it to Annie, who instead used her own sleeve. Pepper couldn't stop looking at the paintings on the wall.

Her entire life had been a gift from Tilda, not Ula. There was a painting of this house, as viewed from somewhere in the surrounding woods, far away. There were two of soft, suspicious rabbits in the yard. There was one of Tilda, standing on the porch, dogs at her side, also painted from afar, from behind. Tilda's hair in the painting was gray.

"When did she do these?" Pepper asked.

"Some of them are from high school," Tilda said. "She used to love watching the rabbits, trying to paint them before they got spooked and ran off. Some she's sent since she left. Every now and then, they get delivered."

"Is that what happened with the money?" Pepper asked.

She heard one of her moms swallow, but she couldn't look at them right now. Tilda met her eyes.

"Yes," she said. "That was before she started doing everything through that lawyer. I was worried you wouldn't keep it."

She looked at her lap again. Pepper had gotten through school on scholarships, studying her ass off in part so she wouldn't have to spend the money. She was always trying to prove herself against the person she thought herself to be. She'd finally spent it on the house, which otherwise she and Ike, newly married academics, wouldn't have been able to afford. Ike had loved it immediately—the breakfast nook, the exposed beams in the living room. Every house they looked at, all he cared about was beams. It felt okay for her to spend it on something for Ike, like she was making up for the fact that he was stuck with her as his wife.

"These paintings will go to you too," Tilda said. "I imagine you've already talked to that lawyer."

Theo raised his head from the floor as if he heard something outside.

"Where do you think she is?" Pepper asked. "I mean, do you think something happened to her?"

Theo stood and trotted to the door, and the other dogs joined him, one still draped with the blanket she'd been under, like a dog dressed up as a ghost for Halloween. Neil went to the window.

"The squirrels," he said. "They like to leave me acorns on the porch."

"I really have no idea," Tilda said. "She could be dead, she could be fine. I have no idea." Neil left the window to put a hand on her shoulder. "No, I don't think she's dead," she said. "She's not. I know it."

Pepper heard in her voice something that had been tightly wound, uncoiling. Pepper felt an unraveling in herself too as she realized letting Ula go was the only way Tilda had to love her. Pepper felt her moms watching her from the couch, holding hands.

"What about the coin?" Annie asked. "I always wondered about that coin."

"She'd read about it," Tilda said. "Something about orphans being left with coins during a war. Our father was Polish, you know," she told Pepper. "His parents came from Warsaw and Americanized their name. He used to have a jar of Polish coins on the dresser. When Ula left, she took the coins with her. Except for the one we left with you, which I told her was a choking hazard, but she insisted."

The dogs were still by the door, but they'd relaxed and lay down again, a pile of greyhounds, their chests all rising and falling at the same time.

"There are more paintings," Tilda said. "Would you like to see them?"

Pepper stood uncertainly. She looked to her moms to follow, but Neil had asked them a question about one of the dog's mouths, and they were examining it with the flashlight from Annie's phone. Pepper followed Tilda up the steep staircase, which led to a hallway.

"When was the last time you saw her?" Pepper asked.

"The day after you were born," Tilda said. "That's when she left."

Tilda stopped at the room at the end of the hall, her back to Pepper. Pepper wasn't sure if Tilda was telling the truth. Ula had come to see Ike seven years ago. Why wouldn't she have visited Tilda then?

"Did something happen?" Pepper said. "That made you stop talking."

Tilda turned, her face unreadable. "This was her room," she said.

Tilda opened the door to the bedroom. The bedroom was in the house's turret; the rounded wall made it feel like a tube. And everything—the walls and floorboards, bed frame and blankets—was white except for the paintings.

The paintings in the bedroom were mostly local landscapes— Pepper recognized the Japanese maple near the playground, the old cemetery with the crumbling headstones, the field near the edge of town. There were a few of that one, each a little different. In one, the field was overrun by geese. In another, it was empty.

"Did she ever ask about me?" Pepper said. She picked up one of the canvases and looked at it more closely. She was trying to seem like she didn't care, and she knew she wasn't succeeding. She didn't want to want to know. But she did.

"I sent her clippings sometimes, early on," Tilda said. "When you were in the paper. When you got that scholarship. Once with your moms when there was a story about the clinic. Your engagement announcement."

Pepper had asked if Ula asked about her. Not if Tilda had told her about her.

"Wait," she said. "My engagement announcement?"

"Just little things like that," Tilda said.

"Did she get it?" Pepper said. Tilda and Ula clearly weren't on the best terms. Maybe Ula had never seen it. But then she'd come to see Ike.

"She knew you were getting married," Tilda said.

Tilda didn't say more. She too was looking at a canvas, trying to disguise her feelings and doing better at it than Pepper. A family trait Pepper could aspire to.

HER MOMS WALKED her in when she got home. Pepper went straight to the bedroom and lay down, not bothering with the light. She could hear her moms talking with Ike in the kitchen but couldn't tell what they were saying.

Tilda had told her the last time she'd seen Ula was the day after Pepper was born. But that didn't make sense. Ula had been here in town since then. Too many things didn't make sense.

Ike came into the room and sat at the edge of the bed. He ran one hand through Pepper's hair, and it caught on a tangle.

"I wish you would've let me go with you," he said.

Pepper couldn't speak. It would've been easier for her if he'd been there, but she didn't deserve for it to be easy. Or it was easier for her to maintain this distance between them, to push him out of this part of her life. Both were true.

"Do you want something?" he asked. "Tea? Whiskey?"

Pepper rolled away from him. In another universe, she was doing this alone. Ike lay down next to her, close but not touching. When she was really upset, being touched only made it worse. She wasn't good at accepting comfort. Ike didn't say anything for a long time. He was good at letting her feel miserable without trying to make it better.

"Tilda told me she sent Ula newspaper clippings," she said. "About me."

"That's how she knew about the wedding," Ike said.

She could feel Ike's breath in her hair. She didn't want to say anything else. There was too much she hadn't told him, too many years in which she'd held her secrets between them like a shield. In another universe, they'd already decided this was an unfixable problem, or they were doing the harder work required to move through it together. In this universe, they'd done neither. The room seemed to bend, like the air above asphalt on a hot day. Sometimes people kept secrets because they were ashamed to say the thing out loud.

"I've seen her," Pepper said, finally. In another universe, she wasn't doing this. There was a universe in which she had no secrets left to reveal.

This time, Ike was the one to roll away.

"You met her too," he said. It wasn't a question.

"No," Pepper said. "I've seen her. I've never met her."

Ike was silent beside her. She couldn't even hear him breathing anymore.

"It was a few months ago." Two months ago. Pepper had seen Ula two months ago, just before she'd disappeared. But it didn't make any sense that Tilda had sent the engagement announcement. The announcement included a photo of Pepper and Ike. Pepper had spent a full week dithering over which one to include. Her hair looked terrible in all of them. "When I saw her," Pepper said, "she didn't know who I was."

She felt Ike roll back toward her. "What do you mean, she didn't know who you were?"

"She didn't recognize me," Pepper said.

"That doesn't make sense," Ike said.

It didn't make sense. "I talked to her," she said. "I was coming home late after a faculty meeting that had dragged on forever and was picking up pizza for us. And there she was. She was getting a slice, and I was behind her in line. She wanted sausage, but they were out and she yelled at the guy at the counter. She was wearing a big furry hat. I bumped into her on purpose and apologized. She looked right at me but didn't react. It was like she had no idea who I was."

Ike sat up next to her. Usually, when Pepper felt miserable, she didn't want to be touched. But now that she did, Ike's hands were balled at his side.

"Why didn't you tell me?" he said.

"I don't know," Pepper said. She could feel tears on her face and was embarrassed for herself. A grown woman, with a life full of privilege and people who loved her, so completely incapable of pulling that love in and holding on to it. "I thought you'd love me less."

Ike exhaled hard through his nose. In another universe, he didn't have such a tiresome wife. "Do you think that little of me?" he said.

Pepper left the bedroom, and Ike followed. In another universe, she was someplace different right now, Paris or Amsterdam or a beach in Costa Rica, with someone else, with none of this on her mind, drinking too much and about to have the best sex of her life with a stranger.

On the kitchen table, there was a fat photo album, bound in faded maroon fabric with little white flowers. Pepper sat but didn't open it.

"What's this?" she said.

"Your moms brought it," he said. "Tilda gave it to them for you. It's her album from when she and Ula were kids."

She gave the album a halfhearted push across the table. "I don't want this," she said.

"That doesn't matter," Ike said. His tone was getting an edge to it. "It's here. You have it." In another universe, he was having a quiet night, an easy night, a glass of good wine with a woman with improbably long, toned legs, which she wrapped around his torso from behind as he tried to read.

Pepper opened the photo album. On the first page: a woman with a gigantic belly, and a young, handsome man kissing it. Pepper's grandparents, already gone. She flipped through the album's pages quickly. Baby Ula with cupcake icing all over her face. Toddler Ula in a little yellow bathing suit, rosy cheeked, playing in mud. Kid Ula, a cast on her left arm, and Tilda next to her, sunburned in a pair of overalls. Ula as a sulky teenager, wearing a dress with a tulle skirt.

Ike put a hand out to stop her flipping pages. Pepper couldn't look at him. In another universe, she was on a boat, a train, she was speeding away from him in her car. The separation felt inevitable, and suddenly—divorced from fantasy—terrifying, wrong. Pepper had spent enough time occupying imaginary universes to know the determining factor in her other selves' happiness wasn't the presence or absence of Ike. The problem wasn't that she thought so little of Ike as much as she thought little of herself, this version of herself. Ula didn't even know who she was. Pepper had been sure of it. But if Pepper looked so much like Ula that strangers could see it, surely Ula would have recognized the resemblance too. Tilda had sent her the clippings, Pepper's photo. Ula must have made the connection that Pepper was her daughter.

It wasn't that Ula didn't know who Pepper was. She just didn't care.

"No more secrets," Ike said. "It's a rule. Starting now."

"Fine," she said.

"Do you promise?" Ike said.

Pepper had been keeping secrets for so long it had become a habit. In another universe, it was a habit she was sure she could break. In this one, she was less certain.

"I promise," she said. But the sense of wrongness inside her continued swelling. Too many things didn't make sense. The loan, the agreement, Ula's conditions—the entire inheritance was an elaborate manipulation.

Pepper knew that they couldn't afford to pay off the loan, that Ike's sabbatical was at stake. She knew they needed to sell the property in London, fix the roof, stave off the myriad disasters that would disappear in the presence of extra cash. But Pepper's only relationship with Ula was in Ula's expectation that Pepper would simply do as she was told. And Pepper couldn't help but wonder what, if Ula was still out there, might happen if she refused.

"I don't think I should sign the agreement yet," she said.

Ike looked at the table. She'd held him away from her for too long. And this universe wasn't fixed in place. This universe always felt like it was on the brink of catastrophe.

"What do you want to do, then?" he asked.

Pepper kept her eyes on the album. She'd stopped on a page of photos of Ula painting. There was only one in which her back wasn't turned to the camera, and in that one she was fixing the photographer with a look of pure disdain.

It was spring break week. Ike had work to do, and so did she. She should sign the agreement, free them of the lien. Let the nagging questions go. In another universe, she would; it was inevitable. But it was also inevitable that Pepper would follow, that in some universe she'd stop retreating into fantasy and allow herself to ask the questions she'd told herself didn't matter for so long.

This universe. This was the universe where she tried.

"I want to go to London," Pepper said.

8

WHILE PEPPER PACKED, Ike made her a list of museums. When Ike was deciding on something, he made lists. Pepper clutched the list on the plane until the sweat from her palms smudged his writing: *giant, merman, blue whale.* There were a lot of skeletal remains to be seen in London. Pepper wasn't sure what Ike would decide about her while she was gone. Her ears popped. She'd read once that an alleged alternate painted into this universe by Ula described the sensation that way, like changing altitudes precipitously. The estate agent for the property in London would meet her shortly after she arrived. Surely, Ula had left her something other than debt. And now she was going to find out what that was.

The property was on the east side of London, and she asked the driver to let her out a few blocks from the address. She was deposited in front of a string of galleries. Everyone in this neighborhood wore jeans that looked too tight. A young guy nearly clipped her with his bike, an old-fashioned contraption painted sky blue with an overlarge basket that was empty.

> you made it

Pepper was always imagining herself into universes without Ike, and here she was—without him. She sent him a photo of the nearest building, whose brick façade was covered with a multistory painting of a creature with both tentacles and wings.

> i made it
>> scott from the magazine called
>> while you were in the air

oh god
what did he want

She stood on the sidewalk as tourists wove their way around her, lining up to pose with the street art.

> he found someone
> a client of ula's
> in germany
> he wants you to go with him

why

Pepper struggled through the pack of tourists, holding her unwieldy duffel bag close to her body. She couldn't think of a reason Scott would want her in Germany. She continued past another building painted with a winged creature, this time human. Ike always knew the answer before she did.

> don't forget the pelicans

There was a park in central London with pelicans—Ike had been deeply excited by this discovery. Pepper turned a corner to find herself on a street full of curry restaurants, each distinguished by a different-colored banner or neon sign. She checked the map on her phone. This was the street where the property was located.

> in medieval europe they thought pelican
> mothers fed their chicks with blood
> pecked from their own chests

Pepper started down the street of restaurants, inhaling the perfume of fenugreek, garlic, ginger. Maybe the property didn't mean anything after all. Maybe Ula just really liked curry.

they thought that because some pelicans
have red pouches
and they press them against their chests
to empty them

In medieval Europe, pelican mothers were believed to sacrifice their own blood for the sake of nourishing their children. That was one version of the myth. Pepper knew there was another, though, in which the pelican mother killed her chicks and then in a fit of guilt used her blood to resurrect them.

She stopped in front of a restaurant and checked the address the attorney had given her. The restaurant had a sign, as did several other restaurants on this street, declaring itself the World's Best Curry House. This was the place. A curry restaurant. She checked the address again. Pepper stood studying the sign until a woman in a shapeless gray suit carrying a large key ring knocked into her.

"It's not the best curry house in the world," the woman said. Pepper followed her into the building's vestibule, where the woman stopped and shook the key ring with frustration. To the left of the door leading to the restaurant was a staircase.

"I'm Pepper," Pepper said.

The woman looked up from her keys.

"You're Pepper!" she said. "Congratulations! You own the world's best curry house!" She found the key she needed and proceeded up the stairs. One of her gray heels was gouged in the back, like she'd gotten it stuck in a grate. "The proprietor of the restaurant just renewed the lease, and that's a seven-year term. Your representative wasn't clear about whether you intend to let the upper flat."

Pepper stood at the edge of the stairs while the woman unlocked the door. She hadn't mentioned the prospect of selling on the phone, but the most recent valuation was enough to give her heart palpitations. The handrail was coated with a film of grease. Part of her had thought maybe Ula was here, waiting for her, which was a stupid thing to think. The estate agent entered the flat, her heels echoing through the empty space. The flat was small and bare, the walls a fresh, bright white. No marks in the plaster where anything had been hanging. Unoccupied.

Pepper walked from room to room, hollowed by her disappointment. The flat was clean, but the radiator was covered in a thick coat of dust. The appliances weren't plugged in. The refrigerator was so old Pepper doubted it would work even if it were. Unoccupied and unlivable. She'd allowed herself to believe this place might mean something, might've been given to her for some reason other than to manipulate her into signing Ula's agreement. But she was wrong. The only thing Ula had given her was an ultimatum: do what I want or else.

"Rents have stabilized, but this area is quite desirable if you can find someone willing to tolerate smelling like curry all the time," the agent said. She was looking at her phone, already moved on to her next appointment. "Do you have any questions?"

"The previous owner," Pepper said. "Did you know her?"

The agent started to laugh but stopped when she realized Pepper wasn't joking. "Oh no," she said. "She handled everything through her solicitor. I don't think she ever set foot in the place."

Through the window, Pepper looked down on the street, where a woman in a hoodie dropped a bag of spray paint and chased the cans as they rolled in every direction.

"Maybe she doesn't like curry," Pepper said.

The agent smiled and shrugged. "Anything else?"

Pepper could still feel the grease from the handrail on her hand. Like the rest of the flat, the bathroom was painted white and showed no signs of recent occupation. The sink only put out cold water. Pepper scrubbed her hands as best she could without soap, and then she saw it—the corner of a photo sticking out from behind the mirror above the sink. Pepper dried her hands on her shirt and pulled it out. It was a Polaroid of a statue, half a man in a wide-brimmed hat rising up out of a brick sidewalk. It looked fairly recent, its colors still vibrant. It looked like it had been left for someone to find.

it's because i'm her daughter
scott thinks people will be more likely
to talk about ula
if i'm there

                    you're not going to see the pelicans
                    are you

PEPPER DIDN'T HAVE time to eat before making the train to Germany, so by the time she arrived in Cologne, she was starving. She found Scott sitting on a bench in the square in the late-afternoon sun outside a sharp-spired Gothic cathedral. When he saw Pepper, he stood and hugged her as if they were friends. He looked the same as before, spoiled and self-satisfied, purple shoes and eyeball cuff links, but red around the eyes.

"He only agreed to meet with me because I told him you'd be here," he said. He was nervous, and Pepper couldn't tell if it was in anticipation of the meeting or something else. "And he won't talk about what happened when she finished the painting, so don't even ask. But also maybe downplay the fact that you've never met her."

"Nice to see you too," Pepper said.

In the time since Pepper had seen Scott, he'd worked through the list of clients he'd gotten from Gordon, which had been less helpful than either of them had hoped. Many of Ula's clients had simply disappeared, and several were dead—three suicides, one aneurysm, two mysterious accidents. One woman had voluntarily institutionalized herself, and the doctors wouldn't tell Scott anything, nor would her family. The clients were mostly wealthy—corporate executives or people with family money, though a few were just devotees who'd written a letter. Ula's fee seemed to operate on a sliding scale. The son of a woman who'd commissioned a portrait and then died driving while intoxicated told Scott his mother had been a grant writer for a cancer research nonprofit. She'd never been a drinker before Ula painted her. She was among the few Americans, and the rest were from all over—Norway,

South Africa, Brazil. The families of Ula's clients were generally uncooperative, bitter at the destructive effect of the experience on their lives.

The breakthrough came when Scott located an American expat in Germany who'd been hospitalized shortly after the completion of his portrait. The man was the son of the founder of a ubiquitous big-box store, and upon his release, he'd moved to Germany. His name was Levi Crow. That was all Scott knew. It seemed the internet had been scrubbed of his name.

"We have a little time," Scott said. He was watching people stream in and out of the cathedral. "If you want to walk around."

Pepper crossed the square and texted Ike a picture of the cathedral. She'd sent him one of the Polaroid as she left London, asking him to forward it to a colleague who specialized in public art, but she hadn't heard back. Maybe it was her reception. She found herself standing in front of a booth that smelled like grease, so she bought herself some food by pointing to what the person in front of her in line had bought. She was rewarded with a gigantic sizzling potato pancake smothered with applesauce. As soon as she took it in her hand, she felt hot grease and cold juice running down her wrist, the contrast in temperatures disorienting. She imagined herself being consumed by fire, licked to death by cool, pleasant tongues of flame.

> it took over 600 years to build that cathedral

were you sleeping

> no
> reading

how's kit

> she's seeing a lot of graves
> there were graves all along the trail

Pepper sat next to Scott on the bench.
"Nice church," he said.
"It took over six hundred years to build," Pepper said.

> kit keeps saying something
> makes me think of you

Pepper took a bite of her pancake and again felt the delicious confusion of hot and cold.

> done brave
> usually after she watches someone die
> but sometimes after she cooks griddle cakes
> or apples
> or whatever
> done brave
> that's basically the opposite of me
> no it isn't

"Do you want some?" She extended the pancake in Scott's direction, but he shook his head. He had a look about him like he was deciding something. "Is your girlfriend still mad?"

Scott gazed at the square, where birds were fighting over trash on the ground. She didn't know what kind of birds they were. Ike would know.

"It's okay," she said. "I don't like to talk about things either." She took another bite, salty and sweet.

Scott kept his eyes on the birds. "She's not mad," he said. "But her dad isn't doing well."

One of the birds pecked viciously at another, who still did not relent.

"Then why are you here?" she said. Ula was famous, even before the stories about other universes. But how many people cared that much about a famous artist if they weren't secretly related to her?

Scott inhaled and stood, and Pepper followed, setting the uneaten pancake on the ground and wiping her hands as best she could on her sole napkin. A man wearing khaki pants and a khaki shirt approached them. Everything about him was nondescript.

Scott extended a hand. "Thank you for coming."

Levi took Scott's hand, then turned to Pepper and froze.

"My god," he said.

"Yes," she said.

"She didn't want me looking at her," Levi said. "Kept telling me other things in the room to look at, as if that might keep me from seeing her face. But of course I saw her anyway. You look just like her."

"Yes," Pepper said. She knew what she looked like. But she didn't know how to react when people looked at her and saw someone else.

Levi sat next to her on the bench, sandwiching her in. He pointed to the cathedral. "The relics of Saint Irmgardis are in the sarcophagus. Do you know about her?"

Pepper shook her head.

"She was a countess," he said. He had a slight drawl, like he'd lived in the South, but a long time ago. "After her parents died, she gave everything away and started performing miracles. And then one day, she stopped and went to live in the hollow of a tree, surrounded by animals. But she was beautiful, she was known for her beauty, and sometimes knights would come from afar and try to seduce her. According to the legend, she would say one word and the knights' castles, kingdoms away, would burst into flames."

"Somehow I suspect even that wasn't a deterrent," Pepper said.

Levi smiled. "She was mostly very quiet, they say. She only started fires when she needed to."

Pepper sat back against the bench. The birds were now picking at what was left of her pancake. One of them darted at her feet and changed direction at the last minute.

"You know why we're here," she said.

"She's really missing, then?" Levi said.

"It's been all over the news," Scott said. "Is there a reason you think she might not be?"

Levi shook his head. "Not really," he said. "But I wasn't

surprised when I heard. Some people, they're just the kind you expect to drop out, you know?"

He was looking at Pepper like she was that kind of person.

"Can you tell us about your time with Ula?" she asked. "What the process was like? Any little detail might be helpful."

Scott cued up a digital recorder, but Levi turned his head.

"It's just that I don't want any more pieces of myself taken away," he said.

Scott pocketed the recorder and closed his eyes when Levi started speaking. Pepper wasn't sure if he was zoning out or if this was the way he listened. It occurred to her that she'd never asked what he thought of the stories about Ula's portraits, realizing it said more about her than it did him that her judgment of him wouldn't have been drastically altered if he was the type who actually believed.

"It was those tortured popes," Levi said. "That's what started it."

"Popes?" Pepper said.

"I had a buddy who collected art," Levi said. "Hedge fund manager. He'd lost a lot, the economy was fucked then. He was after this painting of a tortured pope. Like a shadow of the man, sitting in a chair and screaming. Francis Bacon was the artist. He was big with the finance guys then. I hadn't heard of Ula Frost, but my buddy had this art magazine, and her name was on the cover. I don't know why I picked it up. I was just drawn to it. And once I read about her work, I couldn't stop thinking about it. I didn't care if it was true. My wife had died not long before. Ovarian cancer."

"I'm sorry," Pepper said. She blinked and saw her—a woman flickering in and out of being, dying one second and healthy the next.

Levi nodded. "I thought. Well, I know how this sounds, but I thought maybe somewhere she was still okay. There was an address. I wrote a letter. I've never been a writer. I just wrote about my wife."

"How long did it take before you heard?" Scott said.

"It was almost a year," Levi said. "I'd all but forgotten about it. And then one day, I got a phone call."

"Gordon Priddy," Scott said.

"Yeah," Levi said. "Gordon was his name. He told me Ula Frost had read my letter and would like me to send photographs of myself."

"You didn't talk to her on the phone?" Scott asked. He screwed up his face. This wasn't how he thought it worked, but Pepper wasn't sure how he'd formed an idea of how it worked in the first place.

"No," Levi said. "Nothing like that. The photos had to be specific. My face straight on, and from each side. And two full-body photos, front and back, both nude."

"And you did it?" Pepper said.

"I was in better shape then," Levi said, which made Pepper laugh. "Really, I wondered if that Gordon guy was some kind of pervert, but honestly I didn't care. My kids had been so angry with me since Laila died. I didn't have anything left."

"Sometimes she talked to people on the phone," Scott said. "Before she decided."

"Huh," Levi said.

Scott blinked a few times, processing. Pepper recognized that look he'd gotten too attached to his ideas about how it worked. It was so exhausting, the work of reconciling yourself to your own wrongness.

"Then I got more instructions," Levi said. "From Gordon. I lived in Atlanta, but she wouldn't paint me at my house. It had to be a hotel, and it had to be a certain distance away, on the other side of the city. The hotel she picked was a dump. The carpet had cigarette burns, there were water stains on the ceiling. I was to arrive every day at exactly 9:00 a.m. and wear the same outfit every time. No hair products, no makeup, not that I wear makeup. I had to shave each day immediately before coming. I was supposed to wear quiet shoes. It took me a while to figure that one out."

One of the birds got brave and pecked at Pepper's shoelace,

and she shooed it as inconspicuously as she could with her toe. Her phone buzzed.

so your friends are here

"How long between getting the instructions and your sitting?" Scott asked.

"Three days," Levi said. "Gordon said she'd be there in three days."

the ones from your office
the art collectors
they want to know where you are

Levi was still talking about his preparations, but Pepper was no longer listening. She didn't care if it was rude. She was picturing Ike, trying to get past those men through a doorway, trying to protect her. It was morning in Connecticut, and she felt the distance between them in her body and fully understood then the desire to have the power to harness time and space.

just tell them what they want to know
don't do anything stupid for me

"What was the room where she painted you like?" Scott said. "Did you notice anything special? Like, was there anything unusual about her brushes or paint?"

do you want me to call
or i can call the police

"I don't know anything about painting," Levi said. "I wouldn't know if there was anything unusual about her paint. She had white sheets draped over everything. The bed and the chairs. The mirror. There were frames hanging on the walls, but she'd turned them around. She didn't listen to music. She didn't say anything while she worked, except when she told me to change position. I couldn't sit. I was always standing. Sometimes she'd tell me to turn to one side."

"You've probably heard that no one knows where she was living," Scott said. "Were there any indicators of where she came from or where she was going when she left? Was she dressed for a different climate? Did she leave anything personal sitting around?"

The bird who'd pecked at Pepper's shoe came back, this time with friends. There were three of them, all gathered around her sneaker. Ike hadn't responded yet. In an alternate universe, these birds were swarming her, pecking her guts out. Tourists strolled out of the cathedral into the sunshine, enjoying their day. Another bird joined and hopped onto Pepper's shoe, but she felt too afraid to move.

"She wore all black," Levi said. "Nothing that made her look out of place, nothing that would draw attention. She had a mole on the index finger of her right hand, the size of a pencil eraser. I didn't see anything else. I couldn't look at her for long without getting in trouble. She didn't have a suitcase. She was there when I got there, and if she left the room, she didn't do it until I was gone."

> are you okay
> i'm freaking
> tell them where i am
> and check in

Scott was writing furiously in his notebook. Levi got up and stuck his hands in the midst of the birds, who backed off as if his hands emitted a force field, then took the remains of Pepper's pancake to a nearby trash can.

"Sorry," he said, returning. "I think even Saint Irmgardis would've taken issue with those birds."

Pepper couldn't think. "Thank you," she said.

"I'm sorry I'm not more helpful," he said. "You must be worried about her."

Pepper felt herself welling. She nodded and excused herself, crossing the square to a man selling bottled water. She handed the man some cash from her pocket. She didn't care if he gave her correct change. In another universe, she'd told Ike she was sorry before she left. She never told him she was sorry. In another universe, she'd never left in the first place.

check in motherfucker

The man handed Pepper change and a napkin and mimicked dabbing his own cheek. Pepper tried to compose herself before rejoining Scott and Levi. According to Scott, Levi was only in his fifties, but he looked much older. His hair was nearly translucent, as if the color had been leached out.

"Can you tell us what happened when she finished the painting?" she asked.

Scott had told her not to ask this, but she couldn't stop herself. She needed another world to exist right then, as much as she needed that water.

Levi looked out at the square and cleared his throat. "I told your friend I wasn't going to talk about that."

The birds had moved on, gathered around a very old man in suspenders, who'd sat with difficulty on a bench across the square and was now feeding them bread from a cloth bag. Pepper couldn't think of a way to convince Levi to tell her something he wasn't ready to say out loud. Her phone was sickeningly silent in her hand. She decided that if she could get Levi to tell her what happened, Ike would be okay.

"My husband is a history professor," she said. "He specializes in the history of sexuality." Levi didn't say anything, but he was listening. "In his field, most of the research focuses on primary sources. Diaries, letters, photographs. Oral history. When we first started dating and he told me he was reading dead women's diaries for the sexy bits, I was so mad about it. He didn't have those women's permission. I don't know why I took it so personally."

Levi was still looking at the square. He had a scar behind one ear. "Do you keep a diary?" he asked.

"I never have," she said. "And I sure as hell never will now that I know some historian could get his hands on it."

Levi smiled. He cleared his throat again.

"I was supposed to visit him one weekend, which I did even though I was having second thoughts. He took me to the library at his university. There was a collection of diaries there, World War II nurses. That's what he was researching then. He sat me down with a translation of one diary from Belgium and asked me to read it. So I did. The nurse was in Hannut near the beginning of the war. The entire diary was about this soldier she was caring for who was burned and all wrapped in gauze. As the diary went on, they fell in love. She fell in love with him before she ever saw his face. They had to wait so long to take off the bandages. Then, very slowly, very carefully, she unraveled him."

"Wow," Levi said.

"I finished reading, and that's when Ike told me it wasn't true. The diary had been found in a barn outside of Antwerp. It had been written by a Belgian Jew. She was twenty-three, and she'd written the whole thing while in hiding."

"It was all a lie?" Levi said.

"Ike tracked down the woman's name," she said. "Her mother had been a nurse, but she wasn't. She must not have known about the bandages. They would've needed changing. But it was a story she told because she needed to tell a story to survive."

She'd died in 1944 in Auschwitz, but Pepper left that part out. Ike had stayed in bed for three days after he'd found the records. He had the same attachment to his diaries as Pepper did to her bones. She wasn't sure now why she'd thought this story might convince Levi. Ike would've been able to spin it better.

Levi looked at her. "You really look so much like her."

"I don't know her that well," Pepper said. "Not as well as I should. But I'd like to find out what happened to her. I think you know what it feels like to have something gnaw at you."

Levi nodded. He took a vial from his pocket, removed a pill, and swallowed it. "Okay," he said. "She painted me. I stood there, in that hotel, for nine days. There wasn't any conversation. I wasn't allowed to see the work in progress. My arms and legs kept falling asleep. Sometimes I thought she wasn't even looking at me. On the ninth day, she told me to close my eyes. It made me feel dizzy to stand with my eyes closed, but I did it anyway. I was used to standing by that point. And then . . ."

Scott leaned forward on the bench. He dug one hand into Pepper's knee so hard it hurt. "Something happened?"

"Something happened," Levi said. "My eyes were closed. I didn't see it. But I could feel it. You know how it feels during a lightning storm? When the air is all charged with electricity? It felt like that. And there was a noise. A storm is all I can think to compare it to. Like thunder. And there was a smell. Not smoke, exactly. But like something had been zapped. She told me I could open my eyes. She said she was finished. I heard someone coughing."

Pepper's phone buzzed.

okay they're gone

"I looked, and it was me," Levi said. He was having trouble speaking now, his voice coming out distorted as if there were a pair of invisible hands around his neck. "Or he looked like me. But he was skinny. Not just a little skinny. Like when you see those kids from third-world countries in commercials. The ones that need sponsors. Round bellies and stick limbs. Starving. This guy was me, but he was starving to death. And I said—I know this makes no sense—but I said to her, 'We need to order room service.' She didn't answer. She just walked out of the room. Didn't take her brushes or anything."

but they know where you are
i'm sorry

"What?" Scott said. He was shaking his head. "What did you do?"

"The guy," Levi said. He coughed into his fist. "He wasn't the right color. Kind of blue. He was there, and he was already dying. He looked at me like he knew me, like he knew where he was and what happened, and he said, 'Kill me.'" Levi was quiet for a minute. He looked at his hands in his lap. "So I killed him. I strangled him. I just . . ." He was quiet again. "I don't know how to explain this, but I knew it was the right thing to do. Still do."

Pepper couldn't think of anything to say. She looked at Levi's hands. They were freckled and soft. Just regular hands. His nails were smoother than her own.

"I sat there for a while," he said. "Then I called the desk and told them I'd killed myself. And that was it."

Scott stood and walked an aimless circle. Pepper had read about the actual science of the many-worlds interpretation, but that was years ago. Volumes had been written about this. The likelihood that the other universes weren't romanticized versions of our own world, centered around us and our individual choices, but ones that were radically different.

are you okay

     i'll be fine

     the one guy hit me tho

which guy

     the one who doesn't look like andy warhol

     he was wearing a sweater

     with snowflakes on it

you should call the police

     it's not bad

     bloody nose

     i felt like i was in a movie

"I don't suppose that tells you much about your mother," Levi said. "Or gives you anything that could help find her. But that's what happened."

The old man who'd been feeding the birds had fallen asleep on the bench, and now the birds were gathered around him as if they were guarding him. Pepper had manipulated Levi into telling this story, which gave her nothing and came at a cost to him. She thought about Ike that day in the library, showing her someone else's story, which was false and true at the same time. It was the moment she'd realized they were both doing the same work—using what remained to reconstruct an unknowable past, hoping to learn something from the dead. Ike had words and she had bodies, or not bodies, but the scaffolding of bodies, the only physical part of us sturdy enough to withstand the passage of time. They were doing the same thing, hoping they'd be able to see past the flaws in their own interpretations and find something true.

"What about the body?" Scott said. "What about the portrait?" He was flipping through his notepad for answers Pepper knew he wouldn't find. "Why wasn't there a DNA test?"

Whatever Levi had taken kicked in, and he rolled his head around too loosely. "I was arrested at the hotel. The body was taken away by the police. And then it disappeared."

"Disappeared," Pepper said.

"It disappeared," Levi said flatly. He said it to Scott, not to her. "The portrait too. I never even saw it."

"Disappeared," Scott said, understanding.

Then Pepper got it. Levi had been in a cushy hospital, not in jail. This was a conversation between two men with money.

Levi stood. "The part that really gets me." He cleared his throat. "This is what I think about. I've had a lot of time for thinking. I wanted the portrait because I thought there might be a place where my wife was still alive. But that doesn't make sense. If the version of me in that world still had Laila and the painting brought him here, then that Laila is alone. It means I lost her twice." He looked up at the cathedral, then shook Scott's hand. "I guess that's all," he said.

> there's something else
> they took the paperwork
> from the lawyer

and the picture i printed
of the polaroid
with the man coming out of the sidewalk
like they recognized it

Levi kissed Pepper on the cheek and started walking away. Then he stopped.

"There wasn't anything to look at in the room," he said. "I stood there for days, and I looked where she told me—the window, the walls, the back of the canvas. I don't know anything about painting. I don't know if this means anything. But there was a ship on the back."

"A ship?" Pepper said.

"A little ship. It was burned into the wood. The frame, I guess you'd call it."

"Thank you," Pepper said.

Across the square, the birds coalesced around something Pepper couldn't see as Levi disappeared into the crowd.

if something happens to me
take all those paintings
and sell them for a bajillion dollars
agreement be damned
move someplace warm
drink cocktails with umbrellas
find waterfalls that aren't on maps
learn a new language
and never think of me again

PEPPER COULDN'T SLEEP on the way to Poland. After his visit from the Everett Group, Ike called his colleague, who immediately placed the location of the statue from the Polaroid—Wrocław. Pepper tried to find a canvas supplier in Wrocław that used a ship insignia, but nothing turned up. She did, however, find a listing for a ship repair company, which didn't make sense. Wrocław wasn't near the sea. Scott was distracted, constantly checking his phone, and agreed to Pepper's plan without question.

There was a series of trains, speeding through the night, the stars blurring by in the dark. Rereading Ike's texts, Pepper felt like she could lift a car. Scott had bought them first-class tickets, so they sat across from each other in wide leather chairs, a table between them. Scott, with his fancy neck pillow, fell easily asleep, leaving Pepper alone, resting her head against the cool window glass. A woman came by and offered coffee, but Pepper didn't need it. She was thinking about Levi Crow. Pepper didn't believe in alternate universes, not the way Ula's followers did. But she believed that Levi Crow believed the story he'd told them.

Levi Crow had been hospitalized after his portrait was painted. Pepper didn't know the whole story—maybe he had a history of mental illness. She didn't know. But something had happened to him. Something related to Ula had been a source of trauma in his life. If it wasn't an alternate Levi appearing, what was it? Scott murmured in his sleep, but Pepper couldn't understand anything he said.

When the train arrived in Wrocław, it was pouring. Scott stowed his expensive headphones and misted his face with a tiny bottle of rosewater. He had his travel umbrella ready before they stepped off the train. Pepper reached into her bag even though she knew she hadn't packed anything that practical. But there, neat in its zippered pouch, was her travel raincoat. Ike had slipped it in, knowing Pepper would forget.

Even in the morning gloom, the city glowed with buildings painted shades of sunset. Two countries away from her original plan, Pepper felt an odd calm, as if this was where she'd meant to come all along. When she looked down, she found little gnome statues tucked off the streets, one sleeping in a four-poster bed. She knelt and took a picture to send to Ike. He'd love this place.

"It used to be called Breslau," Pepper told Scott. She was just reciting what she'd read on the train. "The city was destroyed in the war, but they rebuilt the whole thing, meticulously. The gnomes are a tribute to an underground protest movement that painted dwarves over government propaganda when the city was controlled by the Soviet Union."

One world destroyed and replaced by another—the entire city a defiant, joyful re-creation.

> from kit:
> april 6 passed 3 graves made 14 miles
> april 7 passed 9 graves made 16 miles
> april 8 passed 6 graves made 9 miles
> april 10 passed 15 graves made 13 miles
> april 11 passed 2 graves made 15 miles
> april 12 passed 8 graves made 17 miles
> thought you might want to start your day
> with a little history :)

Scott followed Pepper through the cobblestone streets, faded against the vividness of the city. He had an unrumpled quality that made Pepper feel out of place walking next to him. She'd overheard him on the phone, arguing with his father. Pepper was here out of necessity, but Scott was half someplace else. It was hard to function split in two, each version of yourself feeling less real by the second.

The rain was the blowing kind, and Pepper's hood kept slipping off her head. She was wet all the way through her shoes by the time she found the place she was looking for. A skinny blue building, nestled between gray and green ones, with a plaque hanging way up high with the image of a ship burned into the wood. They entered the building and climbed the staircase in single file, because there wasn't room for them to walk side by side.

"Can't imagine getting any ship parts up these stairs," Scott said.

After sleeping on the train, Scott was now waking to the work ahead of them. Pepper, on the other hand, was bleary with exhaustion, her eyes raw in her skull. The door said, in stenciled print, *Naprawa Statków.* Ship Repair.

She knocked and ran a hand through her hair. It would look crazy when it dried. She leaned close to the door, listening, but all was quiet. It was still early, just after eight. And maybe this place had nothing to do with Ula Frost. Outside, a bus honked. Scott shrugged and knocked again, more loudly.

They heard something thump against the floor, and what was probably swearing, but Pepper didn't speak Polish and had managed to learn only a few words and phrases on the train. *Cześć. Do widzenia. Przepraszam.* The door opened.

Pepper wasn't sure what she'd been expecting, but it was definitely not a shirtless man with ropy forearms and the torso of an underwear model in a pair of faded jeans.

"Cześć," she said.

The man let loose with a string of Polish, and it took Pepper too long to remember the translation app she'd put on her phone. The man was in his twenties and had sunken, watery blue eyes and a distinctly square chin. They'd woken him. He blinked a few times and focused on her face. That same look Levi Crow had given her—a kind of recognition that made her feel as if she'd never seen herself properly. The man sighed.

"English?" he said.

"Yes, proszę," Pepper said.

He stepped aside and motioned for them to enter. The room smelled like sweaty socks and reminded Pepper of a dorm. There was a poster for what looked like a Polish gangster film on one wall, unwashed dishes stacked across the counter, empty beer bottles on the floor. At one end of the room, there was what appeared to be an antique loom.

Pepper looked for a place to sit, but there weren't any chairs. "We're so sorry to disturb you."

The man introduced himself as Bartosz and put on a rumpled eagle T-shirt. "You are here because of Ula."

"Yes," Scott said. He was trying to avoid touching anything. "You know Ula Frost?"

Bartosz started gathering trash as if he were embarrassed, then changed his mind and stopped. "Of course," he said. "I know Ula since I was little kid."

"Have you seen her?" Pepper asked. "Recently? When was the last time you saw her?"

He opened the refrigerator and removed a block of hard cheese with a black rind. From the counter, he took a knife. He pointed it at Pepper, and she watched the edge glint. "You want?" She shook her head as he held the cheese in one hand and began curling off slices with the knife. "It has been few weeks now. More than one month, maybe."

"Do you know where she is?" Pepper asked. "It's very important that we find her."

"You look like her," Bartosz said. He held a slice of cheese in his mouth. "Very much like her."

"Yes," Pepper said. She remembered Ike's texts about Kit. *Done brave.* "She's my mother." It felt less like a lie every time she said it. "We need to find her."

"I am sorry not to help you," Bartosz said. He ate another slice of cheese. The way he was cutting made Pepper nervous. He was using too much pressure, getting the knife's blade too close to his palm. "Though I am not sure she would want me to if I could."

Pepper scanned the room for anything that might be helpful. There were stacks all over the place—magazines and mail, receipts and scraps of paper, none of which Pepper could read.

"Your sign says ship repair," Scott said. He was looking at the loom. "What is it that you do, exactly?"

Bartosz sliced off another hunk of cheese and shook his head. "No ships," he said. "My grandfather, he worked on ships."

"But not you," Pepper said.

Pepper hadn't realized he'd put a kettle on the stove, and the unexpected whistling startled her. Bartosz raised his eyebrows and poured water into a mug with no handle.

"There are no ships here," he said. "We are not near the sea."

Pepper knew that, and he knew Pepper knew that. The room filled with the scent of fennel and coriander as steam rose from the mug.

"You must be close," Pepper said, "if you've known Ula since you were a child."

"I know her enough," he said, looking through the steam. She wondered if Ula had prepared him for this, trained him as a child to be evasive when people came asking questions, as they inevitably would. She wondered if Ula would've done the same with her.

Pepper scanned the room again. On the wall near the futon, there was a faded cross-stitch hanging in a golden hoop, blue flowers that looked like hearts.

"This is beautiful," she said.

"My mother," Bartosz said. The musculature of his jaw moved beneath the skin.

"Does she live nearby?" Pepper said. "My colleague has an interest in folk art."

Scott shot her a look, but Pepper kept her eyes on Bartosz's jaw. Men and their mothers, this was something she understood. Ike had once started quietly crying as they walked through campus together, having been reminded of his mother by the scent of clove cigarettes, which she'd sometimes smoked in what she thought was secret when he was a kid.

"She made canvas," Bartosz said. "A family trade. She was the one who was best at it. She was the one Ula liked." He took a long drink of tea.

"But now Ula has you instead."

His jaw hardened, and he nodded.

"This is what you use?" She pointed at the loom, and he nodded again. His face twitched with memory. She wished she had something to give him. "I'm sure Scott would be very interested to see how this works." She smiled brightly at Scott. She could already feel her hair puffing up around her head as it dried. "Scott?"

"Yes!" Scott said, picking up on Pepper's cue. "I'd love to see this baby in action. You must've been well trained, if Ula uses your work."

Bartosz sipped his tea and straightened with pride. Scott was looking at Pepper, but she made herself busy attending to her hair. Bartosz crossed the space and squatted in front of the loom, revealing the small of his back.

"This was my grandmother's," he said. "Very old. I have made changes. You understand looms, yes?"

"Of course," Scott said.

Bartosz embarked on a brief history of the use of cotton and flax in painters' canvases and the modifications he'd made to the loom over the years, first to make the work easier for his mother as she aged, then for his substantially larger hands. Pepper shuffled to the side of the room as he moved on to Venetian sail canvases and gesso and pretended to look in the mirror while scanning the papers on the table beneath it.

"That's fascinating," Scott said.

The stack on the table seemed to be bills—Pepper could only recognize the numbers. Maybe a bank statement. She scanned everything she could see for names and dates, anything that looked familiar.

"And have you made any changes in the technique your mother taught you?" Scott said.

Bartosz lit up—this was how he kept their relationship alive. He launched into an impassioned speech that was nearly impossible to understand. Scott nodded vigorously. There was more clutter by the sink, and Pepper moved from the mirror toward the little kitchen. Bartosz was spitting as he replicated the sound of a beater hitting the fell of cloth. Pepper glimpsed a piece of paper with the mark of a ship at the top, like a letterhead. Bartosz took Scott's hands and placed them on the wood. He had strong feelings about warp. Pepper swiped the paper and stuffed it in her bag. Bartosz turned back. Pepper pulled out a tube of lipstick and applied it using her reflection in the refrigerator.

"Do you make the frames yourself too?" she asked.

"I do," Bartosz said. He was flushed now. He looked like he was ready to run a marathon. "Ula brings me the wood. She says it is haunted."

"Haunted?" Pepper said.

"Ah," Bartosz said. He went back for his tea. "Everything in Wrocław is haunted. But the ghosts do not bother with locals, so you try to blend in, okay? Ula, I think, she does not blend in. I would believe ghosts come to her." He went through a doorway and returned with a frame as wide as his shoulders. "Here is one," he said.

He handed it to Pepper, and as she took it, her body suddenly registered her jet lag. She couldn't run on nerves forever. The wood of the frame was dark and weightier than it looked. The finish was smooth and uneven, sanded by hand. She turned it over and found a sailed ship seared into the surface.

"I mark them," Bartosz said. "This is art too. Would you like a cup of tea?"

Pepper's eyes burned again. The wood was heavy in her hands. She didn't believe in ghosts, but she felt something as she held it, an object that was meant for Ula, that Ula had chosen. "I'm sorry," she said. "We can't stay. Thank you, though. You've been very helpful." She handed the frame back, but the heaviness it had imparted didn't lift.

"Anything for Ula," Bartosz said, showing them out. "She has been good to me. She was very good to my mother."

Pepper and Scott didn't speak as they descended the staircase. Neither of them said anything until they were around the corner, safely out of listening distance.

"Well, I know about looms now," Scott said.

It wasn't raining anymore. Pepper's whole body felt leaden and warm, like she'd been put under a spell. She reached into her bag.

"What's that?" Scott said.

"It looks like an invoice," she said. There was a column of numbers, a line, a fee. At the bottom there was a name, U. Mróz, and what looked like an address. She took out her phone. She typed in the word almost automatically, like she was playing with a Ouija board. "Mróz," she said. "Polish for *frost.*"

9

THE ADDRESS ON the invoice led them to a quiet street east of the center of the Old Town. Pepper spotted another gnome statue on the corner. This one was hunched, covering his eyes. She wasn't ready for this. She needed a shower, a nap, time.

> you okay?
> are you eating a lot of sausages
> that's what they eat in poland, right
>
> isaac

On the sidewalk, they crossed paths with a middle-aged woman whose head was wrapped in a scarf. She spotted Pepper with a look of alarm, then nodded and continued down the sidewalk.

> so many sausages
> please eat something that's not a sausage
> on my behalf

The number listed on the invoice was halfway down the block and, to Pepper's relief, not a curry restaurant. It was a church, or it had been a church. It was smallish, and the windows on the side depicted suffering men in shades of rose and blue. There was no sign outside. There was a scaly dragon carved into the stone above the solid wooden door. The door didn't have a knocker.

"This is . . . not what I was expecting," Scott said, looking up and down the street. He'd been tense the whole way there, walking too fast for Pepper. He wasn't after the same thing she was, but he was in more of a hurry to get there.

"Do we knock?" Pepper said.

Scott shrugged. The wood of the door hurt Pepper's knuckles. It was so thick she doubted they'd be heard even if someone were inside.

They stood and waited, and Pepper tried to focus on the grain of the wood. In another universe, she was in her lab, where it was quiet and familiar, where she knew what to expect. The problem with this universe was that it was so unpredictable. Any moment now, Ula Frost might answer the door, take one look, and fold her into her arms. Any moment now, Ula Frost might answer the door and start screaming at her. Each possibility seemed equally undesirable.

No one came to the door. Scott knocked again, and again they were met with silence. He walked around to either side of the building, then the back, looking for another entrance. Pepper stayed on the sidewalk, staring up at the dragon's scales.

i have important news

The street was empty and still, as if the neighborhood were abandoned.

does it involve sausages
                    i know kit's secret
is she an outlaw
i desperately want her to be an outlaw

Pepper thought she could smell sausages, cooking somewhere, the scent wafting through an open window.

                    she's not an outlaw
        dang
                    but she was MARRIED before

WHAT
              she was married and he died of cholera
              and she thought she'd do better
              if no one knew
              and they thought she was a virgin
wow
can't wait till she finds a new fella
and you get to their wedding night
              i'll keep you posted xo

Pepper imagined Kit, carrying her lie as a form of asylum. The church door in front of her was reinforced with metal bands. Churches were supposed to be places of sanctuary, she thought. Maybe she could just go inside.

The door was unlocked. Pepper entered alone and found herself in a shadowy vestibule. In front of her was another set of doors. Beside each door was a pedestal with a basin on top, for holy water. The basins were empty. Pepper could feel the church's history around her, its past hanging over its present, a sense that other people had stood in this exact spot for other reasons, in other kinds of pain, over and over for a very long time. She could feel some part of them still lingering here, like ghosts. She waited for Scott to join her, but he didn't. The vestibule had been stripped of whatever furniture it once had, leaving only the bare gray stone. Pepper opened the next set of doors.

The windows were all covered with white sheets, which made it hard to see. Pepper pulled one down, revealing a stained-glass image of a man being pierced in the chest by a sword. The glass was full of reds and blues and cast the room in violet light. Almost everything in the room was white, either painted or draped with a sheet. It took Pepper too long to make sense of it. It looked like the place had been turned over. A few white chairs were on their sides near the altar, the only original fixture of the church left in place. On the wall behind it was the outline of a crucifix, the paint in the place where it had hung cleaner than the paint around it. One of the chairs was broken, its white surface splintered to reveal ashen wood underneath. The floor had been painted white too, but when Pepper knelt, she could see the designs on the tiles—a cross, a swastika. She closed her eyes and saw Ula in this space, where Pepper stood now. But it wasn't really Ula, it was Pepper herself. She was conflating their images in her mind.

Pepper stopped and listened. There were brushes scattered across the floor, in front of a long filing cabinet against one wall. Someone had been here, looking for something. There were ancillary rooms tucked around her—the sacristy, the confessionals. Pepper heard the doors creak open behind her.

"Please tell me you didn't pick the lock," Scott said. He took a few steps and stopped. "Jesus."

"It wasn't locked," Pepper said. The room felt wrong to her, though she wasn't the type to have that kind of feeling. She was just scared. She thought about Kit, walking miles and miles alongside her wagon, past graves, hungry or hurting or crazed with exhaustion, making griddle cakes for men and little kids who might die, who were sick and shitting themselves to death, watching people get crushed by wagons or bit by snakes, each dead companion discarded and left behind, with no shelter from any of it, no respite in sight. Kit, despite all those things, walking and walking and walking, her secret tightly coiled inside her, because it was necessary. Pepper started pulling sheets from the other windows. Scott was snapping pictures of the mess with his phone.

"I think we have to call someone," he said.

"Like who?" Pepper said.

"Like the police," Scott said.

Pepper heard a noise again, a quiet scritch from one of the confessionals. Scott was too busy looking at his phone to notice. Pepper tossed a sheet on the floor in front of her to muffle her footsteps. The confessionals were covered with white sheets that swayed softly, though Pepper couldn't see any air vents. Pepper's moms hadn't been big churchgoers, but they took her to midnight mass every year on Christmas Eve, and one year she'd gotten up under the guise of needing to use the bathroom but had instead slid herself into a confessional while everyone else was shaking hands with their neighbors. The confessional had smelled like aftershave—a distinctly male smell that was so different from that of Pepper's own home. She remembered touching the screen that divided sinner from priest, unsure which side she was on.

Pepper got as close to the confessional as felt safe and listened for human sounds. She looked around for something heavy to pick up, but who was she kidding, if there was someone in there who wanted to hurt her she wouldn't have a chance. She imagined a version of herself in another world, tougher than this one, who was capable of fighting back.

Pepper lunged forward and jerked down the sheet. The confessional was empty. Scott looked up from his phone.

"What are you doing?" he said.

"I thought I heard someone," Pepper said.

On the floor, there was a pile of pink insulation, and when Pepper looked closer, she could see the tiny seeds of mouse shit.

"Why didn't you say something?" Scott asked.

Pepper didn't answer, and she pulled the sheet from the other confessional without hesitation, now that she knew Scott was watching. It, too, was empty, save for one embossed red hymnal.

"This building is owned by a corporation," Scott said. "Not one I found before, but it must be one of her shells."

Pepper rested a hand against the stone wall. It was cool to the touch. She inhaled, wondering what Ula Frost smelled like, if she wore perfume or smelled like popcorn like Annie or something else. The only lingering scent here was that of turpentine.

"Do you think she worked here?" she said.

"There are brushes," Scott said.

But no paintings. Pepper opened one of the filing cabinets against the wall. It was full of supplies—paper and paint and brushes and tape, all mixed together, like someone had picked through them.

"Do you think someone came in here and took her?" Pepper said. In another universe, Ula had opened the door and was showing them a work in progress right now. In another universe, Pepper had never learned her identity and never would, that freedom granted to her by Ula like a gift.

"I don't know," Scott said. "Someone's been here. But how would you find signs of a struggle in this mess?"

There wasn't any blood. The chairs and sheets weren't displaced in a way that suggested someone had been dragged. The sheets on the windows had all been in place, so no indication of an attempt to use a window as an escape. Pepper saw a flash of Ula again, this time painting a canvas propped on the altar.

Scott was now going through the file cabinets, taking pictures of each drawer's contents. Pepper ascended a short rise of stairs to the sacristy behind the altar. The door had been removed from its hinges, but the room beyond was dark. Pepper reached in and felt for a light switch. The air in the room felt different, as though it were moving.

She found the switch, but before she could hit it, there was a clumsy clatter, like a stack of magazines hitting the floor. Pepper rushed in senseless, Scott by her side now, both of them stumbling into the sacristy as a pair of legs tumbled out the window. Men's boots, black leather, and the pants were black and frayed at the hems. The shoes disappeared, and they heard the body drop to the sidewalk outside, the sound of a grunt.

Pepper tried to identify the intruder from the window, but the angle of its outward tilt made it impossible for her to see straight down.

"I'll go," Scott said, already running out the door.

Pepper stayed put, listening to the boots clomping against the sidewalk. She only got a glimpse as they rounded the corner, and only from behind. Black pants, black sweater, black cap. Average height, average body. The boots had been small, smaller than Ike's, closer to Pepper's size. She watched Scott sprint down the sidewalk and stop at the corner and spin. The intruder was already gone.

In the sacristy there was a bed against one wall, a mattress on a skeletal frame. All of the bedding had been stripped and strewn across the floor. There was a makeshift kitchen against the opposite wall, a mini fridge and a card table with a microwave and dirty dishes—at least a dozen disposable cups, as if there'd been a party. Pepper sat on the mattress and waited for Scott to return. The nightstand was chipped and its lone drawer had been yanked out, the contents scattered. Most of the papers looked like legal documents based on the letterhead, but there were also two light blue envelopes, worn in the way of paper that's been handled a lot, both of which read *Miś* in elegant, dripping cursive. Pepper took the blue envelopes and stuffed them in her jacket's inner pocket without thinking.

Scott joined her and sat beside her on the naked mattress, still catching his breath. He picked up the papers and sifted through them, returned them to the drawer that was now on the floor.

"I'm starting to think this was a bad idea," he said.

"You're starting to think?" Pepper said.

"We have to call the police," he said. "This is a crime scene. We're just fucking up evidence right now."

In an alternate universe, they'd called the police first thing, and clues to Ula's whereabouts were being bagged and cataloged. Pepper hadn't believed before now that Ula might be in serious danger. No one who knew her seemed surprised by the idea that she might intentionally disappear. The window was still open, and Pepper could hear people outside, greeting each other like long-lost friends. It was only Wednesday. If she got on a plane tomorrow, she'd still have the weekend in the lab before spring break was over. She could sign the agreement for the lawyer, cross one problem off her list. Ula didn't want Pepper to sell the paintings she'd inherit, but between London and Poland, Pepper hadn't found any paintings to sell. Maybe if Pepper let them work, the police would actually find Ula, and Pepper wouldn't have to worry about the inheritance at all.

Scott got up and left the sacristy to make his call. The mattress beneath Pepper was lumpy and thin. She'd read, on her way to Cologne, that another church there housed the remains of Saint Ursula, who'd been shot with a bow and arrow, along with the remains of her eleven thousand virginal handmaidens. There were bones of mastiffs mixed in, the ribs arranged to form words. Pepper hadn't had time to see them. She stood. Relics were often kept in a sarcophagus, but some cathedrals Pepper had visited had larger crypts for sacred remains, passageways or tunnels that were occasionally sealed and forgotten.

Pepper looked around for anything that seemed out of place, beyond the obvious mess. A place where there should be a door, a crack in the floor or the wall. A spot that had been patched and painted. She knocked on the walls, and they all felt solid. There wasn't anything hidden here. Pepper was just trying to distract herself from the fact of her own impotence.

Outside the sacristy, Scott was leading a man in a uniform into the church. He must've already been in the area.

"It is ghost, no?" the man was saying.

"Oh," Scott said. "No, we saw a person. But we heard about that. That the city is haunted."

"Yes, but this place," the officer said, waving his arms around. He was talking to Pepper now too. "There is vampire ghost."

"A ghost," Pepper said, "or a vampire?"

"Both," the officer said. Another man, also in uniform, joined him. He took one look around the room and sighed. There was a lot of work to be done here. The first officer was blond and husky. The second had a sharp face and pillowy lips.

"You tell them about vampire ghost?" the second officer said.

"It would come to people and squeeze them so hard to leave marks," the first officer said.

The second shook his head. "Such a story. It was shoemaker. He cut his own throat—a sin, you know? And his wife sewed it up, to hide it from neighbors. She would not let him be seen. But secrets," he said. "Secrets always lead to stories."

"But the marks," the first officer said. "The vampire ghost left marks. So they dug up body. It had grown extra toe. They cut off head. Then, squeezing stopped."

Pepper and Scott stood in the center of the church, surrounded by the mess. Scott nodded intently.

"Okay," he said. "So do you need anything from us?"

"No," the first officer said. He was nudging a sheet on the floor with his shoe. "We will call if we have questions. Mess like this, it will take time."

THERE WAS AN event at the University of Wrocław, which meant no vacancies at the nearby hotels. The fifth hotel Pepper and Scott tried had one room remaining, and they were too tired to keep looking, so they agreed to share. Scott slid his credit card, facedown, across the counter.

"Afraid I'll learn your middle name?" Pepper said.

Scott only smirked, and Pepper didn't tell him she already knew that Scott was his middle name and Randall his first, same as his father. She let her bag drop to the floor and noticed something sticking out of one of the pockets. A business card, white with gold foil stamping, modest block print—THE EVERETT GROUP. There wasn't a phone number or an address. Just the name.

Pepper scanned the lobby. There was a woman in a black sequined gown, standing alone, waiting for someone. There was a couple quietly arguing with a college-age girl who was on the verge of tears. But no one else. She'd had her bag with her the whole trip. She hadn't left it unattended.

"What's that?" Scott said.

Pepper handed him the card. "It was the Everett Group," she said. "It's the only thing that makes sense."

"It wasn't the Everett Group," Scott said.

"What makes you so sure?" she said.

The man at the desk returned Scott's credit card and gave them one room key to share.

"I'll call the police in the morning," Scott said. "To see if they've found anything. I'm sure she'll turn up."

"You're just saying that to make me feel better," she said.

"No, I'm not," he said. "If the Everett Group did something to Ula, because they want her work . . ." He stopped, thinking it through. "They'd want her dead, right? So the paintings would go to you. But they'd also want people to know she's dead. Because otherwise, there's a whole long process before you inherit her work."

Pepper hadn't told Scott about the loan or the agreement, and the way he'd hidden his credit card made her think she was right not to. "So unless her body turns up, that's probably not what happened."

"Right," Scott said.

"That doesn't make me feel better," Pepper said.

"I'm not trying to make you feel better," he said.

He looked like he was going to touch her, which is when she realized her hands were shaking. The elevator was out of order, and they had to take the stairs. Scott reached for her bag, but Pepper didn't even trust him with that.

THE HOTEL'S EXTERIOR was traced with neon lights, which made the room feel lurid and cheap. The windows were covered with tattered red drapes. The towels left on the bed were thin from use but rolled and tied with satin ribbon.

> you there
>
> are you asking
> or reassuring me

Pepper didn't believe in hauntings, but her body felt as if it were possessed by something that was still having its way with her.

> i can't sleep in this stupid bed without you
> if i were there i'd just be kicking you
> for snoring or whatever
> true
> did you find anything

a mess
but no ula
can i quit now

        don't quit
        i'm reading about joan of arc
        be like joan

lol

        she faced plenty of resistance
        but she was so persistent in her belief
        charles vii totally let a teenage girl lead a war
but don't historians think she had
a condition
like neurological
or psychiatric

        i wasn't going to mention that
and i'm not on a mission from god
also would prefer not to be burned alive

        reasonable
how's kit
has she found a new husband yet

        oh
what does that mean

        well it turns out kit died
i assumed that
otherwise she'd be like 170
which seems improbable
though apparently vampire ghosts exist
so who knows

        no i mean she died of cholera
        i thought there was another volume
        of her diary
        but then i started reading one of her
        companions'
        she did not like kit at all
        a little too happy about kit's death
        if you ask me

oh

are you okay

> yeah
>
> my own fault for getting attached
>
> should've seen it coming

Ike offered to call, but Pepper couldn't handle hearing his voice and was irritated when her phone then rang. But it wasn't Ike—it was a local number, and when she answered, she was met with the sound of a fax machine.

"Who in the world is faxing you?" Scott said. His eyes were unfocused. He was holding a collection of essays about Ula's work, but Pepper realized he hadn't been reading at all.

"No idea," Pepper said. "Someone in Poland."

Pepper turned off her phone and checked to make sure the door was locked, her body increasingly suffused with strangeness. It wasn't the fax—it was everything, her bones felt different. It was probably just the jet lag. She lay on the bed and closed her eyes. Jet lag and too many unanswerable questions.

In another universe, a universe less exhausting and more comprehensible than this one, Pepper was consulting for a television show about a forensic anthropologist, a character with a job like Pepper's but who for inexplicable reasons carried a gun. The lead actor adored Pepper, her relentless attention to detail and realism, and though she resisted him, rejected the trappings of his celebrity, he was patient and persistent, and finally she allowed herself to love him in return. They spent their weeks off at remote tropical bungalows, rooms on stilts with little portholes in the floor so they could look down and watch the stingrays. She lay in the sun and let fresh fruit drip juice onto her skin, then let him lick the juice off. She had a whole collection of oversize sunglasses and people she paid to tame her unruly hair. She'd never liked to be photographed, and yet now she was always smiling like a fool. In every photo, her happiness was so visibly sincere.

In a different universe, she'd been recruited for an important government job—her expertise was essential in avoiding a pandemic—and she wore suits with plunging necklines and had clandestine cocktails at D.C. bars, late at night, with men with alluring accents. She spoke more languages than any of them expected. They would trace with their fingertips the underside of her arm, and she would walk out, powerfully, leaving them with their longing. She could see that Pepper now, as sleep took over her displaced body, striding effortlessly in her stilettos, full of purpose and resolve. That Pepper was so fulfilled, so different from her—charming and confident, in control. A completely different person.

10

PEPPER WOKE EARLY with a headache that felt like a demonic possession and took her jacket into the bathroom, where she removed the faded blue envelopes she'd taken from the church. They'd been opened by a letter opener and a precise hand, the resultant edges sharp enough to give Pepper a paper cut on her thumb. She stuck it in her mouth and sucked her own blood, which tasted unexpectedly bitter.

Each envelope contained a few sheets of pale blue paper, folded into perfect thirds. At the top of each first page, an address had been written in the upper-left corner, like a business letter. The handwriting was the same as on the envelopes—studied, swoopy cursive. The writing was in Polish. She should've shown them to Scott. She shouldn't have taken them in the first place. She tucked the letters into her shirt and slipped on her shoes, leaving Scott sleeping with his mouth open, one arm draped across Pepper's side of the bed.

At the front desk, she was greeted by an elderly man with big ears and a shiny bald spot, who grinned hugely as she approached.

"Dzień dobry!" he said. His name tag identified him as Kacper. He reached across the desk, took Pepper's hand, and squeezed it.

"Good morning," she said.

He took the lid off an etched glass bowl and waved his hand over it. "Mint?" he asked.

He looked disappointed when she shook her head. She slid the letters out of her shirt and placed them on the desk.

"I need to find someone who can translate these into English," she said. "Do you know anyone I could contact?"

Kacper puffed his chest and took one of the envelopes. "My English," he said, "is very good. Excellent. Let us see?"

Pepper looked around, but it was early enough that the lobby was empty. In a room to the right, someone was clanking around at a coffee machine. Kacper took the first letter from the envelope. He cleared his throat in an official, performative way.

"My bear," he said. "Sorceress of time. I am in fever at the thought of you. My body." He stopped and cleared his throat again. "My body . . ." Kacper scanned the text, his expression shifting from worried to a shade of appalled. He folded the letter carefully and placed it back in the envelope. "Apologies," he said. "My English fails me. I fear I cannot be of service."

Pepper took the letters and put them back in her shirt. Kacper no longer met her eyes. "Can you recommend someone who could?"

He busied himself with the computer, suddenly absorbed in something on the screen. "No, no, I do not think so," he said. "No one here would be able. It is not the work of a hotel, madam. Will you be checking out today?"

Outside, the street was cloaked in fog.

"I don't know," she said. "Thank you."

She wandered into the breakfast room, where coffee was dripping into a stained pot, and numbly took a paper cup from the stack. There wasn't enough coffee in the pot yet. All she could do was wait. She checked her email to find she'd received two faxes overnight, again from a Polish number, this time sent to the fax in her office, which she'd set up to forward to email. She was waiting for documents related to the process of repatriating her burials. But these faxes were scanned covers from old issues of *Ekphrasis*.

Pepper searched the covers for mentions of Ula, but both issues had been published before Ula had made a name for herself. She couldn't think of a reason the Everett Group would send them to her. Maybe Bartosz had sent them and the issues had something to do with folk art or looms. Pepper didn't know anyone else in Poland. She was about to look up the issues on her phone when a bony hand gripped her arm and yanked her toward a closet. She was being pulled by a young woman with several piercings in one ear and none in the other. The woman was wearing a uniform dress, which she'd affixed with an enamel pin in the shape of a raised middle finger.

"I will translate," she said. Her name tag said *Jola*. She pulled Pepper all the way into the closet and shut the door behind her, leaving them in total darkness for a moment before she switched on the light. Pepper took one of the letters from her shirt again.

"Here," she said.

Jola skimmed the letter and smiled. "This is love letter," she said. "It is to you?" She gave Pepper an appraising look, as if she might be able to see the qualities that made her worthy of devotion.

"No," Pepper said. The closet smelled like ammonia. There was a stack of unused sponges on one shelf, wrapped individually in plastic. "It's to someone I know." Everything on the shelves was arranged in neat lines as if by ruler. "My mother."

Jola clutched the letter to her chest. "No!" she said. "I cannot read this to you. You will die." She tucked her chin to her chest and giggled. "If I read this about my mother, I would die."

The smell of ammonia wasn't helping Pepper's headache. "I'm pretty sure I can handle it."

Jola read from the letter. "Nothing compares to the dew of your body. I am trapped in your head, I search for you in my dreams. I press my whole self against your breasts, your nipples . . ."

"Nope, that's enough," Pepper said. "You were right. That's plenty."

Pain flashed through her head like barbed light, and Pepper steadied herself by thinking how Ike would laugh at this. If Ike were here, they'd both be laughing, doubled over by it.

"Can you . . ." Pepper thought for a second. "Can you read them both and let me know if there's anything in there that won't make me want to die?"

Jola put a hand on Pepper's shoulder. "It is better this way."

She read all the way through the first letter without speaking, though she did fan herself twice in the middle. "I am sorry," she said. "It is all the same. Worse even than what I read to you." Pepper handed her the second letter, and Jola read. On the second page, she gasped and closed her eyes. "My goodness," she said, and continued reading. She got all the way to the end and frowned. "This," she said, pointing to the final sentences. "This is different. It says, 'I wait on you and wait on you and wait on you. I wait with kind of violence. When will you come?' And that is the end."

Pepper pointed to the address at the top. "Do you know where this is?"

Jola nodded. "I know this building," she said. "You will know when you see it. Like Hansel and Gretel's house."

Pepper thanked her and escaped the closet, dizzy from the smell of industrial cleaners. Scott was in the little room, pouring coffee into a paper cup. Jola winked at him and set to work emptying a trash can.

"What was that about?" he said.

"Girl talk," Pepper said.

"I told the man at the desk we'd stay another night," he said. "I'm going down to the police station. I think I'll have better luck in person than over the phone. Want to come?"

Pepper felt the edges of the envelopes scraping her chest. She should tell him, now, so they could find the letter writer together. She opened her mouth, but the words stalled in her throat.

"No," she said. "I have a headache."

JOLA HAD SAID the house was like Hansel and Gretel's house when what she'd meant was that it was like the house of the witch who tried to eat them. The trim was painted in gumdrop colors, the pillars around the door in candy cane stripes. Pepper stood in a cold drizzle on the steps. She considered taking a picture. It would be easier if she pretended she was a tourist in her own life. The door knocker was shaped like a skull, and Pepper curled her fingers around the jagged mandible and through the teeth and rapped it against the door.

The man who opened it had a face that was flat except for his nose, his eyebrows so pale and eyes so small as to give the appearance of an unbroken surface. He reached out and stroked Pepper's cheek.

"I knew you'd come," he said.

"Cześć," Pepper said. The man stepped back to let her enter, but she stayed on the porch. "Do you know who I am?"

"Of course," the man said. He touched her face a second time, and Pepper felt that weirdness in her bones again. Her body became more foreign to her every time it was treated with such familiarity by someone she didn't know. "Of course I do. Proszę, come in."

Pepper stepped into the foyer, which was painted a nauseating shade of pink. Inside, the house smelled floury and sweet, like a baking cake. The walls were lined with small canvases, each of them painted black with splatters of white and gold, like fragments of the night sky.

"You're Rafał?" Pepper asked. It was the name signed on the letters.

"Rafał Lisiewicz," he said. He took Pepper's hand and pressed his wet lips to it before leading her into a sitting room painted electric blue. One wall was covered in a photographic mural, a lush expanse of garden, flowers all in bloom. "Your mother, she hates this house. Too much color," he said. "I know many artists, and she is only one who cannot stand to be around color. Like noise, to her. May I offer you tea?"

"No, thank you," Pepper said. She'd drunk so much coffee in an effort to drown her headache she felt as if her whole body was buzzing. She sat on a love seat covered with a floral sheet. There was a stack of art books on the coffee table, all with nudes on the covers. Ike would be delighted. "Can you tell me the last time you saw Ula?"

Rafał settled into a high-backed chair that looked like a throne. He traced his fingers over the gilded armrests. He appeared to be in his forties—younger than Ula—and Pepper noticed now that he had a tattoo on his arm, a creature with brown fur under his sleeve.

"It has been too long," he said. "She has not come in too long." He went a surprising length of time without blinking, which made Pepper's eyes sting.

"Okay," Pepper said. "Can you be more specific? She was reported missing by her assistant after he hadn't heard from her in three weeks. And that was two weeks ago. Has it been more than five weeks since you saw her? Has she been in touch with you during that time?"

Rafał stood and crossed to a mirror on one wall, an ornate gold frame. "She would never paint me, you know," he said. "I asked her, all the time. But she said no. I do not know how such a thing works. I would like very much to see how it works. I imagine a Rafał in different universe sometimes. I think he must have many children and live by the sea."

Pepper scanned the room while Rafał studied his reflection. There was a rifle propped in one corner, being devoured by rust. On the mantel, a trail of stones, leading nowhere. Behind Pepper there was a large canvas, similar to the ones in the foyer, but this one had what appeared to be a black hole in the center, sucking in stardust and light.

"Are you a painter?" she asked.

"I dabble," Rafał said. "But this, you see behind you. This is not my work."

He didn't say whose work it was, but Pepper had seen enough of Ula's to know it wasn't likely hers. She looked at the painting again, but something about it made her feel off-kilter. "Can you tell me how you and Ula met?"

Rafał resettled in his chair. "It is brilliant story, really. Like in movies. She was caught in the rain, and I had umbrella. Of course, she fought me when I came to her rescue. She was soaking wet, like a rat. I brought her here to dry off. She didn't say a word. She came in, walked upstairs, and when I went to bring her a towel, she was standing there, naked as a baby."

"That is quite a story," Pepper said. Her headache was creeping back. She imagined Ula, standing in this room, examining the sprays of irises and sunflowers on the wall, but again, her imagination was limited, and the image of Ula in her mind was actually her. She rose and pretended to look at the stones on the mantel. "So you're not sure how long it's been since you've seen her?" From the mantel, she could see into the dining room. There was a bouquet of white flowers in a large white vase on the table. A white knit cardigan was draped over the back of one of the chairs.

"It has been too long," Rafał said again.

He stood and approached the mantel, put one hand on her back, high at first, and slid it downward. Pepper felt small and weak in her body. Maybe she had cholera too, she thought. It'd be just like her to die of dysentery in a strange country on spring break. She wondered if Kit was still brave while she was dying, how long she kept walking, at what point the train abandoned her or if she left them on her own. Under the dining room table, she saw a pair of quilted satin slippers, also white.

Pepper wasn't dying of cholera. She stepped out of Rafał's reach.

"Are those yours?" she asked, pointing at the sweater and slippers. She tried to walk into the dining room, but Rafał blocked her with his body. He touched her face again, which activated the pain in Pepper's head.

"You look very much like her," he said. "It is not too early for a drink. Would you have a drink with me?"

"You don't seem very worried," Pepper said. "A lot of people are worried, but not you. Have you been to her studio recently?"

"I have never been to her studio," Rafał said. "She would never let me come to her."

"She would never let you?" Pepper said.

"It is not me who makes the rules," Rafał said. He slipped his fingers around Pepper's elbow. "And they are always changing. She is changeable woman, your mother. One day all desire, another day distracted. One day she insists on wearing gloves, another day nothing at all. Sometimes sweet as candy. Sometimes she is witch. It is impossible to predict which Ula you will get."

"You talk like she's going to walk through the door at any moment," Pepper said.

And at that, a door in the back of the house opened with a clatter. Pepper moved toward it, but again Rafał blocked her path.

"You must go," he said.

"Is that her?" Pepper said.

"It is time for you to leave," Rafał said. His hand on her elbow tightened enough for it to hurt. "Proszę."

Between her fear and the headache, Pepper's vision flashed, a single, brief image of this man in another world, still awful, holding too tight to a different woman's arm. Why would he be any different? He'd said Ula was changeable, and Pepper was too, always waging a nonsense war between the version of herself she wanted to be and the version of herself she feared. She could be the kind of person who refused to go. She jerked her arm away and darted past him, toward the sound of a door now closing.

There was a woman in the kitchen, holding two cloth bags full of groceries, a spray of carrot greens sticking out of one. She was delicate, with dark eyes and dark hair, a sweep of bangs, rosy lips. Not Ula. She had a pointed face, and she took one look at Pepper and shouted something in Polish, and Rafał appeared in the room.

Pepper couldn't understand what they were saying, only that this was an argument they'd had before. She backed away toward the dining room. The woman took a tea towel that was hanging from the stove handle and threw it on the floor. Rafał turned and motioned with his head toward the front door.

"You must go now," he said to Pepper.

As they passed through the sitting room, Pepper looked again at the painting of the black hole and wished for it to suck her through. This entire trip had been a waste. She'd spent so much time assigning meaning where it didn't exist.

Rafał opened the door, and Pepper turned to leave without

speaking. But he grabbed her arm again, not so hard this time, and leaned in close. He took something from his pocket. Everyone had secrets tucked into their pockets and sleeves.

"She sent me this," he said. "This is why I do not worry. She sent note. She is okay."

He pressed a folded piece of paper into Pepper's hand and closed the door before she had time to unfold it. She stood on the steps and looked out. This city was like a labyrinth. She wasn't sure she remembered the way back to the hotel. The paper was warm from being pressed against Rafał's skin. She opened it and read.

> *If I disappear, don't worry. I don't want you to find me. I'm fine.*

WHEN PEPPER ARRIVED back at the hotel, Scott was waiting for her in the lobby.

"Where were you?" he said.

"Wandering," Pepper said. She was still trying to make sense of the note. She knew she should tell him, but the story had already coiled itself inside her.

"I have some news," he said. "The police didn't find anything at the church. They dusted the whole place for prints, and it's just Ula's all over everything."

"How do they have her prints?" Pepper said.

"They were in a database," Scott said. "Someone got them off one of her paintings. There's a whole book analyzing them."

"I've never seen that," Pepper said. Her head was still pounding. The hotel kept the neon lights on during the day, and she could hear their buzz, even from inside.

"But the real news is that people have seen her," he said. "Since she disappeared. They went around the neighborhood, and people have seen her."

Pepper sat, her head a buzzing light. "In the neighborhood," she said. It didn't make sense. Why would Ula cut off contact from everyone who expected her but stay where people would recognize her?

"She's been to the market, and she's been in one of the cafés. All over, really. The police have several witnesses. So it seems like she's fine."

Pepper stuck her hand in her pocket and ran her fingers over the note. Ula was fine. She disappeared on purpose, prepared Rafał for it, even. And the mess she'd created in Pepper's life was for nothing.

"But what about the Everett Group?" she said. "Someone turned over that church. It had to be them." She never had this kind of feeling, but she knew. They were missing something. "Why would they bother with me if Ula was fine?"

"There's no reason to believe they've done anything but harass you," Scott said. "The police checked them out. They're a legit group of art collectors. Men with money have their own way of operating."

The lobby sofa was stiff, and Pepper could feel it holding her upright. There was an older woman at the desk, pointing at a map. Kacper was patiently drawing a line from one place to another.

"So we can go home," Scott said. "I mean, I know you wanted to meet her, but—"

"I didn't want to meet her," Pepper snapped. "I only came here because I was already in London."

Scott didn't say anything to that, and Pepper didn't care. She hadn't told him about the lien or the lawyer's agreement; she hadn't told him about her problems with Ike. She didn't owe him anything.

"It's your girlfriend, right?" she said.

"What?" he said.

"You're leaving because of her," Pepper said. "Even though we have no idea where Ula is." Kacper looked at her from the desk, which is how she knew she was getting too loud. He turned his attention to an ancient fax machine, which now made a sound like the inside of Pepper's head.

"Ula is fine," Scott said. He was always so sure of himself. That he seemed relieved and Pepper wasn't only made her angrier.

"She's not," Pepper said. Her career was based on evidence; she didn't believe in hunches or feelings. But this she could feel in her bones. "And what about your story? Don't you want to find her and interview her?"

"The story was that she was missing," Scott said. "And even if we did find her, do you think there's any chance she'd actually talk to me?" Scott stood, checking his phone. "There's a flight in the morning," he said. "I'm going back to the square to take some pictures. Do you want to come?"

Pepper shook her head, and Scott left her alone. She went back to the room, which was flushed red from the light bleeding through the curtains. Her moms had left her a message, but she couldn't talk to them, and they knew that, knew talking to them only made her homesick when she traveled. Sometimes they left messages with only the sound of a clicker, because they'd accidentally clicker-trained Pepper to sit when she was three, while training a puppy, and the sound of a clicker had since reminded her of their laughter. She'd received another fax, another page from *Ekphrasis,* this one mentioning Ula's early work on display in her hometown. She hadn't shown the other faxes to Scott and now no longer wanted to. Maybe someone else at *Ekphrasis* knew he'd flake out and was trying to help her. She closed her eyes but could still see webs of light, which made her crazy, so she opened them again. She took out Ula's note and reread it. Something about it wasn't right.

Pepper sat at the hotel desk and copied the note in her own handwriting. *I don't want you to find me,* she wrote. *I'm fine.* Gordon had said her handwriting was like Ula's, but the writing in the note wasn't like Pepper's at all, no connections between letters, the words all in print. And there was something else—the writing looked rushed, shaky in spots. Like it had been written in a hurry, or by a pained hand, or under duress.

Pepper closed her eyes again. It was crazy. She watched too much TV, that inane show about the anthropologist who knew things way outside the scope of an anthropologist's job. Ula had been seen; she was here somewhere in the city, safe. She didn't want to be found. Pepper told herself that, but every time she closed her eyes, she saw the same image, an image of Ula, clawing at the air as someone dragged her. Or maybe not, Pepper thought. Maybe this was her mind conflating them again, another instance of Pepper's brain botching the translation, tagging Ula when what she was really seeing was herself.

11

SCOTT TOLD PEPPER he'd made plans for them for dinner. Pepper dug the sole dress she'd brought out of her bag, which was packed more haphazardly than she'd remembered. The dress was hopelessly wrinkled, even after hanging in the shower's steam. Scott smelled like sage and wore slim gray pants that had nary a crease. Pepper applied lipstick and made the best of her hair, though that was basically pointless here, where fog enveloped the streets like a blanket. Once, on a beach trip with her moms in middle school, she'd gotten so worked up about her humidity-crazed hair she'd thrown herself onto a hotel bed and sobbed, and Annie had patiently braided it in a crown around her face, not once mocking her as she'd deserved. Pepper had left the letters on the desk when Scott came back to the hotel, which he'd picked up, scanned, and put back down. This had never been that important to him.

They walked in the mist to a restaurant with a wooden chef statue outside. The chef was lacquered with glossy paint, and he greeted them with a handlebar mustache and a carefree grin, a red apron tied below his big belly. Scott gave the hostess his name, and she led them through a room with orange-and-yellow stained glass windows to a set of stairs, where they descended into a stone-lined cellar with arched doorways in every direction. It smelled like meat and dampness. They were seated at a table with three chairs and a checkered tablecloth.

"I'm starting to feel like there's something you're not telling me," Pepper said.

"You're the expert on that," Scott said.

There were a few antique barrels around the room, and old mirrors on the walls, along with an odd assortment of art—a painting of a chicken, a harsh, charcoal sketch of a ballerina. Scott's eyes moved across the walls.

"Do you paint?" he asked.

"Me?" Pepper said.

"You must've thought about it," he said. "Whatever they say Ula can do. Maybe you can do it too."

"I was never good at art," Pepper said. "I took a class in grad school as an elective. The teacher would set up a whole long table with junk for us to draw—bicycle wheels and soup cans, ropes. A still life. Everyone else would pick one section and work on it. But I would draw the entire table's worth of stuff, just shrink the whole scene down to fit on the page, with plenty of white space around it. The teacher was always telling me I was very compressed."

Scott unfolded, then refolded his cloth napkin. The waitress arrived with a bottle of wine, which they hadn't ordered. Scott tried to explain, but she waved a hand with an authority that made Scott shut up, so they sat there as she poured their glasses, along with the third. The bottle's label was old and plain, which made Pepper think it was expensive.

"I hope your magazine is covering this," she said once the waitress had gone. Scott didn't answer. "I was bad at perspective too. I could never figure out which way the lines were supposed to go. The teacher would puzzle over the drawings. Even he couldn't figure out what I'd done. That thing where a picture looks almost right, but something's off about it."

Scott stood. A woman approached the table. She was in her sixties, at least, but she had a well-maintained quality that made it difficult to guess her age. She was willowy and wearing a draped linen dress and simple gold jewelry. Her white hair was styled in a long bob. She took Scott's face in her hands and kissed him briefly on the mouth. Then she turned to Pepper.

"You need no introduction," she said.

Pepper straightened and caught her reflection in one of the mirrors. There was a part of her she still couldn't see, that was visible to too many people around her.

"I've heard that a lot the last few days," Pepper said. "But I'll introduce myself anyway." She extended her hand. The woman's handshake was neither gentle nor firm.

"Iphigenia Freitas," the woman said. She stared at Scott until he pulled out the third chair for her, then sat.

Pepper dropped her napkin on her lap and drank.

"You are drinking the wine too fast, my dear," Iphigenia said. "This wine is not meant to be drunk like your American wines."

"There are some good American wines," Pepper said, and drank more. "How do you and Scott know each other?"

Iphigenia's eyes landed on Scott, who kept his own eyes on his glass of wine.

"His father is an acquaintance of mine," she said. "Actually, I've been following you both since shortly after you arrived."

Scott looked up, surprised. "What?" he said. His expression was the same as Rafał's when the woman with the groceries came home. "Pepper, she told me she knew Ula."

"I do know Ula," Iphigenia said. "There was no lie."

The waitress appeared to take their orders, and Iphigenia ordered in Polish without looking at the menu. Pepper decided to err on the side of familiarity: pappardelle. She wasn't in the mood for more surprises. Scott pointed at a random spot on the menu.

When the waitress was gone, Iphigenia started again. "You must forgive me," she said. "I know my interest must come as a surprise. But I simply could not bear to go another day without speaking to you."

"Well, here I am," Pepper said. "Speak away."

Scott raised his eyebrows, but Pepper was decidedly not in the mood to be chastened.

"I'm here in two capacities," Iphigenia said. "First, as a client of your mother's."

"She painted your portrait?" Scott said. Iphigenia nodded. "You weren't on the list."

"I do not know what list you speak of," Iphigenia said.

"And the second?" Pepper said.

"As a member of the Everett Group," Iphigenia said. "Like

his father." She motioned to Scott, and Pepper's vision briefly blurred. The business card slipped into her bag, his sureness of the Everett Group's benignity. "I believe you've already met some of our associates?"

Pepper raised a hand for the waitress, a middle-aged woman with tired eyes. In an alternate universe, Pepper grabbed the wine bottle and took this woman by the wrist into the kitchen, where they drank the expensive wine themselves and the woman smuggled Pepper out a back door. In this universe, Pepper did nothing, so the waitress refilled her glass, which was the only one that was empty. Pepper had talked to Ike before dinner, and he'd agreed with Scott's logic about the improbability of the Everett Group's involvement in Ula's disappearance.

"I'm surprised your good friend Scott didn't tell you," Pepper said. "The police have witnesses who've seen Ula. So I'm off the hook on this one. Her work is her own, and I for one hope she lives to a ripe old age so I never have to deal with her numerous assets."

"Her assets," Iphigenia said. "Yes. I have already heard. That must come as a relief." She stopped and smoothed her dress, her eyes fluttering with self-consciousness.

Pepper drank. "Not that I could've sold them in the first place."

Iphigenia looked to Scott as if he might have an answer. "Why not?"

"It's a conditional inheritance," Pepper said. "I can't sell a damn thing." For the first time, she was glad for it, thrilled for something to be entirely out of her control. Thrilled to lob a secret in Scott's stupid, smug face.

Iphigenia gripped her butter knife with an expression that reminded Pepper of a student who'd just made sense of something for the first time.

"But you never told me she painted you," Scott said. He was trying too hard to avoid looking at Pepper. "So you already have one of her pieces in your collection. When was this? Can you talk about it?" He reached into his bag for his recorder, but Iphigenia shook her head.

"Ah, ah," she said. "But yes. I can talk about it." She sipped her wine. "Saúde," she said, holding up her glass. She dabbed her mouth with her napkin and began. "I did not send a letter. I was not one who obsessed about my own ghosts. There are many who do, but not me. I live in this world, and I had always been content in it. I inherited my money. I live by the sea. I have friends and lovers. I eat fruit while watching the sun move across the water. I leave my days with salt on my skin. I met her at a party. It was a party for a man I did not know, who was dying. He wanted to have a last celebration before the end. Someone I knew brought me. It seemed terribly rude to me to come to this kind of party without knowing the host, but my friend assured me it was how he wanted it. He wanted strangers there, drinking too much, slinking off with other strangers in the dark. The party was in Greece, and the trees were hung with lanterns. It was hard to see, though. The lanterns weren't very bright. Some people wore masks. I lost my friend, and I didn't know anyone else, and I sat with a glass of champagne and watched people dance. There was grief in everything at this party. It was loud and joyous, and yet you could feel it. There was grief in the dancing. Even the olives tasted like grief.

"I sat at a table with my champagne, and a woman sat next to me. I thought she must be an artist because she seemed very comfortable with mess. Her clothes were rumpled, her hair was . . ." She gestured vaguely at Pepper's head. "I asked her how she knew the host, and she told me she was a painter, like him. I had seen some of his work, but it was not to my taste, very political. I asked what she painted. 'People,' she told me. She painted portraits. I'd never had a portrait painted of myself. I thought it might be fun. I asked her, how much would it cost, for her to paint me. She looked me over and gave me a number. I told her she was charging me extra because of my shoes, which I'll admit were very expensive. She said she charged what her clients needed to pay to believe it was worth it, which made me laugh. And I agreed. She told me the name of a hotel and gave me instructions. I was to go to the hotel at a certain time and take off my clothes. Why nude? I asked

her. She told me she could tell any clothes I chose would be a dis-
traction. I did as she asked. It seemed like an adventure. I was in
Greece, paying too much for a strange woman whose friend was
dying to paint me nude. It would make a good story one day."

She stopped and sipped her wine. She smiled at someone across
the room, a smile of recognition, but the recipient turned away
in confusion. She'd mistaken him for someone else. She continued. "She painted me all day. I asked her how long it would take,
and she didn't answer. Her demeanor was not unpleasant but
very focused. I didn't know much about painting at the time, but
it seemed to me that she was working quickly. I could smell the
paint. That's something I remember. The exact scent of the paint.
She painted all day. No breaks for food. I wanted to complain and
I would have, but there was something about her focus that made
me stay quiet. I was afraid to break the spell. It was early evening
when she told me to close my eyes. I asked her why, and she said,
'Just do it.' And I did. It's hard to describe what happened next.
My hair was full of static—I could feel it lifting away from my
head. I had that feeling you get when you shuffle across a rug in
winter, as if the next thing I touched would shock me."

The waitress arrived at the table with their food. Iphigenia
had ordered soup with giant prawns bobbing at the surface. It
turned out that what Scott had pointed to was a large platter of
sliced meats nestled among cornichons. Iphigenia smelled her
soup but didn't taste it. She closed her eyes. "There was a sound,
like an animal crying. I grew up in Portugal, in the country-
side, and sometimes as a child I could hear a small animal being
taken by a wild boar. It sounded like that. I opened my eyes,
even though she hadn't given me permission. And there I was."
She'd been speaking with perfect calm, but now she looked at
Pepper with spooked eyes. "She was just like me. Same haircut,
same lips. But she was wearing finer clothes than I had. And she
looked somehow younger, more relaxed. She was happier than
I was. Or she had been, in whatever life she occupied in that
other world. She was happier than I had ever been. It was plain
to see."

She reached into her soup bowl with her fingers, plucked out a prawn, and sucked its head. "Ula left without ceremony. I had already paid her. The painting was still wet. The other me wasn't upset. She was more curious than anything. 'What's this all about?' she asked me. The kind of woman who . . . what is the phrase?"

She mimicked dodging hits, like a boxer, with surprising grace.

"Roll with the punches," Scott said.

"Yes," Iphigenia said. "She rolled with the punches."

She ate her soup without slurping. Pepper felt as though all the punches were landing and she wasn't rolling with them at all. Iphigenia spoke with total conviction. Pepper didn't know how to explain the story away. She looked at Scott across the table, unsure why they were there. What could this woman possibly want from her? She took a bite of pasta but had a hard time swallowing it. What were all the Peppers in other universes eating right now? And how much happier were their lives?

"She must've been confused," Scott said. "That's the part of this that's hardest for me to get my head around. How strange it would be to find yourself in another world suddenly, with no way to get back to your own."

"Yes," Iphigenia said. "It did not take long for the grief and anger to set in. That's what I've heard from the others as well."

"The others?" Scott said.

"The other clients," she said. "I've tracked down a few. I wasn't obsessed before I met Ula. I didn't even know who she was. But after, it was different. I couldn't sleep. I read everything. And I found a few like me. I knew they'd be there, late at night, on their computers, looking for someone who understood. Their experiences were much the same. Once their ghosts realized they were trapped here, it was all over. Mine, she stayed two days and she was gone. I have no idea where; she didn't have any identification or money. Others stayed longer, raged more, tried to find a way back, or out. And they did, one way or another." She made that face again, like she was calculating something in her head. "Sometimes I think maybe, if it were me, it would be nice. A chance to start over. But I'd miss my cat. The people in my life not as much, but I might die of a broken heart knowing I'd left my cat behind and would never see her again. I don't allow myself to think about it for long."

Scott picked at the slices of meat on his plate, all of it pink and glistening. He pierced a cornichon with a miniature fork and snapped it between his teeth.

"I don't know what to think about any of this," he said.

Iphigenia finished her wine. "There are mysteries we can solve and mysteries we cannot," she said.

Pepper thought she was going to say more, but she didn't. Across the room, a group of men in suits erupted into laughter.

"If you already knew Ula isn't missing anymore," Pepper said, "why did you want to have dinner with us? There isn't anything I can do for you."

Iphigenia held up her wineglass and examined it from below.

"There are whispers," she said. She set the glass down and turned toward Pepper, excising Scott from the conversation with her body. "In the Everett Group. I am the only woman, which surprised me when I joined. That was not the only surprise."

Scott reached out and touched Iphigenia's arm, but she corrected him sharply with her eyes. He folded his hands and put them in his lap.

"I believed I was joining a society of art collectors," she said. "And the Everett Group collects Ula's work, yes. But it is more than that."

Scott inhaled and scanned the room, like he was looking for help, an escape, an idea. "There's no benefit to this," he said.

Iphigenia ignored him. "The members of the Everett Group are people with money, men who like to collect. They are also heads of state, visionaries, billionaires. Men with power and control. But there is never enough. Not in this world."

"But in other worlds," Pepper said.

Iphigenia nodded. Ike had researched the Everett Group after they'd first approached Pepper but had found very little about them. The only hit for Roscoe Larsen was a photo of him at the opening of the world's largest particle accelerator. There were a few other names associated with the group, all of them men who'd funded politicians Pepper despised, or who'd been the architects of some war, or who made a fortune exploiting child laborers. Pepper took another bite of food and bit the inside of her cheek, hard enough to draw blood. Pepper had never believed in other universes the way Ula's followers did. But if it were possible to access other versions of our world, it would be possible to access their resources, their technology, their environments not utterly fucked by laziness and greed. Their weapons. Of course there would be people trying to find an entry point. The inside of Pepper's cheek bled. The blood didn't taste right.

"Once my ghost disappeared, I took my painting and had it stored securely," Iphigenia said. "It was impossible to look at myself that way. I could never see myself in the painting. I understand now she was painting that other version of me the whole time. But there are whispers."

The waitress came again and asked about the food. No one was eating. The waitress seemed satisfied that no one complained. Maybe this was one of those places, Pepper thought, where you brought people to break up with them or deliver other bad news.

"What kind of whispers?" she asked.

"There is a painting," Iphigenia said. "It is here in Wrocław. There is a museum of postal history, in the same building as the Polish Post. It does not receive many visitors, I imagine. I do not know why they have this painting, though in the Everett Group, they say Ula has long been obsessed with postal mail. Some say she had an affair with the postmaster. In any case, there is a painting in this museum of hers. It's separate from the other exhibits, in a staircase, between the floors, in a protective case. The plaque says it's on loan. We have inquired, of course, but the owner remains anonymous."

"Is it a portrait?" Pepper said. Seemed easy enough to find the owner if it was a portrait.

"It's a self-portrait," Iphigenia said. "It's a portrait of Ula, young, maybe even a teenager, holding an infant. It's called *Self-Portrait with Nothing.*"

Scott had been working on a slice of meat and at this coughed, ejecting a chewed piece across the table. Pepper felt all the adjacent universes, jumbling around in space. She also felt a little drunk.

"That's nice," she said. "That's a nice title for a painting."

"There is only a small plaque by the painting, which says it was painted twenty-two years ago. I do not know where they got the date, or if it's accurate. Ula would not have been so young when she painted it if the date is true. But every time I look at this painting, I can feel in my body that it was the first."

"The first . . . ," Pepper said. She knew what Iphigenia meant. She didn't need an explanation.

Pepper used her fork to stab the spongy noodles in front of her. The fork went in with little resistance. She had no idea how anything worked. She imagined a baby version of herself, ripped out of some alternate mother's arms and into this world. She didn't know how it worked. She couldn't swallow. There was blood in her mouth, and it tasted wrong to her. The water on the table was warm. She missed ice.

Iphigenia was looking at her, but Pepper could only shake her head. She couldn't speak.

"I am sorry," Iphigenia said. "I think if I were you, I would not want to know this. But you should. The whispers. The Everett Group believes the destruction of a portrait could have a catastrophic effect."

The lights seemed to dim for a moment and brighten again.

"Based on what?" Pepper said.

Iphigenia shrugged. "I am not in the inner circle," she said.

"Victor Morgan," Scott said. He slid some meat around his plate with his fork. He was still avoiding Pepper's eyes. "He was found dead, with his portrait slashed next to him. And there've been others. No one knows what the destruction does for sure."

"But you think something happens?" Pepper asked. "What is

the evidence?" She didn't know why she was asking him. She'd been right not to trust him. She wasn't thinking clearly. What did the Everett Group know? For men with that kind of money to treat this so seriously—they must have some kind of evidence to support the claims about Ula's work.

Scott shook his head. "Victor Morgan was found with pills," he said.

Iphigenia took Pepper by the wrist. She was stronger than she looked. "Listen," she said. "There are whispers. This painting may be the key. But there are reasons to believe it isn't safe."

Pepper stood. She didn't have a plan in mind, just felt her body moving—toward the stairs, up the stairs, toward the exit, out the exit. Outside, she braced herself against the smiling chef statue and made herself breathe. It was afternoon in Connecticut. She didn't know where Ike would be.

808 808 808

No answer. Pepper gulped in a mouthful of air like water. She missed ice. She missed Ike. She'd been horrible to him, and if she were home, they'd be doing something boring, she'd be irritated with him for one reason or another, fantasizing about another universe, but still, she wanted him right now.

But he was far away. And not answering.

Scott appeared through the doorway and wrapped his arms around himself.

"It's cold," he said.

"Is it?" Pepper said.

She turned away from him, but it was obvious that she was crying. She shouldn't have drunk so much so fast, even though she knew that wasn't her real problem. Scott moved closer as if he were considering a hug, but she didn't want to be hugged, especially not by him.

When Pepper looked up, Iphigenia was standing next to them. She was very quiet, like a ghost.

"I paid the bill," she said. "I'm sorry. I shouldn't have upset you. Perhaps someday we will meet again. You could come visit. We will sit in the sun without these cares and drink our wine very slowly."

Pepper didn't have anything to wipe her nose with so she let it run onto her lip. "Maybe someday," she said. "I'd be interested in seeing your portrait."

"Oh, that," Iphigenia said. "It's a funny thing. I told you, after my ghost disappeared, I had it stored. It was in a special room at the bank. Excessively secure, they promised. And one day, I thought to myself, *I don't remember what it looks like anymore.* Though of course I did. I was just making an excuse. But when I went to see it, it was gone."

"What do you mean, gone?" Scott said.

"It was simply gone," Iphigenia said. "The bank, they did their best to investigate. But they didn't keep their security footage for long. And I have no idea when it was taken." She shook her head and laughed. "Honestly, I was relieved. I went home and laughed my head off. It was almost like I could pretend the whole thing never happened," she said. "Almost."

With that, she kissed Pepper on the cheek and disappeared into the fog, which hung in the air, still and strange.

Pepper stood looking out at the nothingness until she realized Scott was right. It was cold.

12

PEPPER DIDN'T PACK so much as cram all her stuff into her bag and hope for the best. Their flight wasn't until noon, so she had time but lacked the will to sort and fold. Scott bundled his clothes in an orderly, practiced way. There were packing cubes involved. Pepper had woken with her head tucked into his armpit, his hand splayed across her back. It'd taken her too long to remember who she was in bed with, and she'd rubbed her own hand across his chest, stopping only when she registered its smoothness. Ike's chest hair was soft and dense, and she liked to draw in it with her fingers. Now she and Scott maneuvered around each other as she gathered her toiletries, each of them moving farther out of the way than necessary to avoid touching.

Ike had texted while she slept

what did i miss

and she hadn't responded yet. It wasn't fair for her to be upset that he wasn't constantly staring at his phone, ready for her next crisis, but she was anyway. She'd been in a state of dread since she'd left the restaurant, more convinced than ever that the Everett Group was involved in Ula's disappearance, even if Ula was no longer disappeared. The fact that Scott had hidden so much only made her more certain. Ike had been dismissive of her worry. Facing this alone left Pepper too raw to manage self-control. She never had this kind of feeling. Of course no one believed her now that she did.

She made herself focus on small, simple tasks. Pack. Check out. Get to the airport. One manageable task at a time, until it was over.

Scott opened all the room's drawers even though Pepper had already checked them.

"Do you feel like breakfast?" he said.

"I'm not hungry," Pepper said. "But I need coffee."

In the hall, a man in boxers was knocking on the door to another room. He kept his face down, though it was clear he'd been crying. No one answered the door. He knocked again. Kacper was at the desk in the lobby, and he avoided eye contact with Pepper as Scott checked out. Pepper couldn't afford to stay if the magazine wasn't paying. At a café down the street, she and Scott found seats among a ramshackle collection of couches. The walls were painted raspberry pink, and there was a framed black-and-white poster of the Rat Pack on one wall.

"Your husband must be happy you're coming home," Scott said.

Pepper watched people walk past the window. It was the middle of the night now in Connecticut. She and Ike couldn't seem to realign themselves. Outside, there was a man in a suit and a hat who looked just like the statue of a man in a suit and hat rising through the sidewalk in the Polaroid she'd found in London. Today was Friday. Tomorrow, she'd wake in her own bed, salvage what was left of the weekend in the lab. It would almost be like it never happened.

"I don't know," Pepper said. "I don't know if he's happy or not."

Scott ordered something from the menu with camembert in the description. Pepper flipped to the page titled *Alkohole,* and her stomach turned. Outside, two girls in matching polka-dot dresses skipped by. There was a woman in a wide-brimmed straw hat with a yellow bird perched on it. A man in a ball cap that covered his face, wearing a blue sweater with gold buttons. A young guy carrying a bundle of purple and orange flowers. Pepper didn't hate Wrocław. Half the time it was an explosion of color, the other half it was wreathed in silvery fog, one version of the city always imprinting itself on the other.

Scott went to poke around a shelf of vinyl records while they waited. Pepper's phone buzzed.

> are you still coming home
> i cleaned the house and everything

Outside: an old man with a cane dragging a beat-up suitcase, a woman in heels so high she towered over the proud man by her side, some teenagers nearly falling over with laughter. One of them was walking with both shoes untied. Another man in a blue sweater and gold buttons.

> it worries me when you don't answer
> like immediately, but in this case at all
> are you mad at me
> why are you awake
> can't sleep

Outside: a woman walking an Irish wolfhound, who trotted along with a stuffed sheep in its mouth. A man and woman holding hands, the man pulling a red wagon with a clapping toddler inside. A man with bulging muscles and a handlebar mustache who looked like he'd been transferred to this universe directly from a cartoon.

> you're mad at me

> i'm not mad

> you're mad
> mad like a hatter

> hatters went mad from mercury poisoning
> from making felt
> camel urine is what they used originally
> but when demand went up hatters started
> using their own

> and then someone noticed
> men who had syphilis made better felt
> because they'd been treated with mercury
> chloride

Outside: a boy on roller skates, a woman carrying a stack of bakery boxes, a woman in a rush, dodging the slow walkers. Another man in a blue sweater with gold buttons. Pepper didn't process it until after he was out of view. She hadn't looked closely enough to know if it was the same man. He'd been wearing a ball cap.

> pepper
> i'm about to eat
> okay
> but why are you mad at me
> because i'm a terrible person
> you're not completely terrible

Pepper watched the window. Kids, families, people on their way to work. No more blue sweaters with gold buttons.

> i feel so loved
> i hate this
> please don't pick a fight right now
> no fighting before getting on a plane
> that's a rule, right?

Across the room, Scott had struck up a conversation with a girl with several piercings on her face and a galaxy of stars tattooed across her back. She was laughing a lot, though Pepper doubted what Scott was saying was funny.

> pepper
> please

A man in a denim vest covered with patches. A man in a pale pink shirt. A woman in a skintight black bodysuit, torn to reveal fishnets underneath. A man in a blue sweater with gold buttons.

> fine
> i give up

of course you do

> that's what you want isn't it

The man in the sweater's face was covered by the bill of a cap. Black pants. He was moving fast. A gold watch that flashed in the sun.

i can't do this right now

Ike didn't respond, and Pepper watched her phone to see if he started composing an answer, but he didn't. Scott returned to the table, grinning.

"Too bad we're leaving," Pepper said. "You could've ended up with two girlfriends."

Scott's grin disappeared. He busied himself reading his phone. The people in the café moved slowly, while everyone outside went by in a blur. Pepper didn't see another blue sweater. Caffeine didn't improve her mood. Her phone was quiet. Ike had probably just gone back to sleep. She tried to make herself think about the work waiting for her at home—papers to grade, next semester's syllabi to plan, details of her research that needed finalizing. But she couldn't hold any of it in her mind for more than a minute.

"What are you going to do about your story?" she said. "Or was that all made up? Something Daddy told you to say so you could help him get his hands on Ula's work? If that's even what they want."

Scott fidgeted with his watch, which probably cost more than Pepper's car. Then he looked at her. "There's still a story."

"I don't believe you," Pepper said. She knew she shouldn't

pick this fight right now, shouldn't have picked a fight with Ike, but she couldn't stop herself.

Scott kept his eyes on his mug. "The magazine is real," he said. "My job is real. I stayed because I had to, but it's not like we even found any paintings."

"There's the one in the postal museum," Pepper said. Pepper had called that morning, but the museum was closed today. Because of course it was. "Don't you at least want to see the self-portrait?"

Scott held his mug with two hands, like a kid. He looked into the steam.

"You've already seen it," Pepper said.

"I'm not sure what you want me to say here, Pepper," he said.

"Why do they even care about the paintings?" Pepper said. She was mad about too many things. She wasn't good at fighting when she was really mad. It was too easy for her to lose the thread. "Why bother with me at all? Shouldn't they be looking for Ula instead? If they want to find other universes, just go straight to the fucking source."

"You think they haven't tried to find her?" Scott was so calm. He closed his eyes and inhaled the scent of his coffee. "She pops up somewhere, a social media sighting. They send people to look. And she's nowhere to be found. Over and over again. The paintings might be as close as anyone can get."

"And the one in the postal museum? Why is that one in danger?"

Scott just looked at her. She was always so slow to figure things out. If Ike were here, he'd already know the answer.

"If destroying a painting does something to the subject," she said, "she won't have a choice. She helps them figure out how it works or they . . . what? Slash it?"

Scott looked at his phone, like it might save him. He was so young, like one of her students. He wasn't part of the inner circle, didn't have any real answers. He was just doing as he was told. Pepper thought she saw a blue sweater, but she'd taken her eyes off the window and couldn't be sure.

"You never needed me for any of this," Pepper said.

"You've been helpful enough," Scott said. "And there were questions. About whether you might have some kind of ability, like her."

"How do you know I don't?" Pepper asked. If she focused her anger hard enough, maybe she could make him burst into flames. It felt possible in the moment.

"Pepper, come on," Scott said. "You can barely handle your life as it is. If you had some kind of ability, you wouldn't make it out of bed."

"I never should've talked to you," she said. She stood and finished her coffee, fast enough to burn her throat.

"Where are you going?" Scott asked.

"None of your business," Pepper said.

She grabbed her bag, tossed some cash on the table, and walked out without looking back. Outside, the sun was too bright and the air too hot. It felt like slipping from one world into another. Someone knocked against Pepper on the sidewalk, so she started walking, part of her brain vaguely recognizing that she was melting down. Her bag wasn't that heavy but now felt like an impossible weight, this unwieldy duffel, another burden on top of all the others. She wasn't trying hard enough to keep it from knocking into the people she passed. She didn't look up. At some point, she realized she was following the feet of a woman who carried a package covered with labels, most of which had been blacked out. The Old Town's colorful buildings blurred by. A few blocks later, the woman dropped her package, and Pepper stopped. She was standing in front of a tall building with an array of satellites scattered across the top. The Central Post Office. She didn't know what the hell she was doing here. She already knew they were closed. Her body had brought her anyway, moving her like a planchette on a Ouija board.

Pepper checked the time. She should have been heading to the airport, but she went to the door instead. She hated the post office. She tried the door, but it was locked, because of course it was. She sat on the concrete. She was too much a mess to cry, even. She'd save it for the plane. She was always good at crying on planes.

Behind her, she heard a noise and turned to see an elderly man in a long, cream-colored cardigan unlock the door. There was a bell on the door, and it jingled. He stood in the doorway and studied her for a moment.

"Zamknięty," he said.

Pepper nodded. Closed. She looked down the street for a taxi. It was time to go. She made herself stand.

"Miss," the man said. He was still standing in the doorway. "English?"

"English," Pepper said.

"You need to come in?" he asked.

Pepper looked at him. "I don't know," she said.

"Come in," the man said. Pepper obeyed. It was nice to have someone tell her what to do. He locked the door behind them. It was so quiet inside. Pepper saw a shelf lined with postal boxes, all different colors. There was a large black carriage with yellow doors in a room off to the side. The man shuffled to the desk and handed her a map. "You look," he said. "I am here, working."

He circled the desk and sat behind it on a stool, so low that Pepper could no longer see him. She checked her phone again. She didn't have much time. She opened the map and followed it through rooms of stamps and radios until she found the stairs. The lights weren't on in this section of the museum, but she went up anyway, into a stairwell lit by a muted ray of sunlight struggling from a window above.

Pepper reached the landing and stopped. There it was. *Self-Portrait with Nothing,* mounted on the wall inside a thick glassy case. Ula looked as she did in the photos in Tilda's album—hair cropped short, expression of teenage disdain—except her ears were pierced, which Pepper didn't remember from the photos. In the painting, she was wearing an oversize black T-shirt, and it hung off one bony shoulder. There were trees in the background, visible through the bedroom window behind her, and a person-size shadow looming, as if she'd stood in front of a mirror and painted both herself and the shadow she'd cast. But Ula wasn't eighteen when she painted this portrait, if the date on the plaque was to be believed. She'd gone back and painted this moment years later, for reasons Pepper would likely never understand. In her arms was a baby, wrapped in a jersey. The baby just looked like a baby. Pepper didn't see herself in its face, because its face was turned away, toward Ula's chest.

Pepper couldn't take her eyes off the painting, even though she was starting to feel unsteady. There was something different about the brushstrokes on Ula's face. The paint on the rest of the portrait was smoothly applied, but the face was rough, as if it had been painted with a tremulous hand. The eyes looked too old to belong to a teenager, the whole face oddly mature, as if Ula couldn't stop herself from painting her present into her past, superimposing one version of herself over another. Pepper put her hand against the case. She heard the old man downstairs cough and pulled back. She could see her fingerprints on the glass, smudged over the baby. The case seemed thick enough. And probably nothing terrible would happen to her if the painting were somehow destroyed. She walked down the stairs. The man rose from his stool.

"Dziękuję," Pepper said.

The man nodded and unlocked the door. "It is good place to be alone with yourself," he said.

Stepping from the cool of the museum into the heat took Pepper's breath away. She needed to find a taxi, fast now, to make sure she got to the airport and through security in time. Small, simple tasks. All she had to do was walk a few blocks and find a cab. The cab would have air-conditioning. Maybe the driver would talk to her, or have the radio turned up. She would stand in a line, board her flight, take something, try to sleep.

There were taxis in sight when she tripped. She registered the fall not so much as pain but force, in her hands and forehead, as they made impact with the concrete. She'd tripped, or someone had tripped her. The sidewalk was damp, and there was trash on the ground, a crumpled soda can and soggy maps and a gray-pink wad of chewing gum, wrinkled like a brain. Pepper's brain was slow to process what was happening. Had she tripped, or had someone tripped her? She didn't trust herself. Then she felt it. A presence behind her. She took a shaky breath and prepared herself to be helped up, but instead there was a yanking sensation at her shoulder as her bag pulled away. Someone had cut the strap of her duffel bag and was taking off with it.

She tried to turn, but a pain exploded out from her forehead. She got to her knees and felt like she might vomit. She thought about the baby in the painting, helpless in her mother's arms. Ula had painted her as a nothing. Her phone and wallet were in her bag, along with her boarding pass. She closed her eyes and waited for the nausea to pass.

THERE WAS A small crowd around Pepper when she opened her eyes. Everything was out of focus, and everyone was speaking Polish, and there was a girl in a dress with a vegetable print, smiling carrots and peppers and tomatoes, clinging to her mother's leg. The girl was wearing glitter jelly sandals, just like a pair Pepper had as a kid. Pepper was kneeling on the sidewalk, a shroud of pain over her head. The mother of the girl with the sandals pulled a tissue from her purse and handed it to Pepper, and she held it to her forehead and felt it soak with blood. She stood even though a man was emphatically signing for her to stay down. She scanned the street for a blue sweater with gold buttons. She hadn't seen who tripped her, but she knew. And no one would believe her. She reached for her phone and remembered it was gone.

"Time?" she asked, and pointed to her wrist.

The woman who'd given her the tissue showed Pepper her phone. Her flight was leaving in half an hour. She'd never make it. It was too late.

The woman brushed Pepper's hair back. "Not so bad," she said. "Hospital?"

Pepper shook her head. She just wanted to go home. The sky

had a yellow tinge, which she hadn't noticed before. The sky looked wrong to her, like it belonged in a different universe. All she wanted to do was go home.

The girl with the jellies tugged on her mother's arm and reached into her purse. She was really rooting around, trying to find something. Her mother spoke to her softly, but the girl didn't respond. And then she lit up. Her hand emerged from the purse holding a lollipop, a flat, translucent green disk. She handed it to Pepper, and Pepper accepted it and touched her fingers to her lips in thanks.

13

THE MOTHER ON the sidewalk tried to get Pepper to wait for the police, but the police hadn't done anything about the Everett Group before, and they weren't going to now. Pepper was a tourist whose bag had been stolen. The crowd dispersed. Pepper remembered how once, in high school, an emergency had come in to the clinic while her moms were both in surgery. A yellow Lab named Lieutenant who'd been run over with a backhoe on a farm by the owner's college-age daughter. The backhoe had degloved the skin from Lieutenant's abdomen—peeled it right off. Pepper had started the IV and administered meds for shock and pain without thinking about it. It wasn't until after, when Lydia had closed her patient and rushed into treatment, that Pepper realized she'd managed it alone.

She wasn't thinking clearly. She still had her passport and some cash in her pocket, so at least there was that. She found the nearest taxi and gave the driver the name of her hotel. When she walked in, Kacper was still at the desk, and he rushed out and held her briefly like a child.

"Dziubku," he said.

Pepper choked on a sob and let him guide her to the lobby sofa.

"Oh dear, oh dear," he was saying. He took a gingham handkerchief from his pocket and held it to her head. Then he took her chin in his hand. "You," he said. "You will be okay." He said this with such gentle authority that Pepper decided to believe him. Okay. She would be okay.

He summoned the cleaning girl, Jola, who calmly assessed the situation, left, and returned with a wet cloth and a bandage.

Like Kacper, whom Pepper hadn't before noticed had the same amber eyes, Jola held Pepper by the chin.

"I do not think you need doctor," she said. "But I should take you anyway?"

Pepper shook her head. Things were starting to come back into focus. She needed to call Ike. She needed to call the airline and figure out a new flight. Small, simple tasks. She needed to be someplace safe. Who was the man in the blue sweater? Surely, Scott had told his father about the conditions of her inheritance by now. There was no reason for the Everett Group to want to hurt her, especially if Ula was no longer missing. But they were still trying to scare her, or keep her here, for some reason. The sense of dread in her body intensified, drowning out her instinct to flee.

Kacper let Pepper use the phone behind the desk. There wasn't another flight until the following morning. Ike didn't answer, so she left a message, telling him only that she'd lost her phone and missed her flight and that she'd be home tomorrow. He was mad, and she deserved it, and if she told him what had happened, he'd worry. Kacper took Pepper to a room, much nicer than the one she and Scott had shared. There was a wide bed and a view of the square and a bird's nest on the windowsill. The bird in the nest cocked its head at Pepper and pecked once at the glass. She put her fingertips on the pane, and the bird pecked again, which made her feel both more and less alone.

In the bathroom, Pepper stood on the cold, white tile and looked in the mirror. She had a gash on her forehead, but it wasn't too deep. The bleeding seemed to have stopped for now, but the skin around it was swollen and already bruising. Small, simple tasks. She washed the cinders out of her hands. She took off her shirt, dappled with her blood, and rinsed it in the sink because she didn't have anything else to wear. And then she lay down on the big, wide bed. She knew if she let herself cry she wouldn't be able to stop, so instead she thought of another universe, where she was currently flying over the ocean, her legs cramped, irritated with the asshole in the seat in front of her who kept reclining into her knees. In another universe, she had escaped this place unharmed, her dread tamped down and explained away, and she was certain, far more certain about this than she was about most things, that the Pepper in that universe was wrong. The bird pecked at the window again, and Pepper watched it, feeling oddly at peace, until she fell asleep.

PEPPER WOKE TO the phone in her room ringing. She sat up, and pain branched across her face. It was late afternoon—she could feel it in the heaviness of the light. The ringing didn't stop. Ike, she thought, calling to find out what the hell she was doing.

"Hello?" she said. Her chest welled in anticipation of Ike's voice. But it wasn't Ike on the phone. It was Kacper.

"Mrs. Rafferty," he said. "There are the policja here to see you."

Pepper cleared her throat. Her mouth felt gummy, and her voice wasn't coming. Kacper must've called the police.

"Thank you," she said. "I'll be down in a minute."

"Wait," Kacper said. Pepper heard a man's voice, arguing with Kacper, and her body woke with fear. How would she know if they were actually police? "They say . . ." Kacper stopped and asked something in Polish, arguing back. "They say they want to come to your room. To speak with you in private."

Pepper looked for the bird on the windowsill, but it was gone now, and for one perfectly clear moment, she wanted nothing more than for the bird to reappear. She didn't want to answer any questions. Maybe she could climb out the window. Then she remembered herself. She was her moms' daughter, well versed in emergencies. She could handle this.

"I'll come down," she said, and hung up the phone.

She checked the mirror in the bathroom. The bruise was spreading across her forehead, and there was nothing she could do to disguise it. Her T-shirt was still damp, but she took it from the shower rod and put it back on, smoothed over the faint but visible outlines of the bloodstains. She grabbed her room key, not bothering with her shoes. She wasn't helpless. She was a professor. She had an advanced degree, a job, a husband, a house, research funding that was about to run out. If she could get her shit together, there would be more. She had graduate students and consulting work with the police at home. Pepper was a competent woman. She could handle a few questions.

She stepped into the hall and the policja were already there, waiting. There were two of them—a compact man with red hair and broken capillaries across his nose and a woman with dark hair in a French braid.

"Mrs. Rafferty," the woman said. "I'm Officer Jagoda. This is Officer Chlebek. May we come in?"

Pepper felt braver in the hall. There were other rooms around her, she could hear people moving inside. She took a step forward. "Can I see your badges?" she said.

Jagoda offered hers without hesitation and nudged Chlebek to follow suit. They looked real enough, but Pepper wouldn't be able to spot a fake.

"May we come in?" Jagoda repeated.

"We can talk here," Pepper said, holding her ground. If she yelled from the hall, other people would hear. If she yelled from inside her room, maybe not. The officers exchanged a look. Chlebek seemed to be urging Jagoda on with his eyes.

"We have some news," Jagoda said. "Do you want to sit?"

"No, I like to stand," Pepper said.

Jagoda focused on her forehead. "You are hurt?"

"A cut," Pepper said. "When the man who stole my bag tripped me, I hit my head."

Jagoda looked at her partner with confusion. They weren't here about that.

"Mrs. Rafferty," Jagoda said. "We spoke with your colleague Mr. Morrow earlier this week. After you discovered a break-in on Ula Frost's property. We understand you are her daughter, yes?"

"I'm her biological daughter," Pepper said. "But I've never met her. I was given up for adoption."

Jagoda was looking at Pepper with increasing concern. "I think you should sit now," she said. "We will go inside?"

"No, thank you," Pepper said. "Could you please explain why you're here? We were told that Ula Frost has been seen recently. So she's not really missing after all."

"Yes," the woman said. "She was seen by some neighbors. But I'm very sorry to inform you that Ms. Frost has been found dead today."

There were kids in one of the rooms off the hallway, and they were arguing in what sounded like Italian. A girl with a high-pitched voice, and a boy. There was some slapping and stomping involved.

"Oh," Pepper said.

A woman in the room with the kids barked out an order, having reached her breaking point, and the children's voices were replaced by those of cartoon characters. Pepper heard a sound effect like someone running fast and crashing into a wall.

"You would like to sit?" Jagoda said.

"Yes, please," Pepper said.

She turned to open her room but fumbled with her key and dropped it. Chlebek retrieved it from the carpet and unlocked the door. Pepper sat on the bed, her damp T-shirt clammy against her skin. The officers remained standing. The pain across Pepper's forehead magnified, an electric pulse. Her hands were numb. The room around her seemed to waver, like she was on the cusp of universes.

"What happened?" she said.

"We received a call this morning that a body had been found in front of the church owned by Ms. Frost," Jagoda said. "We believe the body was left there some time in the night."

"What do you mean, it was left there?" Pepper asked. "You don't think she died there?"

As she said this, her body clicked into a calm. This was Pepper's area of expertise. She could handle this, the facts of the case. She could recalibrate this into science.

Jagoda cleared her throat. "The body was badly burned,"

she said. "There is no evidence of fire at the place where it was found."

Pepper closed her eyes. She could see a burned body—the tissue, the bones. She had seen burned bodies before.

"How do you know it's her?" she said. "How extensive is the damage? Has a forensic specialist examined the remains?"

Jagoda paused, pressed her lips together tight. "We were able to match the dental records. Ms. Frost's dentist lives in the neighborhood. She used a different name, but he identified her from a photograph."

Pepper tried to process this information. How extensively did the body need to be burned for the police to have to rely on dental records? She had papers on it, in her office, the way burned bodies were scored, how different kinds of dental restorations withstood various temperature ranges.

"I see," Pepper said. She looked for the bird, but it was still missing. "Can I view the remains?"

Jagoda blinked at her. "We do not usually allow family to view the victim in such cases," she said. "We will have an expert to tell us more later this week."

"It is not good to see, Mrs. Rafferty," Chlebek said. He'd been quiet—his English was not as fluent as Jagoda's—but now he felt the need to interject. "Not this."

Pepper looked at him. These officers must have thought she was insane. But she was here, in this universe, for a reason. And this would be the only chance she'd ever get to see her mother.

"It's Dr. Rafferty," she said. "I do this kind of work, at home." She wrote down Detective Marchand's number. "You can call to verify. But I'd like to see the remains. I'll sign whatever paperwork you need."

Chlebek gestured to the hall with his head, and he and Jagoda excused themselves to discuss. Pepper sat on the bed and stared at her bare feet. Had the victim been alive or dead when she was burned? How was the body transported, and was there significance to the position in which it was found? What were the weather conditions, and could they have contaminated the remains? It was misty that morning, but she didn't think it had rained. She would be okay if she kept her mind focused this way. Was there evidence of trauma, and was it possible to differentiate between antemortem trauma and postmortem trauma from the fire?

There was the sound of a police radio in the hall. Jagoda came back into the room.

"Okay," she said. "You may come."

"Thank you," Pepper said. She stood and gathered her passport and key and walked to the door. She could handle this. She was handling this fine. Jagoda stopped her with a hand.

"What?" Pepper said.

"You would like to wear your shoes?" Jagoda said.

THEY APPROACHED A building that looked like a fortress, built from ancient blocks of gray stone. Pepper imagined what Ike would say if he were there with her in the police car, the facts he'd recite about the building's construction, its foreboding tower, the people who'd died inside. The police car came to a stop, and Pepper saw the building with the tower was actually a train station. The police station next to it was squat and brown. Inside, a warren of cubicles spanned the room, the walls painted with a single orange stripe. The office equipment was dated, and Pepper could hear a fax machine somewhere in the back. The officers led her down an empty hallway to a room where they asked her to wait.

The room was lined with dull yellow tile. There was a metal table, two metal chairs, and on one wall, a mirror. An interrogation room. Pepper hadn't done anything wrong, but still it made her nervous. She reached for her pocket out of habit, but her phone had not miraculously materialized while she wasn't looking. What would she even text Ike now if she could? It was easier for her to do this alone, without him gently urging her to be more present than she wanted to be.

The interrogation room door opened, and Jagoda appeared with a man in a tie and neon running shoes.

"This is Dr. Brodowski," Jagoda said. "He is our examiner."

The man gave Pepper a little bow and said, "Hello." He had enormous muttonchops, which again made Pepper think of Ike, whom she sometimes suspected had gone into history because of his wholehearted love of Civil War–era facial hair.

"He doesn't speak much English," Jagoda said. "But he will show you the body."

Brodowski nodded at Pepper and began walking down the hall. "Yes?" he said, and she followed. The room where he took her was cold. She could feel it in the moisture of her T-shirt against her skin. In the anteroom, he gave her a thin blue gown to put on over her clothes, a cap for her hair, gloves, and a mask. Like work, she thought. All she had to do was focus on the work.

He took her through a pair of swinging doors into a room with a long exam table, covered with a crisp white sheet. Pepper's eyes went straight to the slope of the skull. Brodowski waited a moment, then lifted the sheet away. The charred remains were laid out with one arm reaching up toward the head and one resting near the ribs. Pepper took a step backward, then took a step forward.

"Is this the position the body was found in?" she asked.

Pepper could see the sheepish smile despite Brodowski's mask. He shook his head, not understanding the question. Pepper approached the table, her hands sweating inside the gloves. The gown scratched at her neck. She tried to keep her mind focused on the scratching. That was the only sensation she would allow herself to notice.

There wasn't much soft tissue remaining, only on the femurs and pelvic bones. To reach this state of degradation, the body must have burned for a long time or been exposed to very high temperatures. The bones would be fragile. This wasn't a body pulled from a house fire. It could've been burned in a car, Pepper thought, where the gasoline would affect the process. Or it could've been burned in some other controlled environment, using an accelerant. A body could sustain its own fire for seven hours. But this body had some help.

Pepper started with the skull, examining the sutures and struc-

ture of the jaw, which suggested the victim was female, as did the
pelvis, when Pepper tipped it from the table. The clavicles were
fully fused, so the victim was at least twenty-five, and signs of
remodeling on the skull as well as the presence of degenerative
changes in the lower lumbar vertebrae and joints of the legs suggested the age was older. Osteoarthritis was common in young
individuals in ancient populations, but not contemporary ones.
The gown scratched at Pepper's neck. There were no signs of frac-
turing in the skull, so she could rule out blunt force trauma. The
room smelled like eucalyptus, which did not mask the scent of
burnt meat. The rest of the bones were unremarkable, except for
the right radius and ulna, both of which displayed the faint scars
of remodeled fractures. Based on the degree of remodeling, the
fractures had likely occurred in the victim's youth. The maxilla
was missing several teeth.

"The dental records?" Pepper said.

Brodowski shook his head. Pepper pointed to her mouth under
the mask. Brodowski nodded and took an envelope from the table
and opened it to reveal two sets of dental X-rays, which he placed
on a light box. Pepper paced back and forth between the table and
the box, comparing the morphology and spacing of the teeth. In
the X-rays, three of the teeth had fillings, probably silver amal-
gam. Those were the teeth that were missing from the victim.

Pepper returned to the body and pointed to the spaces where
the teeth should have been. Brodowski shrugged. She felt the
gown scratching at her neck. She felt the room contracting around
her. If she could just focus on the feeling of the gown on her neck,
the thought of Ike and how much he'd like Brodowski's muttonchops, the smell of eucalyptus, the work at hand, she could get
through this.

She pointed at the file on the table, and Brodowski nodded. It
was all in Polish. There was a standard diagram of the skeleton,
with circles drawn at the jaw and right arm. He'd marked the
anomalies. He'd also collected samples of tissue and bone, an
array of vials on top of paperwork for an external lab. He was
doing everything right. And this body didn't tell Pepper any-

thing she didn't know. She hadn't learned anything from this body about Ula or herself, except that Ula had arthritis, and that though Pepper tried hard not to care that she was a nothing in Ula's life, she did and it fucking hurt despite every worthless attempt she'd made to pretend otherwise. The room was getting smaller, and it smelled like eucalyptus and burnt meat, and the gown was scratching at her neck.

Pepper escaped into the anteroom, which smelled only like disinfectant. She tugged off the gloves and mask and cap and gown. Her hands were shaking. It was all just work, she told herself, but her body wouldn't listen, and Brodowski waved his hands at her to stop what she was doing, to stop shaking, but she couldn't, and then she realized she was bracing herself against a cart of sterile tools, that's what Brodowski was waving about, and he took her by the arm and eased her into a chair with wheels that spun to one side as she sat.

KACPER BROUGHT PEPPER a bowl of potato soup, a hunk of bread with a crust so thick she could barely tear it, and a little metal tin of salve for her forehead. The salve smelled like anise and honey. Pepper sat over the soup and felt the steam on her face. She held a piece of bread in her mouth until it turned gummy and spit it into a napkin. She couldn't swallow. Her moms would give her ice cream now if they could, but it was too late to call them—they'd only worry. The pain in her forehead had spread through her body, a pair of opened wings, beating downward. She lay on the bed and made a mental list of everything she should have looked at more carefully when she'd examined the remains. She hadn't checked the phalanges of the hands for signs of trauma, to determine if Ula had tried to defend herself. She hadn't scored the bones based on their damage from the fire, to assess if one part of the body burned hotter or longer than the others. She hadn't written anything down.

Somewhere, in an alternate universe, in many alternate universes, Ula was still alive. Somewhere she had died long ago.

Somewhere Ula had never abandoned Pepper, and she'd never known her moms, and she had a complicated relationship with Ula instead. Maybe she dreaded talking to her on the phone, because Ula picked at her about her career, why she wasn't more ambitious or assertive or artistic, or whatever mothers picked at their daughters about. Somewhere Michael Orlando was still alive too, and he sent her cards on her birthday. Somewhere maybe they were all alive and happy together, and there was a lake they went to every year in the summer, even when they were fighting about some trivial slight one of them had inflicted on another. Somewhere Pepper was braver, and more open, the kind of woman who never withheld anything, because she only wanted people in her life who liked her as she was. Somewhere she didn't constantly see the world through the lens of Ula's vision at the expense of the people who actually loved her. Somewhere she was here, in this hotel room, only more competent, capable of finding an answer to the question of what happened to Ula. The Pepper in this universe had no way to link Ula's death to the Everett Group, whom Jagoda insisted they'd already cleared of suspicion, or anyone else. *Self-Portrait* was secure at the postal museum. But now with Ula undeniably gone, Pepper would have control of the rest of her work, and in some universe—this one, which still felt less real than the others—she was the only thing standing between whatever keys that work might contain and the people who wanted to use them for their own profit.

Pepper reexamined the bones in her mind. The sutures of the skull, the missing teeth, the pitting in the vertebrae, the fractured arm. She sat up. She grabbed the phone on the nightstand. It took her a few tries to figure out how to make an international call, but she got it. It was afternoon in Connecticut. She had no idea if Ike would be home, but she called the house phone because she didn't want to bother him otherwise.

The phone stopped ringing, but there was no voice at the other end. For a few seconds, all Pepper could hear was fumbling.

"Ike?" she said.

"Sorry," he said, and coughed. "I just walked in the door. Where are you?"

"The hotel," Pepper said. "I need you to check something for me. Can you get that photo album from Tilda's?"

"What?" Ike said. "I'm carrying groceries."

"I just need you to check something in the photo album," she said. "Please. It's important."

"Are you okay?" he said.

"There was a picture of Ula as a kid," she said. "Six or seven? There were a lot of people in the background, like a party. She had a cast on her arm. I need to know which arm."

She heard the rustling of bags and wondered what Ike was feeding himself. Pasta and eggs, probably. A few years ago, he'd taught a summer course in Amsterdam, and while he was gone, Pepper had subsisted mostly on birthday cake. The woman at the bakery had offered to pipe on the recipient's name, and in her shame, Pepper had given a fake one.

"Fine, hold on." The receiver clicked against the counter, probably next to a book about the history of grenades or liquid rocket propellant. Someone in the room next to Pepper's was watching TV, and Pepper could hear the voices but with no clarity, the dividing wall transmuting words into murmurs.

There were more fumbling noises. "Okay, I have the album," Ike said. "Let me see." He coughed again. She wondered if he was taking his allergy medication. The pollen had been worse than usual this year. She could hear the pages turning. Ike's fingers were sinewy, and he had a faded tattoo of a blue heart on his left ring finger that he'd gotten at age twenty-one as a sign of devotion to a girlfriend who wasn't Pepper. In an alternate universe, they were still together. Probably he was happier that way, even though they'd have their own problems, having grown apart in the ways people do, inside of a love sturdy enough to survive the differences. Pepper had never been the type to inspire tattoo-worthy devotion.

"Okay," he said. "This is it. She's probably ten. You're not good at kids' ages."

"I know," she said. "Which arm?"

"Left," he said. "It's her left arm."

"*Her* left? You're sure?" Pepper tried hard to remember. The remains she examined had fractures in the right radius and ulna. She was pretty sure. Had she made sure the bones were placed on the correct side? She thought she had.

"The cast is low?" she said. "It's not the humerus, right? It's from wrist to elbow?"

"I know where the humerus is," Ike said. "I'm married to you. What is happening? Does this have something to do with the lawyer?"

"What lawyer?" Pepper said. "Ula's lawyer?" She needed to call Jagoda and verify the fracture was on the right side.

"The lawyer was here earlier," Ike said. "That's why I didn't answer when you called. Those guys from the Everett Group took our original copy of the paperwork, so I reread everything last night and realized something."

"What?" Pepper said. Jagoda had given her a card, but she couldn't find it.

"You're named as the executor in Ula's will. And the executor is the person who enforces the conditions of the bequest. There was never anyone but you to enforce Ula's condition. You'll end up in possession of the paintings whether you sign the agreement or not. What is happening?"

"Ula is dead," Pepper said. It came out like she was saying something normal, but with a little choke at the end. Ula was dead, and now the paintings would be hers whether she wanted them or not, and the Everett Group already knew that.

"What?" Ike said.

"They found her body burned," Pepper said. She thought if she said it fast, she might be able to get it all out. "In front of the church. The dental records match. They let me see her, and there was a fracture, but it was on the wrong side."

"Pepper, are you okay?" Ike asked. "Wait, what did you say? That doesn't make sense."

"I know it doesn't make sense," she said. "But it was the right arm. The fractures were in the right arm. I'm almost positive. I am positive. I hit my head, but I can still tell left from right."

"What do you mean you hit your head?" Ike said.

"I got mugged," Pepper said. "I tripped, hit my head, someone took my bag. It's not important. But I can see the ulna in my mind. It was the right damn ulna."

"Whoa," Ike said. "Someone attacked you? Like, are you really hurt? Did you see a doctor?"

"No, I'm fine," Pepper said. "It's just a cut. But my bag is gone. My phone was inside. I missed my flight, came back to the hotel. The guy brought me potato soup. I'm fine."

She was fine, but she needed to think. The teeth matched. Pepper had looked at the records herself. But maybe the dentist had been confused and it wasn't Ula in the first place, or maybe somehow the records had been swapped.

"When were you going to tell me this?" Ike said.

"I don't have my phone," Pepper said. "You didn't answer when I called. I wasn't going to leave a message that said I fell and split my forehead."

"Pepper," Ike said. She could hear him breathing. It wasn't happy breathing. She needed to talk to the dentist. Why was it always dentists? Dentists and post offices, the recurring themes of Pepper's life. There had to be an explanation for the dental records. It was too late to find the dentist tonight. She'd have to wait until morning.

"Are you there?" Pepper said.

"You should've told me," Ike said. "You promised. How many times are we going to do this?"

The TV next door sounded like it was showing the news. Pepper couldn't understand what the anchor was saying, but he had that newscaster tone, straightforward and serious.

"I don't know," Pepper said. "I didn't want you to worry."

Ike sighed. "It's a rule now," he said. "If you get injured in a foreign country, you tell me." He coughed. "Are you coming home in the morning?"

"I don't think I can," she said. "I have to find the dentist. I'll call the airline now and book something for the afternoon."

Ike didn't have anything to say to this. The television next door played footage of a helicopter, chopping at the air.

"Fine," Ike said. "Let me know the flight number. But I can't guarantee I'll be able to pick you up."

The helicopter stopped, the television suddenly muted or clicked off. Pepper felt the exact distance between her and Ike then, in the sound of his voice, which hurtled across thousands of miles to reach her, alone in a hotel room, with these words, in this moment.

"I can get a ride," she said. Sometimes, at home, when she was in a mood, Ike would blast a pop song, grab her hands, and start bobbing around, and then she'd have to start bobbing around, and then everything would be better.

"Sure," he said. "Okay." He was a lousy dancer, self-conscious about it on top of having no rhythm. "I'm sorry about Ula." He sounded like a colleague, offering requisite condolences. "I have groceries to put away. Good night."

PEPPER SLEPT POORLY and woke to the sound of the lamp from the hotel room's desk crashing against the floor. The lamp was green glass and had a pull chain that made a satisfying sound when turned on and off.

"Shhh," someone said. There were footsteps and whispers. Pepper's head was partially under the duvet, and she slunk down farther, while pretending to still be asleep.

"I saw that," a voice said. It was a woman's voice, and familiar. It didn't sound like Iphigenia, but Iphigenia had said she was the only female member of the Everett Group. Pepper could sense the woman wasn't alone. "Just open your eyes already."

Pepper could see sunlight through her eyelids. She could feel her pulse in her stomach. She opened her eyes. Ula Frost was standing over her bed.

Someone across the room put her hands on her hips and nudged the broken lamp under the desk with her foot. It was also Ula Frost. And over by the window, looking supremely bored, another Ula. Pepper scanned the room and counted, twice. There were three Ula Frosts in her hotel room. She closed her eyes. Sometimes when she was having a nightmare, she recognized she was having a nightmare from inside the dream and was able to wake herself. She told herself, *Wake up*. She opened her eyes again. All the Ulas were still there.

The Ula closest to the bed sat at the edge and put a hand on Pepper's forehead. She smelled like laundry detergent. Her face was androgynous, long with thin lips, and her graying hair was lanky and unkempt. Everyone was right, Pepper thought. They did look alike, though this Ula had deep creases in her neck, and the skin around her mouth sagged. This was how Pepper would age.

"I know," Ula said. The other two were leaning in, watching. Pepper could feel their eyes on her. They were all taller than she was by a few inches. Pepper hadn't imagined Ula as taller. "But get up. We need your help."

Pepper sat up and gathered the covers around her. She'd slept in the hotel robe after washing her clothes in the sink. She only had the one pair of underwear now.

"What the hell," she said.

"The short version," Ula said, "is that I've been painting self-portraits."

TWO

14

THE ULA PERCHED at the edge of the bed took Pepper's hand. "It's so nice to meet you, at last. But seriously, get up."

Across the room, the bored-looking Ula sat on the desk and dangled her legs, muscled like a runner's. The third Ula found Pepper's clothes, hanging from the shower rod. Pepper assessed each of them—their eyes, their ears, their bone structure. Maybe Ula had hired look-alikes. But the only differences between them were so subtle. The one rummaging through Pepper's clothes had an intricate skeleton key tattooed on the length of her forearm. The one on the desk had more age spots than the others. None appeared to have altered their appearances in other ways.

The Ula at the bed was not a patient one. "Now," she said.

Pepper got up, pulling the hotel robe tight around her naked body. She approached the Ula who was examining her underwear. This Ula handed them to Pepper with a frown, and Pepper took her clothes into the bathroom. She locked the door behind her and sat on the toilet seat. She'd left home ambivalent about meeting one Ula Frost. Now she had three. Someone knocked on the door.

"Occupied," Pepper said. She stood and checked the mirror. The cut on her forehead was scabbing, the surrounding bruise blooming into shades of purple and blue. She got dressed quickly, afraid one of the Ulas might barge in.

"Yes, okay, I realize this must come as a surprise," Ula said through the door. Pepper had a sense this was the Ula from the bed—her biological mother, the head Ula. "You thought I was dead."

"The teeth," Pepper said. "They have your dental records."

"I knew that dentist would come in handy," Ula said.

"He has a gut," another Ula said. She had a more affected way of speaking, like a stage actress. "It hangs over you when he's working on your teeth."

"Sometimes they come through already dead," the head Ula said. "I saved one, just in case. She was already dead when she got here."

Pepper sat again and felt the cold tile, the realness of her body. This was all real. She'd left home firm in her skepticism, but at some point, without realizing it, her doubt had receded. She'd tried to explain the stories away, and she'd failed. There was no window in this bathroom. The only way out was through the door.

"Are you going to join us?" Ula asked. "We've been waiting a long time to meet you."

Pepper had met Ula before, only Ula hadn't recognized her. But which Ula had that been? The door was white, and there were fingerprints around the knob, smudges from other guests who'd come before Pepper. She'd left her own, and more would after she was gone.

"I think I'm going to need the long version," she said.

"I'm afraid we don't have time for that," Ula said. "Those goons from the Everett Group know where you are, my dear."

Ula tried to open the door, and Pepper watched the doorknob move, first to the right, then to the left. She put her head on her knees. If the men from the Everett Group wanted Ula for their purposes, it made some sense that she'd fake her own death. But she must have known they'd come for Pepper next.

Pepper opened the door. The Ulas were standing side by side. A team of Ulas. A pack of them. Pepper had steadied herself during a rough stretch of grad school by memorizing the collective nouns of the animal kingdom. A bloat of hippos, a parliament of owls. What was the appropriate collective noun for an assembly of mothers you never wanted?

There was a knock on the room's door. The Ulas froze. A

descent of woodpeckers, a maelstrom of salamanders, a shiver of sharks. Pepper put an eye to the peephole and saw Kacper.

She turned to find the head Ula urging the others into the bathroom. The one with the tattoo wasn't eager to cooperate. She backed away in defiance, but the head Ula gave her a harsh look, and the tattooed Ula exhaled hard through her nose and complied.

"Mrs. Rafferty," Kacper said, when Pepper opened the door. She could still hear the Ulas, a whisper escalating quickly to a raised voice. The bathroom door could open at any moment. Kacper tried to step in, but Pepper stood firm in the doorway. He touched her forehead tenderly. "It looks better today."

"The ointment helped," she said. "Thank you."

He was holding a small white shopping bag, which he extended to her. It was heavier than she'd expected.

"Delivered this morning," he said.

She opened the bag to find a new phone.

"Your husband," he said. "He called the desk to ask we make sure you got it."

The phone would need to be charged and set up. There were more sounds from the bathroom, an unmistakable voice, water running. Pepper took the phone and its charger from the box and gave the packaging back to Kacper.

"Thank you," Pepper said. "I'll be checking out soon."

Another sound, but loud and distinct this time, like something hitting a wall. Kacper tried to look past her, but Pepper pulled the door closed, leaving only a crack between them.

"Excuse me," she said. "I had an overnight guest." She winked, like an idiot. She was hopeless at intrigue. She heard the bathroom door open.

"Your husband," Kacper said. He handed her a sheet of paper.

"Thank you," Pepper said, and shut the door in his face.

Behind her, the Ulas spilled from the bathroom and scattered across the room. Pepper folded the paper and slipped it into her pocket.

"You wouldn't dare," the head Ula said.

"Fuck you," the tattooed Ula said in response.

They separated, as far apart as the room would allow. The head Ula took Pepper by the face.

"We're good?" she said. "Let's go."

THE ULAS WERE all dressed in black—the one with strong legs in a swingy dress, the tattooed one in jeans and a T-shirt with holes in it. The head Ula wore wide-leg pants and an open knit sweater. Pepper left them in the room while she went to the desk to check out. Kacper avoided small talk this time. Pepper just hoped the credit card Ike had called in wouldn't be declined. She'd tucked the phone inside her shirt. She didn't want the Ulas to know she had it. The plan was for them to leave, one by one, down the back stairs, which led to an employee-only exit at the rear of the hotel. But as Pepper turned away from the desk, a man took hold of her arm. She recognized him by his hair. Roscoe, from the Everett Group.

"Dr. Rafferty," he said. "How funny to meet you here."

Ha ha ha, Pepper thought. *So funny.* She tried to signal Kacper with her eyes, but he'd dismissed her from the desk with an expression of grandfatherly disappointment. She scanned the room and saw the bald man with horn-rimmed glasses, Christian. He was wearing a blue sweater with gold buttons. He shook his head as if to warn her not to make a scene.

Pepper thought about the swarm of Ulas loitering in her room. "Actually," she said, "I was hoping I'd run into you again. I seem to have lost my bag. Maybe you could help?"

Christian's eyes narrowed, and the split in Pepper's forehead throbbed.

"Let us go somewhere and chat, yes?" Roscoe said.

Pepper glanced back at Kacper, who was now examining an invoice with a uniformed man leaning against a hand truck loaded with boxes. But then Pepper saw something else: an Ula, peering around the corner from the staircase. It was the one who'd sat on the desk in the room, who had the legs of an athlete. Pepper turned back to the men.

"I'm sorry," she said. "I missed my flight once. My husband will be furious if I miss it again."

"Ah yes," Roscoe said. "Your husband. Such a helpful man. I wouldn't mind visiting with him again. Would you, Christian?"

"I will visit him again," Christian said. "If I must."

Pepper imagined Ike, sitting in the hush of the library, stacks of dusty wagon train diaries around him. Once, they were in the yard and something flew at Pepper's head, and she, always anticipating disaster, had swatted at it frantically, knocking it out of the air. It wasn't until after that she'd seen it was a butterfly, mostly orange, with a few black spots, motionless on the overgrown clover. She'd hated herself instantly, but Ike was there, and he'd picked it up gently and held it in a cupped palm, and then it had flown away.

"See," he'd said. "You didn't kill it. You just stunned it."

"A little walk," Roscoe said. "That is all. We will take a walk and chat, and you will go home to your Isaac. I do not think you want trouble. Why would you want trouble? You are a woman of science. You must see what an extraordinary opportunity we have to understand this phenomenon. You must see how such a discovery will benefit all of mankind."

Pepper didn't want to think through the implications of allowing Andy Warhol access to other worlds, but in her mind, there was a clear, unbidden image of him standing in front of a dark, swirling void. "Ula is dead," Pepper said. "There's nothing I can do to help you with that."

Roscoe smiled. "I think we both know that is very convenient," he said. "A burned body is clever, but not clever enough. And it seems unlikely to us that, having you so close, she would not try to make contact."

Pepper willed herself to not look back to the staircase. "Why do you think she'd contact me?" She said it a little more loudly than necessary. "She hasn't my entire life." Until now. They'd kept Pepper here as bait, and Ula had done exactly what they'd wanted.

"She has sent you money, has she not? She is a hard woman to predict. We suspect she will make herself known, if she needs to."

Roscoe put a hand on Pepper's back and pressed her toward the door. Christian was close, close enough to grab her if she tried anything. Did they really think Ula would attempt to protect her?

They were almost through the lobby when a sound exploded from the stairwell, loud enough to make them all jump, like a tray of dishes shattering against the floor. Kacper dropped the invoice and rushed in the direction of the noise. Roscoe stopped in confusion, and Christian skulked after Kacper, and in that moment, Pepper dodged into the side room, past the coffee-maker and the little bowls of sugar and cream, straight into the supply closet, where she closed the door.

Pepper groped in the dark, unsuccessfully, for a mop handle as she heard footsteps—quick, male—follow into the side room and stop. Finding only the hotel's sad breakfast spread, the pursuer cursed in another language and headed elsewhere. But Pepper wasn't alone for long, and she pressed herself against a shelf stocked with soaps when the door opened. Jola spit when she saw Pepper.

"Was that you?" she said.

Pepper grabbed her wrist and pulled her inside. "Was what me?" she said.

"With the television," Jola said. "Someone threw television down the stairs." She took the broom that was propped in the corner, her eyes all accusation.

"I was in the lobby the whole time," Pepper said. "I just checked out." She offered her receipt as proof. "But there are these men."

Jola sighed. "It is always men," she said. "You wait."

She was gone a few minutes, long enough for Pepper to activate the phone. It was partially charged, enough to get her through a few hours. She unfolded the note Kacper had given her, which Ike must've faxed.

⌐Ⴈ Ⴜ>ᒋᒷᒷ ⌂◻ⴹᒷ◻

Jola reappeared at the door, holding a chef's coat and hat. Pepper buttoned the coat over her clothes while Jola leaned around the corner. There was no time to decipher Ike's message.

"Come now," Jola said.

She led Pepper through the hotel's kitchen to a door that opened into an alley. She took a cigarette from her pocket.

"This man, he wears a blue sweater?" she asked.

"Yes," Pepper said.

"He is at end of alley. When I am talking to him, you go other way. This is plan?"

Pepper tucked her hair under the chef's hat. "It's definitely a plan," she said, though it was a plan that almost certainly wouldn't work. The smarter course of action would be to call the police. But she was here now, at the door, at the cusp of the alley. In another universe, a better version of Pepper was still standing in the storage closet waiting for help to arrive. That version of Pepper would live and spend a long afternoon at the police station before going home to Ike, whom she might properly appreciate in the aftermath of this ordeal. If all else failed, that version of her would continue on, correcting the unforgivable mistakes this Pepper insisted on making.

Jola slipped into the alley and held up one hand. Pepper kept the door cracked until she heard Jola's voice lilting in flirtation. There was the flicker of a lighter. Pepper peeked enough to see Jola take a long drag from her cigarette and circle Christian, who followed Jola until he was facing away from the door. Pepper was suddenly aware of the sound of her own feet against the ground. It was hard to walk quickly and quietly at the same time. She was at the end of the alley when she felt it, another hand grabbing her forearm, pulling her away from the alley and toward the street.

A woman in a black dress, now wearing a black straw hat and sunglasses. Her toned legs were familiar, her nails cut so they ended in sharp points. She said nothing and pulled Pepper into the street without looking. There was a handful of taxis, and a man on a bike with balloons tied to the basket who almost hit them and who swore at them as he swerved into the curb. The Ula maintained her focus and now pulled Pepper into the bakery directly opposite the hotel. She continued on, behind the case of glossy pastries and petit fours, into a room where a few guys wearing bandannas were stacking trays of proofing bread. One of them asked Ula a question, but Ula ignored him, moving briskly past them and out the bakery's back door. Pepper went along, keeping pace. There were a few more alleys and another shortcut through a restaurant, a kitchen that smelled like cabbage, filled with employees eating bowls of rice with fried eggs on top. Then they were far enough away from the hotel that Pepper felt the Ula's grip on her arm relax. They continued along the sidewalk, at a less frenzied pace, and as they walked, Pepper saw a second Ula emerge from another alley, another back door. The Ula in jeans, now wearing a pair of aviators and a fedora. Eventually, the third Ula appeared, with cat-eye sunglasses and a scarf tied over her hair. They were staggered on the sidewalk but confined to one side of the street. It felt like a funeral procession. A procession of Ulas, Pepper thought. A wake of them. A vexation, a strangle, a shroud.

They walked for a long time, and the Ula at Pepper's side was silent the whole time. This Ula wore ballet flats and had very cold hands, and her gait made Pepper unpleasantly aware of the lack of grace in her own movements. She shed the chef outfit. She wasn't sure what part of the city they were in now. The buildings were mostly old and industrial.

Then they turned a corner and the formation changed, one Ula hanging back a few hundred feet, one moving ahead. The Ula with Pepper tightened her grip again, pinning Pepper in place with her talons. Pepper watched as the forward Ula circled to the rear of what looked like an abandoned warehouse. A minute later, the loading dock door rolled open. The Ula kept hold of Pepper's arm and continued down the sidewalk while the second Ula entered. They went in one by one, each entering a few minutes after the one before, like clockwork. Pepper and her Ula were last. The neighborhood was quiet, though there must have been people who'd seen them.

As soon as they were inside, the Ula with the talons pulled down the dock door behind them.

"You get the other side," she told Pepper, and latched a lock to the door's left.

Pepper did as she was told. She was sweaty, and her feet hurt. She needed a cold paper towel for the back of her neck, a bowl of ice cream, a quiet room in which she could process the existence of three Ula Frosts. The lock was rusty, and the residue clung to her palm. She wasn't sure if they were locking the men from the Everett Group out or locking Pepper in. Behind her, someone turned on a lamp. The warehouse was a vast space filled with shadows. There were some birds up in the rafters, broken windows way up high. She turned, expecting to see three Ula Frosts. But there were more than that.

Pepper scanned the room and counted, twice. There were nine. Nine Ula Frosts in front of her.

"That was an adventure," the head Ula said. She removed her sunglasses and scarf and gave them to one of the new Ulas, who dragged to her a chair from a stack against a wall. "Now, where were we?"

Pepper looked around the room. Ula had been painting self-portraits. The floor was studded with large drains. The other Ulas watched Pepper with varying degrees of curiosity.

"I should get in touch with Ike," she said. She felt fully incapable of communicating anything right now, but it seemed important to make it clear that someone would notice if she went missing. "He thinks I'm on my way home."

"Who's Ike?" Ula said.

Every Ula was blank-faced at the name. Pepper blinked, hoping some of them might be gone when she opened her eyes.

Ike had met one of them, but no one showed any signs of recognition.

"My husband," Pepper said.

"Oh," Ula said. "Right. There'll be time for that later. You're not going back today, anyway."

"I'm not?" Pepper said.

"Of course not," Ula said. "They'll be waiting for you at the airport. Our priority, beloved child, is keeping you safe."

The other Ulas nodded in unison. They were all the same person, but they weren't. Pepper needed a cold paper towel for the back of her neck. She took a deep breath and got herself a chair from a stack that was swathed in cobwebs. This wasn't their regular base of operations. Above her, Pepper noticed a long metal rail studded with hooks. This also wasn't a warehouse—it was a slaughterhouse. Ike had once collaborated on a project about the lives of immigrants who worked in Chicago's Union Stock Yard at the turn of the twentieth century. It had opened at Christmastime because it was considered festive. Ike had shown Pepper photos of the hogs in pens on the roof. They were driven up there after arrival so they could cool down before they were killed.

"Back to work," the head Ula said. She pulled a list from her pocket. Pepper looked for the mole Levi Crow had described, but she was wearing a pair of black lace gloves. "Fake my own death: check." Another Ula handed her a pen, and she made a deliberate line across the page. Small, simple tasks. "Next: get the painting."

"What painting?" Pepper said.

"Oh boy," one of the Ulas said.

"Shush," said another.

She saw the Ulas exchanging looks. The room was tense, a slack rope the Ulas had pulled taut. The head Ula leveled them with her eyes, and they all looked at their feet in unison.

"There is a painting," she said. "Those men from the Everett Group, they are less concerned with aesthetics than with what they believe they might learn from my work. And there is one piece they want above all others."

One of the Ulas unwrapped a stick of gum from her pocket. Another cleared her throat—an injured throat-clearing—and the gum-chewing Ula took the pack from her pocket and tossed it to her. Pepper wondered what the gossip was like among them. If ever there was a culture begging for an ethnographic study, it was this one.

"It's a self-portrait," the head Ula said. "And there's no telling what could happen if they were able to extract knowledge about the unlocking of universes from it. Mayhem! They cannot be trusted with that power." She looked intently at the list as if she might be too busy reading what Pepper could see was only three lines to answer further questions.

"Is it the one at the postal museum?" she asked.

The head Ula looked up. Behind her, Pepper noticed two low concrete partitions, running parallel to form a narrow corral. At the end, there was a massive grate in the floor.

"Oh," Ula said. "Oh, you know about it, then? Yes, that's the one."

"*Self-Portrait with Nothing*," Pepper said. From the Ulas, there was a communal inhalation. Pepper was the nothing, they all knew, and though she didn't say that out loud, it rang like a goddamn siren in her head.

"I've never been very good with titles," the head Ula said. "I'd just leave them all untitled if I could. But I can't. There's a convention. Otherwise, how would anyone know which one you're talking about?"

"Actually," Pepper said, "I heard a rumor about that painting the other day."

"Rumors, rumors," Ula muttered. She was studying her list again. "Everyone wants to pretend they know something when they know nothing at all."

Pepper waited for Ula to ask what the rumor was, but she didn't. "The rumor is that the painting was the first," Pepper said. She withheld the part about the painting being in danger. Ula's expression remained unchanged. Now a couple of the Ulas were chewing gum, and the pack was floating around the room. Some of them moved oddly, with too much effort, like they were underwater. One of the Ulas threw the pack at another who wore thick-lensed glasses, and that Ula dropped it. That was the clumsy Ula, Pepper noted. "Was it?" she asked.

The head Ula sighed. At home, Pepper spent an unreasonable amount of energy avoiding interactions that made her feel like a pest, though Ike was always quick to remind her that the feeling was, in most cases, her own projection. Pepper was not important enough in the lives of the people she casually encountered to register that level of annoyance. But she wasn't projecting now.

"Here is the story of the painting," Ula said, "if you *must* know. Many years ago, I began painting a self-portrait, returning through the work to you—my darling, my flower—to a moment I could never return to in life. But the more I painted, the more I could feel I wasn't painting myself in that moment, with you in my arms. I wasn't painting myself at all. Something was happening, my cherished blossom, fruit of my heart—a powerful energy shifting around me. Then I understood: I was painting a version of myself someplace else. Of course, I didn't expect her to just show up here. But she did! And that is the portrait hanging in the postal museum. Does that answer your question?"

"It answers one question," Pepper said. "But I have more."

"Questions!" Ula said. "When will the questions ever end?"

The head Ula was the dramatic one, Pepper filed in her mind. "I've hardly asked any questions," she said. Had she asked a lot of questions? She didn't think she had. "Feel free to jump in," she added to the other Ulas in the room. She didn't want them to feel left out. It was strange how quiet they were.

"Fine," Ula said. "What now?"

Pepper didn't want to ask the question, but she knew if she didn't, it would nag at her forever. "When you painted the baby," she said, "did a version of me come through too?"

Ula looked at her face in a way Pepper had grown used to this week, as if she knew her, but with an unexpected intensity, like she knew her more intimately than was possible.

"That's not how it works," Ula said. "The subject has to be there. There are rules, you know."

Pepper didn't know, which is why she'd asked. "So there are no . . . extras of me?" she asked.

"I've already answered that question," Ula said. One of the other Ulas popped her gum, and another tsked at her.

"Okay," Pepper said. "So that was, what, twenty-two years ago? Which one was first?"

She scanned the room, but none of the Ulas volunteered. One of them turned away, her body rigid. Pepper could see her digging her nails into the palms of her hands.

The head Ula puffed her cheeks and blew a stream of air through her lips. "Let's move on."

The Ula who'd turned away spun back. Pepper wasn't sure how to interpret what was happening. This Ula was angry— furious—but she was also too submissive to the head Ula to speak. There were rules and, presumably, consequences for violating those rules.

The head Ula observed Pepper observing this. "It's a touchy subject, dear," she said. "We're all terribly emotional about it." This seemed directed at the angry Ula. "The truth is, I lost one recently. We lost Number One."

"You lost her?" Pepper said. The other Ulas broke synchronization, and the energy in the room went unstable. The angry Ula turned and began pacing hard through the concrete corral. Another chewed her nails. One Ula started taking more chairs from the stack and banging them into rows.

"She was my right-hand woman for many years. Devoted, loyal. The only one who never took off." She glared at the angry Ula, who became perceptibly angrier but remained silent. "And then one day she was gone."

Pepper blinked and saw an extra Ula flicker in and out of the room. Maybe she was the one Ike had met. Any of these Ulas could be mistaken for the real one by an outsider.

"The Everett Group?" she said.

"It seems unlikely," the head Ula said. "If they thought they had me, why would they still be looking for me? I'm sure she's fine. She did so much for me, but there was always a discontent in her. I can't say I'm surprised." Pepper watched the other Ulas, but they were visibly avoiding reaction. "And I still have nine extras, which comes in handy."

"Eight?" Pepper said.

"What?" Ula said.

"There are nine of you total, so that makes eight extras."

"Oh," Ula said. "When you have too many of yourself, it's easy to lose count."

Pepper looked at the other Ulas, who seemed a little hurt.

"So when did the rest of them arrive?" Pepper said.

"Well, not right away," Ula said. "For many years, it was just me and One. Once I'd painted her here, I realized what a gold mine I'd discovered. Only a fool would fail to take advantage. I had to focus on taking commissions from the public. Art is fine, but no one can live without money. I have quite a following. Of course, I shun fame. But I am very famous."

"I've heard," Pepper said. She couldn't get a handle on this woman. It was like watching a bad play—everything Ula said felt overly rehearsed. She pressed on. "And what about the people you painted? Did you ever worry about how it would affect their lives?"

"Why on earth would I worry about that?" Ula said. "They were desperate, and desperate to throw their money at me. I gave them what they paid for. That is the beginning and end of my obligation."

Pepper thought about Levi Crow, the mother who'd died drunk driving, Iphigenia, who hadn't even understood then what she was paying for. Pepper had never wanted more mothers than she already had, and Ula was only confirming this instinct.

Still, there was something about the way Ula looked at her that made her feel like she was missing something.

"So why did you stop painting for other people?" she asked. "And when did you paint all these self-portraits?"

Pepper caught one of the Ulas blowing a bubble. When she saw Pepper watching, she sucked the bubble inward like she was inhaling it.

"Oh, my buttercup," Ula said. "I simply got bored. There wasn't anything fun about painting strangers and leaving just when things got good. And I liked having an extra of me. So why not more? But after One, they never stuck around for long. So I just kept painting them."

Ula stood and disappeared without explanation into a room at one end of the building. The slaughterhouse was quiet for a long minute, the alternates statuesque in their positions, until Pepper heard Ula tossing things around. She still had so many questions. Which Ula had been to Connecticut, and why, and why hadn't she acknowledged Pepper when she'd seen her? And was Ula really this flippant about the damage she'd done to those she'd painted? Especially to these other Ulas, who'd been ripped from their own realities. There were so many of them.

Ula emerged from the back room. "Has anyone seen a rabbit's foot? I can't find my lucky rabbit's foot."

The Ulas immediately checked their pockets. One, who carried a large black handbag, rummaged around inside.

"You don't seem like the superstitious sort," Pepper said.

"It's from home," Ula said. "I always carry it. It was in the church when we trashed it, but I'm certain I took it with me."

She bored into Pepper with that intense look again. It wasn't an expression of familiarity, exactly, but there was so much pain in it, a pain beyond anything Pepper could understand. Pepper looked away as she welled with homesickness. If she were home, her moms would give her ice cream, a sundae even, with butterscotch sauce and whipped cream and sprinkles and as many cherries as she wanted. She was an adult woman, but they always kept cherries on hand, just in case. She wanted to pet a dog. She wanted to feel Ike next to her, close but not touching. She just wanted to be near him.

The phone in her pocket buzzed, and she coughed to cover the sound.

"Is there a restroom?" Pepper asked.

"In the office," Ula said. She turned her attention to a row of overturned troughs against one wall. There were hiding places everywhere. Pepper let herself be swallowed by the shadows. The office was set up like the sacristy at the church—an austere bed against one wall, a makeshift kitchen against the other. Pepper found the lockless bathroom and wedged the door shut with her foot.

> you are not on a plane rn
>
> are you stalking me
>
> yes
>
> because i was worried
>
> you were not going to be on a plane rn
>
> i missed my flight
>
> again
>
> are you okay
>
> your moms have called nine million times
>
> they're probably on their way to poland
>
> by now

She could hear Ula outside, her voice clipped with frustration. The other Ulas didn't seem to be responding. She couldn't quite articulate to herself why she felt compelled to hide this from them. Pepper had come to Poland to find Ula, and now she had. Too many Ulas, bound in a knot Pepper couldn't hope to untangle, none of it right. But she knew that wasn't the real source of wrongness in her body. There was a different, nebulous dread thrumming through her, like that feeling she got when she was missing something. It wasn't even the Everett Group. Something that she couldn't see yet was wrong.

did you book another flight
i'm looking now
there are a couple more today
think i'm going to have to stay
till tomorrow
another day???
you realize tomorrow is sunday, right
and you have a job

Pepper did realize these things, and though normally she feared very little more than even a slightly disapproving email from her department head, she knew she couldn't leave now. She also knew, with an unsettling certainty, that she couldn't tell Ike why. Outside, the Ulas were dragging something heavy across the floor.

it's the police
what about the police
they want me to stay
in case they have questions
do they think you did it
that doesn't make sense
they could just call you
i know
but i have to stay
but why

Pepper focused on the feeling of her foot pressed against the door. She pulled up a pigpen diagram and decoded the note Ike had sent through Kacper: *I'm still here.* She couldn't keep something from Ike again. Of all the things in this universe she couldn't do, that was the one thing she couldn't do most. She'd promised. But she remembered with visceral specificity the feeling of standing in that square in Germany, her fingers coated with grease, waiting for him to respond. Those men were still out there. If she told Ike about the Ulas, he'd either think she was crazy or worse—believe her and get on a plane, knitting himself into her danger. An alarm went off in her body. In every universe, Ike was worth losing if it meant keeping him safe.

i can't tell you

Outside, Ula gave muted commands. Pepper felt the distance between her and Ike unfurling as she watched her phone. She didn't expect a response. The other Ulas were having a discussion. Their voices were so similar, but Pepper was starting to recognize differences in inflection and tone.

i'm sorry
if something happens to me

Someone banged on the bathroom door, and Pepper felt the pressure against her foot.

i'm sorry too
more than sorry
come home when you feel like it
i guess
you're on your own

The pressure against Pepper's foot increased, and she turned off the phone and slid it back inside her pocket. She flushed the toilet and moved her foot, and the door swung open so hard it clattered against the wall.

"What are you doing in here?" Ula said. Pepper wasn't sure what she expected to see.

"Sorry," she said. She pretended to button her jeans. "I'm not feeling well."

Ula huffed and led her back to the slaughterhouse floor. The Ulas were carrying sleeping bags up from a dark cellar even though it was still early. It was too risky for them to leave today, Ula explained. They'd camp here until Ula decided it was safe.

One of the Ulas, whose fingernails were painted dark sparkly blue, brought Pepper a sleeping bag. The bag had camo print on the outside, silver thermal lining on the inside. The blue-nailed Ula moved her sleeping bag close to Pepper's, then unzipped Pepper's at the bottom.

"In case you don't like having your feet covered," she said.

"How did you know that about me?" Pepper asked. Her feet were always hot. The first time she'd admitted it to Ike, not long after they started dating, Ike had responded by taking a jar of marinara from the refrigerator and pressing it against her soles. Was it possible the Peppers in other universes were more similar to her than she'd thought?

Blue lay on the floor and gazed at Pepper's face. "I just do," she said.

15

THE HEAD ULA, or Ula Zero as Pepper now thought of her, disappeared back into the office, so Pepper took advantage, circulating around the room and talking to the others, because she wanted to be able to tell the difference between them. The blue-nailed Ula, whom Pepper mentally nicknamed Blue, had been an art teacher and had named her daughter, who'd been raised mostly by her parents, Frida. When Ula painted Blue into this universe, only One and Two were there to greet her. "I couldn't accept what they were telling me," she told Pepper. "I thought I'd been in an accident, or that I'd been drugged. I tried to get on a plane home to find Frida. I just went to the airport. I didn't have money or a passport or ID. I didn't get very far. And then I wandered into a hotel lobby and found a television showing the news in English. I didn't recognize the president. In my universe, there's a different president."

She returned to Ula for a few weeks before leaving again, shortly after Ula admitted to her there was no way back home. Pepper understood the instinct to flee. Ula Zero wasn't easy to get along with. And Blue didn't realize there had been so many others, then.

She showed Pepper a drawing she'd done of Frida, which she kept tucked in the pocket of her jeans. Just like Pepper, only Frida had given up on taming her unruly hair and kept it short instead. Pepper liked the way it made her face look.

"The eyes and nose aren't quite right," Blue said. "I've lost some manual dexterity since I've been here."

Despite growing up in a different house, with a different family, Frida was like Pepper, observant and analytical. She was a sociologist who studied women's roles in marriage in Scandinavian countries. She had a partner named Emil whom Blue thought was boring, but he was devoted to Frida, and brought her flowers every Sunday, as his father had to his own mother. When Blue had been ripped from her life, Frida was seven months pregnant.

From Poland, Blue had gone to Denmark and lived there quietly, imagining herself to be continuing Frida's work sometimes as she bicycled past families sharing meals outside, under a strange universe's sun. She had fake identification and worked in a flower shop. She was good at arranging. Most of the others, she'd since learned, had followed similar paths. But they'd come back, one by one, after the news broke of Ula's disappearance. They had to see for themselves. It was hard to let go of the hope that maybe, somehow, there was still a chance to escape this world. They didn't know each other very well. But they were back now.

The next Ula went by Ursula and had been a story artist for an animated film studio in her universe. In this one, she drew custom caricatures, sold through an online shop that had been featured on a handful of design blogs. When Pepper asked questions, she tapped her foot, but the tapping was slightly arrhythmic. She wore a brace on her right knee. Ursula took Pepper back to a rusted conveyor belt and, from inside the gears, pulled a leather-bound sketchbook. She'd been working on a flip-book story about a girl from another dimension, plucked from her own world and set down in this one. The girl was drawn with big eyes and wild hair, and as she struggled to make sense of her new world, she discovered she had the power to see multiple universes at once, all of them superimposed over one another, like a stack of transparencies. Pepper flipped through the pages. Toward the end of the book, the girl began to look warped, but Pepper wasn't sure if the effect was intentional.

Ursula took the sketchbook back with a severity that surprised Pepper. She'd done something wrong, hadn't reacted as Ursula wanted.

"I suppose it takes a trained eye to properly appreciate it," Ursula said, and turned away.

The next Ula was the one with the skeleton key tattoo. She, like Ula Zero, was not impressed with Pepper's questions and, instead of answering, did pull-ups on the slaughterhouse rail, raising her neck dangerously close to the hooks. Pepper told Key that in ancient Rome, women were often the keepers of keys, which they wore on chatelaines along with nail cleaners and ear scoops. Key blinked at her but did not slow her pace. The rumor was that she'd been the first to return when Ula was reported missing. No one knew what she'd left behind in her universe, only that she wasn't wasting time if there was a way back.

The next Ula was busy with her hair, which she arranged over an eczematous spot on her scalp using a contraband compact mirror she'd stowed in her purse. Ula Zero disallowed mirrors for what she claimed were safety reasons. Compact had been a photographer in her own universe, her photographs revealing aspects of her subjects they'd never seen before.

"I was more famous there than she is here," she said. She kept her eyes on her reflection. "But those days are behind me."

Pepper watched her attend to her hair until the raw spot disappeared. In this universe, Compact ran the projector for a small movie theater in Prague. She liked sitting in the booth, alone and awash in the flicker of light. In the pile of her belongings, she had a big furry hat, which Pepper recognized.

"I saw you once," Pepper said. "At home. You don't remember."

She took Pepper by the chin and applied lipstick. She didn't have the same strength in her hands as Ursula or Key. "I was looking for something," she said, but didn't elaborate. In the mirror, Pepper saw that the lipstick complemented the colors of the bruise on her forehead. Compact snapped the lid back on the lipstick, avoiding Pepper's gaze. "She never mentioned you. You looked familiar, but then . . ." She swept her arm across the room. "So many people do. It's not always best to engage."

Pepper had thought that she'd seen Ula, and that Ula had looked at her like she was nothing. She'd been carrying the weight of it inside her ever since. But it had never been Ula in the first place. Or not *her* Ula, at least.

"What were you looking for?" Pepper said.

"A portrait," she said. She put the lipstick and mirror back in her bag and reorganized its contents.

"Which portrait?" Pepper asked. She was thinking about the self-portrait in the postal museum but then realized: there were more. There were a lot more.

"Ula seems to have misplaced them," Compact said. "She told us she sold them—an auction, anonymous buyers. Fed the same bullshit story, it turns out, to each of us. But none of us has been able to locate a single portrait. Funny how that works out."

The Ulas had returned, carrying with them an implausible hope of finding a way back to their original universes, but Pepper still didn't understand how the portraits fit in. No one, as far as Pepper was aware, knew for sure what happened when a painting was destroyed. Victor Morgan was found dead next to his slashed portrait, which was enough to give pause but wasn't definitive evidence. Did Compact want to find her portrait so she could protect it from destruction by the Everett Group? Or was the prospect of obliteration a preferable alternative to being stranded in the wrong universe indefinitely?

The next Ula was the one who'd walked Pepper from the hotel to the slaughterhouse, the one with talons and ballet flats. Pepper found her doing a backbend between the concrete partitions of the corral, contorting her wiry body into an improbable position, despite having one of her shoulders wrapped in a flesh-colored bandage. Talons had been a choreographer, Pepper learned. Her pieces were known to transfix audiences, as if the movement of her dancers onstage had a spell-casting effect. Audiences in her universe would leave the theater dazed or weeping, have unmooring, feverish dreams, wake the next morning and overthrow their lives. Talons had a son named Mick, who hadn't spoken to her for several years before she'd been torn away.

"It is impossible for a woman to be both a great artist and a good mother," she told Pepper. "You shouldn't even try."

"I'm not an artist," Pepper told her. "Or a mother."

Talons looked her up and down. Mick had chosen to go into

psychiatry, which disappointed her. He was big on setting clear boundaries, which, she explained to Pepper, she chose not to observe. In this universe, she worked night shifts for a temp service. It suited her best to avoid work that involved interaction with the public.

Pepper followed the next Ula as she scoured the room, making a neat pile of her belongings. They'd all been here before, at one time or another, and had stashed in the nooks the possessions they didn't want Ula Zero to find. This Ula had an unreadable ticket that was torn at one end, a sweater with moth holes in it, a few Polaroids, a matchbook. There was a tiny hole in her nostril, her skin haunted by a piercing done in a universe now inaccessible to her. Key, having finished her exercises, scolded this Ula, adamant that they were to leave everything as it was. The other Ulas turned their backs, as if this was a scene they'd witnessed before.

"Fuck her," this Ula said, stuffing her mementos into a black backpack. "My parents died in a car accident," she told Pepper. "I was only three." Pepper imagined her grandparents, a slightly different version of the couple she'd seen in the photo album, with slightly different hair, driving too fast, or being careful and dying anyway, leaving Ula and Tilda behind. "I never really knew them. Tilda remembered. She tried to tell me about them, but I was never much of a listener."

This Ula had been raised, along with Tilda, by their mother's sister, Magdalene, who lived in Vermont.

"Eight and I are different from the rest," she told Pepper. "All our lives diverged at different moments, but our diversion points were the earliest." Blue hadn't mentioned this, and now Pepper watched her, across the room, helping the clumsy Ula with the jammed zipper on her sleeping bag. "Magda and her husband had five kids. I think growing up in a big family changed me. I didn't have the luxury of being left alone. But sometimes I wonder. How I might've been different in that universe if they'd never died. If I would've become more like myself."

Vermont also had kids, though having grown up in a different state, she'd never met Michael Orlando. She'd married a man named Wyatt, who'd left her when the kids were young. The kids were good kids, she told Pepper. She looked like she might say more about them, but then her jaw set with anger. They were probably doing fine without her, Vermont said, though Pepper didn't believe she believed this.

In this universe, Vermont worked at a ski resort near Munich. It was easier for her to exist in this world if no one could recognize her as someone she was not.

The sky outside the broken windows began to darken, and Pepper hunkered down in her sleeping bag, which did nothing to diminish the feel of the hard, cold concrete beneath her. The Ulas settled on their pallets with books and mixed nuts, bags of beef jerky. Blue brought Pepper peanut butter crackers and a pillow.

"Do you like tea?" she asked. "We don't even know what you like."

Pepper wasn't sure what she liked either. She always wondered if she liked teas made with flower petals because she actually liked the flavor, or because she'd decided she liked it based on a social experience or sense of collective identity and she couldn't tell the difference. Her brain was too tired now, though, to spin around the anthropological conceptualization of identity, and she said yes to the tea, and when Blue brought it, warm and honeyed, it tasted right. Pepper always drank her tea unsweetened.

Her brain was so tired, and it spun anyway. What if she was wrong about everything she liked? What if she was wrong about her feeling of wrongness and had made Ike hate her for nothing?

Blue set a hand on Pepper's hair, then took it away.

"Sorry," she said. "You just look so familiar."

PEPPER WOKE THE next morning to the sound of sleeping Ulas. Some of them slept on their stomachs, like Pepper. Some of them snored. Pepper didn't know how her actual mother slept, because Ula Zero was still cordoned off in the office. It was harder to stay asleep on a cold concrete floor. The Ulas all woke at the exact same time. Pepper rolled her sleeping bag, watching them. There were still two Ulas she hadn't talked to yet, who'd evaded her the previous day. But Pepper had a compulsive need for completion, cataloging the Ulas the way she cataloged burials at home. It was always easier for her to cope with the strangeness of her life if she could pretend it was work instead.

Pepper found the clumsy Ula struggling again with the zipper of her sleeping bag. Her demeanor was jittery and hyperaware, and she avoided answering Pepper's questions, instead adjusting her thick-lensed glasses and chattering on about various restaurants in Wrocław, the antique trams, the carousel in the Old Town, the hippos at the zoo. Specs had been the second to come through, next after the one who'd recently disappeared, and though she'd left like the others, unlike the others, she'd returned a few months later after failing repeatedly to keep a job or apartment. Ula had allowed her to stay here at the warehouse, not at the church or wherever she and One spent most of their time. Ula and One had been together a long time before the others arrived. They were their own clique.

When Pepper asked about the universe she'd come from, Specs's eyelid twitched.

"I don't like to think about that place," Specs said with an unexpected harshness. "This one is better. You have no idea how good you have it. You should be ashamed to complain about anything. Don't complain about anything, ever."

Pepper hadn't complained about anything but apologized to Specs anyway. Specs gave the zipper a yank and the slider broke off. She looked to the office door before pocketing it, and Pepper rolled the bedding and stuffed it back in its bag before anyone else could see.

Pepper trailed the final Ula as she made herself busy around the room, restacking chairs, whisking other Ulas into conversation every time Pepper got close. Pepper finally got her alone after Blue cornered her and made the introduction.

"You're wasting your time," this Ula said. "I have nothing of interest to offer you."

She looked more like the image of Ula Pepper had in her mind than the others. Her hair was the same length as Pepper's and cut with the same layers, and she was somehow both plain and intense at the same time. She was the one who looked most like Pepper, though she wore an orthotic boot and thus walked with a limp.

"What did you do?" Pepper asked. "In your universe."

"I was a painter," Boot said.

"Did you do the same kind of work?" Pepper said.

Boot gave her a grim look. "No," she said.

"Then what did you paint?" Pepper said. "Were you successful?"

Boot was opening a granola bar she'd stowed in her bag. The others were still waiting for Ula Zero to wake up so they could get to the kitchen. This Ula was practical. She'd learned in her time here with Ula not to depend on her.

"Our lives were very similar," she told Pepper. "I grew up in the same house. I went to the same schools. I got pregnant just like she did." She stopped. Pepper recognized that look of hardening against what was about to come. "I didn't keep it. And then I was successful. No magic, no hiding. But I had the life I wanted."

Pepper felt a wave move through her body, the erasure of a version of herself she'd imagined into being. There were universes in which she'd never been conceived, and universes in which she'd been conceived but had never been born. Ula had been better off in that universe. She just didn't want to say it out loud.

"I see," Pepper said.

"But here you are," Boot said. She lowered her voice. "She told me you died at birth in this universe."

Pepper felt like she was flickering. Why would Ula want the others to think she didn't exist?

"Not in this universe," Pepper said. "In this universe, I'm alive."

"Though you don't seem like you're doing particularly well," Boot said.

"I guess not," Pepper said. She'd checked her phone inside her sleeping bag that morning and found no new messages from Ike, which filled her with an uneasy mix of relief and despair. Maybe she'd just stay here. Maybe there was a limit to the number of times your terrible decisions could rearrange space, and she'd already split this universe so many times now there was no way for her to go home. Maybe in an alternate universe, yet another Ula was painting Pepper right this second, and that Ula didn't have Ula Zero's restraint, and this Pepper was about to be ripped away from here. Ripped away from Ike, his inexplicably loud sneezes and his endless trivia, his rhythmless dancing and the way he thumped his leg like a dog when she scratched his back in the right spot. Pepper's eyes burned at the thought of it.

Boot adjusted her orthotic. In this universe, she did freelance graphic design. When Ula had been reported missing, she'd been living in Amsterdam, but she never stayed in one place for long.

"Are you okay?" Pepper said. "Can I do something to help?"

"It's nothing," Boot said. "We deteriorate over time."

The door to the office opened. Ula Zero stood in the doorway, her hair plastered against one side of her head.

"Don't just stand around," she said. "Get moving."

THE ULAS FELL into a morning routine, established out of necessity since they'd all returned. Compact arranged breakfast, while Boot and Vermont finished clearing the warehouse floor. None of the Ulas had been able to go shopping with the threat of the Everett Group looming, but there was a stash of instant oatmeal, dried apricots, and coffee. Talons found a lone Pop-Tart in a cabinet, and though Pepper worried there'd be a fight over it, it went to Specs without conflict, either out of deference or pity—Pepper wasn't sure.

Pepper was impressed by the level of organization and cooperation among the Ulas, despite their difficult histories with Ula Zero. Each of them had left on her own terms, unwilling to live alongside the woman who'd stolen her life, but now they were coexisting in a tenuous peace.

"Why didn't you just leave again?" Pepper asked Blue. Blue was stirring cups of instant coffee and passing them down the line. "When you came back and realized she was fine?"

Talons took one sip and passed her cup down to Key.

"We found a common enemy," Talons said.

"Ula?" Pepper said. They had every reason to hate her. She couldn't understand why they'd stick around this time.

"The Everett Group," Key said. She hadn't spoken directly to Pepper before. Her voice was hoarse. She drank the terrible coffee without hesitation. "They want that painting in the museum. We know that much. We don't know what could happen if they get it. We could all be in danger."

Boot took a coffee and looked into it with suspicion.

Vermont was drinking a cup of plain hot water. "Can't get home if you're Andy Warhol's physics project."

"Can't trust that bitch to make good choices either," Key said as Ula Zero rematerialized from her office, bowl of brightly colored cereal in hand.

Today, each of the higher-functioning Ulas had a task to accomplish and assigned times at which she would leave and return. It wouldn't do to have too many Ulas coming or going at once. They had to be strategic about it. Though these Ulas were different from each other in a multitude of ways, the predilection for order seemed to be a common thread.

Ursula, the story artist, left first, just after 8:00 a.m., long blond wig and sun visor pulled over her hair, for a municipal building where she was researching something about the Central Post Office. The day's tasks centered around this—the Ulas' quest to recover *Self-Portrait with Nothing*, which Ula Zero insisted was key to preventing the Everett Group from gaining power over them and, potentially, other worlds. At 9:00 a.m., Vermont left for the library, where she was sent periodically to print news reports about Ula. Ula Zero was particularly gleeful about this today. She was waiting to read her obituary.

At 10:00 a.m., Compact, having completed her rotation cleaning the kitchen and bathroom, set out on a surveillance mission. She and Talons, the two most attuned to small details and body language, were both assigned to this task. They'd been following two members of the Everett Group whom they'd discovered were staying at a hotel in the Old Town. But Compact had been gone for less than a minute before she came racing back through the loading dock, slamming the rolling door down with the weight of her body.

She tried to yell something, but she was too out of breath to be understandable. She fumbled with the lock at the side of the door. Someone had chased her and was now banging on the metal, the sound of which thundered across the slaughterhouse floor. The Ulas who remained dispersed to all the doors and windows, checking locks, moving at the exact same pace. Pepper was the only one without an assignment and stood alone in the center of the building. The banging on the door continued. A man was talking, but the rusty door was eating his words. Talons opened the hatch to the cellar, and the Ulas scuttled down until only Ula Zero and Key remained. Ula Zero held Pepper by the arm.

The hatch door's hinge creaked shut, and the sound of women's voices muffled as Key covered the hatch with an industrial mat.

"They'll be fine," Ula Zero said. "They know what to do. But you can't stay. We have work to do." She and Key rechecked the doors before having a private conference out of Pepper's earshot. Key didn't argue and pulled from a trough a couple of oversize hoodies, giving Pepper a spare. The hood made it hard to see. Then Key opened the rolling door.

"Just do what I do," she said.

"I don't love the sound of that," Pepper said.

"No one cares what you love right now," Ula Zero said.

There was a pause while the women stepped back and waited. It was too quiet—Pepper could hear the air whistling through Ula Zero's nose. But the peace was abruptly punctuated by the clunk of heavy boots, and in stormed Christian, like a man who'd seen too many buddy cop movies, checking the corners, flattening his back against the wall. He'd found a new sweater, this one a red-and-blue Fair Isle. He was committed to the look; Pepper would give him that. He took in the three women, indistinguishable in their black hoods, with an expression of disbelief.

And then Key ran, not at him but away toward the troughs against the back wall. Christian began to follow, but Ula Zero pushed Pepper at the rolling door, and he started to follow them instead. In response, Key changed course and ran in the direction of the office, and Christian again followed her, which gave Ula Zero and Pepper enough time to get out. There was a white Volkswagen bus parked in the dock, still running. Christian's plan must have been to grab whomever he could find and go. Ula pulled the door open and shoved Pepper into the driver's seat.

"Wait here," she said, and returned to the building.

The bus's radio was still on, throbbing out techno, and Pepper switched it off so she could think. She could drive away now, alone, and get help. She could call the police. A crash carried out from inside the slaughterhouse. Before she could decide, Ula Zero was back, hopping into the passenger seat.

"You're going to have to drive," she said.

"I don't think that's legal," Pepper said.

Ula put the bus in reverse and stretched her leg over to stomp on the gas. Pepper drove.

Pepper had driven the autobahn once, years ago, when she and Ike had rented a car, but he'd sprained his ankle while hiking in the Alps. She'd been terrified the whole time, but Ike had kept saying it wasn't an adventure if it wasn't at least a little unpleasant, their motto when things went spectacularly wrong. Things were always going spectacularly wrong when they traveled—

injuries and storms and lost reservations—but somehow the disastrous trips were always the ones they remembered as being the most fun.

"The gnomes are going to outrun us at this pace," Ula said.

"I'm driving a stolen car," Pepper said. "I think it's better for both of us if we don't get pulled over."

"The police are corrupt," Ula said. "This bus doesn't look like money."

Pepper shed her hood after they rounded the corner and did her best to keep cool as Ula squinted at the street signs and directed her through the labyrinth of the city. There was blood on one of Ula's lace gloves, but Pepper didn't ask. They drove to the Old Town and abandoned the VW. In a shop filled with tourists, Ula bought a baseball cap and Pepper a headscarf with a folk motif. They took a bus and got off in a residential neighborhood in the southern part of the city. Ula dragged Pepper along, walking briskly through the streets. Eventually, they stopped in front of a block of modern-looking apartments, white stone bisected by a long strip of varnished wood. Ula checked under a few mats until she found a key and let herself in. Inside, the apartment was sparse and cold—stainless steel appliances, white furniture, white walls. On the table in the entryway, a straight vase with a few blossoming branches. The chandelier over the dining table was made of a dizzying number of crystals. In the foyer, there was a pair of black leather boots—the boots Pepper had seen tumbling out the window of the church the day she and Scott had discovered it.

"Is this place yours?" Pepper said.

"Mind your own business," Ula said. Seeing Pepper's reaction, she sighed. She slipped off her shoes, rinsed the blood from her hand in the kitchen sink without removing the lace glove, and sat on a white sofa so pristine Pepper wondered if it had ever been used before. "Sit next to me," she said.

Pepper sat, but not close. Ula reached over and put a hand in her hair. Pepper remembered what Rafał had said, that Ula was changeable. Ula closed her eyes.

"My little duck," she said. "What a monster you must think I am." Touching Pepper's hair seemed to calm Ula, so Pepper let her. "I'm not always like this," she said. "I haven't always been like this." She seemed so tired now, a battery drained all the way down. "It was different when you were little."

"I never met you when I was little," Pepper said.

Ula opened her eyes. "No," she said. "Of course not."

"You told the others I was dead," she said.

Ula's jaw went hard. "I had to," she said. "You understand. It was all to protect you. If they'd known about you." Her body tensed. "Some of them are missing their own versions of you. Who knows what kind of chaos they would've brought into your life."

Pepper bit the inside of her cheek. Ula had never shown interest in her before now. She had no idea which Ula had been to see Ike, and even if it was this one, even if it was her mother, she hadn't bothered to take five minutes to see Pepper at the same time. She didn't want to feel so raw about it, but she did anyway.

"Why didn't you ever contact me?" Pepper said. It was a pathetic question, and she felt pathetic for asking it. This woman was so careless; her attention or affection wasn't something Pepper should crave. She already had so much in her life already. How could she want more?

Ula blinked. Pepper couldn't tell if it was confusion or if she was trying to blink something away. "I wanted to see you," she said. "I've wanted to see you for a long time." It wasn't a reason. She kept her hand in Pepper's hair, and her breathing slowed. "Of course I did, darling. I've never stopped thinking about you. Not for a single day." She tipped her head back on a cushion. "I might just rest awhile."

"That's fine," Pepper said. "Will the others . . ." She didn't want to be worried, but she was anyway. It was a lot of Ulas to worry about. "Will the others come here?"

"They don't know about this place," Ula said. "I can't share everything with them. For safety's sake, of course. But they'll be fine. Once the coast is clear. There are protocols."

She shifted and put her head on the armrest, and Pepper stood so she'd have room for her legs.

"My life is very hard, you know," Ula said.

"I know," Pepper said, though she didn't. She didn't know anything. Ula had said she'd thought about her every day, and it only made Pepper feel angry. It was a lie. She'd never bothered with Pepper before now, except to manipulate her; it had to be. Ula closed her eyes. She was the kind of person who fell asleep fast, without going over and over every stupid thing she'd ever said. Pepper was quiet. Ula was a liar, but Pepper knew the real reason for her anger wasn't that she wanted Ula's honesty. She was angry at herself for wanting the lie to be true.

She waited until Ula was asleep to rummage through the kitchen, where she found fast-food wrappers in the trash but no food in the refrigerator. Two beers, though, which wasn't nothing. Pepper cracked one open and padded around the apartment, until she found a bedroom with a white ruffle duvet-covered bed. The duvet smelled freshly laundered. Pepper sank into the down and drank. She checked her phone and found more faxed *Ekphrasis* pages but still nothing from Ike. She could hear Ula snoring in the living room, and it sounded wrong to her. There was something wrong about it.

But maybe the source of wrongness was Pepper, her sense of hearing twisted by her own pathetic desires. She'd spent so much of her life fashioning herself into a person who didn't care about Ula, who didn't want her love or approval, even though she knew, deep down, she did. She was ashamed of that part of herself, but it existed. And now that she was here, with the mother she'd imagined a thousand times, offering some semblance of love, she was numb to the connection. Maybe she'd done such a good job protecting herself from the chance of being hurt more by this woman that she'd also made it impossible for herself to accept whatever Ula was now willing or able to give. Ula sounded wrong to Pepper, but it was Pepper's own hearing to blame.

Pepper couldn't relax, but she also couldn't think about alternate universes anymore, so instead she skimmed academic journals on her phone, landing on an article about the definition of rarity in the diagnosis of ancient disease. Even though the archaeological record was by nature incomplete, occasionally it could present a fuller picture of a disease's prevalence, because osteologists could detect bone diseases that were asymptomatic and thus unseen by physicians and underrepresented in the contemporary medical record. Even so, the authors cautioned, the true prevalence of any phenomenon would always be impossible to assess when a population was already lost to time. The conclusion to the paper, which Pepper read more than once as her exhaustion closed in, was that while those who studied the past could get close to understanding what had happened, it was crucial to proceed with the understanding that they could never truly see the full picture.

16

ULA ZERO SLEPT the entire afternoon, into the night, and though Pepper's body was on high alert, pumping her full of stress hormones at the mere sound of the freezer's ice maker, she finally fell asleep herself around midnight. Ula woke her an hour later.

"Rise and shine, sleepyhead," Ula said tenderly.

She was showered and changed into a different, all-black outfit. She touched Pepper's face. Maybe this was what it was like with biological mothers, this vacillation between resentment and love. Pepper had friends who had this kind of volatile relationship with their mothers, who'd complain about them endlessly but also call them immediately over the slightest crisis. Pepper's own moms never made her feel the way Ula Zero did, though they'd had little patience for Pepper's brattiness when they used to drag her on the annual camping trip. She sat up and felt for her shoes, and the distance between her and her moms solidified in her chest. She was unprepared for the intensity and specificity of the feeling. She wanted Annie's scratched, puffy hands, the snack Lydia made with cereal and peanut butter and powdered sugar. She wanted them both cackling over an embarrassing sitcom; she wanted the taste of envelope glue as she helped them with condolence cards for clients. She turned away, wiping her face with her sleeve. Ula sat next to her on the bed.

"Oh, darling," she said. She held Pepper close to her, which made Pepper stiffen. She ran her hand over Pepper's hair. "We don't have time for this right now."

Pepper pulled away.

"I know," Ula said. "But I'm thinking of you. It's only a matter of time before those goons find us here. We have to end this. We have to get that painting."

Pepper heard cars driving by outside, the sound of a bus's brakes hissing. It was the middle of the night. "The painting in the postal museum," she said.

"That's right, my beautiful princess," Ula said. She was looking through Pepper. "It's time. We have to get our painting now."

Outside, Pepper heard two people walking, trying to be quiet about it. The sound stopped at the apartment door. She could feel her pulse in her eyelid. Then she heard a door open and close. The next apartment over. Pepper didn't want to help this woman with whatever she had arranged. But she also didn't want to worry about every single noise she heard, forever. She didn't want to be in this place anymore. She wanted to go home and not have Ula hang like a loose thread in her life anymore. She wanted to see what life felt like without this looming over her.

"Fine," Pepper said. "Let's go."

PEPPER AND ULA Zero took the scenic route, as Ike would've called it, weaving a circuitous path through the maze of Wrocław's streets to the museum. It was almost three, and the streets were quiet and hazy, only a few drunks left, having been evicted from the familiar embrace of their favorite pubs. Pepper recognized the array of satellites on the museum roof, artifacts of long-ceased communication.

"There aren't any cameras outside," Ula said. "But there are some inside. We've been trying to find a way to disable them, but none of us is any good at the technical stuff." She tried the door, which was locked.

"Why do the cameras matter?" Pepper said. Then she realized. "You're going to steal it?"

"Of course I'm going to steal it," Ula said. "What did you think we were here for?"

"Right now?" Pepper said.

Ula gave Pepper that hard look again, like she couldn't believe she had to tolerate Pepper's company.

"But you painted it," Pepper said.

"Yes, but I don't own it," Ula said.

"But who owns it?" Pepper asked. "Can't you just get them to give it to you? You're Ula Frost!" Pepper felt a desperation awake in her. Sure, she'd been attacked by some shady dudes who wanted control of multiple universes and examined the charred remains of one of her mother's alternates. But the postal museum was in the same building as the post office. Stealing was bad enough, but stealing from a state agency seemed extra ill-advised. Pepper could pretend she was conducting an ethnographic study for only so long. She was pretty sure she couldn't maintain that level of dissociation in a Polish prison.

Ula huffed. "If I knew who owned it, I wouldn't have to steal it," she said.

"That doesn't make sense," Pepper said. If Ula insisted on talking to Pepper like a child, she could do the same. "How do you not know who owns it if you painted it? Did you sell it? Did you lose it?"

"Sure," Ula said. "I sold it to someone, and they must've sold it to someone else. The important point here is that I don't know who currently owns it, but if Andy Warhol and his friends get ahold of it, we're all screwed. What would happen to you if they tore it apart in the name of science? What would happen to any of us? We need to get the painting, and we need to do it now."

Pepper looked up and down the street. The fog was denser than usual. It didn't sound like anyone else was around, but she couldn't see that far. Maybe the Everett Group was already there, waiting for them.

"So what's your plan?" Pepper said.

"Plan?" Ula said.

"Oh my god," Pepper said. "You don't even have a plan?"

"Well . . . ," Ula said. "We haven't gotten to that yet! It's your fault. Everything would've been fine if you hadn't shown up. They thought I was dead. You led them right to me!"

"You came to my hotel," Pepper said. "You marched me to your hideout!"

Was this what biological mothers did? Pepper wondered. Argued with you in the middle of the night about whether it was your fault you needed to break into a government facility and steal a painting? She supposed it would qualify as a bonding ritual.

Ula was pacing in front of the museum furiously. From the end of the street, they heard footsteps, voices. Ula froze.

"I'm going," she said. "I'll take care of it. You get in there and grab the painting."

"How in the world do you expect me to do that?" Pepper said. The situation felt increasingly unreal. Could she steal a painting? Maybe. Maybe she could if none of this was real.

"Break a window," Ula said. "How you get in doesn't matter if you're fast."

"Why don't you just paint another one?" Pepper asked. "You could tell those men it's the real one. You painted it once. They wouldn't know the difference."

"I can't," Ula said. "It wouldn't work that way."

"Why not?" Pepper said. The voices and footsteps were getting closer.

Ula inhaled slowly. She stood very close to Pepper. The voices slurred in Polish. They were just regular people, people who were still capable of having a good time.

"Listen, you ungrateful little bitch," Ula said. "I've spent my entire life protecting you. I've done everything for you. You don't even know. And now you're going to do this for me." She stopped. Pepper was all adrenaline now. The woman standing in front of her hated her. "I'm going to take care of them. Get the fucking painting. I want to go home."

She turned and disappeared into the mist, leaving Pepper on the museum's doorstep. The door was locked. The windows were barred. The painting was housed inside a thick protective case. She didn't know what to do. Her aloneness closed in on her. Ula's voice replayed in her head: *I want to go home.* There was no way out of here without the painting, no other way to make this universe safe again. Pepper wanted to go home. She didn't know what to do.

SOS SOS SOS

It wasn't the ideal time to be slow-texting, but Pepper was out of ideas.

> i know you're not talking to me
> I KNOW
> and i know i'm a terrible wife
> a terrible ungrateful person
> and i never tell you how much i love you
> which i do
> a lot
> i'm not good at anything
> and i broke my promise
> and i'm sorry
> you should have a better life
> without me
> but also
> right now i really need to do an art heist
> it's my only way out of here
> and i could use some help
>> wait what
>> an art heist
> there's this painting
> it's a long story
>> an art heist
> those hideous men are after this painting
> hoo boy when i tell you the title
> and also there are all these ulas
> there are nine of them
> which i was afraid to tell you before
> she's been painting self-portraits for years

i know this doesn't make any sense
but i have to get the painting
which is in the post office
which I am outside of right now
in the middle of the night
in poland
alone

Pepper could hear Ula talking to the drunks, chatting away like they were old friends. Ula was being as sweet as pie to them.

processing

They were heading in a different direction now, their voices trailing away. Ula was leading them away.

it's too bad it's not daylight savings
i don't see how that's relevant
because there's an extra hour
and security cameras rewrite that hour
on their tapes
i always thought that would be a good time
for a heist
okay
but it's not daylight savings
yeah
so what do I do
not steal the painting?
i've considered that
and
i've come to the conclusion that maybe
i should just steal it
never a dull moment
at least i can say that about our life
it's not an adventure if it's not at least
a little unpleasant

The voices and footsteps were gone now, Ula off with the drunks or elsewhere, embedded in the fog.

> what's the situation on the ground
> lol
>
> the door is locked
> and there are bars on the windows
> is the door the only way in
> is there more than one door

Pepper hadn't thought about another entrance, because she wasn't very good at art heists. She circled the building. There was a bay of loading docks, but all the doors looked heavy and loud. There was also a door on the side of the building, predictably locked, but this one was wooden and rickety-looking.

> there's a door on the side
> maybe i could jimmy it open
> but then probably there are alarms?
> probably!
> this is crazy, you know
> i'm still processing the nine ulas thing
> same

Pepper scanned the ground. There was some broken amber-colored glass, crumpled and soggy pieces of paper. There was a yellow umbrella someone had tossed that was already rusting. There was a crushed paper coffee cup. Pepper picked up the broken umbrella.

> i have a broken umbrella
> thank god
> there are pointy metal bits
> this would be better if you'd had time
> to dig a tunnel or something
> agreed

the thing about heists
is that you have to plan the getaway
there was one in sweden
where the guys stole a helicopter
but you probably don't have access to
a helicopter
not at the moment
there was also a heist in antwerp
very elaborate planning
they had copied keys
and fake security footage
I don't have those things
they got busted from dna
on a half-eaten sandwich
well i'm not going to eat a sandwich right
now
so at least you have that going for you
ISAAC
okay let me think
historic heists
do you have any smoke bombs
negative
prosthetics
negative
a speedboat
i'm not near water
face cream?
what
one time people hid diamonds in face cream
i'm trying to steal a painting
so that's not helpful then
negative
in the 1600s this irish dude
tried to steal the crown jewels
dressed like a priest
with a prostitute pretending to be his wife

        it didn't work
        but charles ii made him a member of court
that's fascinating
        but unhelpful
yeah
think i'm just gonna use this broken
umbrella
and try to pick the lock or something

    Pepper pulled out one of the metal ribs from the umbrella, cutting the palm of her hand in the process. Now she'd probably get tetanus too, which was perfect. Dying of tetanus in a Polish jail, the perfect way to end spring break. She took the rib and jammed it between the door and the frame, wrenching it back and forth. And then she heard a siren and saw the flashing lights.

welp
            oh no
i'm going to be arrested now
            i can't tell if you're kidding or what
the painting is called self-portrait with
nothing
in case someone asks later
            pepper
i'm the nothing btw
            are you serious
            pepper
            pepper????
            i love you too
            btw

17

THE ARRESTING OFFICERS took Pepper's phone, and she could hear it buzzing away in the front seat. She watched for Ula through the window as they drove away. Maybe this was her plan all along—let Pepper get arrested to distract the police while she went in and took the painting herself. Pepper had kept her expectations for Ula low, but an unasked grief still echoed through her body. Out of all the possibilities she'd imagined for Ula, this reality had never occurred to her.

In the hall at the police station, they passed Dr. Brodowski, carrying a sticky pastry with strawberries on top. He indicated in Polish for the officers to stop. Pepper didn't understand, but he took a wadded tissue from his pocket and dabbed at her bleeding hand. He asked the officers a question, and they answered in a dismissive tone. He gave Pepper a puzzled look, but that was all he had time for before they put Pepper in the interrogation room and locked the door behind her.

The interrogation room was pleasantly cool. Pepper wondered what they'd done with her phone. They'd taken her passport too. Maybe they'd find her in some database and call Ike. Maybe the funereal lawyer who'd come to the house would help. But everyone who could help was so far away, and now that she was sitting in a pleasantly cool room with no one demanding anything from her and no one to disappoint, she thought it wouldn't be so terrible to stay awhile. It was Sunday night at home, and before long, undergrads would be sitting in her lab, peeling skin from spring break sunburns, waiting for her lecture on genetic skeletal anomalies. The bruise on her reflection's forehead was getting greener. Here, she was safe.

She put her head on the table, which was also pleasantly cool, and realized she was tired, and closed her eyes.

When she opened her eyes, Officer Jagoda was removing the cuffs from her wrists. Her hair was no longer in a French braid but loose and kinked around her face. Pepper, tucked in a small and necessary fugue, hadn't heard her come in.

"They put them too tight," Jagoda said.

"I didn't notice," Pepper said.

Jagoda opened an antiseptic wipe and cleaned Pepper's palm before applying a Band-Aid. She was looking at Pepper with intense concern. "You were trying to break into the postal museum," she said.

There wasn't much point in lying. "Yes," Pepper said.

"Because of your painting?" Jagoda said.

Pepper didn't understand. Jagoda set Pepper's passport on the table between them. "You are Pepper Rafferty?" she said.

Pepper could only nod.

"There is a painting in the postal museum that belongs to you," Jagoda continued. "This is the painting?" She set something else on the table, a sheet of paper printed with a pixelated image of *Self-Portrait with Nothing*. "The man at the museum said this painting is on loan from Pepper Rafferty. So I do not understand why you would want to break in."

Pepper watched her reflection in the two-way mirror, as if her reflection might be an alternate self who understood the many things Pepper did not. Why would Ula want her to steal a painting that already belonged to her? It didn't make sense. "I can't explain," she said.

"I know," Jagoda said, with more sympathy than Pepper expected. "I lost my mother recently too. It has been very hard." She looked at her hands in her lap.

"I'm sorry," Pepper said. "Were you close?"

Jagoda shook her head. "I did not understand her most of my life. I did not try to understand her. At the end, it was different, but you know. It is still very hard. No one is perfect when it comes to mothers."

Pepper ran her fingers over the bandage on her hand. Sitting next to this woman's grief softened her into silence.

"We are not going to charge you," Jagoda said. "You have been injured, and your mother has died. I do not think you are in your mind."

She put a hand on Pepper's hand, which made Pepper feel the rawness of the wound. At every point during this trip, someone had taken care of her—when she was not in her mind, when she was too much in her mind, so many times when she didn't deserve it.

"Thank you," Pepper said.

"If you like," Jagoda said, "the man from the museum said you may take the painting with you. I can have an officer drive you back."

The veneer of comfort receded, allowing the panic in Pepper's body to reemerge. What would happen if she walked out of the museum with the painting? What would happen if she left it?

"I don't know," Pepper said. "I don't know what to do."

Jagoda stood, and Pepper stood along with her. "Things that feel impossible now," she said, "when you do those things, later, you do not regret them."

You only regret not doing them, Pepper thought, though she wasn't sure what felt most impossible to her. She could stay or she could leave, but either way she was abandoning something.

Jagoda signaled for a male officer to come. "To the museum?"

"To the museum," Pepper said.

THE MORNING SKY was all pink as Pepper rode back to the postal museum. In the future, Ike would be in charge of all postal transactions. Her phone's battery was getting low, but she texted him anyway.

i'm out

of jail?????
are you okay

except for the tetanus
        okay good
        are you coming home yet
quick stop at the post office
        pepper
they're giving me the painting
bc apparently i own it?
and have been loaning it to them
all along!
        well that makes as much sense as anything
        else
agreed
but then i'm going STRAIGHT TO THE
MOTHERFUCKING AIRPORT
        lol GOOD CALL
i'm going to turn off my phone
so it doesn't die
but i'll update you when i can
        i'm v much looking forward to making
        ALL the prison jokes
        i'm gonna give you a little time first
        but prepare yourself
i honestly cannot wait

THE MAN AT the postal museum had the painting wrapped for Pepper when she arrived. The officer who'd driven her offered to take her to the airport, which Pepper suspected was to keep her from causing any more trouble, and she accepted. She didn't know how she'd get the painting on the plane or what she'd do with it once she got home. The painting felt like a horror movie virus—she'd never be safe until she passed it off to someone else, someone unsuspecting and undeserving of its cost. Ula Zero and the Everett Group couldn't be far behind. But it would be easier to come up with a solution when she wasn't looking over her shoulder every five seconds. All she had to do now was focus on small, simple tasks.

Pepper struggled out of the police car with the wrapped painting, with no help from the officer, who sped off as soon as her door was closed. Around her, people streamed through the airport's entrance, dragging their luggage, zombified by the malaise of air travel. Normally, she'd be anxious about winging it this way—she only had her passport and phone. She didn't have her wallet, couldn't buy herself food, hadn't even changed clothes in two days. But Pepper wasn't anxious. She was leaving the Ulas behind. Maybe it wasn't the right thing to do, but she'd spent her entire life fighting an instinct to flee, and now she was embracing it. A man wearing a tie and a leather jacket bumped into her mindlessly, and she wanted to hug him. A woman pulled wearily at two whining children, and Pepper wanted to pick them up and spin them around. She was going home.

Then, from the corner of her eye, she saw someone in black. A moment later, from the other side, a second dark blur. *No*, she told herself. *Black is just a popular color for clothing. It's what people who live in cities wear.* She took a step toward the door and found her path blocked by another figure in black. A woman in an oversize black hoodie. She didn't need to look around to know she was surrounded. A few people paused on their way in, wondering if all these women in black were part of some kind of performance art. But no. They were here for Pepper.

Pepper had a slow-motion vision of her stopping this now, throwing herself onto the ground and screaming and flailing. Certainly, if she made a big enough scene, security would be dispatched and cart her off to put an end to the disruption. But even as she saw it, she knew it was a Pepper in a different universe. The Pepper in this universe, the Pepper who'd given in to the instinct to run, knew she couldn't follow through with it. The Ula in front took Pepper by the arm and led her to a maroon van, running in the Kiss and Fly zone. Pepper felt the talons against her skin, felt two more Ulas following, close enough that she could hear their breathing, blocking any chance of escape. One of them, whom Pepper recognized as Key when her sleeve slipped back, took the painting and shoved it in the van first, which made it difficult to then climb inside. Talons gave Pepper a shove toward the back of the van. Pepper settled and watched the others awkwardly navigate into their seats.

The Ula in the driver's seat squealed off. No one bothered with seat belts. From the passenger seat, Ula Zero pulled off her hood and glared at Pepper.

"I trusted you," she said. "I won't make that mistake again."

"You left me," Pepper said. She knew better than to argue with this woman, but maybe that was part of the deal with mothers and daughters. "And I still got the painting."

Ula Zero had no response to this and sat fuming in the front. Pepper wondered what kind of grand overtures the other Ulas had been required to make in order to acquire forgiveness for their faults and indiscretions. The Ula to Pepper's right put a hand on her knee, but Pepper couldn't look. The semblance of tenderness set her on the edge of tears.

"So let's get this thing stashed someplace," Pepper said. It wouldn't be a permanent solution, but Pepper didn't know what a permanent solution to the problem would be. The only permanent solution she could think of would be for Ula and the painting to stop existing. "I just want to go home now."

"I just want to go home," Ula Zero said. "Exactly."

It started to drizzle, and they drove through the streets while the rain played against the windshield. The driver was taking them back toward the slaughterhouse, but once they got close, she veered into a vacant lot. Whatever had once stood here had been demolished, and there was rubble and steel beams and construction equipment at one side. The Ula to Pepper's right gave her knee a quick squeeze. Pepper looked down and saw the blue nail polish.

The van had three rows of two seats, and a final row of four. Ula Zero moved from the front to the last row, taking the painting with her, and tore at its wrapping while the other Ulas shifted toward the driver's seat. Every part of the interior was gray. The mood in the van was somber, with none of the bickering Pepper expected. These women were used to navigating tight spaces, but there was something else happening, a tension that was on the verge of snapping. There were five of them, not counting Ula Zero. Pepper wondered where the others were. She didn't think Specs was there, and she worried briefly about her being left alone.

Ula Zero motioned for Pepper to join her in the back, where the painting was propped against two seats. The other Ulas stayed silent in the front, a ruin of mothers, watching.

Pepper looked at the painting. The windshield wipers squeaked. She was struck by how young and vulnerable Ula looked in it. The baby in the painting had her tiny hand clenched around one of Ula's thumbs. But this was Pepper and Ula in a different universe. That's how Ula Zero had said the portrait worked—she had painted not herself but a version of herself who'd been elsewhere. Pepper compared the two Ulas, trying to see how they were different. Ula Zero had the same three dark moles on her neck, piercings at the same points on her earlobes. The main difference was that the Ula in the painting looked so desperately unhappy, while the Ula kneeling next to Pepper looked joyful now, almost rhapsodic as she examined the face, the brushstrokes. She took a utility knife from her pocket and clicked it open. She extended the knife to Pepper.

"You should be the one to do it," she said, moving to the third row. "I don't know what'll happen to me. No one's sure how it works. But we have to try. I don't want to fuck it up partway through."

Pepper took the knife blade first and held it against her palm, resisting the temptation to squeeze hard enough to cut herself again. "Do what?" she said. She turned the knife around.

"Destroy it," Ula said. She took a deep breath and closed her eyes.

Pepper held the knife tight in her hand and felt the rigidity of her arm. Iphigenia had said the destruction of a portrait could lead to disaster but had failed to specify what *disaster* might mean. The Ula in the painting was hard and scared, but she held her nothing protectively. It was the creation of the painting that was her disaster.

A shadow loomed over her, as if the Ula who did the painting was already making her presence known across the divide.

Ula Zero opened her eyes and looked at Pepper expectantly.

"What if something terrible happens?" Pepper said. She twisted so her body was in front of the painting.

"Nothing terrible is going to happen," Ula said. "Just do it."

Pepper wasn't sure if she believed the Everett Group, but she was equally distrustful of Ula. She looked at the painting. The skin on the baby's neck was mottled. The nails on young Ula's hands looked chewed. The trees in the background gave a sense of sway. The painting radiated a hum of possibility. The painting was beautiful.

"I don't think I should," Pepper said.

"Fine," Ula Zero said. "One of you do it." She reached for the knife, but Pepper moved her hand away. "Give me the goddamn knife," she said.

There wasn't enough space in the van for Ula Zero to maneuver around her.

"Why do you have to destroy it?" Pepper asked. "Can't we just hide it?"

The other Ulas remained motionless in the front, but Pepper could feel their energy, like someone had turned on a Tesla coil.

"You stupid girl," Ula Zero said. "You don't understand anything. Destroying the painting is the only way." Her jaw set with determination. "Give me the goddamn knife." She lunged at Pepper, and Pepper fell back across the row of seats. There was a Polish coin on the van's muddy floor mat, a tarnished eagle wearing a crown. Pepper extended the knife blade defensively. She wasn't sure why she was fighting for this. All she had was a feeling of wrongness. If she did what Ula said, she could go home.

Then Ula Zero coughed into her lace-gloved hand, and when she took her hand away, Pepper could see that a piece of her lower lip had crumbled, a wad of flesh now wet in Ula's palm. *We deteriorate over time.*

Pepper scrambled upright and pressed her back against the painting. Ula Zero leaned in.

Pepper waved the knife. "You're not really her," she said.

Ula Zero didn't flinch, didn't speak, didn't laugh a maniacal laugh. She just kept leaning toward Pepper, serious and slow. She didn't know Pepper owned the portrait, because she had nothing to do with Pepper owning it. It must've been handled by the lawyer, on the real Ula's instruction, like the property in London.

"Which one of you is really her?" Pepper looked at the other Ulas. Their faces were shadowed by their hoods, but they were turning to each other now. Pepper could feel the betrayal like a fog. They didn't know. Blue, almost imperceptibly, shook her head.

"None of them is," Ula Zero said. "She's not here. She never would've allowed this."

"Where is she?" The windows were steamed up, obliterating the outside world.

"She's not here," Ula Zero said again. "She never appreciated any of us. Never thought about what she was doing. I was the first, and I did everything for her. She promised she'd send me back. But she's a liar!" She was getting louder now, spitting as she talked, her anger verging on animalistic. "She never cared about anything but herself. Not you. In my universe, I was better. I kept you and raised you, and you weren't like—"

"Like what?" Pepper said. She couldn't imagine a version of herself raised by this woman. Maybe she was funnier, she thought. Sometimes people who have very hard lives turn out funny.

"She wasn't . . . whatever you are," Ula said. "I don't know. She was mine. And now I'm going back to her. Give me the goddamn knife."

She lunged at Pepper for the last time, but Pepper, devoid of most skills and virtues, was faster, and when she dodged out of the way, Ula hit her head against the window. Pepper kept hold of the knife while she grabbed the painting and wrenched the van door open and ran. She could hear her moms' voices in her head, scolding her for running with a sharp object. She took one last look at all the Ulas, still packed together and frozen at the front of the van. Then someone moved and closed the door.

Pepper ran through the lot with the knife and the painting, past the construction equipment, past the steel beams and the rubble. It was like trying to run with a suitcase. It was still raining, and Pepper felt the puddles soaking through her shoes. All it would take was for someone to start driving. There was a dog with matted fur prowling at the edge of the lot, sniffing an empty bag. It raised its head and watched Pepper with curiosity. Pepper kept running. The buildings in this neighborhood were industrial and dreary. At least she'd worn sensible shoes. She heard a vehicle pulling up behind her. If it came down to it, would she be able to use the knife to defend herself? She was almost certain she wouldn't. She'd taken gross anatomy in grad school, cut through the tissue of a woman who'd died at twenty-five to find her uterus, but a living body was a different thing. Pepper was only competent with the dead.

The vehicle continued past her, a silver car, splashing dirty street water at her ankles. She lowered the knife. She felt like she was going to pass out. It was hard to pretend nothing was real when every part of your body burned with fear and exertion. She heard someone running behind her and spun around.

"You shouldn't run with a knife," Blue said, panting.

BLUE KNEW THE neighborhood, and she knew where to hide. They waited awhile in the courtyard of an office park before winding through alleys and boarding a bus. Pepper tucked the knife behind the painting. The rain had stopped, but she and Blue were both soaked. A few people looked at her, a wet, frazzled woman carrying a large, partially wrapped painting, still out of breath, more from nerves than anything else. Pepper tried to fix her face with indifference. Blue kept her eyes on the window.

They got off at the botanical garden, and Pepper followed Blue past tangles of flowers to a bridge that was enclosed by the limp branches of a weeping tree. Ike would know what kind of tree it was. On the bridge, the air was cool and green-smelling. The light came through the leaves in needles. Pepper could hear water moving beneath them, the feeling around them like the air before a storm, even though the storm was over.

"You're not her, are you?" she said. There was too much happening to process. She needed processing time. The only thing her brain could fully grasp was that through all of this, she still hadn't met her mother.

Blue pulled back one of her sleeves to reveal a gauze bandage, which she unwrapped to expose a patch of crumbling skin.

"I haven't been here as long as most of the others," she said. "But we all fall apart in the end."

Haaa, Pepper thought. If Ike were here, they might be able to laugh at the absurdity of this. It wasn't so funny alone.

"Do you know where she is?" Pepper asked. She didn't like the way Ula Zero had said, *She's not here.* But maybe this universe's Ula had some kind of power over her alternates.

Blue was shaking her head, puzzling through it. "I wasn't the first to come back. Six was already here. Four. Two never really left." Pepper tried to match numbers to names. Key. Compact. Specs. Blue took a weeping branch and began to strip it of its leaves. "She told us One was gone, and we believed her. It made sense. She'd been trying to get back for so long. Ula claimed she sold all the portraits, but we've looked for the records. We've been fucking looking." She stopped. Pepper could see the same anger she saw in the other Ulas as she unwrapped and rewrapped her gauze. Blue was just better at controlling it. "Galleries, the banks. Everyone has looked in different places, but none of us has found any records." The time Pepper saw Compact in Connecticut— that's what she was doing. "But we looked and looked. I thought One finally snapped. Just not like this."

"No one realized?" Pepper said. The whole time, the feeling of wrongness. Pepper hadn't trusted herself.

"It was a pretty convincing impersonation," Blue said. "But the gloves." She rubbed at her bandage. "Ula never wore gloves."

"How long ago did you come back?" Pepper said.

"Just after she was reported missing," Blue said. "A few days after I saw the news."

Haaaa, Pepper thought again. The original problem had been the problem all along. Ula Zero must not have known about the calls to Gordon. Maybe Ula had concealed them from her as a kind of built-in security system.

"Is there some other place she could be?" Pepper asked. She thought about the flat in London, the church, the slaughter-house, the apartment. "Is there any other property she owns? Or places where she spent her time?"

Blue kept picking at the leaves, which piled at their feet. "I got the feeling there was a lot she didn't tell us."

Haaa, Pepper thought yet again. *Haaaa. Haaaaaaa.*

18

you're not going to believe this
but i missed my flight
again

                    pepper i love you
                    but WHAT IN THE WORLD
there was a knife fight involved
didn't even make it inside the airport
                    where are you
                    are you safe
at a hotel
different hotel than before
and guess what?????
i'm STILL trying to find ula
                    didn't you already find like nine of her
yep!
but it turns out none of them are real?
haaaaaaa
                    lolol
                    this would only happen to you
that does not make me feel better
                    sorry!
i can't do this
                    do what
find ula
or literally anything
i'm not good at anything
i'm not good at solving problems
i'm not a good daughter or a good wife
i'm not good at telling you things

or saying i love you
basically anything involving words
i'm wearing smelly clothes
and my hair is awful
and i've been here failing for a week
i don't even know what i like
                    pepper
i might be spiraling a little
also i'm probably gonna get fired
                    breathe
no
YOU breathe
                    LISTEN
                    1. you are very good with bones (heh)
                    2. who cares about your hair and clothes
                    3. i don't love you because you're good with
                    words
phew
                    you've let students stay at our house
                    on at least three different occasions
                    you walked that one girl
                    to the counseling center
                    because she was too afraid to go alone
                    you sneak jars of kimchi and herring
                    into the clinic fridge so your moms
                    will find them
                    even though you gag thinking about herring
                    because you know it makes their day
                    that one time we found the baby deer
oh god
                    and you held it until your moms could come
                    to euthanize
                    you leave songs on my voice mail
                    when i'm grumpy
                    and i KNOW you hate leaving voice mail
also i'm a terrible singer

                    and yet you do it anyway
                    you hike with me even though mosquitoes
                    eat you
                    but you like dogs
                    and heavy blankets
                    you like cilantro
                    and desserts made with lavender
                    or roses
                    which is crazy because that all tastes like
                    soap
                    you know what you like
                    the thing you're bad at is seeing yourself
                    but everyone's bad at that
                    and that's why you have me
        are you finished
                            yes
        you can keep listing nice things about me
        if you want
        i'm not trying to make you stop
                        don't you have an ula to find
        yeah
        but just in case
        and with the acknowledgment that i'm bad
        at words
        this universe with us together
        definitely my favorite universe
        and i love you like a snake loves the sun
                            pepper
        i can't move without you

ACCORDING TO BLUE, Ula Zero had gone out alone every evening at exactly 9:00 p.m. She never took anything with her, never brought anything back, and she never told anyone where she was going. If she was keeping the real Ula somewhere, Pepper reasoned, all they had to do was find her and then follow her.

Easy peasy. They took a cab and checked the church, which was still cordoned off with police tape. The drapes at the apartment were wide open, with no sign of activity inside. The slaughter-house was the only place Blue could think that the Ulas would gather. They decided to wait until dark to stake it out.

Blue had gone to Ula's bank and claimed her wallet had been stolen, and the manager, who recognized her as Ula from the numerous times she'd demanded to see a manager on previous visits, allowed her to withdraw cash while waiting for a replacement card. While she and Pepper waited, she went to the drugstore near their hotel and bought herself a new, steelier shade of blue nail polish. Pepper ordered room service. This hotel, like Pepper's first in Wrocław, had neon lights outside, but it was fancier, with a bathroom whose walls were inexplicably made entirely of glass. Pepper's sandwich was the best sandwich of her life—pastrami with sauerkraut and garlic honey sauce. So at least there was that, Pepper thought. The best sandwich of her life was something.

Blue finished her nails and started on Pepper's toes. She told Pepper nail polish had been Frida's thing, and stopped partway through Pepper's left foot and went to the bathroom, where she sat on the edge of the tub and cried. There was no privacy in the room—Pepper could see everything through the glass. She blew on her toenails and heel-walked to the bathroom, where she sat on the floor. Blue had sent their clothes to be laundered, and they were both in plush white robes. The floor was pleasantly cool, and Blue calmed in Pepper's company.

"It started when I gave her the sex talk," Blue said. Pepper wadded some toilet paper, and Blue wiped her nose, trying not to smudge her nails. "I was rambling about condoms, and she got out all her nail polish and went to town."

"My sex talk involved pictures of cat penises," Pepper said. Annie had been gleeful about it, showing her the photos in one of her vet school textbooks. "They're barbed to keep the female cat from escaping. I think it was supposed to deter me from wanting to have sex."

"Did it?" Blue asked.

"No," Pepper said. Blue sank down next to Pepper on the floor. "In fact, my extensive knowledge of the penises of the animal kingdom eventually helped me seduce my husband."

"Frida knows all the species that are monogamous," Blue said. "Black vultures are her favorite. Emil liked that about her."

Pepper didn't know how to comfort someone who was an entire universe away from the people she loved most. "When you're finished, we should have room service bring us ice cream," she said.

Blue resumed painting Pepper's foot. "That sounds perfect."

AT DUSK, THEY took a tram across town to the slaughterhouse and waited in the shadows across the street with paper cups of coffee. Nothing happened at eight, nothing happened at nine, nothing happened at ten or eleven. There was no light or noise from inside, and when Blue finally went in to investigate, she found the place empty, the hatch to the cellar wide open. She and Pepper stood on the dark loading dock. There was no sign of the van. Blue couldn't think of any other place the Ulas would be.

Out of ideas, Pepper and Blue walked through the neighborhood. It was nearly midnight, and only a few lights were on in the buildings they passed. In one window, Pepper saw a woman peeling off a T-shirt to reveal a lilac-colored bra. In another, two men gesticulating at one another wildly. In a brick apartment building, a flashlight flickered on and off. When Pepper looked across the street, she saw another flashlight flickering back, answering in code.

Pepper froze in the middle of the street.

"You're in the middle of the street," Blue said.

"A code!" Pepper said. She grabbed Blue by the hands and started jumping up and down. "She's been sending me messages! They have to be from her! It's a code!"

Blue was also jumping up and down, despite not understanding what Pepper was talking about.

"A code!" she said. "Okay!"

"I figured something out," Pepper said.

Blue stopped jumping. She looked at Pepper for a moment, then pulled her close.

"You did great," she said quietly. She petted Pepper's crazy hair. "You're doing just fine."

PEPPER WENT STRAIGHT to the hotel business center and printed every fax she'd received from a Wrocław number. One was from the first hotel, a receipt from her solo visit. She'd gotten seven from a different local number, buried in the myriad unread emails in her in-box. She leafed through the scanned *Ekphrasis* pages she'd been sent. The first two were covers from old issues, one featuring a photo of a woman's face that was partially covered by a torn photo of a similar but slightly incongruous face. Pepper squinted at the page as if there might be a clue hidden somewhere in the background. Then it jumped out at her like a Magic Eye illusion—the issue number, twenty, had been lightly circled. The second cover was marked in the same way, the circle barely perceptible but definitely there. This was, to Pepper's surprise, the first issue of the magazine. The cover featured a piece of art that was composed of a bloodstained bandage.

The third fax was from a roundup of notable small-town museums, which included a mention of the historical society that housed Ula's early work. But there were no markings on the page that Pepper could find. She looked for circled words, dates, punctuation—nothing. The fourth fax appeared to be from a feature on the history of dogs in art. The page Pepper had been sent focused on a mosaic of dogs found in Pompeii with the phrase *Cave Canem* at the bottom. *Beware of Dog*. There wasn't anything Pepper could see circled or marked on this one either, though the quality of the scan was low and it was possible she was missing something. She listed out the page numbers of the articles. She listed out the dates and issue numbers. Except for the covers, they were all from the '80s and '90s, and none were published later than 1996. The page numbers were all over the place.

The fifth fax was from an article about Fernande Olivier, a French artist who was better known as a model and mistress of Picasso. Pepper got distracted reading this one, as she'd never known he and Olivier had adopted a child—a thirteen-year-old girl who, upon Olivier's discovery of explicit drawings of her done by Picasso, had been promptly returned to the orphanage. Pepper found no markings on this page either. There was no obvious thread between this article and the one about dogs. Maybe the *Beware of Dog* was meant to be about Picasso, Pepper thought. She knew she was reaching. Maybe there was no point to any of this. The remaining two faxes didn't connect in any way that made sense. One was about an edition of *Alice's Adventures in Wonderland* illustrated by Dalí, and the other about the use of forensics to detect forgeries and identify stolen art.

Pepper wrote the edition numbers in a row. She wrote out the page numbers, covers excluded: 18–52–124–79–63. She wrote out the dates. The phone number that sent the messages was unlisted. They'd been sent to the fax in Pepper's office, the number for which was on the department website. Pepper paced the hotel's business center, past the glass-topped tables, the computers with hallucinogenic strips of color undulating across their screens. The only other person working was a man with dark hair and a skinny black tie who could've been a spy if he hadn't been so unusually tall. He didn't look up from his screen. Pepper recited each set of numbers in her head. She'd studied linguistics. Her sadistic professor had made them translate passages of Klingon with only two sentences as a key. Every code had a key. She just had to figure out what the key was.

She sat on the floor and arranged the papers in a row. The man at the computer was typing at an alarming speed. Maybe if she rearranged them. Maybe if she added the page numbers up. There didn't seem to be a meaningful pattern across any of the numbers. The man at the computer rose and stood by Pepper's side, which would've made her uncomfortable if she hadn't been so desperate to get this right. The man pointed at the page from the piece about Dalí's *Wonderland*. He chuckled.

"That pig," he said. He had an unplaceable accent and an unexpected expression of delight. "Is floating!" He returned to his seat. Pepper picked up the page. He was wrong—the pig looked like it was floating, but really it was simply atop a tree. In the upper-left corner of the lithograph was a girl, presumably Alice, jumping rope. Pepper scanned the page for the illustration's name: *Pig and Pepper.*

The title of the piece was *Pig and Pepper.* Pepper looked back at the other faxes in disbelief. Her hometown, dogs, an orphan, forensics. A secret code needed a key, and the key to this code was Pepper. The first two faxes were covers from issues published before Pepper had been born, but not the rest. The issue in the third fax was from 1996, when Pepper was sixteen, the next two 1989 and 1985. Pepper took the list of dates and translated it into a list of her ages the year each issue was published. Pepper wrote the list out again, this time as ages: 16–9–5–11–14. They could all correspond to letters. Like pigpen, a simple substitution cipher. With the edition numbers: 20–1 p–i–e–k–n. Maybe the two edition numbers were meant to be translated as letters as well? Two and one? Twenty-one? Or she was supposed to add them to get three? The man in the business center strained to see over his screen. Pepper was scribbling out different options, which she realized was probably distracting.

"Piękna," the man said. "Beautiful."

"What?" Pepper said.

"You have secret admirer?" he said. "The message means *beautiful.*"

Pepper gathered the pages. Why would Ula send her a message that said only *beautiful*? That didn't help her at all. She was just wasting her time with this. It didn't mean anything. It was probably something to do with Scott's dad, one of his minions at the magazine faxing random articles to scare or confuse her. She was reading too much into it because she needed to.

"It is lot of work for love letter," the man said, and resumed typing.

Pepper went back to the room. It was almost 3:00 a.m., and

Blue was lying on top of the bed's covers, flat on her back, her hands folded over her chest, like a body positioned to look peaceful in a casket.

"Any progress?" she asked, her eyes still closed.

"Beautiful," Pepper said. "That's all I have. All I have is nothing, as usual."

She threw her scribbled pages on the bed. Blue sat up and took them.

"Piękna," she said.

"Yes," Pepper said. "It means *beautiful*."

"Yes," Blue said. "It means *beautiful*. It's also the name of a street. 201 Piękna is the address of her apartment."

Pepper looked at *Self-Portrait*, propped against the glass bathroom wall. In it, the baby's head was turned away, as if out of some instinct to keep herself from being seen. The Ula in the painting stared back at Pepper, her resentment so sharp Pepper could feel it from across the room.

"Well, that's a relief," Pepper said.

19

IN THE MORNING, Pepper called the hotel desk and asked if they had anything she could use to wrap a painting. They sent up a roll of wrapping paper printed with the words *Sto Lat*.

"One hundred years," Blue translated. "It's a way to say *happy birthday*."

Pepper wrapped the painting as carefully as she could. The paper was lime green, with pink and red flowers. The painting looked festive and neat when she was finished, like it was on its way to a party, which somehow made Pepper feel better about the endeavor. She was just a regular gal on her way to a birthday party, carrying a priceless work of art that a gang of power-hungry billionaires would kill for, as would her mother's doppelgänger from another universe. All very festive.

She'd woken to several emails from school—two from her department head, one from the dean, and a handful from students. Ike had made calls to let the relevant administrators know Pepper was dealing with a family emergency, and there were concerns. Questions about her classes, paperwork to be filed if the absence would be longer. There was no good way to explain the situation via email, so she decided to ignore them, for now. Together she and Blue would visit the apartment. But then, Pepper knew, it was time to go. She had an obligation to the remains in the boxes in her lab—to make sure the story they contained was told, to send them home. She'd run out of time, and now this universe was on the verge of splitting itself again. It was impossible to inhabit two universes at once.

Pepper and Blue took a cab, and sat with the painting spanning the back seat, crowding their knees. Blue reached over and put one hand on Pepper's, which filled her with longing for her moms. She consoled herself by thinking about how they would spend their day. She imagined Lydia seeing a puppy for an exam, the puppy so excited by her voice it peed on the exam table. She imagined Annie in surgery, neutering a cat. She liked to listen to country music in surgery. She liked to sing along. Pepper could hear her, her drawn-out Texan twang. They'd both be there when she got home. Whatever happened, Pepper thought, they'd both be there when she got home.

The cab rolled through the misty streets, the driver stopping occasionally to shout at pedestrians. He was listening to a news show, which Pepper couldn't understand, which was fine because she could only handle one tiny piece of the universe at a time right now. Eventually, the streets started to look familiar. Blue kept her hand on Pepper's.

The cab stopped in front of the apartment building. "I've been here," Pepper said. "She brought me here. There weren't signs of anyone else inside. She wouldn't have brought me here if this is where she's keeping Ula."

They got out of the cab, Pepper wrestling the painting with some effort. She looked under the mat for the key, but of course it wasn't there.

"We should've told the cabdriver to stay," Pepper said.

"We don't need a cab," Blue said. She took something from her pocket and started working on the door, glancing behind her.

"Do you know what you're doing?" Pepper asked.

"When Frida was in middle school," she said, "she got on this spy kick. My parents got her about a million books about spies. She had books about cracking safes, about surveillance. She got in trouble for spying on the neighbors a few times. Someone would see a little face pressed against their living room window and call my mother. She'd come home with dirty feet because she always went barefoot, so no one would find the tracks made by her jellies. For her birthday that year, we took a spy class. There was a lesson on picking locks, which I thought was a questionable thing to teach kids, but I wasn't going to say anything." She was still at it, fishing away at the lock with an unfolded paper clip. "I haven't had a lot of opportunities to practice this skill."

"I think Frida and I would be friends," Pepper said.

"You would," Blue said. "She liked the idea of being able to observe the world without participating. But you know how that goes."

"What do you mean?" Pepper said.

Blue closed her eyes, working the lock by feel. "Eventually, the world requires your participation. The observation is just training."

The lock made a popping sound, and Blue stopped and tried the knob. The door opened.

"You're my favorite," Pepper said. "In case there was any doubt."

"They're not all bad," Blue said. "I mean, we're a real mixed bag of bitches, to be sure. But it's a miracle any of us manage to function in the first place."

Inside, the apartment looked untouched since Pepper's last visit. The branches in the vase on the entry table had dropped a few blossoms, and the blossoms lay wilted in pools of scattered pollen. The boots were still in the foyer. Pepper closed the door as quietly as possible. They stood together and listened, but there was no noise, not even from next door. Pepper and Blue checked each room, one by one. The apartment was chilly, the air conditioner set low. The all-white décor created a false sense of brightness. In one room, Pepper found a sketchbook tucked into a drawer. It was full of sketches of Rafał, some of them nude. Ula had sketched him from a variety of angles, capturing expressions that seemed too intimate for a technical exercise. Pepper stuffed the sketchbook back in its place, trying to block from her mind its value to the art world.

There were no signs that anyone else had been in the apartment. The bed Pepper had slept in was still as she'd left it, messily made. The refrigerator was empty but for one lonely beer, Pepper's bottle still in the recycling bin. Pepper sat on the couch where Ula Zero had slept. She'd been so tired that day, a sign of the deterioration process Pepper hadn't been able to interpret. She'd misinterpreted so many things.

"This was a waste," she said. Blue was in the kitchen, rummaging. "Maybe the message wasn't from Ula in the first place. It could've been from anyone who knows this place exists. A warning from the Everett Group. It doesn't necessarily mean more than that."

"There's a lot of car theft in Poland," Blue said.

"Who even knows if she could drive," Pepper said. "Ula Zero could barely see the street signs. Maybe the real Ula has bad eyes too. I don't know anything about her." The white couch was uncomfortable, but Pepper felt her body sinking. Probably Ula Zero couldn't see because she was deteriorating. Maybe the Ulas were toxic and Pepper was deteriorating now too. "I'll call the police from the airport and try to explain. Not that they'll believe me. But they might have better luck finding Ula if I can convince them she's alive."

Blue was going through kitchen cabinets, banging them open and shut. Pepper closed her eyes, and the warmth of exhaustion crept outward through her body. She tried to remember the last time she'd had a decent night's sleep. She wasn't thinking clearly anymore. She wasn't the type of person to wreck her life based on a feeling. This would all make more sense once she was home and spent a night in her own bed, with the painting someplace safe, away from her. She opened her eyes, ready to go, at last. Blue was standing in front of her, holding a key.

"There's a lot of car theft in Poland," she said. "A place like this, an expensive place, will have a garage."

THE GARAGES WERE at the end of the block, a separate building that looked like a bank of storage units. One of the garages at the end was open, and a woman in tight jeans and a black tube top was working on a cherry-red muscle car, opera blaring from the car's speakers. She gave Pepper and Blue a two-finger salute as they passed and resumed yanking on something under the car's hood. Pepper found the garage that matched the number on the key. The key unlocked a silver box to the right of the door, which contained a cracked white button. Pepper pressed the button and pinned the painting against her legs as the door slowly rose.

Inside the garage, there was a car—an old, taupe-colored Audi, with a creased dent on the passenger-side door. There were boxes stacked against the wall to the left, labeled with writing that had smudged past readability. On the right wall, a pegboard loaded with tools for painting, organized by size, smallest to largest. There were cobwebs clotted in every corner. But no Ula, which Pepper knew had been a foolish thing to expect. She felt the weight of the gift-wrapped painting in her hands, its haunted frame, a finality drifting through her like a ghost. This might be as close as she ever got to her. She would continue on in the universe she'd always known, living with the specter of Ula instead of the reality.

Blue was squinting through the car's dusty windshield when something fell in the back of the garage. An oil can rolled out from behind the car, trickling goop onto the concrete. Pepper left the painting on the hood and followed the oil can, around the car, to the rear of the garage. And there, on the floor, behind the rusting Audi, she found Ula Frost.

Ula's hands were tied behind her back, her ankles bound in front of her, a strip of gray cloth taut across her mouth. She was hollow-cheeked and dirty, but Pepper knew she was from this universe by the way she looked at Pepper, like she recognized her. Everyone here seemed to recognize her, but this was different. This was Ula Frost.

Pepper stood stunned for a moment before snapping back into herself. There was a pair of scissors on the pegboard, which she used to cut the ties on Ula's hands, then mouth.

"It's about time," Ula said. There was a mole on her right index finger. Her ears were unpierced. She was leaning back against the wall, her hair matted with knots of spider silk. "I thought you were supposed to be some kind of forensics expert."

She took the scissors from Pepper and cut the tie at her ankles herself. She tried to stand but stumbled and slid back down the wall. "She hasn't been feeding me much," she said. "I'd kill with no hesitation for a cheeseburger right now. I assume you've called the police?"

Pepper's phone didn't get reception here. Blue was still on the opposite side of the car, hesitant to get any closer. She looked at Pepper.

"Will you be okay," she asked, "if I go?"

Pepper didn't know how to answer the question. She nodded without looking back. Pepper heard Blue a moment later, the opera paused, speaking halting Polish to the woman with the muscle car. Pepper knelt next to Ula, who was lounging in a position of boredom.

"She's not happy with you," Ula said. "At all. I hope you've hidden that painting someplace good."

Pepper felt the distance between her and the painting across the garage. "How did you know I had it?"

"She wouldn't be so agitated if she knew where it was," Ula said. "You should've left it alone. It was safe in that museum. I put it there for a reason."

"Someone was going to take it," Pepper said. "It may as well have been me."

"Listen," Ula said. She sat up with surprising force and grabbed Pepper by the shoulder, digging her overgrown nails into Pepper's skin. "If something happens to you, everything goes to Tilda, and that means Tilda is in danger. I take no responsibility for what happens to you, but you'd better fucking believe I'm not going to let anything happen to Tilda. So you're going to get that painting from wherever you left it, and you're going to put it someplace no one can find it. Make yourself useful. As a gift to me. You took your sweet time figuring out where I was. You owe me."

Pepper sank to the garage floor, which was cool and damp through her jeans. By the wall, tucked in the stack of boxes, she saw an old fax machine partially covered by a drop cloth.

"You faxed me," she said.

"She didn't have me tied up so tight at first," Ula said. She pressed her wrists at Pepper's face, as if Pepper had been the one to inflict the punishment. "Then she caught me honking the horn."

"But why me?" Pepper said. "Why didn't you fax the police, or Rafał or someone?"

"The Everett Group may as well own the police," Ula said. "They think they're so virtuous." She rolled her eyes. "Like if they had access to other worlds they'd do something other than exploit them. And she saw Rafał, from time to time. It had to be something she wouldn't understand."

Rafał was wrong, Pepper thought. Ula wasn't changeable at all—it was just that there were so many of her. She listened for a siren, but the street outside was quiet. She didn't hear Blue talking to the woman with the muscle car anymore either. She felt something on her shoulder where Ula had grabbed her and saw a spindly spider, creeping. In a different universe, she would've been paralyzed with fear, but in this one, she calmly brushed it away. The dance of the tarantella originated as a kind of ritual healing for women, to remove the lustful effects of a spider bite. Pepper could hear Ike's voice in her head, which made the situation almost bearable.

"I hate just sitting here," Ula said. "I've been sitting in this goddamn garage for too long. I probably have rickets."

Pepper knew rickets. She could identify rickets in a skeleton without having to think. Abnormally short stature, curvature to the long bones, deformities in the sternum and ribs.

"In adults, it's called *osteomalacia*," she said. "You'll be fine with some supplements."

Ula grunted, which Pepper interpreted as disappointment that her condition wasn't more dramatic.

"I still can't believe it took you so long to figure it out," Ula said. "You were supposed to be smart, with all your fancy degrees. A waste of money, if you ask me. You can't believe how I've suffered, trapped in this place. I expected better. I really did."

Pepper saw a spider moving toward her from the corner of her eye.

"I'm sorry," she said, and put her head back through the cobwebs to wait.

20

BLUE DIDN'T COME back.

"What's taking so long?" Ula said.

Pepper felt another spider crawling on the back of her neck and swatted it away. "I don't know," she said.

Outside the garage, it was quiet. Suspiciously quiet. Pepper knew she should get up and check, but the feeling of wrongness in her body was so heavy she couldn't move. She felt something on her neck again and turned her head. A tiny spider was crawling up the wall. A baby, Pepper thought. It was almost cute. Then it was joined by two more baby spiders, and several dozen after that. Pepper stood.

"Stay here," she said.

"It's not like I can go anywhere," Ula said.

Pepper felt a streak of teenage rebellion rising inside her. She'd only known this woman for three minutes. This is just what it was like with mothers, she told herself. She tried to hold on to the frustration as she approached the door. Frustration was easier to move through than fear. She'd barely made it around the car when the garage door began closing and Ula Zero ducked in beneath it. One of her sleeves was soaked with blood.

Pepper jumped back toward the pegboard, leaving the painting on the car's hood. The wrapping paper was so cheery.

"Is that it?" Ula Zero said. "God, I didn't think you'd make this so easy for me."

"For fuck's sake, did you bring that fucking thing here?" Ula said from behind the car.

"Where's the other Ula?" Pepper asked. She tried to remember Blue's number, but the numbers shuffled in her mind.

"She was the worst one," Ula Zero said.

"She's not the worst one," Ula said. Pepper glanced back and saw her, still holding the scissors. "You're clearly the worst one. She's not even the second-worst one."

Pepper never had any siblings, but she had friends who had sisters, and she knew she didn't want to be between two sisters who were fighting. That's what these Ulas were like—two sisters who hated each other because they were so alike.

"You don't know who the worst one is," Ula Zero said. "You're the worst one. You've always been the worst one. Look at what you've done to us." She grimaced so Ula could see her mouth, the ragged gap left by the decay of her lip. She'd been here the longest. She was the most warped by distance and time. "You don't care about any of it. It was just a stupid hobby for you. Ruining all our lives. You never cared about any of us past what we could do for you."

On the ground, Ula sighed with exasperation as if she were dealing with a tantruming toddler. "No one ever appreciates me," she said. "I've never been truly appreciated for my talent."

Ula Zero was circling the car now, past the boxes, on the opposite side of the car from Pepper. Pepper tried to think how she could protect both Ula and the painting at the same time. She took a chisel from the pegboard. It wasn't very sharp, but when she approached Ula from her side of the car, Ula Zero backed away toward the garage door. Someday, Pepper thought, a historian would write about this. Scientists would study the bodies of the Ulas, their DNA, their brains, their bones. The tools in this garage would be carted off to a lab and analyzed by machines. Someday people smarter than Pepper would be able to make sense of this.

With Pepper squarely in front of Ula, Ula Zero calculated the distance and darted toward the painting on the car's hood. Pepper tried to cut her off, but Ula Zero got there first. The wrapping paper tore as she snatched it away, a swath falling down to reveal the upper-left corner of the painting, which Pepper now noticed was a tree from Tilda and Neil's backyard. In this universe, the tree grew apricots; in the universe of the painting, pears.

"Happy birthday," Ula Zero said. "I've waited so long for this moment." She pulled something from her pocket, flipped it open to reveal a blade.

"Don't you dare," Ula said, rising. She didn't seem so weak after all. The weakness had been an act, a manipulation to garner Pepper's pity.

Ula Zero tore more paper from the painting, moving frantically as Ula charged. She slashed the knife toward the painting, but Ula threw a can of varnish, which thunked as it hit Ula Zero in the temple. Ula Zero fell back, crying out as she lost her grip on the painting.

"This belongs to me," Ula said, recovering the painting from the floor while Ula Zero clutched at her head. "I made it. It's mine."

Ula Zero scrambled to get up, knife still in hand, as Ula maneuvered past her with the painting toward the door. She pressed the button, but nothing happened, and then she hit it again and again with a punishing impatience, like someone trapped in an elevator, unable to accept her own impotence.

"Never mind!" she said, giving up on the button. "Never mind. The police are coming. It's a real sign of the times when I'd rather deal with the police than you."

Ula Zero came to her feet and laughed. "No one called the police," she said. She motioned at Pepper. "She didn't call the police."

Ula glared at Pepper. She hadn't called the police. And neither, Pepper understood with a sinking she couldn't process now, had Blue.

"You really fucked this up," Ula said. She looked at her the same way Ula Zero had outside the museum.

"Yes, I did," Pepper said. Maybe none of this was real.

"Open the door," Ula said.

To get to the door, Pepper would have to put herself between the Ulas, both of whom were holding sharp objects. The sharp objects were real. Pepper stepped back and circled the car. There was nothing useful on the pegboard, but the trunk was unlocked.

"What are you doing?" Ula said.

In the trunk, Pepper found two folded towels, a stack of newspapers, and a crowbar. The crowbar was solid in Pepper's hand. She could do this. She held it in front of her as she made her way back toward the door. Get to the door, open the door, exit the door. Small, simple tasks. She was nearly there when Ula Zero, still breathless and furious, lunged at the painting. Pepper was too far away. Ula, undeteriorated occupant of her original universe, slashed at Ula Zero with the scissors, cutting her shallowly across the chest.

Ula Zero reeled backward. "That's mine!" she screamed. "Give it to me!"

"Nothing belongs to you," Ula taunted. "Nothing here belongs to you."

"Actually, the painting belongs to me," Pepper said. Both of the Ulas stopped and stared at her. "Technically speaking. I own it."

The Ulas both kept their eyes on Pepper. She'd redirected their anger, maybe long enough for them to get out. Ula Zero was holding one hand to her chest, bleeding through her fingers. She looked down at the blood. "You've killed me," she moaned.

"I don't think it's that deep," Pepper said, and immediately knew it was a mistake.

Ula Zero, now enraged, flew at Pepper with her knife. Pepper held up her crowbar defensively, and in response, Ula Zero changed course and threw herself at Ula, knife first, plunging it into her stomach. Ula collapsed onto the garage floor. Pepper saw the baby spiders on the wall above her fanning out in every direction. Pepper hit Ula Zero in the back with the crowbar, and she gasped and stumbled backward. There was a noise outside, a car door shutting.

"You're not going to keep me here!" Ula Zero said. "I'm going home to my daughter." There was a lot of blood on the floor around Ula. A very bad amount of blood. Once more, Ula Zero lunged at the painting, and Pepper was too stunned to stop her.

Ula Zero dug into the painting with her fingers, into the crook of young Ula's arm, where the baby tucked her head toward her mother's warm body. It wasn't the real Ula in the painting. It was a portrait of Ula Zero. The baby in the painting was Ula Zero's baby, not Pepper, not a nothing to her at all. She managed to get one finger through the canvas, and that's when the room started to change. Pepper felt the air around her vibrate and braced herself for disaster. The hair on her arms stood on end rose and her ears popped, like on an airplane during liftoff. Ula Zero clawed through the canvas, all animal desperation, and then there was a loud crack, like the sound of a lightning strike, and she was gone.

Pepper stood still in the garage. Where had she gone? The air smelled like a storm. Outside, she heard more car doors closing. Then, a siren, distant at first, but moving nearer. She knelt on the floor by Ula, who was holding her wound. There was no disaster other than this one.

"How many people die from stab wounds to the abdomen?" Ula asked. There was a lot of blood, but maybe not a bleeding-to-death amount of blood.

"I don't know the statistics for that," Pepper said.

"I thought you were some kind of medical expert," Ula said.

"Bones," Pepper said. "I know about bones. And the diseases that affect them."

Pepper heard men yelling, and the door lurched and creaked upward. The officers who approached had their guns trained on Pepper until Ula said, "No, you idiots. It wasn't her. She's my daughter."

THE AMBULANCE BLARED through the streets. Pepper had no idea how far they were from a hospital. The paramedic kept asking questions about Ula's medical history that Pepper couldn't answer. There was a history of heart disease, she remembered Tilda saying, and colon cancer. Ula's mouth was covered with an oxygen mask, so she couldn't speak. With Ula lying down and her shirt cut off, Pepper could see the jut of her ribs. Her body was straight like Pepper's, hipless. She seemed to be having trouble breathing. The paramedics were speaking to each other in Polish, and it wasn't chitchat. One of them was holding pressure on the stab wound, the other injecting things into the IV line. Pepper sat next to Ula, helpless but unusually calm. Death was her area of expertise.

"In some cultures," Pepper said, "with very high infant mortality rates, families wait weeks or even months to name their infants."

Ula gazed at her over the mask, her eyes not entirely focused. Pepper thought it was better if she kept talking, though.

"Some ancient cultures buried infants under the entryways of their dwellings," she continued. "It was part of a ritual of transition. In those cultures, where people walked over the remains under the entryways, the demographics of the population are often skewed in the skeletal record because few infant remains are found intact."

Ula's eyes softened. She pulled down the mask. "Make sure they go all out for me," she said. "It would make me feel better to know there'll be some fanfare. Tilda will know what to do."

Pepper could only nod.

"You're not much like me," Ula said. "Too softhearted, like her. It's not what's best for you. Sometimes you have to be tough enough to walk away from things."

Pepper thought that was bullshit but didn't say it. Staying required strength too. Every good thing in her life came from staying, from the work of resisting that part of herself she'd believed was sown into her body from Ula's.

"Do you understand?" Ula said.

The paramedic put the mask back over her mouth, but Ula swatted him away. Pepper didn't understand.

"Why did you paint so many versions of yourself?" Pepper said. "And why couldn't you just let them go? Where are their portraits?"

Ula held out her hand, so Pepper took it. It was colder than she'd expected. Maybe she did understand. She understood wanting to find a different version of herself, a version of herself who'd stopped this from happening, the versions she could only imagine. The better versions. Ula had painted Blue, which was as much proof as Pepper needed that better versions existed.

Ula closed her eyes. Her color was bad. Pepper mostly dealt with dead people, but she knew her color was bad. Ula opened her eyes again.

"Tilda stopped talking to me," she said. "And I was lonely. They kept leaving. I just wanted the company."

She arched her back as pain shot through her body. The paramedic put the mask back over her face and held it in place while he injected something else into the IV. Pepper kept holding Ula's hand until they reached the hospital and the paramedics rushed Ula in, leaving Pepper behind.

THE HALL WAS long and quiet, white walls with a burnt-orange floor. A nurse at the desk spotted the blood on Pepper's hands and led her to a bathroom, where she turned on the water and tested it herself to make sure it wasn't too hot or too cold. When Pepper finished washing, the nurse was ready with a paper towel.

There was a television in the waiting room tuned to a game show that involved people in skintight silver jumpsuits and helmets contorting themselves to fit through oddly shaped holes in a wall that moved toward them more quickly than Pepper would've liked. As the wall got close, a siren wailed like an emergency. Pepper couldn't look away. She didn't notice the doctor until he was standing right in front of her.

When Pepper stood, he took her hands. That's how she knew. She'd already thought Ula was dead once. She'd done this before. But she thought it might feel less shitty with practice.

There were police down the hall, Pepper could see, talking to someone from the medical team. There would be questions to answer, papers to sign. Her hands were clean, but there was blood on her clothes. The doctor, not realizing she didn't speak Polish, was speaking to her seriously in a language she didn't understand. It was too much. She turned away from him, and there was Ike.

"Are you okay?" he said. He rushed toward her and squeezed her harder than she could remember ever being squeezed before. He didn't notice the bloody shirt until he pulled away and immediately started patting her down for injuries.

"I'm not hurt," Pepper said. "But Ula . . ."

Ike looked at the doctor, who nodded. Ike nodded back.

"I am sorry," the doctor said. "I did not realize. You understood what I said?"

No, Pepper shook her head, she did not understand. "Przepraszam," she said. She'd learned almost nothing during this trip, but at least she could say *sorry*.

"Miss Frost said something," the doctor said. "Before she passed."

On the television, a group of silver-clad teammates toppled as a wall barreled into them. Pepper was full up on things she couldn't process. The audience erupted into cheers. She felt Ike's hand clenched around her own but couldn't look at him.

"What did she say?" Ike asked.

"She said *smok*," the doctor said. "It is word for *dragon*. I don't know if that means anything to you, but I thought you should know. Someone will come soon to talk to you more. Take your time." He nodded again and left them.

Pepper turned to Ike. His hair was flat on one side of his head and his eyes were bloodshot and heavy. "What are you doing here?"

"I can't sleep in that stupid bed without you," Ike said.

"But I always kick you," Pepper said. "For snoring."

"It turns out I don't sleep well when I snore," he said. "You play a crucial role in my circadian rhythm."

Pepper nodded. It was contagious.

"You don't have to do anything right now," Ike said. "I'm just going to stand here next to you and not hold your hand."

A list of credits scrolled up the television screen. Pepper had missed who'd won.

"You can hold my hand," she said. "If you want." And he did, and then he held her against his warm body and put a hand in her hair, which was the exact moment when the universe felt real again, and even then Pepper couldn't cry.

21

WHEN PEPPER AND Ike arrived back at the hotel, hours later, it was surrounded by men holding cameras. Pepper told the cab-driver to keep going.

The news had broken while they were still at the hospital. Pepper had seen pieces of Ula's work flash on the screen. It was one thing to speculate about the possibility of other worlds. It was an entirely different thing when there were bodies in a morgue, identical save for a few crucial differences. The doctors had asked Pepper what to do with them—they were already fielding requests from universities and government agencies. Pepper didn't know. For Ula, a funeral, the fanfare she wanted. But for Blue—Pepper needed some time.

She asked the cabdriver to drop them in the square.

"Are you taking me to see the sights?" Ike asked.

Pepper started walking. "I just want to walk," she said.

Ike kept pace. "We're going to have to go back there and deal with this," he said. "Eventually."

"Eventually," Pepper repeated.

As the sun began to set, they walked past buildings painted the color of sunset, outward from the center of the city. Ike didn't ask where they were going or try to make Pepper feel better, though Pepper now failed to register any feeling in her body at all. She didn't know how many Ulas she was supposed to be feeling for yet. She'd thought some of the others would have turned up by now. There were still seven of them out there, by her count, more trapped than ever. Any hope of finding their portraits had died with Ula.

They walked past a woman playing a fiddle, the music aching like the sound of universes splitting apart. They walked past a couple kissing—soft grazing kisses—over and over, in the middle of the sidewalk. They walked past a boy who was sitting cross-legged facing a stoop, being punished for some misdeed, while his mother swiped at her phone, waiting out the time. They walked past men in suits, a woman in a white raincoat with a strawberry print, a small girl who found a puddle and jumped in it gleefully with both feet. And then Pepper saw something out of the corner of her eye. Someone in all black. She turned to check. Yes, a woman in a black hoodie, the oversize hood obscuring her face.

They kept walking. When they turned the corner, Pepper saw another woman in black join them. Now she had a purpose; she was walking a path she'd taken before. Ike didn't notice—he was looking at his phone.

"Ike," she said.

"Sorry," he said. "I was looking up *smok*."

There were three women in black now, all following at a discreet distance. Pepper felt them falling in line, an apparition of Ulas, trailing them.

"If there's a Smok Street," she said, "I don't want to know. Just cram some Xanax down my throat and put me on a plane immediately."

"There's a story about a Polish dragon," Ike said. "The Wawel Dragon."

"I read about that," Pepper said. "A collection of bones in Kraków, probably Pleistocene-era. People claim they're from a dragon. It's a tourist attraction."

"In one of the stories," Ike said, "the dragon liked to eat young girls. He ate every girl in the city but one, the king's daughter. Then a shoemaker fed the dragon a lamb stuffed with sulfur, and the dragon was so thirsty he drank half the river and exploded." He held out his phone to show Pepper the illustration. There were four Ulas now, all walking at the exact same pace.

"Ike," she said.

"Sorry," he said. "I just thought it might mean something."

Pepper stopped, as did all the Ulas in the street, whom Ike now noticed.

"She couldn't have been talking about the church," she said. "I've been there. She knew I'd been there."

"Pepper," Ike said.

"I know," she said. "Are there any alleged dragon remains in Wrocław? Or something else dragon-related? A relic of Saint George?"

They started walking again. Ike's fingers tapped the screen as he searched, but his eyes were roaming. "This is freaking me out," he said.

"You get used to it," Pepper said.

"There's a pizza place called Pizzeria Dragon," he said.

"That can't be it," Pepper said.

The space between the Ulas began to close as if their proximity to the church was pulling them together, like magnets. Pepper looked back. Ulas, all in black, a black ribbon waving behind her on the sidewalk.

The church was still surrounded by red-and-white police tape but no media yet. Locals had been leaving flowers outside the door in the spot where the charred remains had been found, white lilies and snapdragons and lavender. Pepper picked up a lavender stem and inhaled.

"This is her studio," Ike said. He reached up and touched the dragon carved over the door.

"This was her studio," Pepper said.

The door was unlocked. Pepper stepped into the shadows of the vestibule. It was so quiet. The basins for holy water were dry. In another universe, the knife hadn't stabbed quite as deep. In another universe, it had been a different Ula in the garage all along, and now the real one was waiting on the other side of this door. In another universe, Pepper made the sign of the cross. She entered the church. One by one, the Ulas followed.

Ike stood closer, and Pepper held his hand as the Ulas removed their hoods and Pepper took roll. Ursula tapped her foot, all vestiges of impatience replaced by uncertainty. Compact's precise hair had an unruly wave on one side. Talons, Vermont, Specs, standing shoulder to shoulder. There was no one Ula loved more than herself. Even Key, who'd already been in the church, waiting, stood closer to the others than necessary. Blue was accounted for in the morgue. The only Ula who was still missing was Boot, whose life across universes had not been complicated by the presence or sudden absence of a child. Maybe she was still on her way back. Maybe she wasn't. Maybe she'd already deteriorated too much in this universe that wasn't her own.

"What now?" Ursula asked.

"Good question," Pepper said.

THE CHURCH DIMMED as the sun set. Pepper and Ike went through drawers and cabinets, checking for anything that might lead them to the missing portraits. The Ulas gathered their things from their secret hiding places—inside the confessionals, in hollowed-out hymnals, in walls where the bricks were loose and easily pried. Pepper told them they could stay if they wanted, though the church likely wouldn't be safe, but the Ulas looked more lost than Pepper did. And Pepper could feel that Tesla-coil buzz of anger again. They were here with a half-life and no chance of getting home. This wasn't their universe.

In the sacristy, Ike found a tall, wide metal cabinet protected with a simple padlock.

"There's nothing good in there," Talons said. "It's all junk."

The Ulas were quietly discussing the places they'd individually looked for clues to the whereabouts of their portraits. Ursula had briefly held a job at an auction house that had sold a drawing by Ula years earlier. Key and Compact had, on separate occasions, broken into Gordon's shed. Museums, accounting firms, internet forums. Every corner of this church, while Ula had slept. Talons had picked the lock on this cabinet already. Pepper found a paper clip and tried picking the lock herself. Maybe the ability to pick locks had a genetic component. She and Ike would have to leave tomorrow, and there was no way for them to guarantee the church would be as they left it when they returned. There were plenty of people who'd want to get a look inside now.

Pepper jiggled the paper clip the way she remembered Blue doing, but nothing happened. Pepper couldn't help anyone, not even herself. She wondered if, in her own universe, Frida felt something at the moment of her mother's death, if there was a connection between them. She wondered if Frida felt as Pepper did now, like she'd walked too far with too little sleep, aware of a pain in her body that was inescapable, lying in wait for the exact right moment to knock her on her ass, but unable to feel it yet, while there was still work to be done.

The padlock popped open, and Pepper was so surprised she let it slip to the tile floor with a clank. She swung the cabinet door open before she had time to think about what might be inside.

Letters. Inside the locker were letters, thousands of them, tied in bundles by kite string and purple yarn and twine. There were so many stacks some fell out when the door opened. All the shelves were stuffed with them, except for the one on the bottom. Pepper knelt on the cold floor. On the bottom shelf, there was a hatbox covered with dust.

Inside: A yearbook, rarely opened based on the condition of the spine, from Ula's sophomore year of high school. A handful of photographs, including one of Ula as a child, holding her parents' hands as they swung her off the ground. An unopened letter addressed to Tilda marked RETURN TO SENDER. A report card on which Mr. Ashcroft had written, *Makes no attempt to work to her ability.* Three notes all in pigpen. Gallery exhibit programs, a copy of a check. Pepper and Ike's engagement announcement, torn from the newspaper. Seeds from an unidentifiable fruit. A deciduous premolar from a dog. A marigold still pressed between sheets of wax paper.

But nothing that provided a clue as to the whereabouts of the portraits. Pepper stuffed the fallen letters back into the locker and clicked the padlock in place.

"These letters need to be in an archive," Ike said.

Pepper sat on the tile and held the box.

"I didn't mean—"

"I know," she said. He was trying so hard not to be a historian. "We'll have them sent to the postal museum. For now."

She looked out the door to the sanctuary where Specs was counting paces, trying to remember where she'd hidden something. She kept having to stop at the altar and go around it, which was throwing off her count.

Pepper stood.

"Does it seem weird to you that almost everything's been emptied out of the place—the pews and the kneelers—but the altar is still here?"

"Not really," Ike said. "Pews are relatively light. That altar looks heavy as fuck."

Pepper went to the sanctuary and examined the floor around the altar. It had been moved, maybe a quarter of an inch, just enough that Pepper could see the difference in the color of the tile, a narrow strip that'd been covered for years and years and then, for some reason, exposed.

"We have to move this," she said.

"Pepper," Ike said.

Pepper started pushing, and the altar moved more easily than she'd expected. Someone had affixed the bottom with sliders.

"What do you think you're going to find under there?" Ike said.

"Dragon bones?" Pepper said.

Ike added his body, pushing at Pepper's side. One day, they'd remember this moment, a moment when everything was terrible but they were together and that's how they survived it. Once they'd gotten the altar a few inches off its original mark, Pepper saw it. An outline in the tile. There was something underneath. The rest of the Ulas joined in.

With the altar moved away, Pepper and Ike knelt by the rectangular outline. One of the Ulas brought a few palette knives, and they wedged them in until the rectangle gave and started to lift.

"Wait," Ike said.

"What?" Pepper said.

"If there's a crypt down there," he said, "shouldn't we get face masks or something? Haven't archaeologists died from inhaling toxins from mummies in pyramids?"

"Are you talking about King Tut's Curse?" Pepper said. "No, that was black magic."

"Pepper," Ike said.

"That guy died from blood poisoning from an infected mosquito bite," she said. "There could be mold or bacteria growing down there, so masks aren't the worst idea, but I doubt it's anything fatal if Ula went down herself."

She used her palette knife to pop the trapdoor open. The space below was dark. Specs offered the flashlight from her stash, which she had because she was afraid of the dark. Pepper aimed it through the opening but still couldn't see anything. She grabbed a pen from a supply cabinet and dropped it, listening for it to hit.

"It's not so deep," she said. "Lower me."

"Absolutely not," Ike said.

"Lower me," Pepper said.

"What if there are snakes!" Ike said.

Pepper kissed Ike, which she hadn't done for a long time, she realized. He tasted like he hadn't brushed his teeth that day. He kissed her back.

"It's not an adventure if it's not at least a little unpleasant," she said.

Ike took Pepper's hands, and she wriggled her lower body through the opening. Ike rearranged his grip, holding her tight at the elbows, and lowered her.

"Can you feel the bottom?" he said.

"No," she said. "But let go anyway."

"I'm not letting go," Ike said.

Pepper could feel the strength of his hands wrapped around her forearms. He wouldn't let go if he didn't have to. He was ready to pull her back up if she said the word.

"Let go, Ike," she said.

He let go. It wasn't a far drop, only a foot or so. Specs tossed down the flashlight, which Pepper failed to catch, but which, she was thankful, didn't break. She flicked it on. She was in a small crypt, old stone walls and the smell of groundwater. There was a stone slab on one side with an open sarcophagus. Pepper looked for an inscription, some indicator of the religious significance of these remains, but there wasn't one.

"You okay?" Ike asked. She could see him above the trapdoor, his head silhouetted against the opening. She held the flashlight under her chin like she was telling a ghost story.

"No snakes," she said.

She put on the gloves she'd stuffed in her pockets and shone the flashlight over the slab. There was one body in the sarcophagus, four more piled beside it. Only one of these bodies was old enough to belong here. The other four were covered in hair, and soft tissue in various states of desiccation. There was one body that belonged here, and four Ulas.

Ula Zero had said sometimes they came through dead. Pepper wondered what it must've been like for Ula, trying to paint a friendlier version of herself into existence, only to be met with herself in dead or dying form. The other Ulas didn't seem to know about this trapdoor. Lugging the bodies down here must have been a task that Ula reserved for herself.

"Are you sure there aren't any snakes?" Ike asked.

"No snakes," Pepper said. "Just a couple of dead Ulas."

The Ulas were facedown on the slab, and she carefully turned one upright. She was wearing earrings shaped like cicadas, pierced through the leathery skin of her ears. Her mouth had dried open in the shape of an *O*. Pepper touched the hair and saw every version of Ula at once, the kind ones and the cruel ones, the creative and the violent, the desperate and the petulant, and the angry and the falling apart, layered liked a stack of transparencies. Pepper tried to separate herself from the part of her brain that generated grief. There were no obvious signs of trauma, on this one, at least. Not every body could survive whatever happened in the wrenching from one universe to another. But Ula had continued to bring them here anyway.

The older remains in the sarcophagus displayed signs of tuberculosis, plaquing on the ribs, which Pepper noted after performing a cursory exam for the sake of her own calm. Maybe there'd been a saint in this church the whole time, in quiet residence under everything happening above it.

She turned and assessed the rest of the crypt, slowly, because she was worried now that she might find something scarier than snakes, like claw marks or signs of a struggle. But the room was ordinary, the walls stressed and damp. Pepper checked the floor too, a packed dirt surface, and found what looked like shoe prints leading to the opposite wall.

"I need a check-in," Ike said.

"You're practically in the room," Pepper said. "If something terrible happened to me, you'd be able to hear it."

"Not reassuring," Ike said.

"I'm fine," Pepper said. "I'm almost done. Just making sure I'm not missing anything."

"You're like that woman from that show," Ike said.

Pepper knew what he meant. She could see the outline of his upper body hanging upside down from the trapdoor, like a bat. In the sixteenth century, he'd once told her, the word for *bat* had been *flittermouse*. The woman from that show always knew what to do, and she was lonely because she chose to be. "Not in this universe," Pepper said.

The footprints stopped at the wall. Pepper held her flashlight close to the stone. She ran her fingers over it. There was an outline of something. She could feel it but not quite see it. She pressed harder, and a chunk of wall crumbled away. A door.

"Can you toss down one of those palette knives?"

Palette knife in hand, Pepper excavated the door. She was doing this all wrong—she should've been taking photos and notes, drawing a diagram, waiting for impartial experts, preserving samples. She could feel the weight of history in her hands. Maybe she would find a prehistoric creature inside, like in Kraków. The material that she removed didn't feel so old, though. It felt like spackle. Finally, Pepper got down to a surface that wasn't chipping away. She pushed, and it gave.

"I'm going into another room now," Pepper called up.

"Another room?" Ike said. "I'm coming down there."

Pepper turned to reassure him, but he was already dropping himself through the opening. Pepper shone the flashlight in his face.

"I'm not letting you die from some mummy's curse alone," he said. He put a hand on the back of her head and smushed her face against his chest.

"I don't know how I ever imagined myself into a universe without you," she said.

"All those other universes are still out there," he said.

And more would be created, on and on, and all Pepper could do was try to be a better version of herself in the universe she was given. A small, simple task. Ike kissed her hair. She held out the flashlight and stepped through the door.

"Oh my god," Ike said.

Pepper stepped out of the room and stepped immediately back in. She shone the flashlight back and forth across the space. It was bigger than the crypt, and the walls were reinforced with metal. It wasn't damp in here. It was cool and dry and smelled like paint.

The room was full of paintings. There were dozens of them, spaced evenly inside cage-like wire racks.

"Oh my god," Pepper said. She stepped forward and took in the first row. There were a few of the buildings in the Old Town. One of a rabbit nestled in tall grass. There was one of a young man on a motorcycle, head turned, helmetless, barely revealing the side of a smiling face, and two more of a man with the same wavy hair, at different ages—one at maybe thirty, bare-chested in khaki pants, standing over a stove and a frying pan, and another at about fifty, sitting on a riverbank with a fishing pole. There was a painting of a hillside lit with lanterns. Dozens more of people or landscapes Pepper didn't recognize.

From the corner, a climate control system emitted an electric hum. Pepper continued through the racks.

"Some of these aren't finished," Ike said. He pulled out one, and Pepper recognized Tilda by her overalls. Ula had painted everything but her face. Pepper pulled out the painting beside it and found it was the same. There was an entire row of them, all unfinished Tildas. Pepper kept pulling them out until she got to one that was different.

"That's you," Ike said.

Pepper didn't believe him. The painting was of a woman wearing Pepper's best suit and standing on the steps of what looked like a courthouse, but not a courthouse Pepper recognized. As with the paintings of Tilda, the face was unfinished. But she was holding something. Pepper got closer. From the woman's hand dangled a chain strung with a Polish coin.

"It's me," Pepper said. She looked again at the portraits of Tilda. In each one, there was something in the painting that wasn't right. The pink cake-like house was purple instead, or Tilda was surrounded by a breed other than greyhounds. The versions of Pepper were similar. There was another painting in which she recognized her favorite dress, but she was wearing it in front of a lake she'd never seen before. This Pepper was also faceless, but she knew her own hands, her own body. She remembered the baby in *Self-Portrait* with her face turned away. Ula Zero had said the subject of the painting had to be present for the transfer from one universe to another to work, but she couldn't have known. She must have been making it up. Instead, it was the combination of events—Ula's vision of her subject in another universe, plus the painting of the face that unlocked them. And Ula had stopped herself short, many times, for Tilda. She could have painted other Peppers into this world, but she'd chosen not to.

Pepper slid her unfinished portraits back into their slots, her hand shaking. There were still more paintings, an entire row. She didn't want to look. Ike pulled the first one out, and she saw her own face. She was so tired of her own face. But then she realized she was wrong. It wasn't her at all. It was Ula. They'd found the self-portraits. Pepper saw the portrait of Blue, and she turned away and couldn't look back.

"There are thirteen of these," Ike said.

"Sounds about right," Pepper said.

"Does that account for all of them?" he said.

"There were fourteen, as far as I know," she said. "But one got destroyed. The destruction does something. It's a way for the subject to go back, or somewhere else."

Ike took her by the shoulder, waiting for her to process. Pepper felt the universes around them faltering, too many on the verge of changing at the same time.

"We'd better do this quick," she said, "before the scientist in me and the historian in you have a chance to think about it."

THEY HANDED UP the portraits, one at a time, and then Ike boosted Pepper and jumped until he caught hold of the opening. The Ulas gathered around the portraits. Ula couldn't have known who she was painting when she painted them, but they were all different, each portrait depicting a different Ula, with different clothes and different hair. One tying her shoes. One with a pencil behind her ear. One doubled over in a deserted street. The Ulas knew which portraits were their own.

"Why are you giving us these?" Ursula asked. She propped hers against a cabinet and paced in front of it, distrustful of this woman who conjured her from a life far away, whose destruction could be her escape.

"It belongs to you," Pepper said. "And if you destroy it, something will happen."

"We'll go home?" Specs said. She took a giant step back from her portrait, like it was toxic.

"I don't know," Pepper said. Not every body could survive whatever happened in the wrenching from one universe to another. And presumably not every body would make it back. Key sat on the floor and, very quietly, cried. These Ulas knew it better than Pepper did. These Ulas had lived with it for years. Even now, she could still feel their anger.

Compact ran her hands through her hair, over and over.

Vermont touched her portrait's face. Specs walked to a far corner and turned her back to the room. Pepper didn't know what
would happen to them if they decided to stay. Ula was gone,
but the Everett Group was still out there. They'd have to refo-
cus their mission. Pepper rummaged through a cabinet in the
sacristy until she found what she was looking for—a very sharp
knife.

These Ulas would have to decide for themselves. There were
no guarantees of safety, in this universe or any other. They were
looking at each other, which is all they had left.

Pepper had brought Blue's portrait up too, and now she stood
in front of it, terrified of what she needed to do. The Ulas in the
unclaimed portraits looked out at her, as if they were waiting for
her decision. Blue's body was in a freezer, and scientists would
be salivating over it. She didn't want to send her back to Frida
this way, but she knew keeping her here wasn't an option. In her
portrait, Blue was holding a board book about colors, a gift for
Frida's baby. Pepper was still in one piece, somehow, but understood this last, necessary act of destruction might finally be her
dissolution.

Pepper returned to the center of the church, to the semicircle
of women standing around their exits. Then she held out the
knife, handle first, and inhaled as the air in the room began to
vibrate, as the universes briefly opened to one another, as new
universes were created and old ones sluiced away.

THREE

22

THREE WEEKS AFTER Pepper came home, she traveled to Oklahoma to repatriate the remains from her lab. The only one of her grad students to go with her was Janet, who'd shown up at the airport with a fresh tattoo of a bird with an egg in its mouth on one forearm. Pepper wasn't sure if her data would show the probability of treponemal disease in the population—the statistical analysis would take time. With the burials packed away, all that was left was interpretation.

There was a ceremony. There was drumming and a blessing, and the remains were interred in the ground, as they had been before, and as each box was opened, the plastic bags unsealed and emptied, Pepper felt the universes around her. A universe in which she'd never gone to Poland, and she'd had an extra week with these remains, and she'd found something statistically significant that would allow her to publish research and present it at a conference and get tenure. Another box was opened. A universe in which the farmer in Kentucky had plowed in a different spot and these remains had never been discovered in the first place. A universe in which they had been discovered, but there'd been no program in place to excavate them at the time, and desperate men had stolen the bones and sold them as souvenirs. A universe in which these people who'd lived six thousand years ago had found their food more plentiful, their infants in better health, where no one had needed to wrap their burning limbs with wet leaves to ease the pain of infection, where they hadn't experienced so much uncertainty and grief. Another box, emptied and put in the ground. There was uncertainty and grief in every universe, though, in the universe where this population had lived longer and with less disease, in the universes where

Pepper and Ike had never been together, or were together in different ways, in the universes where there were still Ulas and Peppers who were oblivious to the others, who knew nothing about all the ripping and the splitting that continued constantly. There were universes where they hated each other and ones where they loved each other more than Pepper could fathom. And in every universe there was still plenty of uncertainty and grief, and kindness and anger and suffering and joy, beautiful things and miracles and tragedies that knocked people on their asses, there were mistakes and forgiveness, second-guessing and the question of what else might be out there—all constants in every universe, all existing at the same time. Pepper felt the innumerable universes around her, and then she let them go, as the boxes were opened, the bones put into the ground and covered with dirt and marked with a single boulder.

The tribal council leader left, as did the tribe members, having finished singing for the spirits. Pepper waited until they were gone before she sat on the ground and cried, and Janet, not sure what Pepper was crying about, sat next to her and waited it out.

VEV VEV VEV

on the runway
WHAT NOW

                i love it when you actually make it
                onto planes
i'll never take sitting on a runway for
granted again
until probably the next time i fly
are you okay

                so listen
                i wanted to do something special for you
don't tell me!

                i have to tell you though
                because i was trying to bake you something

                    a homecoming cake
                    but the blender exploded
wait what
why were you using the blender for baking
                    LISTEN
lolol
                    it'll all be cleaned up
                    by the time you get home
                    but we need a new blender
remember that time i made creme brulee
and set the curtain on fire
                    that was worse!
and you threw a bag of flour at it
                    it was effective in extinguishing the fire
very true
remember the time you dropped your keys
down the gutter
and we had to knock out a screen to get in
                    and that asshole down the street
                    called the police
                    because he thought we were breaking in
good thing i'm white
that time we were driving through canada
and got a flat tire in the middle of nowhere
                    you were so mad
                    because you wanted to see a moose
                    and there were no moose
i've still never seen a moose
in real life
                    moose can kick in any direction
                    including sideways!
remember that time we were hiking
and a snake bit my ankle
                    and you decided it was venomous
                    and you were dying
                    even though it definitely wasn't venomous

and you sucked on the bite
even though that's not what you're
supposed to do
                    are you just listing all of our stupidest
                    memories
no
i'm thinking about all the times
i was really happy
with you
and didn't realize it at the time
there are a lot of them
                    i still can't believe i sucked on your ankle
i know
me either

PEPPER STOPPED AT Tilda's on her way home because Tilda wanted to give her a house key. One of the dogs, a brindle greyhound named Fern who'd always been shy around Pepper, charged out the screen door and past Pepper into the yard as she arrived.

"Get back here," Tilda said, emerging from the house. She had an orange flower tucked in her hair, and a bee immediately tried to land on it. "Shoo," Tilda said. She took Fern by the collar. The bee moved on. "Can you give me a hand?"

Pepper followed Tilda as she semi-dragged Fern up the porch stairs and into the living room. Theo, who had a plastic cone around his neck, clattered it against Pepper's legs as he greeted her.

"He had a cyst removed," Tilda said. "It's mostly healed, but he still won't leave it alone. It's always something."

She got Fern onto a blanket spread in the middle of the floor, and Pepper then saw the problem: nail clippers.

"They're all reasonably cooperative," Tilda said. "Except Fern. Fern's the squirrely one."

Pepper knelt by Fern's side. "It's okay, Fern," she said. "I'm a professional."

Fern remained suspicious but quit struggling when Tilda revealed a plate of cut-up hot dog.

"I only do this when they make me," Tilda said. "Don't you dare rat me out to your mothers."

Pepper sat on the blanket and stroked one of Fern's soft paws to get the dog used to her touch. Fern yanked her foot back at first but relaxed after a bit of petting. Pepper picked up the clippers and let Fern give them a sniff.

"Did you have a good trip?" Tilda said.

Pepper trimmed the first nail but almost hit the quick. Fern pulled back, justifiably, and Pepper started over with the gentle foot-petting.

"There's this mountain in Oklahoma with a boulder chained to the side," Pepper said. "People say it's chained there so it doesn't roll down and crush the entire town below it." She clipped the next nail, more conservatively this time, but again she almost hit the quick. She held the paw up to the light. Fern's nails were already short. Short enough that trimming wasn't necessary.

"I hope it's a sturdy chain," Tilda said.

"It turns out there's no real threat," Pepper said. She clipped the next nail, but just barely. Fern lifted her head. She was on to Pepper. Pepper fed her a little piece of hot dog. "They put the chain there to attract tourists."

She started on the next nail but changed her mind, and set the clippers down, abandoning the pretense. Some things still seemed impossible to say out loud, but the Pepper in this universe had decided to try. It was a miracle this universe was even intact. And you could only spend so much time blaming yourself on other people. "Can I ask you something?"

Tilda took one of the hot dog pieces and put it in her mouth. "Not bad," she said. She fed one to Theo, who scraped his cone on the floor as he lay across Pepper's feet. "Are you going to ask why I stopped talking to her?"

"Yes," Pepper said. Tilda offered her a hot dog piece, which she accepted. The hot dog was pleasantly salty despite being a temperature Pepper found gross.

Tilda fiddled with the clippers. The third dog appeared from behind the couch, hoovered off the remaining hot dog pieces, and ran. Tilda watched him without moving. "It was a fight we'd had before," she said. They were out of treats, and out of nails for Pepper to pretend to cut. All they could do was look at each other. "She always had a reason, an excuse. But you'd just gotten married, and I thought it was time."

"Time," Pepper said. She knew what Tilda meant. She just hadn't expected it to be about her.

"I wanted to have a relationship with you, a real relationship. It was time. But she said no." Theo rolled on the floor between them, and Pepper put a hand on his bony chest. "We'd had the fight before. But she could tell that this time it was different. So there were threats." She waved her hands vaguely. "Letters from the lawyer. Ula was always good at manipulating people into doing what she wanted. Including me. But that was it. I couldn't keep doing what she wanted and pretend it was fine. It wasn't fine. It wasn't ever fine. And I told her that. Maybe it makes me a bad person, but I ran out of hope that someday she'd change."

"I don't think you're a bad person," Pepper said.

Tilda also put a hand on Theo's chest, next to Pepper's. There was a universe in which Ula had said yes to Tilda's request and so much grief had been avoided. A universe in which Tilda had tried but Pepper had been too scared and stubborn to accept her. Tilda was right, though—Ula hadn't changed, in this universe, at least. But she'd missed her sister. Pepper put her hand on Tilda's. It was hard, but it was also nice. It wasn't something she got to do in every universe.

"I don't want to forget," Tilda said. She took a key from her pocket and gave it to Pepper. It was on a silver key chain engraved with Pepper's initials.

"Are you going someplace?" Pepper asked.

"Not anytime soon," Tilda said. "Just thought you should have it."

Pepper slipped the key in her pocket and stood, and the dogs gathered around her. Even Fern. "Next week?" she said. "Those nails won't trim themselves."

Tilda opened the door. "Next week."

IKE WAS GRINNING on the porch when Pepper got home. She was relieved to find the reporters had cleared out, at last. There'd been a swarm of them when they'd returned from Poland, and she'd spent the intervening weeks redirecting them to Gordon Priddy, who was basking in his newfound celebrity. She'd seen him when he came by her moms' clinic to ask for a reference for a large animal vet. Ula had left him an unexpectedly generous sum of money, and he was planning to buy himself a horse. After he'd done a little traveling first. There were some fountains in Italy he wanted to see.

On the porch, Ike was holding a glass of lemonade that sweat on her hand when she took it.

"Are you ready?" he said.

"Is she?" Pepper said.

Inside, Pepper was greeted with chaos. Her moms were there, both of them on the floor, bodies buckled with laughter. A puppy with a heart-shaped spot on its back and a roll of toilet paper in its mouth ran circles around Pepper's feet, making it difficult to walk. Another puppy was on the couch, trying to drag off a throw pillow, which Annie kept removing from its mouth. Specs was crawling after the puppy with the toilet paper. The puppies had come from one of Pepper's moms' clients who refused to get her own dog spayed and was then dismayed when she began moaning one night, under the sink in the laundry room, and birthed eight puppies she had no intention of keeping. She didn't know who the father was. Her dog was a boxer, but it was too soon to guess about the father's breed. Maybe some kind of terrier, Lydia thought. The puppies seemed to have a penchant for digging.

Pepper thought Ike would say no when she suggested fostering them, especially since Specs, the only Ula who wanted to stay, had come home with them, but as it turned out, he'd secretly wanted a dog for years. The littlest puppy began to growl, protecting Ike from an advancing Specs, who was on all fours pretending, albeit poorly, to be a dog. Pepper thought about what Tilda had said, about giving up hope that Ula would change. Specs seemed to be finding her sense of humor, at least. The runt planted itself on Ike's foot, and it stayed there, teeth locked around his shoelaces, when he started walking.

"How was the trip?" Annie asked.

Pepper sat on the floor, and three puppies immediately pounced on her. She collapsed onto her back and let them attack her face.

"I'm happy to be home," she said.

Specs lured the puppy with the heart-shaped spot into her lap. "Can we go now?" she said.

THE APARTMENT WAS across from the field at the edge of town, the upper level of an older house whose owners had recently moved to Florida. Ike and Pepper's moms had brought over some furniture while Pepper was away, and when they got there, Specs walked from room to room, touching her bed, her sofa, the folding chairs around the kitchen table, but not sitting on anything. She seemed not entirely convinced it was real. From the living room window, Pepper could see the field, where a young couple was spreading out a blanket for a picnic. The young man waited for his companion to sit, then squatted awkwardly beside her. It had rained the night before, and the ground was wet. The woman came to her knees and touched the seat of her jeans, and they both laughed.

The puppy with the heart-shaped spot ran into the room with a dish towel in its mouth.

"Are you sure I can keep her?" Specs said.

She sat on the floor, and the puppy leaped into her lap and tried to climb atop her shoulder, like a parrot.

"This is a good place for a dog," Pepper said. "It's a good neighborhood for walking."

The puppy switched from licking Specs's face to sticking its tongue in her ear. Specs threw a toy and watched the puppy race after it, but again seemed tentative, as if she were afraid to allow herself to get too attached. The Everett Group had shown up, as Pepper feared, just after they'd returned from Poland. Pepper knew they would come, knew she was only one person and couldn't rid the world of them, knew it was all she could do to keep herself and the people she loved safe. But she also knew that being a better version of herself in the universe she was given meant she could no longer deny that Ula's legacy was now intertwined with her own.

When the Everett Group showed up, Boot was with them. She was there for her portrait, and Pepper gave it to her, knowing Boot intended to hand it over to the Everett Group. Boot was looking for answers, answers Ula had denied her for too long, and it wasn't Pepper's place to take that away from her. But Pepper knew the Everett Group wouldn't stop there. She had to find a way to protect what Ula had left behind—the paintings from the church, the bodies from the crypt. Specs. And she still hadn't found research funding for the fall.

She'd been considering taking some time away from teaching, even though the university had an influx of students who were applying in hopes of taking a class with her. She'd even gotten calls from a producer who wanted to hire her as a consultant for a show about a forensic anthropologist. But then a colleague of Ike's approached Pepper, eager to sit down with Specs and discuss the differences between her historic time line and their own. And Dr. Levin from the sociology department called with a similar request, and a woman from the chemistry department Pepper knew because their coffee orders had gotten mixed up at the campus café asked about running a few tests on samples of the destroyed portraits.

Pepper reached out to a handful of philanthropic organizations to fund the project, which would be collaborative and interdisciplinary. There was an art historian Ike had known since grad school, a geneticist Pepper met at a conference who specialized in the epigenetics of identical twins. The funding wasn't hard to find, nor was support from the university. There was enough money for high-end security, in conjunction with a few major museums and labs who already had the infrastructure, and Pepper could select her collaborators, visiting scientists with a sincere desire to better understand the universe, people who could potentially insulate the world from whatever the Everett Group might find. Plus, Ike would be on sabbatical, and though she wasn't fully convinced they wouldn't get sick of each other, she liked the idea of seeing his face more. There were letters in Wrocław he wanted to read.

Soon, she'd sit again in a lab and examine skeletal remains that looked very much like her mother's. It was, after all, her area of expertise. And because the project would be under the auspices of the university, it would be transparent and visible enough that it seemed unlikely paintings or bodies would go missing. Specs and her portrait were as safe as Pepper could make them.

Pepper pulled Specs up from the floor and led her to the couch.

"Are you sure you're going to be okay alone?" she asked.

Specs sat, cautiously, and the couch remained real. She'd gotten a haircut and new glasses with big, dark frames. It had been a week since the last time someone had recognized her as an Ula.

"I haven't lived alone in a long time," she said. "I wasn't good at it. But I think I'd like to try."

She had a list of things she wanted to do, places she wanted to visit, which she'd made together with her therapist. In her universe, it had taken so much energy just to survive. Now she was going to get houseplants and take a cooking class. She was going to learn how to ride a bike. She was going to walk on a beach.

"You know you can always call us if you need anything," Pepper said.

Through the window, she could see the couple now standing,

debating what to do next. A flock of geese landed at one end of the field and began approaching them menacingly. The woman turned to face them and appeared to start honking, and the geese sped up, honking back. Ula had painted this field over and over, every time in a different way. Pepper wondered if she'd foreseen this moment, if this was inside the scope of her vision.

"I don't think I'll be too lonely," Specs said. The puppy was biting at her pant leg. It was too short to make it onto the couch by itself, so Specs helped it up. The puppy flopped over dramatically, closed its eyes, and fell immediately asleep. Specs seemed to relax then, with the dog sleeping in her lap, like they all belonged there. "But I won't be a stranger."

Through the window, Pepper saw the geese prepare to take flight as the couple repacked their belongings. And then, all at once, the geese were in the sky, leaving a new version of the field behind.

ACKNOWLEDGMENTS

My immeasurable gratitude to:

My agent, Stacia Decker — this book would not exist without you.

My editor, Lee Harris, and the many extraordinary people at Tordotcom whose time and dedication helped make this book a reality, including Matt Rusin, Alexis Saarela, Michael Dudding, Jordan Hanley, Christine Foltzer, and Irene Gallo. To Jaya Miceli, for the most beautiful cover I've ever seen.

The early readers of this book, whose generosity and insight made it better, including: Jaida Temperly, Jo Volpe, Molly Pascal, and my writing group at the C. H. Booth Library.

The friends, some of them virtual, whose commiseration, encouragement, and good company sustained me through this process.

My teachers and classmates at Syracuse University, who taught me to be both a better writer and a better human.

My family, especially my mother, Sue Pokwatka, who provided financial planning advice to a fictional character. To Rainer and Gulliver: you didn't help with this book at all, but I love you so much.

Finally, to Jason, for keeping me alive and never letting me give up.